MONEY

○ ○ ○ ○ ○ ○ ○ ○ ○ ○ ○
○ ○ ○ ○ ○ ○ ○ ○ ○ ○ ○

Martin Amis is the author of twelve novels, the memoir *Experience*, two collections of stories and six collections of non-fiction, most recently *The Second Plane*. He lives in New York.

MARTIN AMIS

Money

A Suicide Note

o o o o o o o o o o o o o o o o o o
o o o o o o o o o o o o o o o o o o

VINTAGE BOOKS
London

Published by Vintage Classics 2012

1 3 5 7 9 10 8 6 4 2

First published in Great Britain in 1984 by Jonathan Cape

Vintage
Random House, 20 Vauxhall Bridge Road,
London SW1V 2SA

www.vintage-classics.info

Addresses for companies within The Random House Group Limited can be found at:
www.randomhouse.co.uk/offices.htm

The Random House Group Limited Reg. No. 954009

A CIP catalogue record for this book
is available from the British Library

ISBN 9780099561026

The Random House Group Limited supports The Forest Stewardship
Council (FSC®), the leading international forest certification organisation.
Our books carrying the FSC label are printed on FSC® certified paper. FSC is
the only forest certification scheme endorsed by the leading environmental
organisations, including Greenpeace. Our paper procurement policy
can be found at www.randomhouse.co.uk/environment

Typeset in Dante MT by Palimpsest Book Production Limited,
Falkirk, Stirlingshire
Printed and bound in Great Britain by
CPI Group (UK) Ltd, Croydon CR0 4YY

To Antonia

This is a suicide note. By the time you lay it aside (and you should always read these things slowly, on the lookout for clues or give-aways), John Self will no longer exist. Or at any rate that's the idea. You never can tell, though, with suicide notes, can you? In the planetary aggregate of all life, there are many more suicide notes than there are suicides. They're like poems in that respect, suicide notes: nearly everyone tries their hand at them some time, with or without the talent. We all write them in our heads. Usually the note is the thing. You complete it, and then resume your time travel. It is the note and not the life that is cancelled out. Or the other way round. Or death. You never can tell, though, can you, with suicide notes.

To whom is the note addressed? To Martina, to Fielding, to Vera, to Alec, to Selina, to Barry – to John Self? No. It is meant for you out there, the dear, the gentle.

M.A.

London, September 1981

As MY cab pulled off FDR Drive, somewhere in the early Hundreds, a low-slung Tomahawk full of black guys came sharking out of lane and sloped in fast right across our bows. We banked, and hit a deep welt or grapple-ridge in the road: to the sound of a rifle-shot the cab roof ducked down and smacked me on the core of my head. I really didn't need that, I tell you, with my head and face and back and heart hurting a lot all the time anyway, and still drunk and crazed and ghosted from the plane.

'Oh man,' I said.

'Yeah,' said the cabbie from behind the shattered plastic of his screen. 'Fuckin A.'

My cabbie was fortyish, lean, balding. Such hair as remained scurried long and damp down his neck and shoulders. To the passenger, that's all city cabbies are – mad necks, mad rugs. This mad neck was explosively pocked and mottled, with a flicker of adolescent virulence in the crimson underhang of the ears. He lounged there in his corner, the long hands limp on the wheel.

'Only need about a hundred guys, a hundred guys like me,' he said, throwing his voice back, 'take out all the niggers and PRs in this fuckin town.'

I listened, on my seat there. Owing to this fresh disease I have called tinnitus, my ears have started hearing things recently, things that aren't strictly auditory. Jet take-offs, breaking glass, ice scratched from the tray. It happens mostly in the morning out

○ ○ ○ I ○ ○ ○

at other times too. It happened to me in the plane, for instance or at least I think it did.

'What?' I shouted. 'A hundred guys? That's not many guys.'

'We could do it. With the right gunge, we could do it.'

'Gunge?'

'Gunge, yeah. Fifty-sixes. Automatics.'

I sat back and rubbed my head. I'd spent *two hours* in Immigration, God damn it. I have this anti-talent for queues. You know the deal. Ho ho ho, I think, as I successfully shoulder and trample my way to the end of the shortest line. But the shortest line is the shortest line for an interesting reason. The people ahead of me are all Venusians, pterodactyls, men and women from an alternative timestream. They all have to be vivisected and body-bagged by the unsmiling 300-pounder in his lit glass box. 'Business or pleasure?' this guy eventually asked me. 'I hope business only,' I said, and meant it. With business I'm usually okay. It's pleasure that gets me into all this expensive trouble . . . Then a half hour in customs, and another half before I firmed up this cab – yeah, and the usual maniac fizzing and crackling at its wheel. I've driven in New York. Five blocks, and you're reduced to tears of barbaric nausea. So what happens to these throwbacks they hire to do it all day for money? You try it. I said,

'Why would you want to go and do a thing like that?'

'Uh?'

'Kill all the niggers and PRs?'

'They think, you know, you drive a yellow cab,' he said, and raised one limp splayed hand from the wheel, 'you must be some kind of a scumbag.'

I sighed and leaned forward. 'You know something?' I asked him. 'You really *are* a scumbag. I thought it was just a swearword until you came along. You're the first real one I've met.'

We pulled over. Rising in his seat he turned towards me gradually. His face was much nastier, tastier, altogether more useful than I had banked on it being – barnacled and girlish with bright eyes and prissy lips, as if there were another face, the real face, beneath his mask of skin.

'Okay. Get out the car. I said out the fuckin car!'

'Yeah yeah,' I said, and shoved my suitcase along the seat.

'Twenty-two dollars,' he said. 'There, the *clock*.'

'I'm not giving you anything, scumbag.'

With no shift in the angle of his gaze he reached beneath the dashboard and tugged the special catch. All four door locks clunked shut with an oily chockful sound.

'Listen to me, you fat fuck,' he began. 'This is Ninety-Ninth and Second. The money. Give me the money.' He said he would drive me uptown twenty blocks and kick me out on the street, right there. He said that by the time the niggers were done, there'd be nothing left of me but a hank of hair and teeth.

I had some notes in my back pocket, from my last trip. I passed a twenty through the smeared screen. He sprang the locks and out I climbed. There was nothing more to say.

So now I stand here with my case, in smiting light and island rain. Behind me massed water looms, and the industrial corsetry of FDR Drive . . . It must be pushing eight o'clock by now but the weepy breath of the day still shields its glow, a guttering glow, very wretched – rained on, leaked on. Across the dirty street three black kids sprawl in the doorway of a dead liquor store. I'm big, though, yes I'm a big mother, and they look too depressed to come and check me out. I take a defiant pull from my pint of duty-free. It's past midnight, my time. God I hate this movie. And it's only just beginning.

I looked for cabs, and no cabs came. I was on First, not Second, and First is uptown. All the cabs would be turned the other way, getting the hell out on Second and Lex. In New York for a half a minute and already I pace the line, the long walk down Ninety-Ninth Street.

You know, I wouldn't have done this a month ago. I wouldn't have done it then. Then I was avoiding. Now I'm just waiting. Things happen to me. They do. They just have to go ahead and happen. You watch – you wait . . . Inflation, they say, is cleaning up this city. Dough is rolling up its sleeves and mucking the place out. But things still happen here. You step off the plane, look around, take a deep breath – and come to in your under-pants, somewhere south of SoHo, or on a midtown traction table with a silver tray and a tasselled tab on your chest and a guy in white saying Good morning, sir. How are you today. That'll be fifteen thousand dollars . . . Things still happen here and something is waiting to happen to me. I can tell. Recently my life feels like a bloodcurdling joke. Recently my life has taken on *form*. Something is waiting. I am waiting. Soon, it will stop waiting – any day now. Awful things can happen any time. This is the awful thing.

Fear walks tall on this planet. Fear walks big and fat and fine. Fear has really got the whammy on all of us down here. Oh it's true, man. Sister, don't kid yourself . . . One of these days I'm going to walk right up to fear. I'm going to walk right up. Someone's got to do it. I'm going to walk right up and say, *Okay, hard-on. No more of this. You've pushed us around for long enough. Here is someone who* would not take it. *It's over. Outside.* Bullies, I'm told, are all cowards deep down. Fear is a bully, but something tells me that fear is no funker. Fear, I suspect, is really incredibly brave. Fear will lead me straight through the door, will prop me up in the alley among the crates and the empties, and show me who's the boss . . . I might lose a tooth or two, I suppose, or he could even break my arm – or fuck up my eye! Fear might get carried away, like I've seen them do, pure damage, with nothing mattering. Maybe I'd need a crew, or a tool, or an equalizer. Now I come to think about it, maybe I'd better let fear be. When it comes to fighting, I'm brave – or reckless or indifferent or just unjust. But fear really scares me. He's too good at fighting, and I'm too frightened anyway.

I walked west for a block, then turned south. On Ninety-Sixth Street I hijacked a cab at the lights – I just yanked open the door and swung my case on to the seat. The cabbie turned: and our eyes met horribly. 'The Ashbery,' I told him, for the second time. 'On Forty-Fifth.' He took me there. I gave the guy the two bucks I owed him, plus a couple more. The money changed hands very eloquently.

'Thank you, friend,' he said.

'You're welcome,' I said. 'Thank *you*.'

I'm sitting on the bed in my hotel room. The room is fine, fine. Absolutely no complaints. It's terrific value.

The pain in my face has split in two but hurts about the same. There's a definite swelling in my jaw now, on my upper west side. It's a fucking abscess or something, maybe a nerve deal or a gum gimmick. Oh Christ, I suppose I'll have to get it fixed. The mouth-doctor I choose is in for a jolt. These croc teeth of mine, these English teeth – they're about as good, I reckon, as those of the average American corpse. It will cost me, what's more. You have to splash out big for everything like that over here, as you know, as I've said. You have to tell yourself before-hand that the sky's the limit. All the people in the street, these extras and bit-part players, they all cost long money to keep on the road. There are taxi-meters, money-clocks, on the ambulances in this city: that's the sort of place I'm dealing with. I can feel another pain starting business in the slopes of my eyes. Hello there, and welcome.

I'm drinking tax-exempt whisky from a toothmug, and

listening to see if I'm still hearing things. The mornings are the worst. This morning was the worst yet. I heard computer fugues, Japanese jam sessions, didgeridoos. What is my head up to? I wish I had some idea what it's got in mind for me. I want to telephone Selina right now and give her a piece of it, a piece of my mind. It's one in the morning over there. But it's one in the morning over here too, in my head anyway. And Selina would be more than a match for me, with my head in the shape it's in . . . Now I've got another evening to deal with. I don't want another evening to deal with. I've already had one, in England and on the plane. I don't need another evening. Alec Llewellyn owes me money. Selina Street owes me money. Barry Self owes me money. Outside I see night has happened quickly. Dah – steady now. The lights don't seem at all fixed or stable, up there in the banked sky.

Refreshed by a brief blackout, I got to my feet and went next door. The mirror looked on, quite unimpressed, as I completed a series of rethinks in the hired glare of the windowless bathroom. I cleaned my teeth, combed my rug, clipped my nails, bathed my eyes, gargled, showered, shaved, changed – and still looked like shit. Jesus, I'm so fat these days. I tell you, I appal myself in the tub and on the can. I sit slumped on the ox-collar seat like a clutch of plumbing, the winded boiler of a thrashed old tramp. How did it happen? It can't just be all the booze and the quick food I put away. No, I must have been pencilled in for this a long time ago. My dad isn't fat. My mother wasn't either. What's the deal? Can money fix it? I need my whole body drilled down and repaired, replaced. I need my body capped is what I need. I'm going to do it, too, the minute I hit the money.

Selina, my Selina, that Selina Street . . . Today somebody told me one of her terrible secrets. I don't want to talk about it yet.

I'll tell you later. I want to go out and drink some more and get a lot tireder first.

The sprung doors parted and I staggered out into the lobby's teak and flicker. Uniformed men stood by impassively like sentries in their trench. I slapped my key on the desk and nodded gravely. I was loaded enough to be unable to tell whether they could tell I was loaded. Would they mind? I was certainly too loaded to care. I moved to the door with boxy, schlep-shouldered strides.

'Mr Self?'

'The same,' I said. 'Yeah?'

'Oh, sir. There was a call for you this afternoon. Caduta Massi? . . . Is that *the* Caduta Massi?

'The same. She – any message or anything?'

'No, sir. No message.'

'Well okay. Thanks.'

'Mm-hm.'

So I walked south down bending Broadway. What's all this *mm-hm* shit? I strode through meat-eating genies of subway breath. I heard the ragged hoot of sirens, the whistles of two-wheelers and skateboarders, pogoists, gocarters, windsurfers. I saw the barrelling cars and cabs, shoved on by the power of their horns. I felt all the contention, the democracy, all the italics, in the air. These are people determined to be themselves, whatever, little shame attaching. Urged out from the line of shufflers and idlers, watchers, pavement men, a big blond screamer flailed at the kerb, denouncing all traffic. His hair was that special mad yellow, like an omelette, a rug omelette. As he shadowboxed he loosely babbled of fraud and betrayal, redundancy, eviction. 'It's my money and I want it!' he said. 'I want my money and I want it now!' The city is full of these guys, these guys and dolls who bawl and holler and weep about bad luck all the hours there are.

I read in a magazine somewhere that they're chronics from the municipal madhouses. They got let out when money went wrong ten years ago . . . Now there's a good joke, a global one, cracked by money. An Arab hikes his zipper in the sheep-pen, gazes contentedly across the stall and says, 'Hey, Basim. Let's hike oil.' Ten years later a big whiteman windmills his arms on Broadway, for all to see.

I hit a topless bar on Forty-Fourth. Ever check out one of these joints? I always expected some kind of Mob frat-house policed by half-clad chambermaids. It isn't like that. They just have a few chicks in knickers dancing on a ramp behind the bar: you sit and drink while they strut their stuff. I kept the whiskies coming, at $3.50 a pop, and sluiced the liquor round my upper west side. I also pressed the cold glass against my writhing cheek. This helps, or seems to. It soothes.

There were three girls working the ramp, spaced out along its mirrored length. The girl dancing topless for my benefit, and for that of the gingery, hermaphroditic figure seated two stools to my right, was short and shy and puppyishly built. Well, let's take a look here. Her skin showed pale in the light, waning sorely to the eye, as if she were given to rashes, allergies. She had large woeful breasts, puckered at the heart, and an eave of loose flesh climbed over the high rim of her pants, which were navy-blue and fluff-flossed, like gym-briefs. Yes, the upper grips of her breasts bore soft crenellations, even whiter than the rest of her. Stretchmarks at twenty, at nineteen: something wrong there, the form showing fatigue, showing error, at a very early stage. She knew all this, my girl. Her normal tomboy face tried to wear the standard sneer of enraptured self-sufficiency and yet was full of disquiet – disquiet of the body, not the other shame. If you want my considered opinion, this chick had no kind of future in the gogo business. She was my girl, though, for the next half hour anyhow. Her two rivals further down the ramp looked a lot more my style, but my face throbbed knowingly each time I turned their way. And I had my girl to consider, her own feelings in the matter. I'm with you, kid, don't worry. You'll do me fine. She smiled in my direction every now and then. The smile was so helpless and uncertain. Yes the smile was so ashamed.

'You want another scotch?' said the matron behind the bar – the old dame with her waxed hair and scrapey voice. The bodystocking or tutu she wore was an unfriendly dull brown or caramel colour. It spoke of spinal supports, hernias.

'Yeah,' I said, and started smoking another cigarette. Unless I specifically inform you otherwise, I'm always smoking another cigarette.

I nursed my cheek for a while with the glass. I muttered and swore. By the time I looked up again my girl was gone. In her stead there writhed a six-foot Mex with wraparound mouth, hot greasy breasts, and a furrow of black hair on her belly which crept like a trail of gunpowder into the sharp white holster of her pants. Now this is a bit more fucking like it, I thought. In my experience you can tell pretty well all you need to know about a woman by the amount of time, thought and money she puts into her pants. Take Selina. And these pants spelt true sack knowhow. She danced like a wet dream, vicious and inane. Her tooth-crammed smile went everywhere and nowhere. The face, the body, the movement, all quite secure in their performance, their art, their pornography.

'You want to buy Dawn a drink?'

I levelled my head. The old dame behind the bar gestured perfunctorily towards the stool beside me, where Dawn indeed perched – Dawn, my girl, now swaddled in a woolly dressing-gown.

'Well what's Dawn drinking?' I asked.

'Champagne!' A squat glass of what looked like glucose on the rocks was smacked down in front of me. 'Six dollars!'

'Six *dollars* . . .' I flattened another twenty on the damp wood.

'Sorry,' said Dawn with a wince. She used the long Boroughs vowel, the out-of-towner vowel. 'I don't like to do this part. It's not nice to a girl.'

'Don't worry.'

'What's your name?'

'John,' I said.

'What do you do, John?'

Oh I see – a conversation. This is some deal. There's a wriggling naked miracle five feet from my nose, but I pay good money to talk with Dawn here in her dressing-gown.

'I'm in pornography,' I said. 'Right up to here.'

'That's interesting.'

'You want another scotch?' The old boot, this headmistress in her therapeutic singlet, loomed over us with my change.

'Why not,' I said.

'You want to buy Dawn another drink?'

'Christ. Yeah, okay – do it.'

'. . . Are you English, John?' asked my girl, with deep understanding, as if this would answer a lot of questions.

'Tell you the truth, Dawn, I'm half American and half asleep. I just climbed off the plane, you know?'

'Me too. I mean the bus. Yesterday. I just climbed off the bus.'

'Where from, Dawn?'

'New Jersey.'

'No kidding? Where in New Jersey? You know, I grew up –'

'You want another scotch?'

I felt my shoulders give. I turned slowly. I said, 'How much does it cost to keep you away from me for ten minutes? Tell me something,' I asked her. But I said a good deal more. She stood her ground, this old dame. She was experienced. I gave her all my face, and it's a face that can usually face them down, wide and grey, full of adolescent archaeology and cheap food and junk money, the face of a fat snake, bearing all the signs of its sins. For several seconds she just gave me her face too, full on, a stark presentation of the eyes, which were harder than mine, oh much harder. With her small fists on the bar she leaned towards me and said:

'*Leroy!*'

Instantly the music gulped out. Various speckled profiles turned my way. Hands on hips, older in the silence, her breasts standing easy now, the dark dancer stared down at me with weathered contempt.

'I'm looking for things.' This was Dawn. 'I'm really interested in pornography.'

'No you're not,' I said. And pornography isn't interested either. 'It's okay, Leroy! Relax, Leroy. Pal, there's no problem. I'm going. Here's money. Dawn, just you take care now.'

I slid to my feet and found no balance. The stool wobbled roundly on its base, like a coin. I waved to the watching women – get your staring done with – and made my diagonal for the door.

Everything was on offer outside. Boylesk, assisted showers, live sex, a we-never-close porno emporium bristling in its static. They even had the real thing out there, in prostitute form. But I wasn't buying, not tonight. I walked back to the hotel *without incident*. Nothing happened. It never does, but it will. The revolving door shoved me into the lobby, and the desk clerk bobbed about in his stockade.

'Hi there,' he said. 'While you were out tonight, sir, Mr Lorne Guyland called.'

Daintily he offered me my key.

'Would that be the real Lorne Guyland, sir?'

'Oh, I wouldn't go that far,' I said, or maybe I just thought it.

The elevator sucked me skyward. My face was still hurting a lot all the time. In my room I picked up the bottle and sank back on the bed. While I waited for the noises to come I thought about travel through air and time, and about Selina . . . Yes, I can fill you in on that now. Perhaps I'll even feel a little better, when I've told you, when it's out.

Earlier today – today? Christ, it feels like childhood – Alec Llewellyn drove me to Heathrow Airport at the wheel of my powerful Fiasco. He's borrowing the car while I'm away, that liar. I was smudged with drink and Serafim, for the plane. I'm scared of flying. I'm scared of landing, too. We didn't talk much. He owes me money . . . We joined the long queue for standby. Something in me hoped that the flight would be full. It wasn't. The ticking computer gimmicked my seat. 'But you'd better hurry,' said the girl. Alec jogged at my side to passport control. He tousled my rug and shooed me through.

'Hey, John,' he called from the other side of the fence. 'Hey, addict!' Beside him an old man stood waving at no one that I could see.

'What?'

'Come here.'

He beckoned. I came panting up to him.

'What?'

'Selina. She's fucking someone else – a lot, all the time.'

'Oh you *liar*.' And I think I even took a weary swipe at his face. Alec is always doing things like this.

'I thought you ought to know,' he said offendedly. He smiled. 'Round from the back, one leg up, her on top. Every which way.'

'Oh yeah? Who? You liar. Why are you – who, who, who?'

But he wouldn't tell me. He just said that it had been going on for a long time, and that it was someone I knew pretty well.

'*You*,' I said, and turned, and ran . . .

There. I don't feel better. I don't feel better at all. I'm rolling over now, to try and get some sleep. London is waking up. So is Selina. The distant fizz or whistle or hiss in the back of my head is starting again, modulating slowly, searching for its scale.

Oh man sometimes I wake up feel like a cat runover.

Are you familiar with the stoical aspects of hard drinking, of heavy drinking? Oh it's heavy. Oh it's hard. It isn't easy. Jesus, I never meant me any harm. All I wanted was a good time.

The disease I host called tinnitus – more reliable and above all cheaper than any alarm call – woke me promptly at nine. Tinnitus woke me on a note of high exasperation, as if it had been trying to wake me for hours. I let my sapless tongue creak up to check out the swelling on my upper west side. About the same, yet tenderer. My throat informed me that I had a snout hangover on, too. The first cigarette would light a trail of gunpowder to the holster, the arsenal inside my chest. I patted my pockets and lit it anyway.

Ten minutes later I came out of that can on all fours, a pale and very penitent crocodile, really sorry about all that stagnant gook and offal I went and quaffed last night. I'd just rolled on my back and was loosening my tie and unbuttoning my shirt when the telephone rang.

'John? Lorne Guyland.'

'Lorne!' I said. Christ, what a croak it was. 'How are you?'

'Good,' he said. 'I'm good, John. How are you?'

'I'm fine, fine.'

'That's good, John. John?'

'Lorne?'

'There are things that worry me, John.'

'Tell me about them, Lorne.'

'I don't happen to be an old man, John.'

'I know that, Lorne.'

'I'm in great shape. Never better.'

'I'm glad, Lorne.'

'That's why I don't like it that you say I'm an old man, John.'

'But I don't say that, Lorne.'

'Well okay. You *imply* it, John, and that's, it's, that's about the same thing. In my book. You also *imply* that I'm not very sexually active and can't satisfy my women. That's just not true, John.'

'I'm sure it's not true, Lorne.'

'Then why imply it? John, I think we should meet and talk about these things. I hate to talk on the telephone.'

'Absolutely. When?'

'I'm a very busy man, John.'

'I respect that, Lorne.'

'You can't expect me to just drop everything, just to, just to meet with you, John.'

'Of course not, Lorne.'

'I lead a full life, John. Full and active. Superactive, John. Six o'clock I'm at the health club. When my programme's done I hit the mat with my judo instructor. Afternoons I work out with the weights. When I'm at the house, it's golf, tennis, water-skiing, scuba-diving, racket-ball and polo. You know, John, sometimes I just get out on that beach and run like a kid. The girls, these chicks I have at the house, when I run in late they scold me, John, like I was a little boy. Then I'm up half the night screwing. Take yesterday . . .'

It went on like this, I swear to God, for an hour and a half. After a while I fell silent. This had no effect on anything. So in the end I just sat through it, smoking cigarettes and having a really bad time.

When it was over, I took a pull of scotch, dabbed the tears away with a paper tissue, and rang down to room service. I asked for coffee. I mean, you have to take it easy on yourself sometimes.

'Coffee how?' came the suspicious reply.

I told him: with milk and sugar. 'How big are the pots?'

'Serve two,' he said.

'Four pots.'

'You got it.'

I lay back on the cot with my frayed, fanlike address book. Using the complimentary pad and pencil, I started making a list of the places where I might expect to find the nomadic Selina. That Selina, she gets around. I wondered, out of interest, how much these calls were going to cost me.

I undressed and ran a tub. Then the impeccable black bellhop arrived with my tray. I came over, initialled the check and slipped the kid a buck. He was in good shape, this kid: he had a pleasant agitation in his step and in his smile. He frowned innocently and sniffed the air.

He could take one look at me – at the ashtray, the bottle, the four pots of coffee, my face, and my gut set like a stone on the white band of the towel – he could take one look at me and be pretty sure I ran on heavy fuel.

There is a dog tethered in the steep airwell beneath my room. A talented barker, he barks boomingly well. I listened to him a lot while I sat there being talked to by Lorne. His half-hourly barking jags reverberate in monstrous warning up the length of the canyon walls. He needs that nether fury. He has big responsibilities – he sounds as though he guards the gates of hell. His lungs are fathomless, his hellhound rage is huge. He needs those lungs – what for? To keep them in, to keep them out.

I'd better give you the lowdown on Selina – and quick. That hot bitch, what am I letting her do to me?

Like many girls (I reckon), and especially those of the small, supple, swervy, bendy, bed-smart variety, Selina lives her life in hardened fear of assault, molestation and rape. The world has ravished her often enough in the past, and she thinks the world wants to ravish her again. Lying between the sheets, or propped at my side during long and anxious journeys in the Fiasco, or seated across the table in the deep lees of high-tab dinners, Selina has frequently refreshed me with tales of insult and violation from her childhood and teenage years – a musk-breathing, toffee-offering sicko on the common, the toolshed interrogations of sweat-soaked parkies, some lumbering retard in the alley or the lane, right up to the narcissist photographers and priapic propboys who used to cruise her at work, and now the scowling punks, soccer trogs and bus-stop boogies malevo-lently lining the streets and more or less constantly pinching her ass or flicking her tits and generally making no bones about the things they need to do . . . It must be tiring knowledge, the realization that half the members of the planet, one on one, can do what the hell they like with you.

And it must be extra tough on a girl like Selina, whose appear-ance, after many hours at the mirror, is a fifty-fifty compromise between the primly juvenile and the grossly provocative. Her tastes are strictly High Street too, with frank promise of brothelly knowhow and top-dollar underwear. I've followed Selina down the strip, when we're shopping, say, and she strolls on ahead, wearing sawn-off jeans and a wash-withered T-shirt, or a frilly frock measuring the brink of her russety thighs, or a transparent coating of gossamer, like a condom, or an abbreviated *school uniform* . . . The men wince and watch, wince and watch. They buckle and half turn away. They shut their eyes and clutch their nuts. And sometimes, when they see me cruise up behind my little friend and slip an arm around her trim and muscular waist, they look at me as if to say – Do something about it, will you?

Don't let her go about the place looking like that. Come on, it's your responsibility.

I have talked to Selina about the way she looks. I have brought to her notice the intimate connections between rape and her summer wardrobe. She laughs about it. She seems flushed, pleased. I keep on having to fight for her honour in pubs and at parties. She gets groped or goosed or propositioned – and there I am once again, wearily raising my scarred dukes. I tell her it's because she goes around the place looking like a nude magazine. She finds this funny too. I don't understand. I sometimes think that Selina would stand stock still in front of an advancing jugger-naut, so long as the driver never once took his eyes off her tits.

In addition to rape, Selina is frightened of mice, spiders, dogs, toadstools, cancer, mastectomy, chipped mugs, ghost stories, visions, portents, fortune tellers, astrology columns, deep water, fires, floods, thrush, poverty, lightning, ectopic pregnancy, rust, hospitals, driving, swimming, flying and ageing. Like her fat pale lover, she never reads a book. She has no job any more: she has no money. She is either twenty-nine or thirty-one or just possibly thirty-three. She is leaving it all very late, and she knows it. She will have to make her move, and she will have to make it soon.

I don't believe Alec, necessarily, but I won't believe Selina, that's for sure. In my experience, the thing about girls is – you never know. No, you never do. Even if you actually catch them, redhanded – bent triple upside down in mid-air over the head-board, say, and brushing their teeth with your best friend's dick – you never know. She'll deny it, indignantly. She'll believe it, too. She'll hold the dick there, like a mike, and tell you that it isn't so.

I have been faithful to Selina Street for over a year, God damn it. Yes I have. I keep trying not to be, but it never works out. I can't find anyone to be unfaithful to her with. They don't want what I have to offer. They want commitment and candour and sympathy and trust and all the other things I seem to be really short of. They are past the point where they'll go to bed with somebody just for the hell of it. Selina is past that point also, long past. She used to be a well-known goer, true, but now she has her future security to think about. She has money to think about. Ah, Selina, come on. Tell me it isn't so.

I worked up a major sweat over the console that morning – yeah, and a major tab, too. Deafened with caffeine, I was just a hot robot, a ticking grid of jet-lag, time-jump and hangover. The telephone happened to be an antique: a dialler. And my fingers were already so sore and chewed that each shirtbutton had felt like a drop of molten solder . . . Half way through the session I was dialling with my left pinkie. 'Room number please,' said the telephonist in her honeying drone, every time, every time. 'Me again,' I said and said. 'Room 101. Me. It's *me*.'

I tried my own number first and repeatedly thereafter. Selina has her keys. She is always in and out . . . I spoke to Mandy and Debby, Selina's shadowy flatmates. I rang her old office. I rang her dancing class. I even rang her gynaecologist. No one knew where she was. On a parallel track I combed the airwaves for Alec Llewellyn. I talked to his wife. I talked to three of his girl-friends. I talked to his probation officer. No luck. Boy, these are pretty thoughts for me to entertain, three thousand miles from home.

The dog barked. My face felt small and clueless between its fat red ears. For a while I slumped back and stared hard at the phone. It held out for several seconds, then it rang. And so naturally I thought *it's her* and made a hurried grab for my girl.

'– Yes?'

'John Self? It's Caduta Massi.'

'At last,' I said. 'Caduta, it's an honour.'

'John, it's good to talk to you. But before we meet I want to sort some things out.'

'Like what, Caduta?'

'For instance, how many children do you think I should have?'

'Well I thought just the one.'

'No, John.'

'More?'

'Many more.'

I said, 'About how many?'

'I think I should have many children, John.'

'Well okay. Sure. Why not. What, say two or three more?'

'We'll see,' said Caduta Massi. 'I'm glad you're amenable to that, John. Thank you.'

'Forget it.'

'And another thing. I think I should have a mother, a white-haired lady in a black dress. But that's not so important.'

'You got it.'

'And another thing. Don't you think I should change my name?'

'What to, Caduta?'

'I don't know yet. But something a little more appropriate.'

'Whatever you say. Caduta – let's meet.'

After that I had them send me up a rack of cocktails and canapes. The same black bellhop walked skilfully into the room with the silver trays on his tense fingertips. I had nothing smaller, so I flicked him a five. He looked at the drinks and he looked at me.

'Have one,' I said, and picked up a glass.

He shook his head, resisting a smile, averting his mobile face.

'What's up?' I said coolly, and drank. 'Little early for you?'

'You party last night?' he asked. He couldn't straighten his face for more than a couple of seconds at a stretch.

'What's your name?'

'Felix.'

'No, Felix,' I said, 'I did it all by myself.'

'. . . You gonna party now?'

'Yeah. But all by myself again. Damn it. I got problems you wouldn't believe. I'm on a different clock to you, Felix. My time, it's way after lunch.'

He lifted his round chin and nodded his head tightly. 'I take one look at you, man,' he said, 'and I know you ain't *never* gonna stop.'

I didn't attempt anything else that day. I drank the drink and ate the grub. I had a shave. I had a handjob, closely structured round my last night with Selina. Or I tried. I couldn't remember much about it, and then all these guys came walking in on the act . . . So me and my sore tooth throbbed our way through a few hours of television – I sat flummoxed and muttering like a superannuated ghost, all shagged out from its hauntings, through sports, soaps, ads, news, the other world. Best was a variety show hosted by a veteran entertainer, someone who was pretty well over the hill when I was a kid. Amazing to think that these guys are still around, still alive, let alone still earning. They don't make them like that any more. No, come on, let's be accurate: only now, in 1981, do they make them like that. They couldn't before – they didn't have the technology. Jesus Christ, this old prong has been sutured and stitched together in a state-of-the-art cosmetics lab. The scalloped blaze of his bridgework matches the macabre brilliance of his flounced dicky. His highlit contacts burn a tigerish green. Check out the tan on the guy – it's like a paintjob. He looks terrific, positively rosy. His Latin rug sweats with vitamins. His falsy ears are sharp and succulent. When I make all the money I'm due to make and go off to California for that well-earned body transplant I've promised myself, I'll mention the name of old green eyes here, and tell the medics, as I go under, *There. That's how I want it. Give me one just like that* . . . But now this aged android starts bringing on a string of even older guys, also spruce and dazzlingly metallic, a chorus line of tuxed fucks called things like Mr Music and Entertainment Himself. Wait a minute. Now I *know* that one has been dead for decades. Come to think of it, the whole show has the suspended air and sickly texture of treated film, that funeral-parlour glow – numb, tranced and shiny, like a corpse. I switched channels and sat there rubbing my face. The screen now showed a crater-field of dead cars, the frazzled heaps pummelled to the sound of tinnitus, a new necropolis of old American gods. I telephoned, and found no answer anywhere.

Time passed until it was time to go. I climbed into my big suit and brushed the hair back off my face. I took one more call that afternoon. It was a curious call, a strange call. I'll tell you about it later. Some whacko. No big deal.

Where is Selina Street? Where is she? She knows where *I* am. My number is up there on the kitchen wall. What is she doing? What is she doing for money? Punishment, that's what this is. Punishment is what I'm taking here.

I ask only one thing. I'm understanding. I'm mature. And it isn't much to ask. I want to get back to London, and track her down, and be alone with my Selina – or not even alone, damn it, merely close to her, close enough to smell her skin, to see the flecked webbing of her lemony eyes, the moulding of her artful lips. Just for a few precious seconds. Just long enough to put in one good, clean punch. That's all I ask.

So now I must go uptown to meet with Fielding Goodney at the Carraway Hotel – Fielding, my moneyman, my contact and my pal. He's the reason I'm here. I'm the reason he's here too. We're going to make lots of money together. Making lots of money – it's not that hard, you know. It's overestimated. Making lots of money is a breeze. You watch.

I came down the steps and into the street. Above, all was ocean brightness: against the flat blue sky the clouds had been sketched by an impressively swift and confident hand. What *talent*. I like the sky and often wonder where I'd be without it. I know: I'd be in England, where we don't have one. Through some physiological fluke – poison and body-chemistry doing a deal in their smoke-filled room – I felt fine, I felt good. Manhattan twanged in its spring ozone, girding itself for the fires of July and the riot heat of August. Let's walk it, I thought, and started off across town.

On masculine Madison (tightly buttoned, like a snooker waistcoat) I took my left and headed north into the infinite trap of air. Cars and cabs swore loudly at each other, looking for trouble, ready to fight, to confront. And here are the streets and their outlandish personnel. Here are the street artists. At the corner of Fifty-Fourth, a big black guy writhed within the glass and steel of a telephone kiosk. He was having a terrible time in there, that much was clear. Often as I approached he slapped the hot outer metal of the booth with his meaty pale palm. He was shouting – what, I didn't know. I bet money was involved. Money is always involved. Maybe drugs or women too. In the cabled tunnels beneath the street and in the abstract airpaths of the sky, how much violence was crackling through New York? How would it level out? Poorly, probably. Every line that linked two lovers would be flexed and snarled between a hundred more whose only terms were obscenity and threat . . . I've hit women. Yes, I know, I know: it isn't cool. Funnily enough, it's hard to do, in a sense. Have *you* ever done it? Girls, ladies, have you ever copped one? It's hard. It's quite a step, particularly the first time. After that, though, it just gets easier and easier. After a while, hitting women is like rolling off a log. But I suppose I'd better stop. I suppose I'd better kick it, one of these days . . . As I passed by, the negro cracked the phone back into its frame and lurched out towards me. Then his head dropped and he slapped the metal once more, but feebly now. Time and temperature flashed above.

Fielding Goodney was already in attendance at the Dimmesdale Room when I strolled into the Carraway a little after six. Erect among the misangled high chairs, he stood with his back to me in the depths of this grotto of glass, two limp fingers raised in a gesture of warning or stipulation. I saw his talking face, bleached to steel by the frosted mirror. A low-browed barman listened responsibly to his orders.

'Just wash the ice with it,' I heard him say. 'None in the glass, all right? Just wash it.'

He turned, and I felt the rush of his health and colour – his Californian, peanut-butter body-tone.

'Hey there, Slick,' he said, and gave me his hand. 'When did you get in?'

'I don't know. Yesterday.'

He looked at me critically. 'You fly Coach?'

'Standby.'

'Pay more money, Slick. Fly in the sharp end, or supersonic. Coach kills. It's a false economy. Nat? Give my friend here a Rain King. And just wash that ice. Relax, Slick, you look fine. Nat, am I wrong?'

'That's right, Mr Goodney.'

Fielding leaned back against the rich wood, his weight satisfyingly disposed on two elbows and one long Yankee leg. He regarded me with his embarrassing eyes, supercandid cornflower blue, the kind made fashionable by the first wave of technicolor American filmstars. His thick unlayered hair was swept back from the high droll forehead. He smiled . . . Speaking as an Englishman, one of the pluses of New York is that it makes you feel surprisingly well educated and upper class. I mean, you're bound to feel a bit brainy and blueblooded, a bit of an exquisite, when you walk through Forty-Second Street or Union Square, or even Sixth Avenue – at noon, the office men, with lunchbox faces and truant eyes. I don't get that feeling with Fielding. I don't get that feeling at all.

'And how old are you?' I asked him.

'I'll be twenty-six in January.'

'Jesus Christ.'

'Don't let that spook you, John. Here's your drink.'

Frowning Nat expectantly slid the glass towards me. The liquid looked as heavy as quicksilver.

'What's in this?'

'Nothing but summer skies, Slick . . . You're still a little lagged, no?' He placed a warm brown hand on my shoulder. 'Let's sit down. Nat: keep them coming.'

I followed him to the table, steadied by that human touch. Fielding adjusted his cuffs and said,

'Any thoughts on the wife?'

'I just spoke to Caduta Massi.'

'No kidding? She called you herself?'

I shrugged and said, 'Yeah, this afternoon.'

'So she's hungry. I love it. What did she say?'

'She said she wanted lots more kids.'

'Uh?'

'In the film. She wants this bunch of kids.'

'That figures,' said Fielding. 'Word was she had herself snipped. Sometime in her late twenties. She was a devout Catholic, also a hot lay. You know – no more abortions.'

'Hey look,' I said. 'I don't know, Fielding. She's a bit old for us, isn't she?'

'Have you seen *The Weird Sister*?'

'Yeah. It was terrible.'

'Sure, the film crapped, but Caduta looked great.'

'That's just it. She looked like a pampered moviestar. I don't want that. I want one of those . . .' I wanted one of those new-deal actresses, the sort that look like averagely scuffed-up house-wives. Critics were forever saying how *sexy* and *real* these actresses looked. I didn't think they looked sexy but I thought they looked real. At least this was my instinct, and my instinct was all I had to go on. 'Who else is there? How about Happy Jonson?'

'No good. She's in the Hermitage.'

'What's up?'

'Depression, deep, practically catatonic. That girl is real blue, Slick.'

'Okay, what about Sunny Wand?'

'Ditto. Fat farm. Two hundred and twenty pounds.'

'Wow . . . Okay, Day Lightbowne.'

'Forget it. She just came out of a two-year analysis. Then she was date-raped in Bridgehampton by her weekend therapist.'

'Date-raped, huh. What kind of deal is that? What, sort of with bananas and stuff?'

'*Date*-raped, Slick. Out on a date, you know? Remember? In fact it's an interesting distinction. With a regular rape, lust plays no part in it. It's all about power, self-assertion, violence – normally these losers can't even perform. But with a date-rape, lust features.' He paused, then went on briskly. 'Anyhow Day Lightbowne was screwed to shreds by her shrink and she's right out of business. I say Caduta, Slick. She's perfect for us. Think about it. Just think about it. Have you spoken with Lorne?'

'Yeah.'

'This is a very difficult time for Lorne.'

'You're not fucking kidding.'

'His career's in turnaround and he just had eighty grand's worth of dental work. He's low right now.'

'Low? What's he like when he's high? Two hours I had him

on the line. Look, Fielding, he's going to roast me. I won't be able to handle him.'

'Stay icy calm, Slick. The truth is, Lorne Guyland will do anything to be in this picture. Have you seen *The Cyborg Sanction*?'

'No.'

'*Pookie Hits the Trail? Dynamite Dick?*'

'Of course not.'

'He'll do anything now. Space opera, road movies, good-ole-boy stuff, TV specials. His agent straps him on the horse and out he rides. This is the first real part that's come his way for four–five years. He's crazy for it.'

'Then why do we want him?'

'Trust me, Slick. With Guyland in, it respectabilizes the whole package. The bottom line is, no Lorne Guyland movie ever lost money. It ups the TV and cable and video sale by 50 per cent, means we clean up in Taiwan and Guadeloupe. I have a bunch of old farts with five hundred grand under the cot. They won't haul it out for Christopher Meadowbrook or Spunk Davis or Butch Beausoleil. Never heard of them. But they'll haul it out for Guyland. Lorne's our man, Slick. Face it.'

'He's a maniac. How do I deal with him?'

'Like this. Say you'll do everything he wants and then when the time comes don't do any of it. If he goes bananas, you shoot the scene then lose the take. You'll have the final cut, John. That I swear.'

Well, this made pretty good sense to me. I said, 'How's the money?'

'The money,' said Fielding, 'the money is beautiful. Ever take any exercise, Slick?'

'Why? Yeah.'

'What kind of stuff?'

'Oh, you know. I swim sometimes. I play tennis.'

'No kidding.' He called for the check. I reached for the squashed notes I kept in my trouser pocket. With a strong left hand Fielding seized my wrist. As I stood up I saw him take a fifty, one of many, from his glowing clip.

Fielding had the car waiting outside – a six-door Autocrat, half a block long, complete with zooty chauffeur and black body-guard riding shotgun. He took me to an old gangster steakhouse in the Heights. It was brilliant. We talked money. Everything looked cool with Fielding's quorum of investors. Fuck it, I thought: worst case, his dad will end up tabbing the whole deal. Fielding's father is called Beryl Goodney and owns half of Virginia. Maybe his mum is called Beryl, too, and owns the other half. Fielding never talks about his own dough, but I've yet to meet a more spectacular *have*: he's got a lot already and he wants a lot more . . . 'In general terms, Slick, how much do you know about money?' I said – very little. 'Let me tell you about it,' he began. And he was away, his voice full of passionate connoisseurship, with many parallels and precedents, Italian banking, liquidity preference, composition fallacy, hyper-inflation, business confidence syndrome, booms and panics, US corporations, the sobriety of financial architecture, the Bust of '29, the suicides on La Salle and Wall Street . . . And I found myself wondering whether Alec has seen the single dead flower in the jamjar beside Selina's bed, or heard her peeing and humming in the quiet bathroom, the black pants like a wire connecting her calves. There seems to be a thing about girls and best friends. I always fancy their best friends too, come to think of it. I certainly fancy Debby and Mandy, and that Helle from the boutique whom Selina hobnobs with. Perhaps you fancy your girl's best friends because your girl and her best friends have a lot in common. They're very alike, except in one particular. You don't go to bed with the best friends all the time. In the sack she can give you one thing your girl can't give you: a change from your girl. Not even Selina can give you that. *Is* Alec fucking her? Well, what do you think? Is she doing him all those nice favours? Could be, no? Here's my theory. I don't think she is. I don't think Selina Street *is* fucking Alec Llewellyn. Why? Because he hasn't got any money. I have. Come on, why do you reckon Selina had soldiered it out with me? For my pot-belly, my bad rug, my personality? She's not in this for her health, now is she? . . . I tell you, these reflections really cheered me up. You know where you are with economic necessity. When I make all this money I'm going to make, my position will be even stronger. Then I can kick Selina out and get someone even better.

Fielding signed the check. I signed some contracts, directing more and more money my way.

He dropped me off on Broadway. Eleven o'clock. What can a grown male do alone at night in Manhattan, except go in search of trouble or pornography?

Me, I spent an improving four hours on Forty-Second Street, dividing my time between a space-game arcade and the basement gogo bar next door. In the arcade the proletarian ghosts of the New York night, these darkness-worshippers, their terrified faces reflected in the screens, stand hunched over their controls. They look like human forms of mutant moles and bats, hooked on the radar, rumble and wow of these stocky new robots who play with you if you give them money. They'll talk too, for a price. *Launch Mission, Circuit Completed, Firestorm, Flashpoint, Timewarp, Crackup, Blackout!* The kids, tramps and loners in here, they are the mineshaft spirits of the new age. Their grandparents must have worked underground. I know mine did. In the gogo bar men and women are eternally ranged against each other, kept apart by a wall of drink, a moat of poison, along which mad matrons and bad bouncers stroll.

At eleven thirty or thereabouts the old barmaid said to me, 'See? She's talking to you, Cheryl's talking to you. You want to buy Cheryl a drink?'

I paid the ten and said nothing. The old barmaid in her brown condom, she might have been last night's sister. That's my life: repetition, repetition. True, the chicks on the ramp provided some variety. None of them wore any pants. At first I assumed that they got paid a lot more for this. Looking at the state of the place, though, and at the state of the chicks, I ended up deciding that they got paid a lot less.

Two hours later I was wheeling around Times Square, looking for damage. I found some too. A very young prostitute approached me. We caught a cab and rode thirty blocks, downtown, west, Chelsea way. I glanced at her only once in the bucking car. She was dark, with lips the colour of blood and Spanish hair too tangled to shine. I consoled myself with the thought that, along with a bottle of Je Rêve, a carton of Executive Lights, and a punch in the tits, I'd be taking back a real wowser of a VD for Selina – Herpes I, Herpes II, Herpes: The Motion Picture. I can recall the rudimentary foyer of some thriving flophouse. I paid for the room, up front. She led me there. The figure of forty dollars was mentioned by her and approved by me. She started getting undressed and so did I. Then I stopped. '. . . But you're pregnant,' I remember saying in childish, open-ended surprise. 'It's all right,' she said. I stared at the strong gleaming belly. You expect it to be so soft but it looks so strong. 'It's not all right,' I said. I made her get dressed and sit on the bed. I held her hand and listened to myself talking crap for an hour and a half. She did a lot of nodding. I had paid her the money. She even listened to some of it: this was easy work, really. Towards the end I thought I might even try and wangle a handjob out of her. She would have obliged readily enough, no doubt. She was like me, myself. She knew she shouldn't do it, she knew she shouldn't go on doing it. But she went on doing it anyway. Me, I couldn't even blame money. What is this state, seeing the difference between good and bad and choosing bad – or consenting to bad, okaying bad?

Nothing happened. I gave her a further ten for carfare. She went off to find more men and money. I returned to the hotel, and lay down fully clothed, and backed off into sleep for the second night running in this town where the locks and light-switches all go the wrong way, and where the sirens say 'you' and whoop! and *ow, ow, ow*.

My head is a city, and various pains have now taken up residence in various parts of my face. A gum-and-bone ache has launched a cooperative on my upper west side. Across the park, neuralgia has rented a duplex in my fashionable east seventies. Downtown, my chin throbs with lofts of jaw-loss. As for my brain, my hundreds, it's Harlem up there, expanding in the summer fires. It boils and swells. One day soon it is going to burst.

Memory's a funny thing, isn't it. You don't agree? I don't agree either. Memory has never amused me much, and I find its tricks more and more wearisome as I grow older. Perhaps memory simply stays the same but has less work to do as the days fill out. My memory's in good shape, I think. It's just that my life is getting less memorable all the time. Can you remember where you left those keys? Why should you? Lying in the tub some slow afternoon, can you remember if you've washed your toes? (Taking a leak is boring, isn't it, after the first few thousand times? Whew, isn't *that* a drag?) I can't remember half the stuff I do any more. But then I don't want to much.

Waking now at noon, for example, I have a strong sense that

I spoke to Selina in the night. It would be just like her to haunt me during the black hours, when I am weak and scared. Selina knows something that everyone ought to know by now. She knows that people are easy to frighten and haunt. People are easy to terrify. Me too, and I'm braver than most. Or drunker, anyway. I got into a fight last night. Put it this way: I'm a lovely boy when I'm asleep. It began in the bar and ended on the street. I started the fight. I finished it too, fortunately – but only just. The guy was much better at fighting than he looked . . . No, Selina didn't call, it didn't happen. I would have remembered. I have this heart condition and it hurts all the time anyway, but this is a new pain, a new squeeze right in the ticker. I didn't know Selina had such power of pain over me. It is that feeling of helplessness, far from home. I've heard it said that absence makes the heart grow fonder. It's true, I think. I certainly miss being promiscuous. I keep trying to remember my last words to her, or hers to me, the night before I left. They can't have been that interesting, that memorable. And when I woke the next day to ready myself for travel, she was gone.

Twelve fifteen and Felix arrived, bearing a cocktail or two on his shoulder-high tray. I drink too much coffee as it is.

'Thanks, pal,' I said, and slipped him a ten.

Oh yeah, and while I remember – I haven't briefed you about that mystery caller of mine yet, have I? Or have I? Oh that's right, I filled you in on the whole thing. That's right. Some whacko. No big deal . . . Wait a minute, I tell a lie. I *haven't* briefed you about it. I would have remembered.

Yesterday afternoon. I was doing then what I'm doing now. It's one of my favourite activities – you might even call it a hobby. I was lying on the bed and drinking cocktails and watching television, all at the same time . . . Television is cretinizing me – I can feel it. Soon I'll be like the TV artists. You know the people I mean. Girls who subliminally model themselves on kid-show presenters, full of faulty melody and joy, Melody and Joy. Men whose manners show newscaster interference, soap stains, film smears. Or the cretinized, those who talk on buses and streets as if TV were real, who call up networks with strange questions, stranger demands . . . If you lose your rug, you can get a false one. If you lose your laugh, you can get a false one. If you lose your mind, you can get a false one.

The telephone rang.

'Yeah?'

There was silence – no, not silence but a faint parched whistle, dreary and remote, like the sound that lives inside my head. Perhaps this was the sound the Atlantic made with all its mass and space.

'Hello? Selina? Say something, for Christ's sake. Who's paying for this call?'

'Money,' said a man's voice. 'Always money, the money.'

'Alec. Who is this?'

'It isn't Selina, man. I'm not Selina.'

I waited.

'Oh, I'm not anybody very special at all. I'm just the guy whose life you fucked up. That's all I am.'

'Who are you? I don't know you.'

'The man says he doesn't know me. How many guys' lives you fucked up recently? Maybe you ought to keep score.'

Where was this coming from? Would the hotel telephonist know? *Had* I fucked up anyone's life recently? Not that I could *recall* . . .

'Come on,' I said, 'who needs this? I'm hanging up.'

'WAIT!' he said – and I thought, at once, with relief: Oh, he's *mad*. So there's no real problem. It's not my fault. Everything's fine, fine.

'Okay, Say your bit.'

'Welcome to New York,' he began. 'Flight 666, Room 101.

Thank you for flying Trans-American. Don't mess with cabbies, don't fight with drunks. Don't walk Ninety-Ninth Street. Don't go to topless bars. You want to buy Dawn a drink? Stay out of those porno stores you've been eyeing. They'll wreck your head. Stay drunk for when we meet. And give me back my fucking money.'

'. . . Wait. Hey. What's your name?'

The line died. I put down the receiver and picked it up again.

'It was a local call, sir,' the girl told me. 'Everything all right, sir?'

'Yes,' I said. 'Thank you. Everything's fine, fine.'

Wow, I thought – this is a new wrinkle. It was a local call, no question. It was very local indeed.

Two forty, and I was out on Broadway, heading north. Now, how bad do you assume I'm feeling? . . . Well, you're wrong. I'm touched by your sympathy (and want much, much more of it: I want sympathy, even though I find it so very hard to behave sympathetically). But you're wrong, brother. Sister, you slipped. I didn't feel too great this morning, true. A ninety-minute visit to Pepper's Burger World, on the other hand, soon sorted that lot out. I had four Wallies, three Blastfurters, and an American Way, plus a nine-pack of beer. I'm a bit full and sleepy, perhaps, but apart from that I'm ready for anything.

I wondered, as I burped up Broadway, I wondered how this town ever got put together. Some guy was dreaming big all right. Starting down in Wall Street and nosing ever upward into the ruins of the old West Side, Broadway snakes through the island, the only curve in this world of grids. Somehow Broadway always contrives to be just that little bit shittier than the zones through which it bends. Look at the East Village: Broadway's shittier than that. Look uptown, look at Columbus: Broadway's shittier.

Broadway is the moulting python of strict New York. I sometimes feel a bit like that myself. Here the fools sway to Manhattan time.

Now what's all this about me playing tennis with Fielding Goodney? Do *you* remember me making this ridiculous arrangement? Remind me. This morning, as I sat sobbing over my first cigarette, Fielding rang and said,

'Okay, Slick. I fixed the court. Let's do it.'

Well of course I kept quiet, and nonchalantly transcribed the address he gave. I happen to have an old pair of sneakers with me, and a T-shirt of sorts. Fielding will supply the trunks. As for tennis, I thought to myself – yeah, I can play that stuff. A mere four or five summers back you could have seen me out there, gambolling around the court. I haven't played since, but I've watched an awful lot of tennis on television.

Carrying my stuff in a plastic duty-free bag, I followed leaning Broadway up past the loops and circuses at the corner of the Park and into the West Side with its vacant lots and gaping car chutes. The numbered streets plodded slowly by. I kept expecting to see a sports complex or a gymnasium, or one of those shady squares of green that surprise you in the streets of London. 'You've screwed up again,' I thought, when I came to the building that Fielding had specified. It was a skyscraper, whose glassy lines climbed like a strip of film into the open blue. I went in anyway and asked the oldtimer.

'A fifteenth,' he said.

What was Fielding playing at? I rode the lift, which barrelled me up through the dead floors marked with an X. In the corridor I passed a familiar face – that of Chip Fournaki, a swarthy pro who usually flopped foul-temperedly in the semis of the major competitions. A few seconds later I passed Nick Karebenkian, Chip's doubles partner.

The door buzzed and I stepped into the loud green of an equatorial anteroom. On the astroturf carpet stood Fielding

Goodney, drinking real orange juice from a tall beaker. His skin had the perennial tan, highlighting the milky down on his limbs and the sharp creases of his pristine shorts and shirt, the chunky bleach of his high-tec footwear.

'Hey, Slick,' he said, and turned towards the glass wall. I joined him. As if from the bridge of a ship we looked down on to the court. It was television: two top grand-slammers thwacking it out, all grunt and sprint. At the far end of the deck was another window. Behind the dark screen sat twenty or thirty people. The court itself must have been three floors deep. A hundred dollars an hour? Two hundred? Three?

'Who are they over there?' I asked.

'They just come in and watch. See that kid down there? Jo'burg out of Texas. Eleventh on the computer. He's under investigation by the TPA. He takes guarantee money to appear in the minor majors. Bribes. It's illegal, but practically the whole top thirty are triple earners. There's going to be a real shitstorm in a couple of years. They should legalize it, fast. I'm a capitalist, Slick. I'm a *good* capitalist. It's supply and demand. Why fight it? Here are your trunks.'

He pointed to the door.

'Oh, Mr Goodney,' I heard the white-smocked lady sing. 'You'll finish prompt, won't you. Sissy Skolimowsky is on at four, and you know what she's like.'

I knew what Sissy Skolimowsky was like too. She was the world champion.

So I slipped into my gear next door. Hippie-red tanktop drummer's T-shirt, Fielding's hideous trunks (they weren't tennis shorts at all, damn it: they were skintight Bermudas, with golfing check), black socks, my cracked and parched sneakers . . . Usually, as I think I've said, New York is a holiday from the nine-to-five of my social shame. But I felt a bad premonition now – intense, adolescent. I tiptoed to the can. The shoes pinched like crazy: my feet must still have jet-lag, jet-swell. I unzipped the trunks and did my thing. The pee looked awful pale against the Vitamin B-steeped mothballs of the curved jug. I turned. There was a mirror. Oh forget it. They won't let you play anyway.

But they did. The lady gave me a startled glance – at the tureen of my gut, no doubt, and at the crushed bullybag in the wide-checked Bermudas – but she gave me my racket and opened the door. I came down the steps and on to the deck. Fielding had already loped hungrily to the far end, holding his barndoor-sized steel bat in one hand and a dozen yellow tennis balls in the other.

'Want to hit for a while?' he shouted, and the first of the balls was burning through the air towards me.

I should have realized that when English people say they can play tennis they don't mean what Americans mean when they say they can play tennis. Americans mean that they can play tennis. Even in my prime I was never more than an all-weather park-player. A certain wrong-footing slyness has sometimes enabled me to dink and poke my way to victory over more talented players. But basically I'm a dog on the court. Fielding was good. Oh, he was good. And there were differences of health, muscle-tone and coordination to be accounted for too. Fielding, tanned, tuned, a king's ransom of orthodonture having passed through his mouth, reared on steaks and on milk sweetened with iron and zinc, twenty-five, leaning into his strokes and imparting topspin with a roll of the wrist. Me, I lolloped and leapt for my life at the other end, 200 pounds of yob genes, booze, snout and fast food, ten years older, charred and choked on heavy fuel, with no more to offer than my block drive and backhand chip. I looked up at the glass window above Fielding's head. The middle-management of Manhattan stared on, their faces as thin as credit cards.

'Okay,' said Fielding. 'You want to serve?'

'You do it.'

I watched Fielding bend forward, pat the ball, then straighten up to aim his gun. *My* serve is no more than a convulsion which occasionally produces a baseline overhead. But Fielding was precise in his stance, measured in his action, with a touch of the severity that all natural ballplayers have. What is it with ballplayers? What is it about roundness that they understand better than we do? The world is round. They understand that too.

His opening serve I didn't see at all. It fizzed past me, losing its definition for a moment on the centre line, before thwacking first bounce into the green canvas behind my back. The passage of the ball seemed to leave a comet's trail of yellow against the artificial green of the court.

'Nice one,' I called, and trudged across in my black socks and checked Bermudas. This time I managed to get a line on Fielding's first serve: it smacked into the tape with a volume that made me whimper – the sound of a strong hand slapping a strong belly. I edged up a few feet as Fielding daintily removed the second ball from the pocket of his tailored shorts. I twirled my racket and swayed around a bit . . . But his second serve was a real dilly too. Hit late and low with what I guessed was a backhand grip, the ball came looping over the net, landed deep, and kicked like a bastard. It jumped so high that I could return it only with a startled half-smash. Fielding had come sauntering up to the net, of course, and angled the ball away with acute dispatch. He aced me again at thirty-love, but on the last point of the game I got another crack at that second serve of his. I stood my ground and lobbed the brute, quite accurately, and Fielding had to stroll back from the service line to retrieve it.

That lob was my last shot, really. I was never a contender after that. We had a rally of sorts: Fielding stood at the centre of his baseline while I hurled myself around the court. *Put it away*, I kept telling him, but there were a good few strokes exchanged before he chose to place the ball beyond my reach.

We switched ends. I didn't meet his eye. I hoped he couldn't hear my hoarse gasps for air. I hoped he couldn't smell – I hoped he couldn't see – the junk-fumes swathing my face like heat-ripple. As I took position I glanced up at our audience in their high aquarium. They were smiling down.

My opening serve flopped into the net, six inches from the ground. My second serve is a dolly and Fielding murdered it in his own sweet time, leaning back before putting all his weight into the stroke. I didn't even chase his return. The same thing happened on the next point. At love-thirty I served so blind and wild that Fielding simply reached out and caught the ball on the volley. He pocketed it and strolled forward a few paces – several paces. I moved wide and, in petulant despair, hit my second serve as if it were my first. And it went in! Fielding was less surprised than I was but he only just got his racket to the ball – and he was so insultingly far advanced that his return was nothing more than a skied half-volley. The yellow ball plopped down invitingly in the centre of my court. I hit it pretty low, hard and deep to Fielding's backhand and lumbered cautiously up to the net. A big mistake. Fielding chose this moment to untether a two-fisted topspin drive. The ball came screaming over the tape, skipped a beat, regathered its tilt and momentum – and punched me in the face. I toppled over backwards and my racket fell with a clatter. For several shocked seconds I lay there like an old dog, an old dog that wants its old belly stroked. Now how's this going to look? I got to my feet. I rubbed my nose.

'You okay, Slick?'

'Yeah. I'm cool,' I murmured. I bent down for my racket, and straightened up. Behind the glass wall the sea-creatures watched from their pool. Sharp faces. That's right, get your staring done with.

And so it went on. I won about half a dozen points – from Fielding's double-faults, from net-cords and shots off the wood, and from telling lies about a couple of the calls. I kept wanting to say: 'Look, Fielding, I know this is costing you a lot of money and everything. But do you mind if I stop? Because I *think I might* DIE if I don't.' I didn't have the breath. After five minutes I was playing with a more or less permanent mouthful of vomit. It was the slowest hour of my life, and I've had some slow hours.

The first set went six-love. So did the second. We were about nine-love in the third when Fielding said,

'You want to play or you just want to hit?'

'. . . Let's hit.'

Finally a bell rang, and Sissy Skolimowsky appeared with her coach. Fielding appeared to know this chunky, white-skinned girl.

'Hi,' she said.

'Hey, Siss,' said Fielding. 'Okay if we watch?'

She was already on the line, starting work. 'You can watch,' she said, 'but you can't listen . . . Shit!'

But I was staggering off by this time. Ten minutes later, I was still slumped wheezing and gagging on a director's chair in the anteroom when Fielding trotted up the steps. He squeezed my shoulder.

'I'm sorry, I . . .'

'Relax, Slick,' he said. 'You just need to sink a couple of thou into your backhand, maybe a grand on your serve. You should quit smoking, drink less, eat right. You should go to high-priced health clubs and fancy massage studios. You should undergo a series of long, painful and expensive operations. You ought to –'

'Look, shut the fuck up, will you. I'm not in the mood.'

'Your funeral, Slick. I just want you to stick around for a while. You'll be a rich man by the time I'm done. I just want you to *enjoy*.'

Pretty soon, Fielding jogged off back to the Carraway. I went and sat next door in the changing-room. I stared at the pimpled tiles. I thought if I could just stay completely still for the next half an hour, then maybe nothing too bad would happen. One twitch, I reckoned, one blink, and the changing-room was in for some restricted special effects . . . Then six huge guys came in – I guess from the squash courts, down the passage somewhere. These gleaming, stinging jocks were all shouting and swearing and farting as they stripped for the shower. I never saw their faces. I couldn't raise my head without copping an open-beaver shot of some armpit or scribble-haired backside. Once I opened my eyes to see a great raw dick dangling two inches from my nose, like a pornographic reprisal. Then they had a ten-minute towel-fight. The chick in the smock even poked her head round the door and hollered at them through the steam . . . I couldn't take it any longer. I weepily gathered my street clothes and crammed them into the duty-free bag. I hit Sixty-Sixth Street in sweat-looped tanktop, knee-length Bermudas, black socks and squelchy gyms. Come to think of it, I must have looked exactly like everyone else. My body craved darkness and silence but the sun's controls were all turned up full blast as I screamed for cabs in the yellow riot of Broadway.

There is only one way to get good at fighting: you have to do it a lot.

The reason why most people are no good at fighting is that they do it so seldom, and, in these days of high specialization, no one really expects to be good at anything unless they work out at it and put in some time. With violence, you have to keep your hand in, you have to have a repertoire. When I was a kid, growing up in Trenton, New Jersey, and later on the streets of Pimlico, I learned these routines one by one. For instance, can you butt people (i.e. hit them in the face with *your* face – a very intimate form of fighting, with tremendous power to appal and astonish)? I took up butting when I was ten. After a while, after butting a few people (you try to hit them with your rugline, hit them in the nose, mouth, cheekbone – it doesn't much matter), I thought, 'Yeah: I can butt people now.' From then on, butting people was suddenly an option. Ditto with ball-kneeing, shin-kicking and eye-forking; they were all new ways of expressing frustration, fury and fear, and of settling arguments in my favour. You have to work at it, though. You learn over the years, by trial and error. You can't get the knack by watching TV. You have to use live ammunition. So, for example, if you ever tangled with me, and a rumble developed, and you tried to butt me, to hit my head with your head, you probably wouldn't be very good at it. It wouldn't hurt. It wouldn't do any damage. All it would do is make me angry. Then I'd hit your head with my head extra hard, and there would be plenty of pain and maybe some damage too.

Besides, I'd probably butt you long before it ever occurred to you to butt me. There's only one rule in street and bar fights: maximum violence, instantly. Don't pussyfoot, don't wait for the war to escalate. Nuke them, right off. Hit them with everything, milk bottle, car tool, clenched keys or coins. The first blow has to give everything. If he takes it, and you go down, then you get all he has to mete out anyway. The worst, the most extreme violence – at once. Extremity is the only element of surprise. Hit them with everything. No quarter.

★

Well I really beat myself up out on the court there, I'll tell you that. For seventy-two hours I just lay in my pit at the hotel. The tinnitus was operational pretty well full time, and that toothache of mine got much more complicated: it would kick me awake with sirens of pain, loud, inordinate, braiding, twisting like currents in a river. I'd fucked my back, too, out on the deck – and there was this incredible welt up the rear of my thigh where I'd fallen and tobogganed across the mat on my can for a few yards, wrong-footed by Fielding. Last but not least, I seemed to have developed an acute gastric condition, maybe from all those frazzled junk-furters. Or maybe it's just a compound hangover, I don't know. For the first day I was pure turbo power, a human hovercraft over the bowl. Oh, I had lift-off . . . The maid lurked but never got a look in, and soon the room was really showing its age.

Felix the bellhop turned out to be a good pal to me here. He ran errands to the pharmacy and liquor store. With his quick presence, his careless intensity of of life, he dotted the wastes of the afternoon. He grew assertive. He even bawled me out when he found me shitfaced in front of *The Money Game* at ten thirty one morning, and looked as though he might prove difficult about ferrying in the booze. I bawled him out back. 'Fuck you, Felix,' I said. 'I'll use room service.' So he did my bidding, rest-lessly, with averted eyes. I was touched. Felix was getting money for this – I'd already passed the kid a twenty. But he would have made a lot more if I'd been liquored up all the time. In my reduced state I couldn't bear the rub of his disapproval and so I tried to take it fairly easy, on the whole.

I had fever. And I had Selina fever too. Lying in that slipped zone where there is neither sleep nor wakefulness, where all thoughts and words are cross-purposed and yet the mind is forever solving, solving, Selina came at me in queries of pink smoke. I saw her performing flesh in fantastic eddies and convulsions, the face with its smile of assent and the complicit look in the flattered eyes, the demonology of her underwear suggesting spiders and silk, her sharp shoulders, her fiery hair, the arched creature doing what that creature does best – and the thrilling proof, so rich in pornography, that she does all this not for passion, not for comfort, far less for love, the proof that she does all this for *money*. I woke babbling in the night – yes, I heard myself say it, solve it, through the dream-mumble – and I said, *I love it. I love her . . . I love her corruption.*

The telephone was a one-way instrument, an instrument of torture. Caduta rang. Lorne Guyland rang. A trio of nutters called Christopher Meadowbrook, Nub Forkner and Herrick Shnexnayder – I had them on the line too. That madman, that real madman, that accredited devo crazoid, he checked in again, three times, four times, son of a *bitch*. He's really got to me, I admit it. I turn hot now when I hear the empty sound at the end of the line, just before he starts his spiel. His voice is abject, bitter, poor – his voice is so *mean*. You can hear self-hatred and shame and suffering there. He maunders. He cries. His graphic and detailed threats come as a big relief. I can deal with threats. 'What do I call you?' I once asked him. 'I'll be Frank,' he said, and laughed for a long time, with no pleasure.

He knew about the tennis, and crowed at length over my humiliation. I assume he was glaring down from the glass gallery, having tailed me to the court. 'Black socks,' he said. 'Man, did you look sick.' His general theme? His theme was that I had ruined his life. I had tricked and cheated him many times. Nothing I could do would ever make it up to him. Only my own ruin could ever do that. I didn't argue. I didn't say much at all. I kept wishing he would ring when I had a decent drunk on: then I'd give him a piece of my mind. Sometimes he sounded big, sometimes he sounded small. Often he sounded damaged. If it came to it – who knows? With a few brandies down me I could probably handle him with my brief but nasty repertoire of sudden street stunts. You never can tell, though, with mad guys. I once got bopped by a mad guy and it was like no blow I have ever felt – qualitatively different, full of an atrocious, a limitless rectitude. Their internal motors are all souped up. They can lift buses and things if they're feeling mad enough.

Fielding rang several times too. He was gentle and solicitous, and scolded himself for having run me ragged on the court. It was my own fault, and I said so. He wasn't toying with me. He was just playing his natural game. Christ, he didn't even break stride.

'Hey,' I said. 'Those guys at the court. In the gallery. Who were they?'

'Why, I really couldn't tell you, Slick. I think they can just come in off the street. Maybe friends of the players, I don't know. Why do you ask?

'One of them rang me up,' I said vaguely.

'Who was he, Slick? A talent scout?'

'Oh yeah,' I said, and made a long arm for the scotch.

Fielding then offered to send over his personal physician to take a look at me, but I saw no good reason to put the doc through that ordeal.

Someone else rang. Someone else rang me here in New York. In my fever, out of the babble, one day, came a human voice.

By now I had learnt to think of the telephone as something hysterical and malevolent in itself, this dumb doll with its ventri-loquial threats and wheedles. Do that, think this, pretend the other. Then came a human voice.

I was lying on the bed, hugely, malely, in my winded Y-fronts. Boy am I butch. I was just lying there sweating and swearing and searching for sleep. Then the telephone did its act, its number.

One of my big beefs about Selina was that her disappearance obliged me to answer this thing whenever it rang. And it also might be Fielding, I supposed, aiming more and more money my way.

'Hello?' said the knowing voice. 'John?'

'. . . Selina! Ooh, right, you bitch. Now you just tell me where the –'

'Bad luck. It's Martina. Martina Twain.'

I felt – I felt several things at once. I felt the flinch of shameful unpreparedness. I smiled, and felt my facial flesh ease out of its recent mould. I felt my abscess for a second, lightly tickled by the strange creasing of my cheek. I felt my head-static quieten – and I felt that I really wasn't up to this, not now, maybe never.

She laughed at my silence. The laugh somehow established me as a waster or gadabout – but not unkindly, I thought. By this time I was sitting up straight and smoking and drinking and generally pulling myself together. For I have to tell you right off that Martina Twain is a real boss chick by anyone's standards – even by your lights and scales, your shadowy values and mores, you, the unknown Earthling, unknown to me. Pal, she's class, with a terrific education on her, plus one of those jackpot bodydeals whereby a tall and slender-framed girl somehow ends up with heavy tits and a big tush. She has a lively tongue in her lively mouth, and deep-flavoured colouring. American, but English-raised. I've always had a remote and hopeless thing for her, ever since film school.

'Martina . . . How are you this year? How did you know I was in town?'

'My husband told me.'

'Oh really,' I said sadly.

'He's in London. He just called this minute. So. Why are you here?'

'Oh I get over pretty often these days. I'm getting a film off the ground at last.'

'Yes, Ossie told me. I'm having some people over for dinner tonight. Do you want to come?'

'Oh yeah? Who'll be there?'

'Mostly writers, I'm afraid.'

'Writers?' I said. A writer lives round my way in London. He looks at me oddly in the street. He gives me the fucking creeps.

'That's right. Writers. There's a lady reviewer from the *Tribeca Times*. There's a Nigerian novelist called Fenton Akimbo. And Stanwyck Mills, the critic.'

'Tonight I can't do,' I said. 'I have to go to this dumb party – with uh, with Butch Beausoleil and Spunk Davis.'

She sounded impressed, or at least her silence did. 'Well I thought you'd probably be busy.'

'Wait a minute. How about breakfast? Things are tight but breakfast I think I can manage.'

We arranged to meet the following morning in the Bartleby on Central Park West. Nine o'clock. At once I grimly instigated my miracle flu cure. You go to bed, wrap up warm, and drink a bottle of scotch. Technically it's meant to be half a bottle, but I wanted to make absolutely sure. I cancelled all calls, put the Don't-Disturb docket on the latch – and I was sleeping like a baby well before ten.

My travelling-clock told me eight fifteen. I leapt out of bed feeling full of fight, really tiptop, apart from the sweats, the jerks, the shivers, a pronounced dizziness – and a sensation, hard to describe and harder to bear, that I had missed my stop on the shuttle and was somehow due yesterday at the next planet but one. Through the back window I warily inspected the span of the morning pale . . . My coffee arrived as I lay smoking in the tub, one leg atremble on the cold white shelf. I slashed myself shaving, then had a big rumble with my rug. I like to recede right out in the open but the slate-grey hanks kept doing bashful curtseys over the scooped zigzag of my brow. So I soaked the brush and plastered it all back. Next door I drank coffee in thick panting gulps. Eight forty. Best outfit: long flared jacket, sharply tapered strides, chunky black brothel-creepers. I didn't take a drink but as I locked my door I rehearsed the way in which I would say hi to Martina and laughingly call for champagne.

I headed east, then north. Whew, the day certainly had a funny colour to it – a harp light, but livid, bilious, as if some knot of eco-scuzz still lingered in its lungs. Go on, cough it out. And the shops were still sleeping . . . Where was the noise, where were the noisemakers? Only thin traffic with thin gimlet eyes. Suddenly feeling much stranger I stopped an old hardhat in his rompers of municipal blue.

'What's up, pal?' I said rockily, and I think I even grasped his arm. 'Where is everybody? Is this a bank holiday? Jesus, it's so dark! Is there some kind of eclipse deal or something?'

'What time you got? It's nine o'clock.'

'That's what I got too.'

'Nine p.m., sonny. It always gets dark here around now. People all gone home.'

I couldn't take this, I don't know why. So I started crying, not easily either but very tight and needing lots of work from the pumps of the chest. With extraordinary forbearance the old man stood his ground, his hands on my shoulders, saying, 'Hang on to it, kid. You're all right, I reckon. Yeah, you'll do. You ain't got a problem here. Listen – there'll be another day.'

And the man was right. On the third morning I woke to find the sheets were dry. Cautiously I opened my eyes and sat up straight. Yes, it had transferred, it had passed over, it had moved on to another place and was now busy somewhere else. And I thought: home, go home.

I slid out of the bag and rang room service. For over a minute I jogged on the spot. Now this is what waking up is *supposed* to be like. Was it my fancy, or had I lost a little bit of weight? I shampooed my rug. I found a bottle of disinfectant and took a swig of it. I did a press-up. I called the airline.

Half way through the first pint of coffee I torched a cigarette. Mmm, tasted good. Fags and fever really don't mix. I reproach myself for lack of self-discipline, but you've got to hand it to me when it comes to cigarettes. During my sickness, I realized, I had maintained my snout-count by sheer willpower. There was a slight downcurve or shortfall on the second carton, but nothing I couldn't fix if I smoked two-handed.

I touched my toes. I poured more coffee and unpeeled the fifth carton of sticky half-and-half. I yawned contentedly. Well then, I asked myself – how about a handjob?

I flipped a couple of men's magazines out of my suitcase and returned to the sack to check them out. Let's see here . . . The whole idea was obviously a very serious mistake. It wasn't any fun at all and gave me an unbelievable neck-ache. Besides, pornography is habit-forming, you know. Oh yes it is. I am a pornography addict, for instance, with a three-mag-a-week and at-least-one-movie habit to sustain. That's why I need all this money. I've got all these chicks to support . . . While I ruefully rubbed my neck in front of the bathroom mirror, and withstood the gaze of my blasted face, I also received another memory from the gibber of my nights of fever here in hot New York. Someone had come to the end of the long passage outside Room 101, once, twice, perhaps many more times, someone had come and mightily shaken the door, and not with the need for entry but in simple rage and warning. Did it happen, or was it just a new kind of dream? I'm getting new kinds all the time now, sadness dreams, drunk dreams, boredom dreams with me or someone else going on and on for ever – and dreams that I can liken only to the strains of search that poets must endure as they wait for their lines to form. I say this tentatively. I don't know what it's like to write a poem. I don't know what it's like to read one either . . . About me and reading (I don't really know why I tell you this – I mean, do you read that much?): I can't read because it hurts my eyes. I can't wear glasses because it hurts my nose. I can't wear contacts because it hurts my nerves. So you see, it all came down to a choice between pain and not reading. I chose not reading. Not reading – that's where I put my money.

I rang Fielding at the Carraway.

'Lorne wants reassuring,' he told me.

'Yeah, well you reassure him for a while. I'm going home.'

'Slick, so soon!'

'I'll be back. I got to sort some things out.'

'What's the problem? Women or money?'

'Both.'

'It's the same problem. When's your flight?'

'Ten.'

'So you leave for the airport at 8.45.'

'No. I arrive at the airport at 8.45. I'm flying Airtrak.'

'*Airtrak*? What do they give you on Airtrak, Slick? A spliff, a salad and a light-show?'

'Well, that's what I'm doing.'

'Listen . . . I want you to meet Butch Beausoleil before you wing out. Can you get to my club around seven? The Berkeley, West Forty-Fourth. Leave your bags at the door and just walk on through.'

Yes and I rang Martina too. She accepted my apologies. They always do, at first. Actually she was very sympathetic. We're meeting for a quick one at the Gustave on Fifth Avenue, six o'clock. I levelled with the girl, and told her how ill and lonely and fucked up I'd really been.

Now this was turning into a busy day. Noon saw me queueing at the stall on Sixth Avenue, queueing with the studes and lumber-jacks for a cheap thin seat on the wide-bodied, crash-prone aircraft. This is the people's airline: we are this airline's people. They brought the prices down across the board and now only the abject fly Airtrak. A uniformed girl with tomato-red hair and an incredible gobbler's mouth disappeared for an ominous few minutes to check out my US Approach card, then bustled back, her moist teeth refreshed by my sound credit rating. I asked,

'What's the movie?'

She tapped out the query with her red nails. 'They got *Pookie Hits the Trail*,' she said.

'Really? Who's in it?'

The tolerant computer knew this too. 'Cash Jones and Lorne Guyland.'

'Come on. Who do you like best?'

'I don't know,' she said. 'They both suck.'

I looked in on a crepuscular but definitely non-gogo bar on Fiftieth Street. For a while I read my ticket. On the next stool a trembling executive sank three dark cocktails quickly and hurried off with a dreadful sigh . . . White wine, me: trying to stay in shape here. It's my first piece of alcohol for – what? – nearly two days. After all that tearful confusion, after feeling like a one-year-old out on the street that night, I couldn't get anything down me. I tried. It tasted of poison, of hemlock. So I just sacked out with a fistful of Serafim. I don't know what I would have done without the old guy in his boiler suit. I really think I might have died, without that human touch . . . Thoughtfully chewing on a pretzel, I suddenly skewered my dodgy back tooth. Knowledge is painful, and I knew then beyond all question that Selina had some other prong on her books. Come on, of course she has. She's smart. She's practical. She'll have some property developer or spaced-out rich kid, some moneyman. She might not even be banging him yet, just keeping him quiet with the odd spangled glimpse of her underwear, the odd audience at the bathtub – yeah, and the odd handjob too, no doubt. After all, this was how she processed me to begin with, when she still had her sugar-daddy ad-exec, plus a twenty-year-old location researcher on the side. Selina knows how to fend them off fondly, she knows how to keep them stacked above her tarmac – she is an old hand at air-traffic control. Then, one day, you get the lot . . . Where is she now? It is six o'clock over there, when the dark comes down. She is dressing herself for the evening, and she is worried. She is worried. The night is young over there, but Selina Street is not so young, not any longer. You know something? I've got to marry her, marry Selina Street. If I don't, probably no one else will, and I'll have ruined another life.

I finished my wine and settled the tab – surprisingly high. But then it seemed I had had six glasses, or vases, of the friendly Californian cordial. I walked back to the hotel through the crowds (here they come again) of Manhattan groundlings, extras and understudies, walk-ons and bit-part players, these unknown Earthlings. Hugely the cast swelled into the street. Incensed cabs cussed and sulked: then I saw banners – BRITS OUT OF BELFAST and I LOVE THE IRA and WHO KILLED BOBBY SANDS? Bobby Sands, the dead hunger-striker. Hunger-striking must look particularly dire to these guys, each of whom has a neck like a birthday cake. 'You talking to me?' I shouted at one of them. 'Stay out of it. Yeah, what do *you* know.' Then I remembered that the Prince of Wales was in town too. It was probably him they had in mind. Some of the banners actually said as much, I now saw. Well, hang on to it, Prince, I thought. Don't listen to these bums. You're all right, I reckon – yeah, you'll do.

Back at the hotel I firmed up a deal with the man behind the desk. In exchange for ten bucks and as many minutes' chat about Lorne Guyland and Caduta Massi, he gave me my room until six without charging an extra day's whack. A lifelong Caduta fan, he also had a lot of time for old Lorne. 'He's been at the top for thirty-five years,' he explained. 'That's what he's got my respect for.' The unloved room looked on in quiet martyrdom as I packed my stuff. Mindful of my meeting with Martina, and determined to keep up the good work of the last two days, I had lugged back a quart of Chablis to keep me lightly fuelled throughout the afternoon. But the room was full of scotch and gin and brandy, and I deplore waste. Why, an African family could stay drunk for a month on the gear I'd be leaving behind. I didn't try Selina. I wanted to give her a nice surprise.

Orderly at first, my packing became brutal and chaotic. Under the couch I found an unopened pint of rum – hidden there by Felix, probably – and started tackling that too. I jumped up and down on the suitcase after I had seriously gouged my thumb in its catch. At some stage I flopped on to the bed and must have dozed off for a few minutes. The telephone woke me. Suavely I took a slug of rum and lit a cigarette in my own good time.

'Oh Christ. You again.'

'You fuck-up,' said the voice. 'Running back home. Wreck some more lives there. What happened? You skip a day? I saw you bawling out on the street. You're finished. It's all over.'

Now this was a break. He'd really caught me in the mood. With a case like this you have to reach down for the language. It's never far away from me. Drink brings it nearer. I took the phone by the throat, leaned forward, and said,

'Okay, blowjob, your turn to listen. Get some help, all right? Go down to your neighbourhood whacko project or sicko facility or scumbag programme and turn yourself in. You're one sick fuck. It's not your fault. It's your chemicals' fault. It's money's fault. They'll give you some nice free pills and you'll feel all right for a little while.'

'More,' he said. 'I like your style. Big man . . . We'll meet one day.'

'Oh I hope so. And when I get through with you, sunshine, there'll be nothing left but a hank of hair and teeth.'

'We'll meet –'

'We'll meet one day. And when that day comes I'll fucking kill you.'

I cracked the receiver down and sat there panting on the bed. I needed to spit. Uch, I hate making these threatening telephone calls. I looked at my watch . . . *Jesus*. I must have gone to sleep for an hour or more – though *sleep* might be pitching it a bit high. *Sleep* is rather an exalted term for what I get up to nowadays. These are blackouts, bub. I upended the rum bottle over my mouth, finished my packing in the sourly twanging light, marshalled my travel documents and buzzed down for the boy.

In the end I had ample time for my farewell to New York. First off, I gave Felix a fifty. He seemed strangely agitated or concerned and for some reason kept trying to make me lie down on the bed. But he was pleased, I hope, by the dough. I love giving money away. If you were here now, I'd probably slip you some cash, twenty, thirty, maybe more. How much do you want? What are you having? What would you give me, sister, brother? Would you put an arm round my shoulder and tell me I was your kind of guy? I'd pay. I'd give you good money for it.

Leaving my bag in the lobby I marched straight off to the

House of the Big One, where I ate seven Fastfurters. They were so delicious that tears filled my eyes as I bolted them down. Next I bought a joint, a popper, a phial of cocaine and a plug of opium from a fat spade in Times Square and snuffed it all up in a gogo bar toilet. This is a dumb move, they say, because the spades mix in strong stuff like devil dust with the dope. But where's the economics in that? What they really do is mix in *weak* stuff with the dope, so that in effect you're only buying a roll-up, a dimestore thermometer, some ground aspirin and a dog turd. Anyway, I snuffled it all up, as I say – and felt a distinct rush, I think, as I came bullocking out of the can.

Urged on by the cars and their brass, I crossed the road and hit the porno emporium on Forty-Third and Broadway. How to describe it? It is a men's room. These 25-cent loop cubicles are toilets, really: you enter your trap, putting money in the slot, you sit down and do what you need to do. The graffiti is written in black magic-marker on yellow cards, to which curious pin-ups are attached. This bitch has a gash so big. Watch the fuckpigs frolic in torrents of scum. Juanita del Pablo gets it in the ass. Who writes these things? Clearly someone on exceptionally cool terms with the opposite sex. Meanwhile, the black janitoriat stroll with jinking moneybags . . . First I sampled an S/M item in booth 4A. They got the chick on her back, bent her triple, and wedged a baseball bat in the tuck behind her knees. Then they gave her electric shocks. It was realistic. Was it real? You saw a writhing line of white static, and the girl certainly screamed and bounced. I split before they gave her an enema, which they were billed to do in the scabrous hate-sheet tacked to the door. If the girl had been a bit better-looking, a bit more my type, I might have stuck around. In the next booth along I caught a quarter's worth of film with a sylvan setting: the romantic interest of the piece focused on the love that flowers between a girl and a donkey. There she was, smiling, as she prepared to go down on this beast of burden. Ay! The donkey didn't look too thrilled about it either. 'I hope you're getting good money, sis,' I mumbled on my way out. She wasn't bad, too . . . Finally I devoted twenty-eight tokens' worth of my time to a relatively straight item, in which a slack-jawed cowboy got the lot, everything from soup to nuts, at the expense of the talented Juanita del Pablo. Just before the male's climax the couple separated with jittery haste. Then she knelt in front of him. One thing was clear: the cowboy must have spent at least six chaste months on a yoghurt ranch eating nothing but icecream and buttermilk, and with a watertight no-handjob clause in his contract. By the time he was through, Juanita looked like the patsy in the custard-pie joke, which I suppose is what she was. The camera proudly lingered as she spat and blinked and coughed . . . Hard to tell, really, who was the biggest loser in this complicated transaction – her, him, them, me.

Now I come jerking and burping up the portalled steps of Fielding's club, having stopped off for a drink or two on the way. You'd think I'd be in pretty terminal shape by now, what with the rum and the dope and all. But not me. No sir, not this baby. You recognize the type by now? Some people get sleepy when they drink a lot, but not us. When we drink a lot, we want to go out and do things . . . *Never do anything* is the rule I try and stick to when I'm drunk. But I'm always doing things. I'm drunk. 'Never do anything': that's a *good* rule. The world might be a better place – and a lot safer for me – if nobody ever did anything . . . So, as I say, I was in capital fettle when the revolving doors hurled me into the hall – to meet Fielding Goodney, and Butch Beausoleil, the real Butch Beausoleil.

There was a white-haired old robot at the desk and we shot the breeze for a while as he checked me out on the intercom. I told him a joke. How does it go now? There's this guy and his car breaks down and he – No, hang on. There's this farmer who keeps his wife locked up in the – Wait, let's start again . . . Anyway, we had a good laugh over this joke when I'd finished or abandoned it, and I was told where to go. Then I got lost for a bit. I went into a room where a lot of people in evening dress were sitting at square tables playing cards or backgammon. I left quickly and knocked over a lamp by the door. The lamp should never have been there in the first place, with its plinth sticking out like that. For a while I thrashed around in some kind of cupboard, but fought my way out in the end. Skipping down the stairs again, I fell heavily on my back. It didn't hurt that much, funnily enough, and I waved away the appalled footman who tried to help me to my feet. I then had a few pretty stern words with the old prong at the desk. He made sure I got there this time all right, personally escorting me to the door of the Pluto Room and saying with a bow,

'This okay now, sir?'

'Fabulous,' I said. 'Look, take this.'

'No thank you, sir.'

'Come on. What's a five?'

'We have a no-tips policy here, sir.'

'Just this once won't harm anyone. No one's looking – come on . . . Okay then – fuck off!'

Well that sorted him out. I chugged into the Pluto Room loosening my tie and craning my neck. Boy, was it dark and hot in here. The bent backs of women and the attentive angles of their men stretched down the bar away from me. I took a bit of a toss on a stool-leg and sprinted face-first into a pillar, but stumbled on until I made out my friend Fielding down at the far end. Dressed in a white tux, he was whispering into the nimbus cast by a miraculously glamorous girl. She wore a low-cut silk dress in a razzy grey – it rippled like television. Her ferociously tanned hair hung in solid curves over the vulnerable valves of her throat and its buzzing body-tone. Giving Fielding no time to intercept me, I swanned straight up to the girl and kissed her lightly on the neck.

'Hi, Butch,' I said. 'How you doing?'

'Well *hi*. John Self. An honour,' said Butch Beausoleil.

'How goes it, old sport,' said Fielding. 'Hey, Slick, you look really lit. Now before I forget, here's a present for you.'

He handed me an envelope. It contained an air ticket, New York–London, first class.

'The flight's at nine,' said Fielding, 'but you'll catch your plane – I guarantee it. Now, John, you look like you could use a drink.'

The kids were on champagne and I soon hollered for another bottle. I spilt a lot of that and hollered for another. Butch was a million laughs – and an obvious goer: you should have seen the way she helped me dab her lap with the napkin, and the way she playfully retrieved the ice-cubes I kept dropping down her front. Whew, the stuff that hot fox was giving out, all miming so fluently with the pornography still fresh in my head. Heat, money, sex and fever – this is it, this is New York, this is first class, this is the sharp end. I was one happy yob up there in the Pluto Room, and then another bottle appeared, and my nose was fizzing with the stuff, and there was another room and terrible confusion, and someone turned me by the shoulder and I felt wetness and could see Fielding's face saying . . .

The yellow cab shouldered its way through the streets of New York, a caged van taking this mad dog home. The driver with his flexed brown arm gouged the car through the lights on amber and gunned us out on to the straight. Never do anything, never do anything. I watched his brown arm, the skin puckered and punctured by its lancing black hairs. I watched unfamiliar city acres surge past in their squares. Eventually the flat signs and white lights of the airport began to swish by my face.

'Wha you fly,' said the driver, and I told him.

I was lying. So far as I could tell – from my watch, and from the red streamers of the ticket-books – both my flights had flown. But a squad of surprises awaited me in the expo aviary of the terminal. The departure of the nine o'clock flight had been delayed, thanks to a timely bomb hoax. They had just started reloading the baggage, and expected to be in the air by eleven. I strolled to the first-class check-in bay. First class, they treat you right. 'How many bags, sir?' asked the chick. 'Just the one,' I said, and turned with an obliging flourish. 'Oh, you poor fucking moron.' 'Sir?' 'No, no bags. Just me,' I said with a dreadful smile . . . I rang Felix at the Ashbery. He would store my stuff with no sweat. I'd be back . . . Under the hot dental lights I traversed the building in search of a bar, having developed the idea of toasting my deliverance from New York. Far and wide did I roam. 'Ten o'clock and you're closed?' I heard myself yelling. 'This is fucking JFK, pal!' By that time I had a couple of navy-blue serge lapels in my fists. The guy reopened the duty-free counter and sold me a pint. I sat drinking it in the departure lounge. Boarding began, first class first. I stood up and entered the tube.

And continued to travel deeper into the tubed night – to travel through the night as the night came the other way, making its violent sweep across the earth. I drank champagne in the wide red throne, friendless in the plane's eye, tastefully curtained off from the coughing, snoring, shrieking, weeping, birth-giving innards of Business, Trimmer and Economy. How I hate my life. I called for divining cards. I've got to stop being young. Why? It's killing me, being young is fucking killing me. I ate my dinner. I watched the film – they gave me a choice and I caught *Pookie*: it was terrible, and old Lorne looked like shit. What happened out there, with Fielding and Butch? Ay, keep it away! Don't let it touch me. I can't give it headroom. I've got to grow up. It's *time*.

'COME ON, John, what's it feel like? You're one of the top commercial directors in the country, you're only thirty-five, you're about to make your first feature, you're working with people like Lorne Guyland and Butch Beausoleil. Come on, John – what's it feel like?'

Actually it didn't feel like anything. It just felt like I was in London again, dumped out of the sky into nothing weather. It didn't feel like anything, but I sipped my beer, smiled at the microphone, and said,

'Well, fantastic, Bill, obviously. Making your first film, it's never easy, but I've got a really good feeling about this project. Things are looking really good.'

'You're telling me. You must feel bloody marvellous.'

'The future certainly looks bright.'

Bill is the London stringer of *Box Office*, the Hollywood trade – hence his celebratory tone. I don't think Bill was feeling very celebratory this morning, though. Exulting in my success looked like pretty hard work. But that's what they paid him for.

'Fill us in a little. Will you be writing the script?'

'Me? Are you kidding? No, the idea is mine, but we'll be using a, the American writer Doris Arthur' – Bill nodded – 'to develop the screenplay. Originally the film was set in London. Now it's New York, so we need a writer who can speak American.'

'Tell me, how do you feel about the prospect of working with Lorne Guyland? Excited?'

No doubt there was irony here, but I said, 'Very excited. Really thrilled. I'm looking to Lorne to help me over this hurdle – Lorne, with his years of experience and his – Hang on. You'd better not put that. Try this. Uh, Lorne is a true professional, one of the old school. Wait. You'd better not put that either. Just say he's a true professional, okay?'

'What about Butch Beausoleil?'

'The big thing about Butch is that she's not just a dumb blonde. She looks like a million dollars but she's also a very intelligent and sensitive young woman. I think she's got a great future in our industry.'

'Last question. Money.'

'Well, as I said, Fielding Goodney is the money genius. This is his first feature too, but he's had a lot of experience in, in money. We're going to bypass the big studios until the distribution stage. We've got this quorum of medium-sized investors. Some of the money will be coming from California, some from Germany and Japan. As you know, this is the new thing in funding.'

'That's right. What's the budget? Six?'

'Twelve.'

'Christ. It's all right for some, isn't it.'

'Yup.'

Bill then buggered off, thank God, and I strolled back to the bar with my empty mug. Eleven thirty, Sunday morning, the Shakespeare. In the booze-lined defile under the bendy mirror, Fat Vince and Fat Paul, two generations of handyman-and-bouncer talent, assembled beer crates with simian stoop. Fat Paul straightened up and I looked into his colourless, moistureless face.

'Same again?' he said.

'Yeah,' I said. 'Hey, and – Fat Paul. Give us a scotch and all.'

'Big one?'

'Nah, just a double'll do.'

Fat Paul placed the drinks on the bar. He folded his arms and leaned forward. He nodded pensively. 'There's a new stripper on today,' he offered. 'Veronica. Jesus. Beautiful.'

'I'll stick around.'

'Here, that – Selina. Still giving her one, are you?'

'Don't ask me, pal.'

We heard the sounds of chains shaking. We turned: a small shadow bided its time behind the locked glass doors.

'Fuck off out of it!' said Fat Paul, in his youthful way.

'No, it's all right,' I said. 'This must be my writer.'

Five days of London time, and still no fix on Selina.

Twenty-four hours ago I ran Alec Llewellyn to ground, but then the trail went cold. Alec, that liar. He was holed up in a service-flat block off Marble Arch – a high-priced dosshouse for middle-management loners and transients, with the strict feel of the ward or the lab: fifty units of downward mobility, observable under controlled conditions. Alec sees himself as one of life's deep divers. Crime, debt, dope – these are the fathoms through which he swims. The pinch of his long fingers over bookmatch and cigarette packet corresponds to the lines of his handsome, nervous, nutcracker face. Yes, he's nervous. He is much weaker than he was a year ago. He could do it all then. He is not sure he can do it all now.

'Where's Selina?'

'I don't know,' said Alec. 'Lying in a pile of cocks somewhere. Wiggling her bum in some penthouse. Take your pick.'

'Who's she fucking?'

'How should I know?'

'You told me it was someone I knew well. Who is it. Who.'

'Doesn't matter who. Think about it, man. I can't believe I've got to sit here telling you this. She's a gold-digger pushing thirty, right? In other words, an exhausted sack artist with shrinking assets. She can't stop digging, she has to keep digging until she strikes. There's nothing else she can do. Okay, marry her. Or try another kind of girl: freckles and A-levels, career woman, divorcée with two kids, fat nurse –'

'Oh you're such a liar. You just don't care what you say. What's it like, being a liar?'

'Not too bad. What's it like being a moron? Where do *you* think she is. Summer school? Walking in the Lake District?'

I looked round the room, at the churned bed, the hairbrush, at the splayed, eviscerated suitcase. Lean Alec, at thirty-six, a father of two, with his education, his privilege – what's he doing in this hired coop? We were drinking pernod, or paranoid, from a litre bottle with Heathrow tab.

'You know,' I said, 'what you told me at the airport, it fucked up my whole trip. Thanks. You really gave me a bad time.'

'That was just a precaution.'

'Uh?'

'She wants all your money.'

This really got me going. 'So what?' I said. 'God damn it, what's that got to do with *you*?'

'. . . *I* want all your money.' He laughed, but the laugh had a lot of wince in it. 'Look, John, this is serious. I hate to ask you this.'

'And I hate to hear it. How much?'

He named the figure – a consternating sum. I said,

'You already owe me money. What's it for? A drug deal? Gambling debt?'

'Alimony! She's got the law batting for her now. We have a

disagreement, I get a squad car full of rozzers coming round here to put her side of it.'

'Wait a minute. You told me you were still fucking her.'

'I am. Between you and me, it's never been better.'

'I don't get it.'

'It's like this. The pigs say I owe her all this money. If I didn't have the money there'd be no problem. But there it is, in the bank. Now I need that money to close a deal. I'm in with some bad guys on this and if I don't come across I'm going to get really worked over. They told me what they were going to do to me.'

I said, with interest, 'What, exactly?'

'No blows to the back of the head. In other words my face comes off. The pigs, they mean business too. Either I cough up on Friday, or it's Brixton.'

'Christ.'

'Give me the money. Come on, man – do it! Do it. How much are you getting for this film? Eighty? A hundred?'

'Nothing yet.'

'Do it. I'd do it for you.'

'Yeah, you keep saying that.'

'I pay you back in ten days. I swear. There's a cheque coming in. This is just a bridging loan.'

'Yes, I know all about this bridging business.'

I did, too. It was always the same. The money Alec was expecting – it looked like my money now. It looked as though it was all marked *me*. But when that money came, it wouldn't look like my money any more. It would look like his money. He wouldn't want to blow it all on me. Money is very versatile. You really have to give money credit for that.

I said some of this to Alec. He wasn't listening. Neither was I. An inner door opened and a long girl wearing a pair of fluted white pants tiptoed into the room. Now here's someone,

I thought, who really *understands* about pants. The tone of her skin was almost laughably exotic. Where was she from? Borneo, Madagascar, Mercury? She held one hand over her face as she groped for her bag. She didn't care who saw her mahogany breasts. They looked as though a lot of people had checked them out by now. Behind her the windowless cubicle shone like a filament. I've been in bathrooms like that, battery bathrooms (as if bathrooms weren't testing enough). You feel like a rat, taking a rat leak, watched by scientists up in rat control.

'Can't find me face,' she said.

'Have a pernod, sweetheart,' said Alec. 'John – Eileen.'

'Just cleaned me teeth,' she said.

She turned and headed back to the bathroom, moving more naturally now. Alec and I silently noted her flowing shoulders and pampered rump.

'Where do these chicks do their sunbathing?' I asked. 'Some island?'

'It's all She-Gloss,' he said, gazing at the closed bathroom door. 'You wouldn't believe it, but her bum is as white as those pants. Eileen wouldn't want anyone to think she sunbathed with no clothes on. She'd think that was dirty. Funny, isn't it.'

'Those are cool pants,' I said briskly. 'Now listen.' I tapped the bottle with a warning finger. 'Maybe I've had it with you and money. How do I know you're not lying? I'd like to know where it goes, this money I keep giving you.' A pair of airline tickets lay curled on the bed. I reached for them. Paris, first class. 'What sort of girl is Eileen? A fat nurse?'

'A career woman. She paid for all that. I owe her too.' He shuddered and made a bedraggled flutter with his hands. 'I've got to get out of this *crap*. You're just a jammy yob riding a fluke. What do you care? Just shut up and give me the fucking *money*.'

This is what I wanted. This was what I needed to see and hear and feel, the salute of his fear as we passed each other by. Me going up, him going down. Perhaps this was what I was paying for.

'Well,' I said, 'let's see what I can do.'

A sharp bell sounded, followed by three grim thuds on the outer door. Instantly Alec stood up and backed off with practised stealth towards the bathroom, miming self-erasure with his palm. He nodded fiercely at me, and vanished.

Holding my glass and cigarette, I unlatched the door and tugged it open. A heavy man with ragged hair was leaning as if exhausted on the jamb, rubbing his eyes with his fists. His smile was mean and weary but not yet quenched of amusement. Yes, he was big, about my weight. His shiny fat suit caught the real light at the end of the corridor.

'Yeah?'

'Mr Llewellyn?' he said, and straightened his neck.

He wasn't expecting me, someone like me. I don't have Alec's gaunt, dandyish look, the scuppered cunning of the top-drawer desperado. He wasn't expecting me, someone of his own kind.

'Who's asking?'

'Is Mr Llewellyn at home, by any chance? Have I caught him in? Mind if I take a look?'

'You're not coming in here.'

'All it is', he said, 'is a little bit of silliness. He's very silly, your friend. Us, we're serious. We get aggravated when people start being silly.' He stepped forward. 'Now let's sort this out.'

'Oy,' I said, and stepped forward myself. 'I know your trade. You buy bounced cheques at half price, then go out on the squeeze.' This was no arm-breaker or face-flayer. He served low down in the money army, a freelancer, a forager. He didn't beat it out of you. He bored it out of you. He bored for money. 'You're hardly legal,' I said. 'You're a cowboy. On your bike.'

The heavy man dropped his head and turned. For a moment I saw him sitting in his parked Culprit or 666, red-faced and winded, thinking how to save his day. But then he spat on the floor and looked up at me wryly.

'You can tell your bent friend he'll be seeing me again. And so will you.'

'Oh you frighteners,' I said. This guy had no future in the frightening business. He just wasn't frightening.

'Soon,' he said, and walked off down the passage stirring his keys.

Feeling braced, I sauntered back into the flat. 'He's gone,' I said as I tipped open the bathroom door.

. . . Ah, pornography. Eileen was up on the basin deck. She was naked. No, she wore white pants. No, she was naked: that milky rift was simply the phantom of her bikini line. This girl (I thought suddenly), she takes pains to be realistic – but then, how hard are dancers working, when they pretend to be marionettes? . . . Her legs dangled over Alec's shoulders in the loutish white light. He turned to me with an expression of vexation and strain. She turned too. Her eyes were flat and reluctantly engaged, as if she were looking into a mirror without much prospect of liking what she saw. Her mouth was even stranger. So *that* was where the pants were hanging out. Their frilled edges curled from her lips like a crushed bouquet.

I left the cheque on the bed. As I walked back down the corridor to the stairs I heard something, exceptionally clear and rhythmical, the sound that imitates consenting pain, the sound of a child riding the brink of its sneeze, I heard something telling me that Eileen was a noisemaker who had slipped her gag.

Now Fat Paul stooped, and worked the big black bolts. And now Doris Arthur stepped into the Shakespeare, wondering where to direct her grateful smile. But Fat Paul kept his head low, like all hell's doormen, like all hell's bouncers . . . Fielding Goodney had told me that Doris was 'a feminist of genius'. I'd assumed that this was merely droll code for sack talent, but now I wasn't so sure. I sipped my drinks and let her seek me out in the blinding gloom. After all, Doris was the beneficiary of a university education, over at Harvard there. She could find her own way. As a rule, I hate people who are the beneficiaries of a university education. I hate people with degrees, O-levels, eleven-pluses, Iowa Tests, shorthand diplomas . . . And you hate me, don't you. Yes you do. Because I'm the new kind, the kind who has money but can never use it for anything but ugliness. To which I say: You never let us in, not really. You might have thought you let us in, but you never did. You just gave us some money.

And told us to get lost . . . As for feminism in general, well, my position here was that of the unbudgeably powerful mob boss who, when piqued by bothersome incursions that threaten to sour the whole deal, calls the Ladies in and calmly says, Okay, so you want a piece of this. What kept you? We thought you were happy doing all that other stuff. You stayed quiet for however many million years it is. *Now* you tell us. But I'm a reasonable man. Some time soon there's a concession coming up in one of our out-of-town operations. If everything goes through okay and you keep your nose clean, who knows, we might be able to . . .

'John Self?'

She stood there, poised, peering. No matter how butch and pushy they get, girls will never lose this air of sensitive expectancy. Or I hope they won't. She wore roomy dungarees and a much-patched flying jacket – anti-rape clothes, mace clothes. They didn't work. Now here's someone, I thought to myself, here's someone who's really worth raping. With a good lawyer you'd only get a couple of years. It's not so bad in the nick these days. They have ping-pong, telly, individual cells.

'Sit down, Doris,' I said, dead cool. 'Let me get you a pint. Fat Paul!'

'No – just water.'

'Designer water, or is from the tap okay?'

'From the tap is fine.'

I heaved myself up and trudged to the bar in my boxy suit. I turned. Doris was looking around with an anthropological eye . . . Some months ago Fielding had sent me a copy of this chick's first book, a slender album of short stories. Young Doris had apparently done all right for herself in the States. The underlined bits of the clippings which Fielding's LA office had enclosed spoke warmly of her originality and offbeat erotic power. The book was called *The Ironic High Style*, for some reason. For some other reason, one of the stories was called that too. I had yawned and blinked my way through several of these tales, late at night, looking for this offbeat erotic power. I read the one called 'The Ironic High Style'. It was about a tramp who spoke exclusively in quotations from Shakespeare. All he did was beg and ponce and scrounge, but he talked Shakespeare while doing it. This old tramp – I can't tell you what a pain in the pipe he was. Anyway, even I could see that her straight dialogue had a lot of swing to it, and that's what Doris was on the payroll for. Fielding had said she was a Jewish princess. She was certainly a little miracle to look at, a North African queen bee, with satanic complexion, hot black eyes, a blazing, tearing mouth . . . Oh, man. No wonder she dressed down. But there's probably nothing you can do about those kinds of looks. They're uncontrollable. They came at me straight through the shimmer of the heat-ripple hangover I was wearing. They peeled away its seven veils.

Like Bill from *Box Office*, Doris took out a pad and gazed

at me encouragingly. 'The original idea,' she whispered. 'You want to tell me a little about it? I mean, where was it set?'

'What?'

'I said where was it set?'

I shrugged. 'Here,' I said.

Together we stared sadly round the half-converted vault – at the rosewood, the moist velvet plush, the curtains limp against the stained glass, the brutal slab of the pool table, the armless bandits, Fat Paul with his pale eyes, his pub face, slack-mouthed as he watched the clock, ticking its way to noon.

'Here. I was born upstairs. My dad owns this place.'

'No kidding.' The toy phrase slipped strangely from those opulent, deep-olive lips. Her teeth are like pearls, pearls in the oyster of the Shakespeare. I inhaled noisily and said,

'It's like this. There's a Father, a Mother, a Son and a Mistress. The Mistress is shared by Father and Son. She was Father's first, but then Son muscled in there too. Son knows about Father but Father doesn't know about Son. Okay? You with me? You see, Father has been –'

'I got it.'

'Fucking her for years, and now Son is too, in secret. Oh yeah, and Mistress has mob connections – she used to strip in a mob club. Anyway, one day, in the restaurant – they all work in a restaurant, or a pub, or a bar, or a club. We haven't decided on that yet. Mistress works there too. Anyway, one day – Mother and Son are pretty close, and Mother has a, a sort of mothering interest in Mistress. Mother doesn't know anything. Anyway, one day, at the restaurant, where they all work, or the pub, or the bar, or the club, there's the daily delivery from the bakery. Father and Son open a case of flour. But it's not flour – it's heroin. Now Father has had mob connections. He just wants to give the stuff back. But Son, he –'

I've done this speech so many times now – keep me fuelled,

and I can drone it out with seamless fluency, making no effort at all. And so my mind was free to wander unpleasantly, as it always wanders now when unengaged by stress or pleasure. My thoughts dance. What is it? A dance of anxiety and supplication, of futile vigil. I think I must have some new cow disease that makes you wonder whether you're real all the time, that makes your life feel like a trick, an act, a joke. I feel, I feel dead. There's a guy who lives round my way who really gives me the fucking creeps. He's a *writer*, too . . . I can't go on sleeping alone – that's certain. I need a human touch. Soon I'll just have to go out and buy one. I wake up at dawn and there's nothing. And when I wake up at night, in minus time . . . better not to ask – better not to say.

Her devilish eyes never leaving mine, Doris swayed out of her jacket and pressed a handkerchief to her glowing brow. Her manly white shirt also glistened in its silk. I stared, and mumbled on. So far as I could see, she was definitively flat-chested. And yet her slenderness, too, was weirdly stirring, especially when you gazed at the athletic, the intricate throat. Selina's throat is fuller, more volatile, more flammable, as indeed are her tits. What *is* it with tits? You don't *need* them, do you. Doris doesn't . . . The pub doors opened and stayed that way. In they file: not so many regulars now, not so many middle-timers in brackish suits with a tabloid under the arm. No, here come the young, in manmade colours and animal health, in city noise and detail, with all *their* clothes and tits and money.

'So in the end,' I was saying, 'we come to the big showdown between Father and Son. Oh yeah, and the –'

'Tell me,' said Doris. 'What's the motivation of the Butch Beausoleil character?'

'Uh?'

'The Mistress. What's her motivation?'

'Uh?'

'Why is she sleeping with these two guys? Father gives her money. Okay. But why the Son. It's a big risk for her. And the Son's such a meatball.'

'*I* don't know,' I said. 'Maybe he's brill in the bag.'

'Pardon me?'

'Maybe he's a hot lay.'

'That's not motivation. That's not something we can show dramatically. The whole point about the Mistress is she's not just a dumb blonde, right? Then why does she behave like one? I don't think an audience would buy it. A considerable woman, wrecking her life for sex? I think we need to provide some motivation.'

Fat Paul cruised past. 'Veronica's on,' he said, and made the big-tits sign: two caved palms, raised and tensed. Doris looked up sweetly.

I said, 'Ah, you chicks. You writers. Come here.'

I led her by her cold knuckly hand. We passed through the damp dust of the velvet curtain, into deeper noise, deeper smoke, deeper drink. Twenty loud people watched the big woman on the small stage. She was spider-dark, and hefty, and good at her job – the face all voided, as it must be. For several minutes she danced slowly, then half-reclined on the waiting straightbacked chair. Now one hand welded the deep breasts, while the other sought the sequins of the pants, and slipped within, working, working. I bent down and whispered into the tracery of Doris's ear.

'Can you see okay, or do you want to sit on my face? Tell me something. What's *her* motivation? What's theirs? Listen. I got the Fiasco outside. Let's have some lunch at your hotel. Then I'll take you upstairs and give you a really long lesson in motivation.'

She looked at me assessingly. She nodded and smiled and

walked out through the drapes, speeded by a loud flathander on her rock-hard rump. I followed, muttering, my eyes on the busy stage. Beautiful, isn't it, the way they're all the same, God bless them? You just need a big body – a big body, and a little nerve.

With her jacket hooked over one shoulder Doris was hurriedly gathering her things. Whoah, baby, I thought. An eager one, eh? Maybe we skip lunch and bunk out right away. Then I saw the tears flying from her face like sweat.

'Thanks,' she said as I approached. 'This is one of the worst times I've had for years.'

'Come on, darling, you know you love it.'

She steadied herself. She spoke with effort, but she managed to get it all out in the end. 'You asshole,' she said. 'I didn't know they were still cranking them out. You think that despite ourselves women like me are attracted to men like you. But I don't want to go to bed with men like you. I don't want men like you to *exist*.'

She swivelled. I lurched forward to intercept her. I failed. I fell over the table instead. This manoeuvre, together with the dozen empty beer beakers and whisky glasses I floundered among, began to persuade me of something. I thought my hangover was lifting. In fact my hangover had sunk without trace beneath another ton of booze. As I climbed upright and started brushing the wet shards from my suit I saw that my father was watching me through the vent of the red curtains. I looked at him confusedly, expectantly. But he gave a weak leer of dismissal and backed off into the shadows with his drink.

Ten minutes later I was still soothing my brow against the cool glossy stone of the Shakespeare urinal. I raised my head, frowning gradually, and mouthed out the graffiti on the lime-green tiles. KILL ALL NIGS. RAPE IS SHIT. FUCK KOFF.

'Who's Koff?' I mumbled to myself. 'Yeah, well, fuck him, whoever he is.'

After my siesta I felt a little better, and clambered quite gamely from the back seat to the front, only pausing to disentangle my ripped trouser-leg from the handbrake. Then I drove myself home – from Pimlico to Portobello in my purple Fiasco. Now my Fiasco, it's a beautiful machine, a vintage-style coupé with oodles of dash and heft and twang. The Fiasco, it's my pride and joy. Acting like a pal, I lend the motor to Alec Llewellyn while I'm in New York. And what do I return to? An igloo of parking-tickets and birdcrap, with a ripped spare, a bad new grinding noise, and every single gauge resignedly flashing. What's the guy been doing to my great, my incomparable Fiasco? It feels as though he's been living in it, subletting it. Some people, they've got no class. You should see the way the boys at the garage simply cover their faces with envy and admiration when the Fiasco is driven – or pushed or towed or, on one occasion, practically coptered – into their trash-strewn mews. It is temperamental, my Fiasco, like all the best racehorses, poets and chefs. You can't expect it to behave like any old Mistral or Alibi. I bought it last year for an enormous amount of money. There are some – Alec is among them, probably – who believe that the Fiasco errs on the side of ostentation, that the Fiasco is in questionable taste. But what do *they* know.

The car and I crawled cursing up the street to my flat. You just cannot park round here any more. Even on a Sunday afternoon you just cannot park round here any more. You *can* doublepark on people: people can doublepark on you. Cars are doubling while houses are halving. Houses divide, into two, into four, into sixteen. If a landlord or developer comes across a decent-sized room he turns it into a labyrinth, a Chinese puzzle. The bell-button grills in the flakey porches look like the dashboards of ancient spaceships. Rooms divide, rooms multiply. Houses split – houses are tripleparked. People are doubling also, dividing, splitting. In double trouble we split out losses. No wonder we're bouncing off the walls.

. . . I like to think of my West London flat as a kind of playboy pad. This has no effect on my flat, which remains a gaff, a lair, a lean-to – a sock. It smells of batch, of bachelordom: even I can nose it (don't let batch into your life, into your bones. After a while, batch gets into your bones). Like an adolescent, throbbing, gaping, my poor flat pines for a female presence. And so do I. Its spirit is broken, and so is mine. (Her dressing-gown, her moisturizing creams, the treasure-chest of her knicker drawer – they're not here any longer, they're all gone now.) My pad has tousled cream carpets, a rhino-and-pylon sofa and an oval bed with black satin counterpane. None of this is mine. The voile walls are not mine. I hire everything. I hire water, heat, light. I hire tea by the teabag. I've lived here for ten years now and nothing is mine. My flat is small and also costs me a lot of money.

Standing in the nordic nook of the kitchen, I can gaze down at the flimsy-limbed joggers heading south towards the Park. It's nearly as bad as New York. Some of these gasping fatsos, these too-little-too-late artists, they look as though they're running up rising ground, climbing ground. My generation, we started all this. Before, everyone was presumably content to feel like death the whole time. Now they want to feel terrific for ever. The Sixties taught us this, that it was hateful to be old. I am a product of the Sixties – an obedient, unsmiling, no-comment product of the Sixties – but in this matter my true sympathies go further back, to those days of yore when no one minded feeling like death the whole time. I peer through the spectral, polluted, nicotine-sodden windows of my sock at these old lollopers in their kiddie gear. Go home, I say. Go home, lie down, and eat lots of potatoes. I had three handjobs yesterday. None was easy. Sometimes you really have to buckle down to it, as you do with all forms of exercise. It's simply a question of willpower. Anyone who's got the balls to stand there and tell me that a handjob isn't exercise just doesn't know what he's talking about. I almost had a heart-attack during number three. I take all kinds of other exercise too. I walk up and down the stairs. I climb into cabs and restaurant booths. I hike to the Butcher's Arms and the London Apprentice. I cough a lot. I throw up pretty frequently, which really takes it out of you. I sneeze, and hit the tub and the can. I get in and out of bed, often several times a day . . . Ah, you saw me at my best in New York, at my most disciplined, decisive and dynamic. Over here, I find I have a tendency to go downhill. There's nothing to do and no one to do nothing with. I never do anything. I wish I could find someone to be unfaithful to Selina with. I thought little Doris, for instance, was dead keen. Women! Drink! It puts you at a big disadvantage with the ladies, being drunk all the time – though Fielding astounded me on the phone the other day by saying what a hit I'd made with Butch Beausoleil. Yes, you saw me at my very best, at my most suave and attractive, over there in New York. Oh for some of that New York spirit! Over there, you can look all fucked-up and shot-eyed and everyone thinks you're just talented and European. I made my mistakes, I admit, as we all do when we go over there to try it on. Like bawling for more drink at two fifteen in thinning restaurants. Like instigating singsongs in bars and falling over all the time in nightclubs and discos. One morning, two trips ago, I attended a breakfast meeting with Fielding and three preliminary moneymen in the office suite of a velvet hotel off Sutton Place. Half way through my synopsis the cork of nausea abruptly popped in my throat. I only just made it to the adjacent can, which was large and acoustical: my imitation of an exploding hippopotamus came through the closed door in full quadraphonic (as Fielding later explained). I got one or two funny glances on my return, but I just butched it out and I don't think it did me any harm. If I were them, I'd enjoy the spectacle. It does my poor old ticker good to see someone really totalled – by his own hand, mind you. Not blasted by outside nature or misfortune, which only frightens me. But they're a bit more puritanical in the States, hence the looks of incredulous solicitude, that morning over juice and scrambled eggs and coffee gurgling in heavy silverware, as I attempted to talk on. I started making an extraordinary noise – I heard that noise again the other day, while trying to force the last drops of ketchup from a plastic tomato. It was no big deal. I simply coughed myself into a crying jag and had to be helped downstairs and into the Autocrat. All good knockabout stuff. I don't like seeing women in this state. You don't see it so much in women, and I'm glad. You see it round my way sometimes, the dead blondes in the scarred pubs . . . What happened that night, that night in the Berkeley? What happened? Something did . . . I've solved one minor mystery. I now know how I managed to make my flight from New York. Fielding rang JFK and informed Trans-American that there was a bomb on board my flight. 'It's no big thing, Slick,' Fielding told me on the phone. 'I always do it when I'm running late. They grill the latecomers but not if you're first class. It's not economical' . . . And then there is the second mystery, the mystery that lingers.

Now on this Sunday afternoon I walk from the kitchen to the bedroom. I open the white slats of the fitted wardrobe and take out the suit I wore on that last night in New York. Not for the first time, I tug the trousers out and flatten them on the bed. On the lateral creases of the crotch there is a large splattered stain, dark tan against the fawn, ending in tapered trickles down either leg. The soiled contours of the material crackle faintly to the touch. What is it? Tapsplash? No. It is champagne, or urine. I think I know the truth. The memory is there somewhere, it has its being – but it is loathsome to the touch. Ay! don't let it touch me! Keep it *away* . . . So I lock the suit in again, back in the slammer with its partners in crime, shut up safe for the night, far from my touch.

Something is missing from the present too. Wouldn't you say? Mobile, spangled and glamorous, my life looks good – on paper, anyhow – but I think we're all agreed that I have a problem. Not so? Then what is it? Brother, sister, do the right thing here and let me in on it. Help me out. You'll tell me it's the booze . . . the booze isn't brill, I warrant, but the booze is nothing new. Something else is new. I feel invaded, duped, fucked around. I hear strange voices and speak in strange tongues. I get thoughts that are way over my head. I feel violated . . . The other morning I opened my tabloid to find that, during my brief absence, the whole of England has been scalded by tumult and mutiny, by social crack-up in the torched slums. Unemployment, I learned, was what had got everyone so mad. *I know how you feel*, I said to myself. *I feel how you feel.* I haven't got that much to do all day myself. I sit here defence-lessly, my mind full of earache and riot. Why? Tell. Inner cities crackle with the money chaos – but I've *got* money, plenty of it, I'm due to make lots more. What's missing? What the hell else is there?

Randomly prompted (and that's how I'm always prompted these days: it is all I have in the way of motivation), I went next door and ran an eye over my book collection: *Home Tax Guide, Treasure Island, The Usurers, Timon of Athens, Consortium, Our*

Mutual Friend, Buy Buy Buy, Silas Marner, Success!, The Pardoner's Tale, Confessions of a Bailiff, The Diamond as Big as the Ritz, The Amethyst Inheritance – and that's about it. (Most of the serious books are the accumulations of Selina's predecessors, except for *The Usurers*, which I remember buying myself.) I stared at my space-age sound system. Many years ago I outgrew rock music, and I have failed to grow into any other kind since. I waited, I hung about, but it just didn't happen. Breakfast television is as yet only a dream, a whisper. I'm going to hang around for that too, maybe. Maybe not. Watching television is one of my main interests, one of my chief skills. Video films are another accomplishment of mine: diabolism, carnage, soft core. I realize, when I can bear to think about it, that all my hobbies are pornographic in tendency. The element of lone gratification is bluntly stressed. Fast food, sex shows, space games, slot machines, video nasties, nude mags, drink, pubs, fighting, television, handjobs. I've got a hunch about these handjobs, or about their exhausting frequency. I need that human touch. There's no human here so I do it myself. At least handjobs are free, complimentary, with no cash attaching.

On the quartz coffee-table serving the spudjacket sofa a deck of unopened mail is carelessly fanned. For how long now in my life has mail confined itself to one topic? When I look at the cards in this pack, when I eventually rip and snarl my way through these trap-faced offers and demands, these begging letters, I want to say, Look, can't we change the subject? Just once, after all these years? Isn't there anything else you can talk about? . . . When did I last get a love letter, for Christ's sake? When did I last write one?

It was half-past six. Time to repent. I called Doris Arthur at her hotel and did a lot of apologizing. How much apology can a person contain? I'm going to need a lot more of this stuff when I return to New York – for Martina . . . Doris let me off pretty lightly. They always do, at first. Besides, she's getting a hundred thousand bucks to stay interested. Then I found a ballpoint, a pad, some envelopes, a sheet of stamps. I flexed my chequebook. As I worked, I whispered to myself and to money.

The last letter bore an ink-written address, referring to me as Mr John Self Esquire. When I'd flicked through this khaki stack on the dreadful morning of my return from New York (sitting there, at London noon, in the emptied flat with a drink in my fist: i.e., a gin and tonic at six a.m. – now this *has* to be good news for both body and soul), looking for a friendly, a helping hand, I had glanced at these gawky graphics and fingered the letter for a tactful forget-me-not from one of the spine-specialists, rug-gurus or ticker-experts I need to use . . . They get foreign chicks to hand-address the mail: it lends a personal touch. But this letter suddenly seemed very personal indeed. I tore its throat open with my heart climbing. And I quote:

> *John Darling*
>   *Take me back. I cant believe you mean't those terrible things you said. How could you think such things of me. Send for me please, I dont know what to do if your not there to look after me.*
>   *Love, Your Selina XXXXXX*
>   *PS. I'm pennyless.*

Dangerously excited, italicized with surefire lust, I poured myself a drink and scanned the letter for clues. The postmark said Stratford-upon-Avon. Its dateline was ten days old. Within, the letterhead proclaimed the Cymbeline, Hotel-Casino, with a seven-figure telephone number in two-five formation . . . What was all this take-me-back stuff? What were these terrible things I was supposed to have said? Not for the first time I tugged myself back to the eve of my departure for New York. What happened? I took Selina out for an expensive dinner. We had a vicious row about money. Back home, there followed a detailed bout of valedictory lovemaking, with Selina game and longsuffering, and me as effusively carnal as ever. Then I had a few nightcaps, as I recall, and composed myself for sleep. In other words, a completely ordinary evening. I might have given her a bit of lip last thing, but that was pretty standard too. When I woke at noon the next day Selina had long taken her leave. I didn't give that a thought either. I had an Irish coffee, packed my things, and left my number on the kitchen wall.

A male voice answered, and levelly agreed to do my bidding.

'I knew it would be you,' she said, with urgent, husky restraint in her low louche voice.

'Come here. Come home,' I said in the same kind of way. 'I want you. Now.'

'Oh my man. How have I lived?'

'Get a taxi.'

'A taxi!'

'Do it.'

'Yes.'

'Soon, then.'

'Yes.'

I walked round the flat. I picked up the letter. My eyes, how they itched and burned. You know something? This was the first time I had ever seen her handwriting – her floppy, amateurish signature, her scribbled kisses. How was it *possible*? I mean, I know we're not the most expressive of couples, but all the same. God damn, two years on and off, and not even a note? God damn. I dropped the letter. I looked up. Had I ever shown her *my* hand? Yes, she'd seen it, on bills, on credit slips, on cheques.

I roved out into the foaming malls. My mission? To buy champagne. Selina, she likes a lot of outlay. You cannot do pornography by halves. Pornography and money enjoy a close concordat, and you have to pay your union dues . . . The Cymbeline, eh? Now I've stayed in that joint myself – with one or other of Selina's forerunners, some model or stylist, some Cindy or Lindy or Judy or Trudy. It's an expense-account, no-account gin palace and gaming den, very expensive, full of yanks and maple-leafers, touts, tarts, hustlers, dirty weekenders. I recommend it. Me, I was up in Stratford making a TV ad for a new kind of flash-friable pork-and-egg bap or roll or hero called a Hamlette. We used some theatre and shot the whole thing on stage. There was the actor, dressed in black, with his skull and globe, being henpecked by that mad chick he's got in trouble. When suddenly a big bimbo wearing cool pants and bra strolls on, carrying a tray with two steaming Hamlettes on it. She gives him the wink – and Bob's your uncle. All my commercials featured a big bim in cool pants and bra. It was sort of my trademark. No one said my ads were subtle. But boy did they sell fast food fast.

Now I ducked from the wet white light into the prisms of the Liquor Locker. Jesus, have they got a lot of booze in here, and a lot of it is bottom line – tubs of Nigerian sherry, quarts of Alaskan port. They even stock a product called Alkohol, sold in cauldrons of label-less plastic. The Liquor Locker must have started up in direct response to the many bagladies, bums and limping dipsoes who haunt this part of town. There were certainly some dreadful faces flickering through the racks. As I tarried in the malt-whisky showroom an old head presaged by spores of woodrot breath came rearing up at me like a sudden salamander of fire and blood. Dah! In his idling voice he used distant tones of entreaty and self-exculpation, pointing to the recent scar that split his heat-bubbled cheek. No you don't, pal, I thought – you can't beg in here: it makes all kinds of unwelcome connections. I'd have given him a quid just to keep him at bay but, sure enough, a member of the pimply triumvirate guarding the till came over with a yawn to drop a heavy hand on the poor guy's shoulder, aiming him back to the streets, where he belonged. Out, old son. Why? Because money says so. I scored three bottles of the tissued French usual. At the desk they cleared my Vantage card in the little paperback which lists the numbers of busted frauds and proven losers . . . Then I clanked next door to the place where a caged chick cashes cheques round the clock but seems to keep half your dough as commission for this fine service. Actually, it's more than half, or feels that way by now. It goes up all the time. One day I'm going to come in here, write a cheque for fifty quid, slide it over, hang about for a while, then ask: 'Come on – what about my money?' And the caged chick will look up and say, 'Can't you read? We keep all that now.'

I walked home the long way round, to kill time before she came – my shop-soiled Selina, my High-Street Selina, once more going cheap in the sales. How I love it. How I love it all. Like Selina, this area is going up in the world. There used to be a third-generation Italian restaurant across the road: it had linen tablecloths and rumpy, strict, black-clad waitresses. It's now a Burger Den. There is already a Burger Hutch on the street. There is a Burger Shack, too, and a Burger Bower. Fast food equals fast money. I know: I helped. Perhaps there is money-room for several more. Every other window reveals a striplit boutique. How many striplit boutiques does a street need – thirty, forty? There used to be a bookshop here, with the merchandise ranked in alphabetical order and subject sections. No longer. The place didn't have what it took: market forces. It is now a striplit boutique, and three tough tanned chicks run it with their needly smiles. There used to be a music shop (flutes, guitars, scores). This has become a souvenir hypermarket. There used to be an auction room: now a video club. A kosher delicatessen – a massage parlour. You get the idea? My way is coming up in the world. I'm pleased. No, I am. A shame about the restaurant – I was a regular patron, and Selina liked it there – but the other stuff was never much use to me and I'm glad it's all gone.

Slipping off the demographic shuttle, I moved into the calmer latticework of dusty squares and sodden hotels. Some of the residential allotments are going up in the world too: they are getting gentrified, humidified, marbleized. Ad-execs, moneymen, sharp-faced young marrieds, they're all moving in and staking out their patch. You even cop the odd sub-celebrity round my way now. An old actor, singing arias of bitterness in the backstreet pubs. There's a chick newsreader whom I sometimes see cramming her kids into the battered Boomerang. Every day a failed chat-show host and an alcoholic ex-quiz-master grimly lunch at the Kebab House in Zilchester Gardens. Oh yeah, and a *writer* lives round my way too. A guy in a pub pointed him out to me, and I've since seen him hanging out in Family Fun, the space-game parlour, and toting his blue laundry bag to the Whirlomat. I don't think they can pay writers that much, do you? . . . He stops and stares at me. His face is cramped and incredulous – also knowing, with a smirk of collusion in his bent smile. He gives me the creeps. *'Know me again would you?'* I once shouted across the street, and gave him a V-sign and a warning fist. He stood his ground, and stared. This writer's name, they tell me, is *Martin Amis*. Never heard of him. Do *you* know his stuff at all?

. . . With a flinch I looked up: still no weather. Sometimes, when the sky is as grey as this – impeccably grey, a denial, really, of the very concept of colour – and the stooped millions lift their heads, it's hard to tell the air from the impurities in our human eyes, as if the sinking climbing paisley curlicues of grit were part of the element itself, rain, spores, tears, film, dirt. Perhaps, at such moments, the sky is no more than the sum of the dirt that lives in our human eyes.

All set. I'm back at my flat now. The sheets have been changed, the socks corralled, the mags stashed. I myself am scrubbed and primped. Soon the bell will ring and Selina will be here with Persian eyes, overnight bag, hot throat, omniscient underwear, scarred wrists, boudoir odours and, quite possibly, the odours of other men. Under the auspices of pornography, however, this is all right, this is okay. This'll do. I ought to wait until I know you a bit better before I reveal what I get up to with Selina in the sack. But I'll probably tell you anyway. Who cares? I don't. Is she an infidel? Does she go to bed with men for money? No, not my Selina. She simply makes blue films while I'm out of town, for private screening in this old head of mine. Tonight I get the lot. I can't say I'm too much bothered, now that pornography is on its way in a cab.

While the champagne cooled in my small but powerful refrigerator, I uncapped a tube of beer and swallowed ten capsules of Vitamin E. I am a vitamin addict, I am a penicillin addict, I am a painkiller addict. Painkillers, now they're some *good* shit . . . Numb, groaning, restless, helpless, I paced the flat. I stood still. I sat down. Using the remote-control console I activated the television. With a premonitory crackle the Prince of Wales surged on to the hired screen. Hi, Prince, I said to myself. When did you get back? This guy is getting married in a month or so. He's pulled a little darling called

Lady Diana. She doesn't look as though she'll give him any trouble – not like my Selina gives me, anyway . . . In a series of clips, the Prince played polo, climbed mountains, flew fighters, bossed battleships. He sat before a fireplace, quietly chatting with his mother, the Chick. Full face to camera, the Prince then answered questions about his childhood and youth. He was, he said, profoundly grateful that he had been taught self-discipline at an early stage in life. Self-discipline, said the Prince, seemed to him absolutely essential to any kind of civilized existence . . . Boy, I wish someone had taught *me* self-discipline – when I was young, when you learn things without really trying. They could have taught me pride, dignity, and French too, while they were at it. I wouldn't have had to lift a finger. But no one ever did teach me all that stuff. I've endeavoured to teach it to myself. I sit around trying to teach myself self-discipline. I can't be doing with it, though (it just isn't enough fun, self-discipline), and I always end up going out for a good time instead.

The door-buzzer sounded and I climbed to my feet, hands busy in my pockets with the money.

'Got laid recently?'

The evening, at last, has reached its promised, its destined stage. We've just got back from dinner at Kreutzer's. This was traditional, a matter of convention. Kreutzer's provides the costly setting of our reunions, our foreplay and our lies. There have been rich meat and bloody wine. There have been brandies, and thick puddings. There has already been some dirty talk. Selina is in high spirits, and as for me, I'm a gurgling wizard of calorific excess.

'Yeah,' she said, after a pause, and sipped her champagne.

'Who? Anyone I know?'

'. . . Yeah.'

'You'd better tell me about it.'

'I was in my room. I was kneeling on the window-seat looking at the common. It's so lovely now. Then this big fat black car pulled up outside the hotel. It was made of chrome and gold. The window went down and a hand with twelve rings appeared and beckoned to me.'

'What were you wearing?' She was wearing an extended black bodice that clasped between her thighs, and chrome stockings, and golden shoes.

'I was wearing a little white frock that belonged to me when I was small. It only comes down to here. I hadn't put on my panties yet because I was just getting dressed from my bath.'

'What did you do then?' She crossed the room and knelt on the bed beside me. With both hands she drew back her hair, disclosing the changeable throat.

'I crossed the room and tiptoed down the stairs. I got into the big fat car.'

'What did he do?' I laid her on her back. The black bodice had forty black buttons, fastened with eye-shaped loops of corded silk. Now it had thirty-nine. Now it had thirty-eight.

'He lifted me on top of him. It was like sitting on a capstan or a water hydrant. He put his hands on my shoulders, and pressed. I thought: he'll never get in, I'll never get round him. But he was so strong, his hands were unbelievable, as heavy as gold. It hurt but I was wet and the hurt was runny and sweet. I thought: I'm a cock, I'm just a cock.'

Later, with her resting body spread out beside me on the satin, I smoked a cigar and finished the champagne and thought about the good life. In a way, in a sense, I think I really do want to live well.

But how is it done?

*

Deep down, I'm a pretty happy guy. Happiness is the relief of pain, they say, and so I guess I'm a pretty happy guy. The relief of pain happens to me pretty frequently. But then so does pain. That's why I get lots of that relief they talk about, and all that happiness.

'You know what I wish?' said Roger Frift. 'I wish you'd take it easy the nights before you see me.'

'What's the matter now?'

I'd better add that Roger is a dinky 26-year-old, and a hyper-active homosexual.

'Your tongue, it's all . . . I mean, it's a question of common good manners. It makes the whole thing so much more unpleasant for me.'

'It's not meant to be pleasant for you. Just do it. Christ, you charge enough.'

'Lie back then. And *relax* . . . God!'

You wouldn't be too relaxed if you were reclining on Roger's electric chair. Roger is my hygienist, my gum-coach. Four times a year with his beaked pincers, skewers and arrow-headed bodkins he goes squeaking and splitting through the roots of my head. We call this deep scaling, or plaque control. What the fuck is this plaque crap anyway? Why can't plaque go and pick on somebody else? It doesn't bother my father. Plaque didn't bother my mother either, so far as I know. My mother died when I was very young. She died when she was very young too, now I come to think about it, which I don't much . . . That tooth on my upper west side, the one that brought me so much pain – it calmed down a few days ago, bringing me happiness instead, oh such happiness. But yesterday it started bringing me pain again. It never really calmed down: I could feel it humming, purring, braiding beneath the skin, planning its comeback. Now Roger, I hope, will fix it, will relieve that pain and bring me happiness again. Selina has this knack also. She brings me pain. She relieves it. Am I happy? I'm not sure. I'm certainly relieved, now she's back. At least, when she's with me, she's not with anyone else. Apparently I denounced and banished her that night, the night before I left for New York. I can't remember. Apparently I called her a whore, cursed her for a gold-digging fuckbag, and kicked her out. She shuffled off into the blackness without a farthing. Convincing, yes? Or not? I can't remember. We don't talk about it much. We talk about money. She wants a joint bank account. What do you reckon?

'Ooh,' said Roger, whose own breath isn't too hot either, if you want to know the truth.

By this time I already had a trio of gurgling gimmicks in my mouth. 'Ow,' I said as best I could. 'Easy.'

'Have you had any discomfort there?'

'Pain, you mean? Pain? Yeah, lots. That's why I'm here.'

'Yes, well you would. Hello, seems to be some mobility there.'

He made mobility sound as if it were a pretty encouraging thing to have, like social mobility, upward mobility. 'Loose, you mean?' I gargled.

'I might just check the vitality of that one.' Roger reached for the robot tendon of the drill fixture. 'Can you feel anything?'

'What sort of thing?'

'Pressure?'

'On the tooth? No.'

'Discomfort? . . . Minimal vitality,' he murmured.

At this I coughed out the braces and sprays and jerked myself upright. 'What are you talking about? Talk right, okay? It's loose and it's dead and it's coming out. Yes? No?'

'I don't do extractions,' he said primly. 'You'll have to see Mrs McGilchrist about that.'

'Then just clean them,' I said.

Roger replaced the nozzles and clips. He hummed while he cleaned. His instruments did their beaky work, their painful fine-tuning. The steel lingered on the trouble spot, the wasted block on my upper west side.

'Mm,' he said when the polishing was done. Daintily he plucked the gadgetry from my mouth. 'The gum's been traumatized by the shape of the root,' he mused. 'Rinse.'

'Traumatized?' I sipped the fizzy liquid and expelled its tactful pink. 'Now you're talking.'

'Well the shape of the root is very unusual.'

'And the gum can't cope with this? The gum has a trauma about it?'

'The tooth is still viable,' he said.

I picked up my coat in the hot floral waiting room – two people there, indistinct and self-sufficient, like all ghosts in waiting rooms. I paid the chick who lurks with knitting in her windowless stall: fifteen pounds, cash, and a video cassette. No receipt. Black economy. I run Selina on the black economy. We don't keep any books: there is nothing, no letter, no notes. There is no gentleman's agreement. There isn't even a handshake. But we both understand.

'Selina,' I had said, two days after her return, '– Alec told me a funny thing on the way to the airport.' Selina hesitated as she took off her coat.

'What? Don't I even get a kiss then?'

'He said you were fucking someone – a lot, all the time.' I sipped my drink and lit another cigarette.

'He's an English aristocrat,' said Selina intently. 'He doubled the family fortune on Wall Street. His servants come round to get me in a –'

'No. This is serious. This is real. He said you'd got someone on the side. Someone I know.'

'Oh you stupid sod. Don't *listen*. You know he made a pass at me once.'

'Did he? Son of a bitch.'

'He kissed my tits. Then he put my hand on his cock. Then he –'

'Christ. Where were you at the time? In bed together?'

'Here, in the kitchen. He came round when you were out.'

I refreshed my drink and said calmly, 'Everyone makes passes at you, Selina. Waiters in restaurants make passes at you. Men in the street make passes at you.'

She shut her eyes and laughed. Then she sobered quickly and said, 'But he's supposed to be your friend.'

'All my friends make passes at you too.'

'You haven't got any friends.'

'Terry's made a pass at you. Keith's made a pass at you. My *dad*'s made a pass at you – and he's family.'

'Just don't *listen* to him. Don't you know how jealous Alec is of you? He's trying to destroy our love.'

This struck me as a novel notion, in all senses. While unscrewing the second bottle of scotch, I thought suddenly, *Something else is missing. What is it?* But all I said was – 'You really think so?'

'You're spilling it! Bloody hell, take it easy. It's hardly six o'clock. Listen. Have you got those forms from the bank yet? How long have you been in here drinking?'

'What forms?'

'You know what forms. I've got to have some independence.'

'Yeah yeah.'

'I'm twenty-eight.'

'Twenty-eight? Well you don't look it.'

'Thank you, darling. I don't think I'm being unreasonable. Gregory gives Debby an allowance. Why are you so frightened of it? You're quite generous over little things, I'll give you that. But as soon as it comes to –'

'Yeah yeah.'

The trouble is, the whole trouble is, Selina's too clever for me. I tried to change the subject. In my experience, with Selina, the only way to change the subject is to go down the Butcher's Arms. How can you change the subject when there's only one subject? Oh yeah – violence. That'll change it. That'll do the trick, for a while. But of course violence is no longer an option. I didn't even consider it for more than a few seconds. I'm serious about this new self-improvement course I've put myself on – very serious. Self-discipline. A more civilized existence.

So I just got out of bed, told her to shut up, and went down the Butcher's Arms.

Tonguing my tooth and twisting my neck for taxis, I now stroll the length of the dental belt, through the stucco of the plaqued streets and carious squares, past railings, embossed porches, pricey clinics, tranquillized Arabs, groggy mouth-sufferers in their Sunday best, their women wearing fur coats and Harlem lacquer, their spruced kids either pained or happy – across the bus-torn slum of Oxford Street into Soho, the huddled land of sex and food and film, down narrowing alleys until I reached the glass preserve of Carburton, Linex & Self.

For me, now, Carburton, Linex & Self is another kind of waiting room. But what a place! You should see how much money we pay each other, how little work we do, and how thick and talentless many of us are. You should see the expenses claims, the air tickets that lie around in here, and the girls. C. L. & S. was a breakthrough when we established the company five years ago. It still is. A lot of outfits tried to do what we did. None of them made it. C. L. & S. is an advertising agency which produces its own television commercials. Sounds easy. *You* try it. I myself was the key figure in all this, with my controversial TV ads for smoking, drinking, junk food and nude magazines. Remember the stir in the flaming summer of '76? My nihilistic commercials attracted prizes and writs. The one on nude mags was never shown, except in court. The publicity and its attendant heft empowered us to make our breakthrough, our breakaway, and we never looked back. Our moneyman Nigel Trotts, down in the basement with a chick, a xerox and a bushel of instant coffee, is the only guy here who works a full whack. And Nigel is a moneyman who does it all for love.

'Nigel has gimmicked a bag-carrier for the Dutch Antilles,' people will say to me at my desk.

'Beautiful,' I'll whisper back, as you're bound to do.

We all seem to make lots of money. Man, do we seem to be coining it here. Even the chicks live like kings. The car is free. The car is on the house. The house is on the mortgage. The mortgage is on the firm – without interest. The interesting thing is: how long can this last? For me, that question carries an awful lot of anxiety – compound interest. It can't be legal, surely. You can't legally treat money in such a way. But we do. Are we greedy! Are we shameless! I once saw Terry Linex, that fat madman, take a grand out of petty cash for a weekend in Dieppe. He got his wife's hysterectomy on X's – and his daughter's orthodontic work. He even gets the family poodle shampooed against tax: security expenses, with Fifi doubling as a guard-dog. We estimate that Keith Carburton spent £17,000 on lunch in fiscal '80, service and VAT *non compris*. You should see their freehold townhouses and bijou Cotswold cottages. You should see their cars – the Tomahawks, the Farragos, and Boomerangs. I've been ripping off the firm and the government too, for five years now, and what have I got? A hired sock, a Fiasco, and the prohibitive Selina. What did I ever do with it, the money? Pissed it away, I just pissed it away. And somehow I still have lots of money.

'I told my wife,' said Terry Linex, parking half his heavy can on my desk, '"You can have *any domestic appliance* you want. But when it goes wrong, *don't come running to me*. Do we understand each other?" I come home Friday night. I go into the kitchen – I said, "What's this, a horror film?" There's a brand-new washing-up machine and all this fucking black gunge all over the floor. "Get on the fucking phone," she says. "Fix it!" So what did I do.'

'What did you do.'

'I sued them. I rang Curtis & Curtis, got Mr Benson at home. Ten minutes later I walk into the kitchen – there's a Pakki on his back with his tongue up the funnel. *No* charge. *No* grief. It's brilliant. I do it all the time now. Took the motor in for a service. Four hundred quid. So what did I do.'

'You sued them.'

'I sued them. Fucking right. "How would you like to pay, sir?" he asked me. "Cash or cheque or credit card?" I said, "I'm not paying. You are. I'm fucking sueing you, mate." They go all pale. Thirty-six quid I ended up paying. I sued the tax-inspector last week.'

'Beautiful,' I said.

'Don't you love it?'

I said I did, and returned to the sorry-looking chaos of my desk. I'm supposed to be tying things up here, sorting things out. The antique desk-drawers are buckled stiff with ripped paperwork: five years without paying any tax – *that's* why I've got all this money . . . The feeling in the office is that I am moving on to better things. Sometimes I wish they had consulted me about this. But they just roll their eyes and whistle and rub their hands encouragingly. I have been interviewed in

Box Office, featured in *Turnover*, profiled in *Market Forces*. My thirty-five-minute short, *Dean Street*, won the guest critics' special-mention award at the Siena Film Festival last year. I am a headliner, a highroller. Peter Sennet did it. Freddie Giles and Ronnie Templeton did it. Jack Conn – he did it. They all live in California now. They have all bled out of the ordinary world. They all have new houses, new wives, new tans, new rugs. In V8 Hyenas and haunchy drophead Acapulcos they cruise the road-margined seas, gunning to the medical zone for their daily DNA boosters and plasma rethinks. Twice or three times a month they wing out for a long weekend on Thousand Island, a world that time forgot, down in the sea of joy. Everyone thinks that this will soon happen to me. Me, I don't see it somehow. I have a sharp sense of my life being in the balance. I may never look back, or I may never recover. I tell you, I am terrified, I am fucking terrified. 'Just give me the fucking money okay!' I want to shout this all the time. And if you fail they don't take you back . . . I was in Cal myself this January – Los Angeles. I did cool deals there and it all looked possible. On the leisure side, though, things didn't go so well, and I got into some seriously bad business. Let me tell you about it sometime. It's a good one . . . I met Fielding on the flight back to New York. We both happened to be travelling first class.

'Where d'you fancy, John? The Breadline? Assisi's? The Mahatma?'

Terry Linex and the boys want to take me out to lunch. Keith Carburton has just walked in, razzing his hands. There has been quite a bit of this sort of thing recently. It feels to me like a new way of superannuating people. But I'm keen. After my morning, I need the fuel, I'm almost out of gas. I go, of course I go – as I will go when the time is right, when I get my big break. I hope it doesn't break me, my big break

. . . So we come bobbing out of cabs in our high-shouldered cashmere overcoats. The girl in dike suit and streaming salmon tie (I think I could go to bed with her, if I liked, but it might be just her professional style to put this idea about) shows us fondly to our table. But it is the wrong table! Before Terry Linex can sue the restaurant, Keith Carburton takes the girl aside. I can hear him dully reminding her how much money we all spend here. The chick is impressed. So am I. Very soon we have another table (an old man is backing away with a napkin still frilling his throat), a better table, circular, nearer the door, and bearing a bottle of free champagne.

'We're sorry about that, sir,' said the girl, and Keith slipped her his pained nod.

'Now this is a bit more bloody like it,' said Terry to himself.

'Right,' said Keith. '*Right*.'

We drink the champagne. We call for another. One by one the girls finish in the bog or the powder parlour and are redirected to the improved table. Mitzi, Keith's assistant. Little Bella, the telephonist. And the predatory Trudi, an all-purpose vamp and PR strategist. (As for the hiring of girls, we have a looks-alone policy over at C. L. & S.) They will have to do a lot of laughing and listening. They can talk a bit, but only so long as we are the heroes of the tales they tell. The quenched light of this joke June, in the shape of a sail or a breast, swells its camber across the room. For a moment we all look terribly overlit in here: we look like monsters. For a moment, the whole restaurant is a pickle-jar of rug glue and dental work. But now the real fun starts. Terry is throwing bread at me, and Nigel is on the floor doing his dog imitation and snuffling at Trudi's stockings. I notice that the middle-aged pair at the next table retract slightly and lower their heads over their food. As they huddle up, I give Terry a squirt from the shaken champagne bottle and join Keith Carburton in a few choruses of 'We are the Champions'. No, the rest of the meal isn't going to be much fun for those two, I'm afraid. I suppose it must have been cool for people like them in places like this before people like us started coming here also. But we're here to stay. *You* try getting us out . . . Now the menus come, dispensed like examination scripts, and we hesitate and fall silent for a little while, frowning and murmuring over the strange print.

Four o'clock. In heavy, motionless, back-breaking light, Linex and Self stood swaying in front of the basement urinal. I heard the slow rasp of Terry's three-foot zip, then the drilling of his leak against the ivory stall. There goes the day again, like so many others, just pissed away.

'Whoar,' said Terry with a wince.

'How's your dick?'

He glanced downwards. 'Still green,' he said in his piping, disembodied, fatman's voice.

'Still that thing you caught in Bali? What was it? Clap?'

'Clap?' he said. 'Clap? No, mate. I caught the bloody *plague*.'

Then his shot face grew serious. 'John. Have you fucked anyone's wife recently? Run over anyone's kids?'

'Uh?' I said, and pushed out a hand to steady myself against the cold wall.

'I mean – is there anyone out to do you a bit of harm?'

'Well yeah.' I shifted my weight. Some days it seemed that everyone was out to do me harm.

'*Real* harm?' he specified. 'Something a little bit serious?'

'No. What is this?'

'I was down the Fancy Rat the other night,' said Terry Linex. 'We think *we* drink. They're nutters down there. It's a scotch contest. I was with this crew of villains, one of them says, "Oy. You've got a business associate, John Self, right?" I says,

"What of it?" He says, "There's some work out on him. Not sure what. But there's some work out on him." Now it's true, as you know, that an awful lot of bollocks gets talked down the Fancy Rat. But there's usually *something* in it . . . Want me to ask around?'

I looked into Terry's fiery face – cheap churned hair, half an ear bitten off, penny-farthing nostrils. His teeth are as randomly angled as shards of glass on a backstreet wall. Terry is one of the new princes, an improviser of fierce genius. His current dream is to hire a handicapped chauffeur: the Disabled sticker would give Linex unlimited parking anywhere he pleased.

'Yeah, do that.'

'Glad to,' he said. 'Better safe than sorry. Know what I mean?'

So now as I plod home through the crumpled afternoon, veering this way and that among my brothers and my sisters, with eyes meeting and not meeting, it's sort of nice to know that it's all official.

'Check,' I said.

Selina looked up at me indignantly. Her lancing eyes returned to the board. She exhaled, and made an irrelevant move with her black-square bishop.

'*Check*,' I said.

'So what?'

'It means your king's threatened. I can take your king.'

'You can have it. It's more bloody trouble than it's worth.'

'You don't understand. The whole –'

'I'm going to have a bath. I hate chess. Where are we going to go? I'm not having Indian or Chinese. Or Greek. Kreutzer's.'

'If you like.' I reset the heavy pieces.

'Your hair looks terrible. You should let me cut it.'

'I know.'

I'd had a twenty-quid rug-rethink that very afternoon. The little faggot sorted through my locks for a while, curled his lip and said, 'How old are you?' Roger Frift asked me the same question. It's the heart, the heart. My heart's wrong, my ticker's wrong. My clock's not right.

I went into the bedroom and browsed through Selina's knicker drawer, intending to spring a selection on her when she emerged from the tub. Hello, these are new. And so are these . . . As I experimentally fingered a disused bodice I felt something solid in the tuck of the lining. What's this? Whalebone? No: a roll of used tenners – two hundred pounds! Now Selina's knicker drawer is a dumb place for Selina to hide things in, because I am always rootling about in there, as Selina well knows.

She came out of the bathroom with a handtowel belted round her waist. I pointed. She barely blinked when she saw the money – negligently scattered on her side of the sack.

'Where d'you get it?'

'I won it!'

'How?'

'At roulette!'

'What's all this about you being penniless?'

'It was my last fiver! I put it on a number on my way out of the door!'

'They only pay thirty to one – what about the other fifty?'

'It was a tip!'

'You said you were working there, right?'

'Right!'

'What as?'

'A croupier!'

I scowled, and paused. Selina had worked as a croupier

before. This is true. The Cymbeline hires little cockteasers to police the tables. This is true also. They doll them up in mini-skirts and see-through blouses. The chicks look as though they'd come across for a cigarette but they're all strict business-heads and are forbidden to tangle with the punters – as I myself established, one night after my girl had gone to bed.

'Look – how do I know you weren't just shacked up there with some guy?'

'Ring Tony Devonshire!'

'Who's Tony Devonshire?'

'The manager!'

'Yeah, well . . .'

'Go on! Ring him up!'

'Yeah yeah.'

'By the way, I thought I asked you to take the rubbish bag down. Will you do it now please. Why can't we have lunch in town tomorrow and then go to your bank and get it all sorted out. That money's all got to go on rent and I still owe my gynaecologist sixty. It would be a lot more sensible if I moved in here. Come on, you're rolling. Look at that. They've shrunk. I can hardly get them on. Whoops. Ooh. I don't think they go with this garter belt anyway, do you?'

I sat down on the crushed money. 'Dah,' I said. 'Come here.'

The Fiasco needs a major overhaul. Selina Street wants a joint bank account. Alec Llewellyn owes me money. Barry Self owes me money. I've got to head back to America, pretty soon, and earn lots more.

I had lunch with Doris Arthur. She was very nice about me making a pass at her. In fact, she was so nice about me making a pass at her that I made a pass at her. It wasn't the drink this time. It was the woman. After the meal we discussed the outline in her hotel room. Basically I have six big scenes in my head that I know how to shoot: Doris's job is to get from one to the other as smoothly as possible. 'You know something?' she said, as she slid out from beneath me and wryly detached my hands from her thighs. 'You've given me a lot of new heart for the struggle. I thought we were winning, but there's clearly a long way to go.' Thanks to Selina, the second pass wasn't nearly as bad as the first pass. But it was still quite bad, thanks to Selina. Selina, she . . . Oh yeah, and I had a few drinks with my lighting man, Kevin Skuse, and Des Blackadder, my grip. Fielding says I should put these guys on retainer immediately, ready for shooting in the autumn. But there's no work around. They seem hungry enough to me and I figure they can wait another month.

Can I? Where has the weather gone, where? Where? You get April, blossom blizzards and sudden sunshafts and swift bruised clouds. You get May and its chilly light, the sky still writhing with change. Then June, summer, rain as thin and sour as motorway wheel-squirt, and no sky at all, just no sky at all. In summer, London is an old man with bad breath. If you listen, you can hear the sob of weariness catching in his lungs. Unlovely London. Even the name holds heavy stress.

Sometimes when I walk the streets – I fight the weather. I take on those weather gods. I beat them up. I kick and punch and snarl. People stare and occasionally they laugh, but I don't mind. Tubbily I execute karate leaps, forearm smashes, aiming for the sky. I do a lot of shouting too. People think I'm mad, but I don't care. I *will not take* it. Here is someone who *will not take* the weather lying down.

For some time now Selina Street has been on at me to open a joint bank account. She hasn't got a bank account and she wants one. She hasn't got any money and she wants some.

She used to have a bank account: it broke my heart to see her dreaded statements and note the pitiable sums she dealt in – £2.43, £1.71, £5. But they took her bank account away. She never had any money in it. Selina maintains that a joint bank account is essential to her dignity and self-respect. I have been disputing this, arguing that her dignity and self-respect can get on perfectly well under the present system, with its merit awards and incentive schemes. Now, the way I see it, girls with no money have two ways of asserting themselves: they can either start fights all the time, or they can simply be unhappy at you until you surrender. (They can't leave: they haven't got the dough.) Selina is not a fighter, maybe because I'm a hitter – or used to be (she doesn't know I've reformed, and I hope she never finds out). And she hasn't the patience to be unhappy at me. That *would* be a long-term project. So Selina has found a third way . . . For a week she used no make-up, wore dumpling tights and porridgy knickers, and went to bed in face-cream, curlers and a dramatically drab nightdress. I didn't find out whether sex was actually off the menu. I never felt like asking.

The day before last, however, I decided to open a joint bank account. I filled out the forms, coldly supervised by the watchful, sharp-shouldered Selina. That morning she went to bed in black stockings, tasselled garter belt, satin thong, silk bolero, muslin gloves, belly necklace and gold choker. I made a real pig of myself, I have to admit. An hour and a half later she turned to me, with one leg still hooked over the headboard, and said, 'Do it, anywhere, anything.' Things had unquestionably improved, what with all this new dignity and self-respect about the place.

★

Last night, then, about twenty to eleven, I was sitting in the Blind Pig. America tomorrow. I was in thoughtful mood – expansive, self-questioning, philosophical, if not downright drunk. Selina was seeing Helle, her pal at the boutique. I had a present for Selina: a spanking new chequebook. I would hold it out towards her, and watch her shine. Selina had a present for me too: some new bag-gimmicks, a selection from Helle's under-the-counter underwear. I was just sitting there, not stirring, not even breathing, like the pub's pet reptile, when who should sit down opposite me but that guy Martin Amis, the writer. He had a glass of wine, and a cigarette – also a book, a paperback. It looked quite serious. So did he, in a way. Small, compact, wears his rug fairly long . . . The pub's two doors were open to the hot night. That seems to be the deal in early summer, tepid days and hot nights. It's a riot. Anything goes.

I was feeling friendly, as I say, so I yawned, sipped my drink, and whispered, 'Sold a million yet?'

He looked up at me with a flash of paranoia, unusual in its candour, its bluntness. I don't blame him really, in this pub. It's full of turks, nutters, martians. The foreigners around here. I know they don't speak English – okay, but do they even speak Earthling? They speak stereo, radio crackle, interference. They speak sonar, bat-chirrup, pterodactylese, fish-purr.

'Sorry?' he said.

'Sold a million yet?'

He relaxed. His off-centre smile refused to own up to something. 'Be serious,' he said.

'What you sell then?'

'Oh, a reasonable amount.'

I burped and shrugged. I burped again. 'Fuck,' I said. 'Pardon me.' I yawned. I stared round the pub. He returned to his book.

'Hey,' I said. 'Every day, do you . . . Do you sort of do it every day, writing? Do you set yourself a time and stuff?'

'No.'

'I wish I could stop fucking burping,' I said. He started reading again.

'Hey,' I said. 'When you, do you sort of make it up, or is it just, you know, like what happens?'

'Neither.'

'Autobiographical,' I said. 'I haven't read any of your books. There's, I don't really get that much time for reading.'

'Fancy,' he said. He started reading again.

'Hey,' I said. 'Your dad, he's a writer too, isn't he? Bet that made it easier.'

'Oh, sure. It's just like taking over the family pub.'

'Uh?'

'Time,' said the man behind the bar. 'Time. Time.'

'Here, you want another?' I asked him. 'Have a scotch.'

'No, I'm fine.'

'Yeah well I'm pretty well pissed myself. My girl'll be back soon. She's having one of her business dinners. She got this, a boutique. They're, she's trying to get people to invest in it.'

He made no reply. I yawned and stretched. I burped. As I got to my feet, I caught the table with my kneecap. His drink wobbled, like a coin, but he caught it. It didn't splash much.

'Fuck,' I said. 'Well, see you around, Martin.'

'No doubt.'

'. . . What's that mean?' I didn't much like his superior tone, come to think of it, or his tan, or his book. Or the way he stares at me in the street.

'Mean?' he said. 'What do you think it means?'

'You calling me a cunt?' I said loudly.

'What?'

'You called me a cunt!'

'You're mistaken.'

'Ah. So you're calling me a liar now. You're calling me a liar!'

'Hey, take it easy, pal. Christ. You're fine. You're great. I'll see you around.'

'. . . Yeah.'

'Take care now.'

'Yeah. All right then, Martin,' I said, and swayed out through the open door.

Eleven o'clock: the rioting hour. Policemen in shirtsleeves (we are all so relaxed, so informal, about crime these days), standing in six-packs round the white vans, the money-ambulances with their single smart red stripes, waited in the turnings off the trench of the main road. Somewhere the kids, the why-bovver boys, were massing to launch their show. Apparently there was a full-scale revolution on this strip last Saturday night. I was dining alone at a window seat in the Burger Bower, and I didn't notice a thing. If you ask me, there's a riot here every night. There always has been and there always will be. At eleven o'clock, London is a storm, a rave, a knees-up, a free-for-all . . . Here they come again. Yes, I say, go on, go on. I'm shattered, you're shattered – it's a gas. Go on.

Rip it up.

'*Right*, Selina,' I explained, when my own riot was done, 'I want you to listen to this and I want you to listen good. While I'm away you young lady are going to *behave*. Do you *read* me, Selina? No more shit! You're on the payroll now and you damn well do as I say, God damn it. *No one* fucks my race! NO ONE fucks with John Self! You hear me? *NO ONE!*'

'Hark at him. I can't hear a word you're saying. Get your great face out of the pillow.'

'Anyone cheats on me, they're soon sorry. They find they've taken on a little more than they –'

'What? Get your – *oof*. Right. You were saying.'

I rolled over with a grunt. Selina said sharply,

'Did you see Martina Twain in New York?'

'Sort of. I was going to, but there was – I had this schedule problem.'

'You think she's the cat's miaow, don't you, with her degrees and her big arse.'

'Yeah, well . . .'

'Fat chance. Forget it, mate. She's all married up. There's only one way to keep the woman you want. You marry them.'

'Yeah yeah.'

I got out of bed and went next door for a nightcap. An hour or two later I thought I heard Selina's voice, a murmur, a moan. I heaved myself off the couch and walked quietly into the bedroom. She was naked now, on the warm sack, stripped of her props and fetishes. I tell you, Helle's boutique really came up with the goods tonight . . . I moved closer. Selina was asleep, contentedly so, uncunning, unperplexed. The child in her was still visible in the resting eyelids and the ghost of her smile – yes, still visible. She is travelling through time, and to where? At that moment Selina stirred, tenderly, oozily, seeking a more perfect horizontal, just as water desires the flattest level.

Selina Street has no money, no money at all. Imagine. Many times in her life she has lacked the price of a busfare, a teabag. She has stolen. She has pawned clothes. She has fucked for money. No money hurts, it stings. Right, dead right, to give her some. She has always said that men use money to dominate women. I have always agreed. That's why I've never wanted to give her any. But right, dead right, to give her money. Here. Have some money . . . I crept to the bedroom window and put a hand between the black curtains. This spring was the coldest of the century. Now June sleet slapped at the bendy glass. Cold out there. When it's cold. That's when you really feel your money.

I STOOD AT the bar with the *Morning Line*, WITCH WHO LIED FOR DR SEX. ITS ONLY. . . PUPPY LOVE. I BACK IRA – RED KEITH. MY SECRET LOVE BY TV'S MIDGE: SEE CENTRE PAGES. Now is this any way to interpret the world? Seems there's a major rumble brewing in Poland. Solidarity is giving Moscow the V-signs and fight-intros. Russia will beat Poland up, I'm sure, if things go on this way. That's what I'd do. I mean, give them an inch . . . The speculation about Lady Diana's trousseau continues. I have no strong views on the trousseau, but I wish they'd show that famous snap again, the one where she's holding the kid in her arms and you can see right through her dress. A barmaid who cudgelled her landlord boyfriend to death with a beer flagon has been sentenced to eighteen months imprisonment (suspended). How come? Because she pleaded Pre-Menstrual Tension. I'd have thought that PMT was enough of a male hazard anyway, without that kind of mollycoddling. Another granny has been mob-raped in her sock by black boys and skinheads. What is the new craze for grannies? This one's eighty-two, for Christ's sake. Getting raped at that age – Jesus, it must be the last thing you need. Here's another piece about that chick who's dying in her teens because, according to the *Line*, she's allergic to the twentieth century. Poor kid . . . Well I have my problems too, sister, but I don't have yours. I'm not allergic to the twentieth century. I am addicted to the twentieth century.

Terminal Three was in terminal chaos, the air and light

suffused with last things, planet panic, money Judgement. We are fleeing Earth for a newer world while there is still hope, while there are still chances. I queued, checked in, climbed the stairs, hit the bar, I got frisked, X-rayed, cleared, I hit the bar, plundered duty-free, walked the chutes, paced the waiting room until we entered the ship, two by two, all types represented, to make our getaway . . . Aboard the travel tube (a new kind of waiting room) we sat in lines, like an audience, to check out the art therapy on offer: toothache muzak, and, adorning the canvas curtain of the home-movie screen, a harbour view from a bracingly talentless brush. Next, the death-defying act from the stewardesses, those bashful girls and their oxygen mime. But the stalls gave the bird to this dance of doom. Unhooked from London, we boiled and shuddered and raced. Away! I thought, as we climbed through the air with the greatest of ease.

I looked down at the pretty patterns that streets don't know they make. Me, I was flying economy, but the plane, churning sideways now, was guzzling gas at seven gallons a mile. Even the Fiasco is more economical than that. I was flying economy, but I too needed my fuel. With cigarette and lighter cocked, I awaited the release of NO SMOKING. Twisting my neck, I monitored the funereal approach of the drinks trolley. I wolfed down my lunch, charming a second helping out of the all-smiles stewardess. I love airline food and further suspect that there's money in it somewhere. I once tried to interest Terry Linex in the idea of opening an airfood restaurant. Obviously you'd need proper seats, trays, mayonnaise sachets, and so on. You could even have video films, semi-darkness, no-smoking sections, paper bags. Linex liked the way I was thinking, but he said that you'd never get the punters in and out quickly enough. The food would never be fast enough to make really fast money . . .

Using the costly head-pincers, I watched the in-flight movie.

The movie was a wreck, of course. The movie was a flapping, squawking, gobbling turkey. I hope my movie is better than that: I certainly hope it makes more money. (An airline sale within three months of release? This has to be a tragedy for everyone involved.) You know, the thing I want more than anything else – you could call it my dream in life – is to make lots of money. I would cheerfully go into the alchemy business, if it existed and made lots of money . . . We travelled on through air and time. Still four hours to kill. Drinking and smoking, alas, do not claim one's undivided attention. That's the only fault I have to find with these activities. Some people, it seems to me, are never satisfied. Not content with her smart new chequebook, Selina now wants a Vantage card. Oh yeah, and a baby. A *baby* . . . I looked around the quarter-empty aircraft. Everyone appeared to be sleeping or reading. I suppose reading must come in quite handy at times like these. The tousled girl in front of me, she was reading a buxom magazine: its text was in French, I think, but even I could tell that the article she scanned was about fellatio technique – blowjob knowhow. The fur coat on the seat beside her was uncontrollably voluminous, like a distending liferaft. She was flying to her man, or maybe she was flying away from him, to another one. The intent, bespectacled young lady to my left, in contrast, was reading a book called *Rousseau's Philosophy*. This gave me a neat opening. I fetched another fistful of miniatures and spent the rest of the flight telling her about *my* philosophy. It was tough, but we got through the time somehow.

'I have travelled widely', said Fielding Goodney, 'in the world of pornography. Always endeavour, Slick, to keep a fix on the addiction industries: you can't lose. The addicts can't win. Dope, liquor, gambling, anything video – these have to be the deep-money veins. Nowadays the responsible businessman keeps a finger on the pulse of dependence. What next? All projections are targeting the low-energy, domestic stuff, the schlep factor. People just can't back going out any more. They're all addicted to staying at home. Hence the shit-food bonanza. Swallow your chemicals, swallow them fast, and get back inside. Or take the junk back with you. Stay off the streets. Stay inside. With pornography . . .'

'. . . Yes?' I said.

I sipped my crimson drink. I lit another cigarette. We were in an Italian restaurant, well south of SoHo – Tribeca somewhere. Fielding said it was a mob joint and I believed him: brocade, matt light, as quiet as a church. I am a standard, no-frills Earthling, but Goodney, in his white suit, suntan and sliding blond hair, stood out like a pink elephant among the sin-sick funeral directors lurking and cruising against the blood-coloured walls. These guys, they seemed to talk without moving their legs. Just then, a middle-aged, blow-dried villain – the usual opera-star face, woozy with loot and mother-love – urged a neon redhead past our table, our good table, to which Fielding had been instantly and officiously steered.

Fielding looked up. He paused. 'Antonio Pisello,' he said, 'Tony Cazzo – from Staten Island. He was shot in the heart five years ago. Know what saved him?' he asked, and jabbed his own ribs with a long straight thumb. 'Credit cards – kept in a deck, with a band. Used to be a bad boy, but now he's pretty well totally legit.'

'And the girl?'

'Willa Glueck. Smart lady. A grand-a-night hooker, semi-retired. For ten years she worked the streets – you know, giving head and hand at a dollar a dick. Then five years at the top, the very top. No one knows how she made the switch. It just doesn't happen. Look at her, the eyes, the mouth – superb. No evidence. I can't figure it. I hate it when I can't *figure* things.'

Indeed, lamentably under-informed, Fielding Goodney. He smiled in innocent self-reproach, then swung sternly and made the reverse V-sign at the watchful waiter. Two more Red Snappers were on their way. We ordered. Fielding held the crimson menu (silken, tasselled and beautified, reminding me and my fingers of Selina and her secrets) in slender brown hands, the wrists cuffed in pale blue and the gold links taut on their chains. Over dinner Fielding explained to me about the lucrative contingencies of pornography, the pandemonium of Forty-Second Street, the Boylesk dealerships on Seventh Avenue with their prodigies of chickens and chains, the Malibu circuit with the crews splashing through the set at dusk for the last degrees of heft and twang and purchase from the beached male lead on the motel floor, the soft proliferations of soft core in worldwide cable and network and its careful codes of airbrush and dick-wipe, the stupendous aberrations of Germany and Japan, the perversion-targeting in video mail-order, the mob snuff-movie operation conceived in Mexico City and dying in the Five Boroughs.

And I asked him, 'These movies – they exist?'

'Sure. But not many, not for long and not any more.' Fielding (I noticed) cut his veal in the normal way, but then passed his fork to the right hand to prong the meat. 'Come on, Slick, be realistic. If there was money there, it had to be tried . . . The girls were vagrants.'

'Ever seen one?'

'You understand what you're asking me? You're asking me if I'm an accessory after the fact to first-degree murder. Not me, Slick. This was organized crime, superorganized. No other way. Snuff movies – now this is *evidence*.'

And then his manner, the force field he gave off, it changed, not for long. He became pointed, intimate. He said,

'Clinching, no? Evidence that it corrupts, pornography,

wouldn't you say?' He relaxed, and so did his manner. 'Too hot, Slick. No one could use them. A distribution problem.'

We went on to discuss *our* distribution problem, which, according to my pal Fielding, was absolutely non-existent. We would simply lease out the finished product: that way, said Fielding, we preserved our artistic freedom while making much, much more money. I thought only the big boys could pull off a gimmick like this, but the kid had it all worked out. His contacts were extraordinary, and not just in movies either. As he talked, and as I hunkered down to a long train of grappa and espresso, I felt the clasp and nuzzle of real money. Money, my bodyguard.

'You know, Slick,' he said, '– sometimes business looks to me like a big dumb dog howling to be played with. Want to know my hunch for the next growth area in the addiction line? Want to make a million? Shall I let you in?'

'Do it,' I said.

'Cuddles,' said Fielding Goodney. 'Cuddling up. Two people lying down and generating warmth and safety. Now how do we market this. A how-to book? A video? Nightshirts? A cuddle studio, with cuddle hostesses? Think about it, Slick. There are millions and millions of dollars out there somewhere in cuddles.'

Fielding caught the unspectacular tab, leaving a twenty on the plate. His hired Autocrat was waiting on the street. At one point Fielding turned to me and said, with midtown flashing against his face, 'Oh, I misled you, Slick, earlier on there. It's murder two not murder one. New York, murder one is just for cops, prison officers, shit like that. Forgive me.' I slipped out near Times Square. I heard Fielding give the driver an address on feminine Park Avenue.

I walked unsteadily through the heat of the pornographic night. As for my own body-clock readings and time-travel co-ordinates, well, it was 6 a.m. in here, and fuming with booze.

I had travelled far that day, through space and through time. Man, how I needed to crash. Among the alleys and rooftops near the Ashbery, Fielding tells me, a nimble maniac sprints and climbs at large. What he needs to do is drop slating and masonry on to the heads of strolling theatre-goers and diners. He has done it five times now. He has had five hits. One was fatal. Murder two. Ultraviolet policemen lie in wait up there but they can't seem to catch him, this rooftop psychopath, adept of eave and sill, of buttress and skyhatch, this infinite-mass artist. So he darts and shinnies his way through the gothic jaggedness of fire-escapes, drainpipes and TV aerials, while beneath him Broadway crackles in late-night styrofoam, and there is no money involved. There is no money for him up there at any point.

Now you've seen me in New York before, and you know how I am out here. I wonder what it is: something to do with the energy, the electricity of the place, all the hustle and razz – it fills me with that get up and go. I'm a different proposition in New York, pulled together, really on the ball. I was at it again first thing this morning, straight down to business despite my jet-lag and the kind of hangover that would have poleaxed any lesser man – worse, even, I think than the hangover I caught in California. The hangover I caught in California was now seven months old, and I still showed no signs of recovering from it. It'll probably be with me till my dying day . . . I told you all about my LA lark, didn't I. It's a good one, isn't it. The big black guy with the baseball bat – remember? Jesus, the risks one takes for a couple of laughs. I often think that the staying-power of my Californian hangover has something to do with an inability to believe I'm still alive.

Lying in bed, with telephone, address book, ashtray and

coffee-cup efficiently arranged on the pouffe of my gut, I now buckled down to the first item of business: Caduta Massi . . . Like everyone else, like you yourself, I had seen Caduta many times up on the big screen, in costume dramas, musicals, Italian sex comedies, Mexican westerns. I had seen Caduta cringe and prance and pout and sneer. I used to beat off nights about her when I was a kid – like everyone else. The more I thought about her, the nearer I got to beating off about her now. She had been a big brawny vision in her youth, with an encouraging hint of rural gullibility in the breadth of her eyes and lips. Over the passing years, time had been kind to Caduta Massi. Over the passing years, time had been cruel to nearly everybody else. Time had been wanton, virulent and spiteful. Time had put the boot in. Now, at forty-odd, she could still play the right kind of romantic lead, given a sufficiently elderly and/or bisexual co-star . . . I hadn't been quick to come around to Caduta, as you know. I would have preferred someone less gorgeous, happy and sane – Sunny Wand, or even Day Lightbowne. I'm not sure why. But Fielding argued that Caduta was crucial to the package, and you have to follow the money in a case like this. Caduta, wife of the erring Lorne Guyland, rival to the busty Butch Beausoleil, mother of the greedy, thieving, addicted Christopher Meadowbrook or Spunk Davis or Nub Forkner – or whoever the hell we ended up with. The role was passive yet quietly central. It was sad. I wanted someone more realistic . . . You see, the impulse behind my concept, my outline, it was personal, it had to do with my life. Autobiographical. Yes, it had to do with this old life of mine.

I rang the Cicero, where Fielding had installed Caduta and her entourage. A man answered. Caduta asked me to come to an address in Little Italy at two o'clock that afternoon. I then threw in a call to my sock in London. Engaged. Engaged . . . According to Fielding, Caduta was in need of reassurance. I was going to give her some, gladly. I just hope I've got a little to spare. Yesterday, after that tearful reunion with my suitcase, I tried to get a negro hand-slapping thing going with Felix. *Why?* I thought. It's for the touch, for the touch. After all we are only human beings down here and we could do with a lot more praise and comfort than we actually get. Earthling reassurance – it's in permanently short supply, don't you think? Be honest, brother. Lady, now tell the truth. When was the last time a fellow-Earther let you rest your head on their heart, caressed your cheek, and said things designed to make you feel deeply okay? It doesn't happen often enough, does it. We'd all like it to happen a lot more often than it does. Can't we do a deal? Oh boy (I bet you're thinking), that head-on-heart stuff, whew, could I use a little of that.

I yawned and stretched – and nearly spilt the coffee. Reaching to steady the cup, I unbalanced the ashtray. Reaching to steady the ashtray, I spilt the coffee, and also hooked my elbow in the telephone's lone dreadlock – so that when, with a final heroic convulsion, I burst out of the bed, the swinging casket somehow smashed into my shin and then dropped like a bomb on to the bare mound of my foot . . . Twenty minutes later, by which time the pain had done its worst, I unpeeled my way through the sodden address book. I sought reassurance that Martina's number wasn't listed there. This was one call, one lost date, one apology, that I begged to be excused. Here we are: Theresa's, TV Repair, Trans-American, Trexacarna – Martina Twain. Now wait just a goddam minute. That wasn't my handwriting. It was – Selina's! . . . *Bitch*. Was this a recrimination, or a taunt? Defiantly I squelched the book shut. Yes and then I made that call.

And still I surfed on Manhattan static. YIELD say the traffic signs – but don't you listen! *Not* yielding, that's the thing. To strive, to seek, to butch it out – it's all a question of willpower. Thus midday discovered me with a second scotch in my hand, a Pakki nightie round my waist, and a half-naked sex-stewardess straddling my thighs. I was in the Happy Isles, on Third Avenue. I had read about the place in *Scum* magazine . . . I felt all right in here: a circular, windowless room, tricked out in some lost pimp's image of a paradisal arbour – tendoned vines, plastic grape-clutches, bamboo ceiling, lagoon lights and canned bird-song. I even found myself humming one of Fat Vince's favourites. What was it? – 'O Twine Me a Bower'. You know, there's a certain sort of man who would come to a joint like this in order to fuck the women in it. But self-improvement isn't nearly as hard as people make out. Take, for instance, a look at me. I'm only here for a handjob.

'Yeah, well what do you do?' I was saying. 'Use the blow-dry *after* the towels, or what?'

I was talking to this chick about her hair and the trouble she had with it. She was asking for trouble, mind you. Flattened by its own weight, its prisms as lively as oil stains or car blood, her solid black rug coursed down the length of her back. When she stood and turned to refreshen my drink, the bristly hem almost covered her double-fisted backside. Man, I wish I had an American rug, instead of this old dishtowel I live my life under . . . The lady had cordially assured me at the outset that I was free 'to party with anybody I liked the look of' (this, except for the half-ounce bikini she wore, being her only hint that what we were sitting in wasn't a beauty parlour or seminar room but actually a brothel. I didn't let on either). I wondered then and I wondered now whether anybody included her. She'd sat on my lap in a friendly way, true, but that was just so I could get a better fix on her rug. Maybe she was simply a bargirl, a cashier, an all-purpose heft-dispenser . . . and maybe I had already got to know her a little too well. By my side nestled a water-proof, see-through plastic bag, containing my wallet: the money, the necessary. I had been obliged to take a blistering shower in a back room jovially serviced by two fat negroes in Hawaii shirts and frazzled straw hats. So I sat there, deloused, in the Happy Isles. Spurred by all this travel and transfer, the disease I have called tinnitus tunnelled deep and desperate into the corners of my head. Both ears were doing their jet imitation, with whistle and whine and the hungry rumble of underfloor fire. I held my new drink up to my forehead, as if to soothe my pulsing, my needing brow – plastic glass, plastic ice, an aeroplane drink. Yeah. I call this living good.

'The second wash,' I persisted, 'can be a big mistake. It expands the follicles and then the cleaning agents dry and harden.'

'Really?' said the girl. 'Is that a fact.'

'Yup,' I said. Hair is one of the things I do know something about. I may not know much about anatomy, but I *am* rug-smart. It's all those stylists, wardrobe girls and make-up technicians I've hung out with, plus my own pricey psychodramas on the topic. I nodded and drank my drink. I looked around. Where were the other candidates? Anyway, I assumed that this unit here in the white bikini was relishing the banter and the rug-wisdom. Chatting with me was presumably a lot more fun than going to bed with me for money – though less profitable, it had to be said. I too was pretty pleased by the way things were going. I was pleased to be sitting here with a strong drink, pleased that I wasn't staked out on the basement floor, playing the romantic lead in a snuff movie. No, it was all very civilized, very civilized indeed.

Now her head dipped as she pried at the fissure of a half-split nail. With that backdrop of hair the small round shoulders gained in defencelessness and pallor – but come on, the Isles was no place for local contrasts. The girl, the lean teenager with W-shaped folds in the vent of her shut armpits, she would suit me right down to the ground. Being the being I am, though, and no other (not yet anyway), I wanted full brothel privileges, the old male deal of dough and careless choice.

'Where are your friends?' I said.

She shrugged, and surveyed the empty bower. Where were mine? Then she raised her face to me and said with sad seriousness,

'Hey. What's your name.'

'I'm Martin,' I said at once . . . I hate my name. I mean, you have a kid, a little baby boy, and the best you can do with it is to name it John? I'm called John Self. But who isn't?

'And what's yours?'

'They call me Moby. You married?'

'No. I guess I'm not the marrying kind.'

'What do you do, Martin?'

'I'm a writer, Moby.'

'But that's really *interesting*,' she said sternly. 'You're a writer? What do you write?'

'Uh. Fiction. Stuff like that.'

'John roar mainstream?' she seemed to say.

'Pardon?'

'I mean are they mainstream novels and stories or thrillers or sci-fi or something like that?'

'What's mainstream?'

She smiled appraisingly and said, 'That's a good question . . . I'm fucking my way through college? English Literature, at NYTE? You write *novels*? *That's* what you do? What did you say your name was?'

By this time I was more than ready to ask Moby what *she* did, and how much it cost – but then I felt the full-thighed waft of a new female presence. I turned. A big bimbo in cool pants and bra came swaying from the shadows of the rear corridor. She was built on the Selina model, with several dirty-minded enlargements, the emphasis all on protuberance, convexity. And I thought: I want. Me, for me. She sat with a sigh on a black plastic mushroom by the bar. A few seconds later a smug, exhausted man in an impeccable business suit went staggering past.

'Take care now, She-She,' he said richly.

'You too, sir,' said She-She, in the brisk commercial tones of hostesses everywhere. 'I'd like to thank you for stopping by. See you again, sir.'

'Oh yes.'

She-She's trick staggered on. His slack, slaked face seemed about to drop off with sheer gravity of dissipation. He obviously hadn't stinted himself with She-She back there. No. He had given his senses all kinds of presents and treats with She-She back there.

'Hey, She-She,' said Moby. 'Martin here's an English writer.'

'Yeah?' said She-She.

'Yeah,' I said. I stood up, in my grey skin, stacked gut and floral wraparound, my hair the colour of London skies – under the bam, under the boo.

'Aren't you excited?' I was asked, ten minutes later.

'Yes and no.'

'Come *on*. Ooh, you must be so *excited*.'

'Well yeah,' I said, 'I suppose I am quite.'

True, I was now lying naked in a locked and candlelit cabana, alone with the industrious She-She, whose fleshy right hand made smoothing motions on the hair-dotted slope of my inner thigh . . . For a while, back there under the bam, I had hesitated before arriving at my selection. Perhaps little Moby would be hurt by my preference for her talented colleague – would walk out, burst into tears, commit suicide. But there doesn't seem to be a self-pity problem in the Happy Isles. You know, I suspect I'm not cut out for brothels. I can't help getting engaged on the human scale, minimal though this is, fight it though I do. I just can't get off the scale . . . Moby and I swapped fond farewells as She-She led me away. I shadowed her down the tapering passage, all its planes carpet-covered, like four floors. She-She then parked me in the aromatic cubicle. Standing at the door with her knuckles on her hips, she bade me recline on the high wall bed, as if for a medical inspection. Yeah, that's what it felt like: a much-dreaded, long-overdue and sinisterly ritzy visit to the dick-doctor. 'Why don't you make yourself more comfort-able?' she asked, with a touch of joshing indignation. Obligingly I leaned back an additional inch or two into the firm and furry pillows. 'No – take off your sarong! Now I'll be with you in just one minute.' So I lay naked in the rinsed airlessness of the room, waiting for She-She's return, and wishing pretty earnestly that I had taken my chances with Moby.

'If I was you,' resumed She-She, 'I'd be very excited.'

'You would, would you.'

'I'd be just wild.'

'Well I'm looking forward to it, certainly.'

'I'll bet.'

'Yes, it should be fun.'

'I'd just be so *excited*.'

I frowned and said, 'About what, exactly?'

She-She gave an incredulous pout.

'I mean, you're a great-looking chick and everything,' I said, 'but –'

'Not *me*. God! Your new Princess!'

'Oh *her*.'

So for some time She-She and I talked very seriously about the future Princess of Wales. The future Princess of Wales is evidently a big hit with the hookers on Third Avenue. She-She was full of admiration of Lady Diana's hairstyle, dress-sense and poise. She also had a lot of time for Prince Charles. She liked Prince Andrew. She liked Prince Edward. She even fancied the Duke of Edinburgh. After an increasingly eerie half hour of this I clapped my hands together and said, rather abruptly perhaps,

'– Right then. So what are you selling?'

'Oh anything you want,' she said, with no change in the speed of her voice. 'What kind of tip you want to give?'

'Well let's see now. What's on offer?'

'Straight French English Greek Turkish. Or Half'n'Half.'

'. . . What's Half'n'Half?'

'Straight with French.'

'What's English?'

'Correction.'

'What's Turkish? – No, don't tell me. Let me have, just give me a – I think I'll just have a handjob.'

'A handjob?' She-She stiffened. 'Okay. If you want. What kind of tip you want to give?'

Naked as I was, I still had my condom-like moneybag on my lap. I had already coughed up forty bucks at the door. How much is a handjob? Come on, what do you reckon? With a shrug I said, 'Fifty dollars?'

'Listen,' She-She told me. 'Why don't you put your clothes on *right now* and get down to Seventh Avenue or Forty-Second Street. You want to spend fifty dollars, maybe they can help you out. Fifty dollars? Nobody gives me fifty dollars.'

'Wait a minute – hey, take it easy,' I said. I confess I was a little shaken by my playmate's tone. For a moment there she had looked and sounded like a rockhard loan-shark reclaiming an ugly debt. 'I'm new to all this, I'm sorry. Why don't you make a suggestion?'

She-She: 'If you give the fifty cash, then seventy-five on the card plus the credit supplement which is 15 per cent else we lose on the rental or we have a spa-cheque policy which works out the same minus the 15 per cent with a ten-dollar supplement. It makes no difference with a gift this size.'

'. . . A hundred and seventy-five dollars? For a *handjob*?'

'Listen, this is Third Avenue, not Seventh. Why don't you put on your clothes and –'

'Yeah yeah.'

Oh, they've worked this one out: some male thought has gone into this all right – more, probably, than went into that bamboo shitbox, the birdsong, the lagoon lights. There you are, naked, and tagging your needs with the sex inspector. It's not that she wants to make you feel cheap. She wants to make you feel the cheapest *ever* . . . Spryly She-She left the room. But she soon came back again. She bore the sliding brace of a credit-card franker. What was going into that crushing ratchet – my US Approach card, or my Johnson? Now, sir, I'll just take an impression of your penis here . . . There was some more budget-balancing over the question of She-She's underwear. The top came off at once. The pants, she said, had not been part of the deal.

'You certainly know how to turn a guy on,' I said, all passion spent, and flicked another twenty into the pool.

To put it at its highest, I was in no more than so-so shape by the time I reached Caduta's. I'd had a couple of drinks, lapped up some fast food, and jumped into a cab. I only had time for fast food. I'm going to kick fast food too, one day. The time has come to kick fast food. Time to fast from it . . . That session with She-She had done me no good at all. Although I had tarried in the Happy Isles for well over an hour, the actual handjob was the work of a moment – forty-five seconds, I'd say. I had to rack my brains to remember a worse one. 'You must have been really excited,' said She-She quietly, as she started plucking tissues from the box. Yes and no. Between ourselves, it was one of those handjobs where you go straight from limpness to orgasm, skipping the hard-on stage. I think She-She must have activated some secret glandular gimmick, to wrap it up quickly. She then attempted a drowsy recap on the Royal Family but I shouldered my way out of there as soon as I could. The trouble with all this is – it's so *unsatisfactory*. Regular handjobs are unsatisfactory too, but they don't cost five bucks a second. Overheads are generally low. Say what you like about handjobs, they don't cost eighty-five quid.

The cab journey downtown was an anguish of effort, of clogged and doddering crisis. When I first came to New York even a traffic jam was interesting. Nowadays, though, I can take or leave a traffic jam in New York. I wish I could work out how to use the subway. I've tried. No matter how hard I concentrate I always end up clambering out of a manhole in Duke Ellington Boulevard with a dustbin-lid on my head. You cannot get around New York and that's the end of it . . . I looked at my watch. I sat sweating and swearing on the sticky back seat. It's heating up here already, yes it's stoking up here nicely for the scorch-riots of August. Of the many directives gummed to the glass partition, one took the trouble to thank me for not smoking. I hate that. I mean, it's a bit previous, isn't it, don't you think? I haven't not smoked yet. As it turned out, I never did not smoke in the end. I lit a cigarette and kept them coming. The frizzy-rugged beaner at the wheel shouted something and threw himself around for a while, but I kept on not not smoking quietly in the back, and nothing happened.

Local rumour maintains that Little Italy is one of the cleanest and safest enclaves in Manhattan. Any junkie or Bowery red-eye comes limping down the street, then five sombre fatboys with baseball bats and axe-handles stride out of the nearest trattoria. Well, Little Italy just felt like more Village to me. The zeds of the fire-escapes looked as though they were used in earnest twice a week – they were grimed to a cinder. In these clogged defiles they could never wash off all the truck-belch and car-fart bubbling upwards in vapours of oil and acid and engine coolant. What is the spangled Caduta doing in a dump like this? She's got a suite at the Cicero, tabbed by Fielding Goodney, with a hairdresser, a bodyguard, and a 73-year-old boyfriend . . . I ran back and forth across the street until I found the dirty door.

'Now, Mr Self, "John": our movie!' said Caduta Massi. 'I see from the outline that the lady is from . . . Bradford. I do not find this convincing at all.'

'Well the outline you saw, Caduta – that was the English version. Now we've switched to New York we can –'

'I prefer Florence. Or Verona.'

'Sure. Okay. Take your pick.'

'And what is the title of the movie?'

'*Good Money*,' I said. Actually, we weren't sure yet. Fielding liked *Good Money*. I liked *Bad Money*. Fielding suggested calling it *Good Money* in the States and *Bad Money* in Europe, but I couldn't see the percentage in that.

'Good,' said Caduta. 'Tell me, John. This Theresa. How old is she?'

'Uh . . . thirtyish?' Yeah, thirty-*nine*. I gazed at Caduta warily.

'Excuse me, but I understand she has a son of twenty.'

'That's true. I suppose she's a little older than that.'

'I myself am forty-one,' said Caduta.

'No kidding,' I said. 'Well, that's perfect.'

'So could you tell me? Why should a woman of this age be taking her clothes off and demanding sex all the time?'

I sat with a cup of coffee on my lap, still half-asphyxiated by what I took to be Neapolitan warmth. The place was crawling with kids – bundles, toddlers, nippers, loping adolescents. There were at least three dad-figures, wearing vests and overalls, in the kitchen next door, hunched over bottles of unlabelled wine and steaming pasta in arterial sauce. They even had a couple of black-clad bagladies sitting silently on straight chairs by the door. I couldn't see any mums about the place. Apart from that, though, the whole crew might have just come in from Ellis Island . . . Caduta herself was clearly the queen bee here. She kept clapping her hands and unleashing her imperious Italian. Like a department-store Santa she shuffled the kids on her lap: the kids, they did their shift, then climbed off. Every now and then a dad would swagger in and talk to her with reverence but also with a certain courtly gaiety. The one-tooth-apiece bagladies murmured and nodded and crossed themselves. Caduta frequently addressed me in Italian too, which didn't make things any clearer.

I coughed and said, 'I'm sorry, Caduta, but what is all this?'

'Mr Guyland. He said there were to be several explicit love scenes.'

'With you?'

She lifted her chin and nodded.

'That's all nonsense, Caduta. There aren't any love scenes in the outline.'

'Lorne Guyland said that Mr Goodney promised him three long love scenes, with full nudity.'

'Good God, how old is Guyland? What's he want to be in the nude for?'

'He is a disgusting person. Listen, Mr Self – John. I need your reassurance that this will not happen.'

'You got it.' I glanced round the room. The bagladies smiled encouragingly. 'Look, Caduta. There are no sex scenes between you and Lorne. There'll probably be a scene or two with you in bed together, in the morning sort of thing – but with sheets, okay?'

'I'll be frank with you, John,' said Caduta Massi. She shooed the children from her lap. 'I am forty-three, as I say. My tits are not so good any more. My belly is good, my ass is good, but the tits?' She waved a hand in the air. 'I have second-degree cellulite on my outside thigh. What have you got to say to that?'

I had nothing to say to it. Caduta was wearing a two-piece suit of grey suede. With a little bounce she drew the skirt up to her hips. I could see the stocking tops, the tender skin, the billion-lira panties. She took a fistful of her outside thigh and squeezed, making the flesh frown.

'See?' she said, and started to unbutton her shirt.

I glanced round the room again. One of the dads popped his head through the doorway. The head smiled, then withdrew. The bagladies stared on, stonily now. One of the children pawed at my lap, as if returning my attention to the lady on the velvet throne.

Holding my eye, Caduta parted the flounces of her shirt. She freed the clip that marked the centrepoint of her cleavage in the hefty brassière. 'Come, John,' she said.

I stood up, I moved forward, I knelt. She gathered my face to her heart. I sensed all the voluminous stirrings in there, deep among the mortal heaviness.

'You never had a mother, did you, John.'

My voice was muted, but what I said was, 'No. I never did.'

There are, at the latest count, four distinct voices in my head. First, of course, is the jabber of money, which might be represented as the blur on the top rung of a typewriter – £%¼ @=&$! – sums, subtractions, compound terrors and greeds. Second is the voice of pornography. This often sounds like the rap of a demented DJ: *the way she moves has got to be good news, can't get loose till I feel the juice – suck and spread, bitch, yeah bounce for me baby* . . . And so on. (One of the subvoices of pornography in my head is the voice of an obsessed black tramp or retard who roams the Times Square beat here in New York. Incomprehensible yet unmistakably lecherous, his gurgled monologue goes like this: Uh guh geh yuh tih ah fuh yuh uh yuh fuh ah ah yuh guh suh muh fuh cuh. I do a lot of that kind of talking in my head too.) Third, the voice of ageing and weather, of time travel through days and days, the ever-weakening voice of stung shame, sad boredom and futile protest . . .

Number four is the real intruder. I don't want any of these voices but I especially don't want this one. It is the most recent. It has to do with quitting work and needing to think about things I never used to think about. It has the unwelcome lilt of paranoia, of rage and weepiness made articulate in spasms of vividness: drunk talk played back sober. And on the TV they keep showing hysterical ads or the fucking news . . . All the voices come from somewhere else. I wish I could flush them out of my head. As with vampires, you have to ask them in. But once they're there, once you've given them headroom, they seem pretty determined to stick around. Don't let them in, these crashers. Don't let them in, whatever you do.

How about that Caduta, though, eh?

Mind you, if you think she behaved strangely, you should have seen me. I had an incredible crying jag. So did Caduta. So did two kids and one baglady. After a while, the dads trooped in. Everyone was beaming and weeping at this display, this proof of human richness. It was all crap too – I knew that. It was all bad art. But what can you expect from me? There are times these days when I feel so starved of warmth that the instructions on a painkiller packet or vitamin tub ('At the first sign of a cold developing be sure to . . .') can make me go all husky and brave. And I certainly appreciated the faceful that Caduta laid on me. I sniffed and rootled around down there for at least ten minutes, and got in several good licks and kisses. But it wasn't a sexual thing. I would never make a pass at Caduta – no, not Caduta – and if you made a pass at her, I'd beat you up. I was still brimming with plangency, chockful of feeling, when I arrived back at the hotel. Caduta's parting words to me – she delivered them like a war bride or mother, keeping pace with my cab as it pulled away – were as follows: 'Protect me, John! Protect me.' I knew what that meant. I seized the telephone and called Lorne Guyland, in high indignation.

'Now, Lorne,' I began, after a female flunky had put the great man on. 'I've just had a meeting with Caduta Massi. Those scenes you suggested to her – she doesn't want to take her clothes off, and I have to say I –'

'WHAT DO YOU MEAN SHE WON'T TAKE HER CLOTHES OFF! SHE'S ONLY A FUCKING TV ACTRESS! I'LL RIP HER FUCKING CLOTHES OFF!'

I held the telephone at arm's length, and stared at it. What impressed me most, I think, was the sheer instantaneousness with which Lorne lost his temper. Suddenly, immediately: no temper – gone, long gone. I'm a short-fuse artist myself, but even I need a little longer than that. It takes at least a couple of seconds before I recognize the last straw. But to some people, clearly, every straw is the last straw. To some people, the first straw is the last straw.

'Lorne, Lorne,' I said, 'bear with me here. Look, there aren't any nude scenes in the script, not with Caduta. With Butch Beausoleil, yes, fine, go ahead, as many as you like. But with Caduta. She's –'

'What script? Nobody showed me no fucking script!'

'Doris Arthur is still working on it, Lorne. But I think I can say that there aren't going to be any nude scenes between you and Caduta. Semi-nude, maybe. But not nude. And that's final.'

While he talked I sank back gratefully with my duty-free. Lorne's superfury had run its course. He had a grip on himself. He was now merely incredibly angry. He said,

'Final? *Final!* Boy, you're really new at this. Now you listen to me, you piece of shit. This is *Lorne Guyland man.* Yeah. Me! Me! I got to have some beef in that role. You don't need *me.* Why don't you get some old fart like Cash Jones?' Lorne laughed. 'I don't know why I say that. I love Cash. Cash and I go way, he's one of my oldest, one of my closest friends. A dear friend, John. Very dear.' Lorne paused. 'Yeah, but when you got Lorne Guyland in a picture, you got to give him some beef, you got to give him some size, you got to give him some – it's got to be like big, you know? You saw my work in *Pookie*, John. I'm glad you called,' Lorne went on weirdly, 'because I want to tell you about another new idea I've gotten. Now I'm not a writer. I've written scenes, of course, in fact I, in fact the idea is this. The young guy, right? I don't know who the fuck you cast and I don't care, but him and I have this fight, right?'

'You and your son. That's right.'

'And in the outline, John, it says that he wins.'

'That's right.'

'Now I don't think that's convincing dramatically, John.'

'Why not?'

'Well, it suggests to the audience that he's stronger than I am.'

'That's right. I mean, he's only twenty and you're – you're a mature man.'

'But I know that kid you've been testing. He's a punk! I could rip him to fucking pieces with my bare hands!'

'But people won't know you could do that, Lorne. They'll think he won because he's forty years younger than you are.'

'Ah! I get it. You think just because I'm not as *young* as he is, *he's stronger than I am*. Crap!'

'*I* don't think that, Lorne. But everyone else will.'

'Okay, okay. I'm a reasonable man. We'll do it this way. And, yeah, I want this whole scene in the nude, we're all nude, that's definite. I won't sacrifice that, that idea. Now. I'm fucking Caduta, right? And I mean really *fucking* her. The woman's in – Wait. No. This is Butch. I just fucked Caduta, now I'm fucking Butch, right? And I mean really *fucking* her. The woman's in tears, right out of control. She's hysterical, John. Then this young *actor* walks in – he's nude too – for the showdown. And I spring out of bed, naked as I am, and I just start to tear him to fucking pieces. I'm damn near killing the guy when Butch, in the nude, starts shouting, "Lorne! Lorne, baby! Honey, what are you doing! Stop, sweetheart, please stop!" And I realize I been – that the *animal* in me, because, John, it's a terrible world we're living in, John, it's a really crazy, awful . . . world. So Butch and Caduta lead me away. I'm damn near in tears on account of what I've done to the guy. Then this young punk comes up behind me and hits me on the head with a car-tool. John? What do you say.'

'Lorne? We'll see.'

'No, No! *You'll* see. Yes you will!'

Crack.

I replaced the receiver and stared at my lap. On it lay a cellophaned wallet of Guyland press handouts – this was where I'd scribbled his number. Running my eye down the page I saw that Lorne had, in his time, on stage or screen, interpreted the roles of Genghis Khan, Al Capone, Marco Polo, Huckleberry Finn, Charlemagne, Paul Revere, Erasmus, Wyatt Earp, Voltaire, Sky Masterson, Einstein, Jack Kennedy, Rembrandt, Babe Ruth,

Oliver Cromwell, Amerigo Vespucci, Zorro, Darwin, Sitting Bull, Freud, Napoleon, Spiderman, Macbeth, Melville, Machiavelli, Michelangelo, Methuselah, Mozart, Merlin, Marx, Mars, Moses and Jesus Christ. I didn't have the lowdown on every last one of these guys but presumably they were all bigshots. Perhaps, then, it wasn't so surprising that Lorne had one or two funny ideas about himself.

Oh, what a *long* day. Dah! what a day. You know what the time is, my time? Four o'clock in the afternoon. Hey, if you were here now, sister mother daughter lover (niece, auntie, granny), maybe we could talk a bit and cuddle down together – nothing dirty. Only spoons. Maybe you'd let me rest my great face in the gentle bracket between the wings of your shoulderblades. That's all I have in mind, believe me. I know you for a pure creature. You don't drink or smoke or screw around that much, I'll bet. Am I wrong? That is what I love in you . . . Now the way I figured it I had six realistic options. I could sack out right away, with some scotch and a few Serafim. I could go back to the Happy Isles and see what little Moby was up to. I could call Doris Arthur. I could catch a live sex show around the corner, in bleeding Seventh Avenue. I could go out and get drunk. I could stay in and get drunk.

In the end I stayed in and got drunk. The trouble was, I did all the other things first. Sometimes I feel that life is passing me by, not slowly either, but with ropes of steam and spark-spattered wheels and a hoarse roar of power or terror. It's passing, yet I'm the one who is doing all the moving. I'm not the station, I'm not the stop: I'm the train. I'm the train.

'Fill me in on the tits, Slick. Tell me about them in incredible detail.'

'No way. Back off, pal. This was a very personal thing between Caduta and me. I'm saying nothing. My lips are sealed.'

'You know, she has a similar set-up in Rome and also in Paris, a little crèche where she can go and queen it once a year. It's a sweet deal for the families. All they have to do is keep the mothers out of the way whenever she shows up and to psych the kids into thinking Caduta's some kind of superwomb. Tell me a little about the tits, Slick. I take it they're bigger than, say, Doris Arthur's?'

Whose aren't? I thought tenderly. We strode on. This was Amsterdam Avenue, with the cross streets moving slowly by. There goes Eighty-Seventh. Here comes Eighty-Eighth. Maintaining a low profile, the Autocrat lurked a steady block behind as we walked north. I had never been on the Upper West Side before, but it still reminded me of something. It reminded me how quiet my rocky tooth had been for at least a week or two now . . . Over a fanatically carnivorous lunch in an Argentinian joint on Eighty-Second Street my friend Fielding had been very reassuring on the whole Lorne–Caduta question. All the conflicts, he explained, would melt away the minute we had a screenplay in our hands. Moviestars invariably fucked you around like this until there was a script to defer to. Then they forgot about characterization and obsessed themselves exclusively with things like line-count, screen-time and close-up allocation. Doris Arthur was back in the States, typing away at her rented cottage in Long Island. I fondly imagined little Doris among her busy lizzies and lazy susans, in racoon hat and frontier dungarees, working the pump, fixing the roof, with half-a-dozen nails and a couple of briar pipes in her syrupy mouth. The first draft, Fielding promised, was only three weeks away.

'Where are we going? What's with all this walking?'

'It's a sunny Sunday, John. We're sightseeing. Tell me. How did Doris strike you? Physically, I mean,' he added, with such soft, sweet-tooth hooding of the eyes that my stride faltered and I said,

'You've been there, huh? Oh boy. What's she like?'

'Listen. You tell me about Caduta's tits and I'll tell you everything there is to know about Doris in the sack. Is it a deal?'

'Well they're big all right and low too but what they mainly are is very deep and heavy. They rest on the ribcage of course and span out a bit lower down but they're still very solid and they –'

'I get the picture, Slick. We can't use them. I thought she might have had them fixed. You're thinking, We don't want some cantilevered old bimbo. We want someone real. But filmstars *aren't* real, John. It isn't in them. You'll see.'

'Right. Doris. Do it.'

'I'm afraid I misled you. I know all there is to know, which is nothing. Doris is gay, Slick.'

I stumbled to a halt and snapped my fingers through the air. 'So *that* was it. Jesus, I knew it was something like that. That *bitch* . . .'

'You made a play?'

'Well sure. Didn't you?'

'No, I knew all along. It was clear from the stories.'

'What stories? Tell me them at least.'

'The short stories, John. *The Ironic High Style*, remember?'

'Oh *them*.'

But here I saw the way the streets were going, how they darkened despite the sun, the juicy air, the innocence of the covering blue. Three blocks back there were canopied doorways, wealth-guards in livery and vistas of brownstone. Now the lanes were carless, lawless. We skirted the spreading sponge of split mattresses and jaw-busted suitcases facedown in the gutter, saw the dark excluded profiles behind windows and chicken wire – this was no-money country, coldwater, walkup. And so sudden, the breakdown, the feelable absence of all agreement, of all consensus – except for that money-hate or anger you get when cities wedge their rich and poor as close as two faces of a knife . . . I marked the poverty and the poverty marked me. And I also sensed – perversely, unnecessarily, wastefully – how *gay* Fielding and I must look, him in his sneakers and strontium rompers and flyaway hair, me with my butch suit, thin jekylls and proud-rounded shoes. Even the hardened faggots of Manhattan (I fancied) were gazing down at us with concern from their lofts and condos and thinking – we're pretty brazen, God knows, but these guys, they'll queer the whole pitch.

'Hey nigger brother!'

Ninety-Eighth Street. I turned my head. Two black guys with a big dog cocked on its leash.

'Fuck this shit, man. I think my dog go bite one of them white dudes.'

'Fielding,' I said tightly. 'Is this smart? Let's get the car. This is fucking pangerland.'

'Walk on, Slick, with your head high. Nothing's happening.'

He was wrong. Fielding was wrong. Something was happening, for sure. When you've brawled around for as long as I have your senses get to know the kind of fix that you can't just walk through or away from. You get to know when you have to give satisfaction. Less than a block ahead the scatterings of low-caste colours had begun to solidify into a group or gauntlet. I saw loud T-shirts, biceps, facial hair. These people, they had nothing to tell us except that we were white and had money. Perhaps they were also saying – you cannot go slumming, not in New York. You just cannot go slumming, because slumming pretends that slums aren't real. They were real. They would show us that much. By now I was obeying instinct or habit, checking the chain for strengths and weaknesses. Avoid the left. Stay kerbside – yeah, that sick-looking little guy there.

Burst in with blending fists and run like a bastard for the green slope ahead. I let my eyes flick sideways. Fielding raised his right arm, an instruction to the Autocrat, but his gaze and stride were direct, unfaltering. The car surged up and then idled on snuffling treads. Fielding slowed. He made an elaborate gesture, explanatory, supercandid. And nothing happened. The path cleared and we walked on through.

'Columbia, Slick . . . Chicago, LA, wherever – in America our seats of learning are surrounded by the worst, the biggest, the most desperate ratshit slums in the civilized world. It seems to be the American way. What does this mean? What is its content? Now over here, John, we get a really superb view of Harlem.'

I took a look at Columbia. I checked it out. I've seen these pillared, high-chinned buildings, their deep chests thrown out in settled cultural pride. The place had nothing to tell me that I didn't already know. With Fielding's wrist on my shoulder I now approached the castle's steep rampart. We leaned on the railing, and peered down through the littered lattice of cross-angled trees, their backs broken in their last attempt to scramble up the cliff. Beyond lay the square miles of Harlem – part two, the other, the hidden half of young Manhattan.

'What happened?' I asked, and lit another cigarette, still heavy from the unburnt fight fuel, the awakened glands.

'It was the car, that's all.'

'Did our guy have a gun on them? I didn't see.'

'Nah. Well, he had his gun ready, I guess. But it was no big deal. The car would do it for a minute or two. That's all we needed.'

I suppose I understood. The Autocrat, the chauffeur, the bodyguard: this showed them the gulf, the magical distance. How did Fielding's gesture go? One palm arched on the heart, the other turned in polite introduction towards the car, saying. 'This is money. Have you all met?' Then the hands brought together, face up, an offering of the simple proof. And they backed off in the stumbling, hurried, slightly reckless way that traffic pulls over for ambulances or royalty. I said,

'Why?'

'Sightseeing. Local colour. The car's all yours, Slick. I'm going to run on back.'

I watched him jog off, the head held high for the first twenty yards, to promote oxygenation, then tucked in low as he measured out the rhythm of his pace. I turned and looked out over the slanted, foreshortened wedge of streets and stocky tenements, and for once the strain in my ears found the appropriate line, the right score. With a low hum of premonition my eyes panned Harlem, as if out there among the smokestacks and flarepaths lay my damage, my special damage, waiting for birth or freedom or power.

There is only one Earthling who really cares about me. At least, this human being loyally follows me around the place, keeps tabs on me and rings me up the whole time. No one else does. Selina's never there. All the others – it's just money. Money is the only thing we have in common. Dollar bills, pound notes, they're suicide notes. *Money* is a suicide note. Now this guy, he talks about money too, but his interest is personal. His interest is very personal indeed.

'You don't think about them,' he'll say. 'You don't think about them. You go slumming, but you never think about them – the others.'

'Who?' I asked him. 'You poor guys?'

'Listen. I've stolen food, out of hunger, just to stay alive. You can do it for a week. After a month you get the look. You look like the sort of guy who has to steal food to stay alive.

And that's it. All over. You can't steal food any more. Why? Because they can tell, the second you walk in the store. They can see no money in you. Not even the memory of money. Imagine.'

'Sounds rough. Just goes to show that it's a really dumb move, being poor. Listen, I've seen all that. This isn't news to me, pal. I've heard this stuff all my life.'

'You're poor. Still you're so poor.'

'You're wrong. I got stacks of dough and I'm going to make lots more. Now you, you sound seriously strapped for cash.'

Telephone Frank turns out to be not only a money expert, or an expert on not having any. He also talks about the chicks a good deal. For example:

'You just take women and use them. Then you toss them aside like a salad.'

'Wrong again. I keep trying to do that – but none of them will stand for it.'

'Women, for you, they're just pornography.'

'Listen, pal, I've got a date. Lots of rich pretty people are expecting me downtown.'

'We'll meet one day.'

'I'm really looking forward to it . . . Okay, Frank, I'll see you around.'

I arrived at Bank Street eight o'clock sharp, in the very last of the light. Overhead the sky still scintillated, but there was a film of green up there among the pinks and blues, an avocado tinge of beautifying city sickness . . . My best suit, me – dark grey with a thin chalk stripe. I additionally sported a wide silver tie furled in buxom Windsor knot. The West Village, where the streets have names.

Bank Street looked like a chunk of sentimental London, black railings and pale blossoms girding the bashful brownstones, even a cautious whiff of twig and leaf in the night-scented air. As I strolled along I watched an elasticated black kid, Felix's age or maybe older, gangle past with his pretty little friend. Negligently he reached into a front garden and yanked a flower from its tree. He offered the pink blossom to his chick, who twirled it in front of her briefly lit face before dropping it to the ground. 'Hey,' he said. 'Hey, that was a beautiful thing I did. That was a beautiful thing I did – with the flower. What you throw it away for, cunt?' He walked on, his spring wound tight now, the shoulders stiff and sullen. She dropped back and crouched to retrieve the shattered thing, gathering dry petals in the dip of her dress.

I had about a half hour to kill, I reckoned. Taking a couple of rights, I found myself on the ramp of lower Eighth Avenue – a medium-poor people's district, I assumed. Shoe Hospital, Asia de Cuba Luncheonette, Agony and Ecstasy Club, ESP Reader and Adviser, Mike's Bike World, also LIQ, BEE and BA. Are the clips on the sidewalk grills *meant* to look like the soles of giant feet? Young men playing chess on the hoods of parked cars. A pale tattoo on a pale old arm. Here they come again, young and old, health and distemper mixing like American prodigies of money and no money, beauty and malformation, Manhattan miracles of heat and cold. Some of the people are in terrible disrepair. Boy, could they use a little investment, a little gentrification. But I love the dense variety. Yes, it stirs me. After this, London feels watery and sparse . . . Now I idled in the yellow light of closed banks, municipality and bad business all done for the day. Why aren't banks as diverse and improvisational as every other American concern? Why can't we have Mike's Bank World? I don't know, but I feel steadier. I've drunk nothing all day. I drank nothing at lunch, despite the horrendous Malvinas Surprise I ordered (a triple mixed grill swaddled in steaks). I want to be at my very best tonight. I've showered and everything and I don't look too bad. That hike with Fielding, that uptown safari really did me good. I need it, I need to be strong. You think I'm paranoid but I tell you, man, there *is* something going on. Are you in on it? I've had this terrible feeling ever since I came to New York last time, a feeling of – a feeling of ulteriority. I try to convince myself that it's conditioning, the poor boy and his fears of success. It's not the film. The film is fine. It'll happen. But something else is not fine, something bigger. It is bigger than what Frank the Phone is doing to me, whatever that is. It is bigger than what Selina is doing to me, whatever that is. It is bigger than what I am doing to me . . . Turning from a storefront window – and why must this always be the way? – I was confronted by a six-foot woman with ginger hair, bobble hat and tadpole veil frilling her chin. Her leaning presence was deliberate, challenging: I think I'd even felt the play of her breath on my neck. '*Yeah?*' I said. But she just stood and stared through her mask . . . Now where have I seen that mad bitch before? Look. Here she comes again. Somewhere, I've seen her somewhere.

I doublebacked through the faggot district, Christopher Street. I skirted the dike district too – or at any rate two big chicks denied me entry to their purple sanctum. Then I found a place that was clearly headlined as a singles' bar, and no one tried to keep me out . . . Now I'd read about these VD workshops in *Scum* and *Miasma*, both of which adopted a markedly high-handed line. Word was a year or two ago that the joints were popping with air-hostesses, models and career women: five minutes, a couple of lite beers, and you'd be in a hotel room or service flat with some little darling doing the splits on your face. Not so! says *Scum*. It might have been that way for a while, *Scum* argued, but after a couple of weeks the Boroughs shitkickers moved in, and the game was up. The chicks moved out. *Miasma* even sent a squad of personable male reporters out on a sweep, and not one of them scored . . . Well, this place looked okay to me, the only hitch being that there weren't any women in it. They were all in the butch bars and the diesel discos. So I joined the half-dozen speechless loners and got to work on the Sidecars. Eight-twenty: no sweat. Here's to you, Martina, I said to myself, and flattened out a twenty on the moist zinc.

You remember Martina, Martina Twain? Now don't tell me you've forgotten. How *is* the memory, pal? Sister, what's the recall like? You remember her, surely. I know I do. She and I go way back. The thing about Martina is – the thing about Martina is that I can't find a voice to summon her with. The voices of money, weather and pornography (all that uncontrollable stuff), they just aren't up to the job when it comes to Martina. I think of her and there is speechless upheaval in me – I feel this way when I'm in Zurich, Frankfurt or Paris and the locals can't speak the lingo. My tongue moves in search of patterns and grids that simply are not there. Then I shout . . . Consider the people I've been around all my life, stylists, models, actors, producers, seat-warmers, air-sniffers, knee-crookers, cuecard-readers, place-men, moneymen – funny men, not straight men. Funny women too, juggling sex, time and dough. Who's straight? I'm not. I am bent gouged pinched and tugged at, and squeezed into this funny shape. Each life is a game of chess that went to hell on the seventh move, and now the flukey play is cramped and slow, a dream of constraint and cross-purpose, with each move forced, all pieces pinned and skewered and zugzwanged . . . But here and there we see these figures who appear to run on the true lines, and they are terrible examples. They're rich, usually.

Her English husband Ossie, now he's rich-for-life but he works in money, in pure money. His job has nothing to do with anything except money, the stuff itself. No fucking around with stocks, shares, commodities, futures. Just money. Sitting in his spectral towers on Sixth Avenue and Cheapside, blond Ossie uses money to buy and sell money. Equipped with only a telephone, he buys money with money, sells money for money. He works in the cracks and vents of currencies, buying and selling on the margin, riding the daily tides of exchange. For these services he is rewarded with money. Lots of it. It is beautiful, and so is he.

I switched from Sidecars to Old Fashioneds. I'm always early for these dinner parties anyway. I leave it late, but never late enough. Barkeep, let's do it again. As I feasted on my drink I sensed the hum, the confectionery of a feminine presence. I turned to find that a girl had joined me at the bar. Now she asked for white wine in her charged voice. I diversified with a Manhattan. New York is full of heart-stopping girls with potent colouring, vanilla teeth, and these big tits they all seem to be issued with as a matter of course. There must be a catch. (There is. Most of them are mad. It pays you to remember this.) This chick on the stool – she looked like Cleopatra. I don't know what it was, but I instantly fingered her for an obvious goer, sack-artist, dick-idolator, and so on. I can always spot them. I glanced at my watch: eight thirty – no, *nine* thirty. Hey there! Time to be moving on.

'Buy you a drink?' I said.

Her face slackened. She gave a tremble of negation.

'White wine?' I said.

'No thanks.'

'What's with all this no thanks? Can't you read? This is a singles' bar.'

'Excuse me!' she said. 'Bartender! Sir! This man is bothering me.'

'Damn right I'm bothering you.' I tapped her shoulder. 'What d'you expect, kid? Why d'you come here anyway? You like the Californian Chablis or these plastic ducks they have on the wall?'

'Hey. Hey. You. Shut up or get out.'

This was the bartender.

'What is this? Am I the only guy in here who can read? It says *singles' bar* out there, in neon. I'm single. She's single. What's the problem?'

'He's drunk.'

This was one of the loners.

'Okay, who said that?'

I slithered lithely from my stool. This deed somehow necessitated a second manoeuvre, that of picking myself up off the floor.

'He just had ten cocktails, for Christ's sake.'

'Here he's . . . Put him . . . Get the . . .'

I felt several hands on my arms, a knee in my back and a tug on my rug. Well, time was travelling anyway, and I thought I might as well be moving on.

Fifteen minutes later, or it may have been twenty, I stood staring at a caged lift: the chest-flexing iron lattice, the accordion doors. I swivelled and strode up to the end of a passage. I rang the bell. I was drunk, okay, but I was getting my second wind by now. That's the thing about drink: some of us can take it, and some of us can't. Put another few down me and I'll be as right as rain. I straightened my tie and guided my hair back with my hands. I rang the bell – a good long ring. Someone clattered down a wooden staircase. The door sucked open.

Ossie was standing there in waistcoat and shirtsleeves. I could see Martina down the end of the passage, aproned, with plates in her hand.

'Hey my man!' I croaked. 'Was coming down a track!'

He took one step forward. 'It's late,' said Ossie. Martina's curious face appeared beyond his shoulder. Ossie said, 'Go home, John. Just *go home.*'

The door cracked shut. What's with him? I wondered. Some

guys . . . Okay, so I'm running a bit behind schedule, but . . . I looked at my watch. It said one fifteen. Then I remembered something. I wasn't only late to arrive – I was late to leave, too.

That's right. I had already been to the dinner party. And something told me I hadn't behaved too well.

Today is my birthday. I am thirty-five years old. According to the last good book I read, this means that I am half way through my time travel, my travel through time. It doesn't feel like that – it doesn't feel like half way. The prestige number-plate on my Fiasco says OAP 5. I've got the mind of a kid, but I'm a pretty senior partner over at Rug & Gut & Gum. It feels as though I have just started out. It feels as though I am just about to end, just about to end. That's what it feels like.

Morning came, and I got up . . . That doesn't sound particularly interesting or difficult, now does it? I bet you do it all the time. Listen, though – I had a problem here. For instance, I was lying face-down under a hedge or bush or some blighted shrub in a soaked allotment full of nettles, crushed cigarette packs, used condoms and empty beercans. It was quite an appropriate place for me to be born again, which is what it felt like. Obviously it hurts, being born: that's why you scream and weep. Next, I had to frisk myself, to make sure I still had my wallet, limbs, face, dick, being. Next, I had to run crying through the concrete concourses in dawn rain until my panic slowed and I recognized the city and myself in the matt and muffled streets. Then I had to find a cab and get back here. The guy wouldn't take me until I showed him money. I didn't blame him. I had dreamed – and who needs dreams with this kind of nightlife? – of torture, laughter, pincer-grips on the frail-tubed spine.

In the bathroom I stripped slowly before the mirror. Face first: there was a grey swelling over my left eye, and my rug was quite badly singed on the same side. A fight? I didn't think so. If there'd been a fight, then I must have won it. My body was all there, trembling, whimpering in the graphic light, but all there. I turned – and gasped. *Dah* . . . Oh, Christ. My back, my great white back was scored with thirty or forty sharp red welts, regularly patterned, as if I'd slept on a bed of nails. Taking a two-fisted grip on my spare tyre, I was able to wrench round some flesh and get a good look at one of these bloodless wounds. An indentation, a red hole: I could insert my quivering pinkie to half-nail depth. I stepped back. No other damage. No new damage. My bumf-crammed wallet was intact: credit cards, eighty-odd dollars, thirty-odd pounds. My hangover was fine. My hangover had come through okay.

So. I had spent the night, or part of it, on a patch of earth in alphabet-land – Avenue B, deep down on the East Side. After an evening of pleasure and profit with my friends in Bank Street, I had clearly gone out for a drink or two. Bad idea! Oh very bad! Someone, at some stage, had worked me over with a tool, a spike or a blunt shiv. My shirt was punctured in places, but not my jacket – my good, my best jacket. It was now eight thirty. I bathed my face with water and felt hot fingers beginning to tickle my back. For ten minutes I vomited elaborately, with steamhammer convulsions that I had no strength to resist or contain. Then for twice that long I sat twitching on the shower's deck, the silver snout tuned to full heat and heft but doing nothing much to wash off my rot. I must be *very unhappy*. That's the only way I can explain my behaviour. Oh man, I must be so depressed. I must be fucking suicidal. And I wish I knew *why*.

Look at my life. I know what you're thinking. You're thinking: But it's terrific! It's great! You're thinking: Some guys have all the luck! Well, I suppose it must look quite cool, what with the aeroplane tickets and the restaurants, the cabs, the filmstars, Selina, the Fiasco, the money. But my life is also my private culture – that's what I'm showing you, after all, that's what I'm letting you into, my private culture. And I mean *look* at my private culture. Look at the state of it. It really isn't very nice in here. And that is why I long to burst out of the world of money and into – into what? Into the world of thought and fascination. How do I get there? Tell me, please. I'll never make it by myself. I just don't know the way.

Nothing much happened for a couple of days, which was fine by me. Nothing happened. Well, I say that, but of course me and my sore back got up to all kinds of stuff.

Me and my sore back composed a letter to Martina. Yes, a letter. I even went out and bought a dictionary on Sixth Avenue to assist me in the project. You know those hangovers where you can't spell *I'm* or *you're*, let alone *sorry* or *again*? It took me about a day each to write, seal, stamp and post this letter of mine, but I managed to get the thing off in the end. I apologized for my behaviour (you know how it is: a few drinks, a few laughs, you step out of line), and asked if I could buy her lunch some time. After all, I pointed out, lunch was the one date we hadn't yet tried. Drinks, breakfast, dinner – but not lunch. I said I would 'quite understand' if she wanted to cut her losses and call it a day. *I* wouldn't let me buy me lunch, I said, and I meant it. Jesus, would *you*?

Me and my sore back had cocktails with Butch Beausoleil. There was no mention of the debacle at the Berkeley Club, thank Christ. Butch looked beautiful – a cauldron of youth and health – and she seems docile enough at this stage. That makes sense. She's getting $750,000. Her only proviso is that she won't do any housework. In the film. She won't sweep a floor. She won't even rinse out a coffee-cup. Chicks' liberation. Who do you want to play opposite you? I asked her. Christopher Meadowbrook, Spunk Davis or Nub Forkner? Butch said that she would favour a dark-complected co-star. The big thing about Butch is that she isn't just a dumb blonde, as she herself stressed. I agreed. She might look like one. She might even behave and talk like one on occasion. But she isn't just a dumb blonde. That's the big thing about Butch.

Me and my sore back have had several meetings now with Fielding's moneymen. We had dinner in La Cage d'Or with Steward Cowrie, Bob Cambist and Ricardo Fisc. We went night-clubbing at Krud's and Parlour 39 with Tab Penman, Bill Levy and Gresham Tanner. They're an odd crew, these moneymen, Miami hotel barons, Nebraskan ranching bosses, Marylander oil kings. Their only topics are moviestars and money. They talk about money in that sharky American style, as if money were the only gauge of anything, the only measure. They're pretty relaxing company, I find. Fielding picks up the checks. Fielding picks up the cheques, too. Each meeting ends with the moneymen all saying things like *I'm in* or *I want in on this* or *You got it* or *Let's do it*. Fielding is already making plans to cut one or two of the smaller guys out of the action.

Oh yeah and me and my sore back got hold of little Selina late one night. It was seven in the morning over there in my sock. Her voice was thin and cold, the way I like it. After a while she cooed and cursed me into peace. I have to tell you that these hot-line, long-distance blowjobs are another of our regrettable routines . . . This particular perversion, I notice, like every other, has been set up on a professional basis in go-getting New York. The small-ad columns of *Scum* magazine are full of remote-control hookers who just sit by a telephone all day for money, like Ossie Twain. You ring them up, give your credit-card number, and they talk dirty to you for however long you can afford. They're probably cheaper than Selina, come to think of it, what with the hotel mark-up. They're here and she's there, after all . . . I was on the point of signing off when Selina started telling me, in accents of alarmingly genuine arousal, about this rich new boyfriend of hers, this transatlantic moneyman, how he took her to hotels and dressed her up and fucked her on the floor like a dog. This was fairly standard stuff, but I deplored her tone. Quit it, I said. Her thin voice teased on. She said that when she wasn't here she was there – with him, doing that. Enough, I said.

'Then marry me,' said Selina, but not nicely.

Fielding smoothed his back against the scalloped seat of the limousine, like a cat. He straightened his cuffs and said firmly,

'I say we go with Spunk.'

'He's not really called that, is he?'

'Sure,' said Fielding, and went on to tell me about two Southern actors called Sod MacGonagall and Fart Klaeber. He gave his laugh, his rich, his million-dollar laugh, reluctant, like all the most lovable laughter. You long to hear this sound. You would do almost anything to inspire it. 'Maybe,' he said, 'maybe for the British market we can call him Scum.'

'It's a problem, you've got to admit.'

'I talked with his agent. He knows Spunk's going to have to have his name fixed sometime. Thing is, he was christened that way, and he hates the whole moviestar bit. He's a tough Bronx kid but he acts up a storm. You want a drink?'

'No thanks.'

'What's the matter? It's five o'clock.'

'No thanks.'

I had my reasons. Do you want to hear the good news first, or the bad news? The good news is that Martina called this morning and we're having lunch tomorrow. The bad news is that the good news made me feel so relieved and excited that I ran out to a bar and drank a bunch of big ones. *Yeah?* you'll say. *And? Nothing new in that.* Agreed, but the bad thing about the bad news is that the alcohol had a really bad effect on me. It didn't make me drunk, which was what I was confidently expecting it to do. It made me hungover instead. It did. I kept incredulously ordering more drinks, in a doomed bid to stave off this conclusion. That's why I had so many. All the more ironic, too, because I woke up this morning feeling bloody marvellous after a really late and heavy night with the TV and the B & F. Was the phenomenon a new jet-lag deal, or the terminal mutiny of my whole bodybag? Oh man, I'd better get to California soon, while the transplant people still have something to work on. Maybe I'd better wing out there right away and have them fix me up with a temporary. And the mind was suffering too. Yes, the mind had its sufferings also. It was crammed with sin and crime, the thoughts nowhere, all in freefall and turnaround. I've got to get this stuff out of my system. No, more than that, much more. I've got to get my system out of my system. That's what I've got to do.

'Concentrate, Slick,' said Fielding. 'This is semi-crucial. The entire package pivots on this. Moneywise, Meadowbrook's the safe choice. I think Nub Forkner would play well with Butch. But Davis is the gamble, the longshot, and that attracts me. Put your instincts to work on it, Slick. I say we go with Spunk.'

'You better give me a scotch.'

This would entail some self-inspection, alas, since the character was loosely based on me, on myself – Doug, the Son, the greedy berk, the addict, the betrayer. It now looked like a straight playoff between Christopher Meadowbrook and Spunk Davis, with maybe Nub Forkner as an outside possibility. Meadowbrook I knew all about, a steady ensemble man but no headliner. You've seen him. He's the guy with the freckly yankee-doodle face and the hint of comic spindliness in his floppy-limbed frame. He usually plays older brothers, blushing patsies, jumpy sidekicks, all-smiles Ivy Leaguers. As Doug, Meadowbrook would be cast violently against type, but that was exactly the sort of doubletake effect I was interested in. The other guy, this Davis character, I had heard of but never seen in action, a Broadway boy with one film in the can. *Prehistoric* was still at the editing stage. We were going to see the roughcut. The *word* was very good. According to Fielding, Davis was hot.

We alighted at an address on doublebarrelled Park Avenue. Our greeter, who looked like a presidential bodyguard, led us through the lobby and into the executive screening parlour – a six-seater with an air of luxury interrogations, one-way mirrors, corporation propaganda. Davis's agent was there, Herrick Shnexnayder, a desperate human being who wore a French smock, a prosciutto cravat and the most complicated double pate-job I have ever come across in ten years of show business. One yellowy hank was swiped forward from the nape of his neck, while the other originated from his luxuriant left sideburn. His head looked like a fudge sundae – I swear to God, he could have put a spoon in his ear and a maraschino cherry on his crown and looked no worse. I drank the limitless champagne on offer (most of it soaked without fuss into the parched coral of my tongue) and listened to Herrick's obsequious banter. Agents, these days, they look like corporation men – but Herrick was more show biz than Coco the Clown. At one point Fielding mentioned money. The agent smiled like a death-dealing doctor and said, 'Oh I think, after *Prehistoric*, we're looking at five.' In other words, Spunk's fee was now half a million dollars. Fielding just nodded and said, 'And what does his availability look like?' His availability looked good, partly because, after *Prehistoric*, no one could afford to hire him.

Prehistoric started with a long pan over a series of cave murals: a man, a woman, a fight, a fuck, a tiger – a spaceship. We backed off. A gang or tribe of pre-fire apepeople were huddled about the place: there was Spunk, sharpening his spear. Square-headed, square-lipped, the dark face dense and sinewy. The next morning – or soon, anyway – Spunk was beamed up on to the bridge of the low-lying spaceship by the mischievous, conical, beep-voiced aliens, who then travelled through time and beamed Spunk down again into Greenwich Village, 1980. It was a summer night, so Spunk didn't look at all conspicuous in his bodyhair, warpaint and loinskin. After staring around and grunting a lot, Spunk reflexively saved a drunken girl from being roughed up in a sidewalk fracas outside a singles' bar. She takes him home to her swish apartment. More grunting. She assumes he is Lithuanian or Albanian or whatever – Christ knows there are some pretty perfunctory Earthlings on the streets of New York. Spunk accepts a glass or two of firewater and is led to the sack, where he proceeds to give her the pasting of a lifetime. Come dawn, the chick has checked out, but Spunk is still hanging in there – bad diet, presumably . . . There followed a brilliant scene, as Spunk staggered out to confront the girl's flatmates. The flatmates are used to the girl's rugged pick-ups, but Spunk (cracking nuts with his teeth, eating unshelled eggs and raw sausages) is a new wrinkle. With various delicate transitions that left me sighing in assent, the film now turned into a gentle parodic love story, the girl civilizing Spunk – teaching him how to dress, eat, speak – and Spunk decivilizing her: teaching her to kick the booze, the pick-ups, the self-destruction, the money (they go primitive for a while, after Spunk has an urban break-down. Even I, in my exalted state, could detect some sentimentality here). Throughout Spunk wore a silent gaze of uncomplaining bafflement and reserve, comic but dignified, formidable. He was especially good at the end, when the aliens (who have been monitoring the whole joke, helping Spunk out at awkward moments) beam him back to BC. He knows what's about to happen, more or less, and tries to explain to the girl with his pitful resources of gesture and language. Thus Spunk stands bereft on the stark crag, with old winds whistling. He frowns, he tenses – he peers into a sloping hollow. The girl sits there muttering and shivering, with her last cigarette and an electric lighter. Credits. I was deeply moved. Moved? I had a nervous breakdown. The tears were still pissing from my eyes when I fled to the can. No doubt about it, no doubt at all: Davis was going to be a big, big name.

In the Autocrat I turned to Fielding and asked huskily. '*Can* he talk? I mean properly?'

'Spunk? Sure. He did Richard the Second off Broadway last fall. He was kind of nervous about his accent, but the articulation? Superb. Okay, Slick. What do you say?'

'I say we go with Spunk.'

We drove straight to a panelled restaurant in the dining district between Fifth and Sixth for an exploratory meeting with Christopher Meadowbrook. It was depressing, after *Prehistoric*. One look at Meadowbrook and I knew he was hopeless for us. The sharp-shouldered chairs in this joint, which reminded me of Selina's torso and its erect triangularity, seemed specifically designed to give clients with sore backs a really rough ride. In the end I did at least as much squirming as Christopher Meadowbrook, and he squirmed a lot. The guy was in shocking shape – that was clear. He didn't look like a goodie. He didn't look like a baddie either. He looked like a weakie, unmanned, pure victim. I once saw this same beseeching looseness of eye and mouth in face of a ragged little faggot on Sunset

Boulevard, scorched and peed-on and limping back for more. After drinks and introductions and a few minutes of jangled smalltalk, as if the three of us were gods or apes or spacemen, Fielding did the bad thing. He left for a light supper with Butch and Caduta at the Cicero. He would later swear that he had cautioned me about this the previous night. No doubt he had, no doubt he had. I looked at him helplessly and he vowed to return at ten.

As soon as we were alone Meadowbrook took my hand, hunkered forward and said, 'I have to have the part, sir. Sir, you have to let me have it.' Then he burst into tears. Now this I didn't need . . . Money, of course. The actor was out for seventy-five big ones. Cocaine debts, he said – though he'd kicked it long ago. A dear friend (oh so very dear) had run out on him. His mother needed an operation. *He* needed an operation. And on it went. I suppose, in theory, I've had worse times, but not many, and not much worse. Jesus, am *I* ever as bad as this? Do I ever show such concerted and repetitive frailty? He sank four cocktails. He instigated a meaningless rumble with the *maitre d'*. A waiter bounced back by handing him a molten soup-plate. Meadowbrook upended the whole fiery mess into his lap and let out a scream of such inhuman power that the restaurant cat (a sleepy, sloth-flattened Persian) kamikazeed through a glass screen into the startled shards of the lobby. Then he went to the john for twenty minutes and squelched back clicking and ticking like a geiger counter. At this point I noticed that he had only one nostril. Abuse has a habit of smacking you in the nose like that, for all to see. Back home there's a guy who works in my nearest off-licence: he's got a conk like a haemorrhaged strawberry. I avoid him. I go to the next off-licence along, where the guy's nose is still okay . . . Now Meadowbrook started making with the Shakespeare. To be or not to be. Tomorrow and tomorrow and tomorrow. Never never never never never.

In despair, and despite the zags and zigs, the lagjag, the alphabet chowder of my own alcothon, I hit the scotch. Fielding returned. Semaphoring his credit card, Meadowbrook made a big thing of catching the tab. 'And lose that soup!' he warned. The card was borne back on a silver tray. It was snipped into four pieces.

'I'm dying here,' said Meadowbrook.

'No rating,' grinned the waiter.

'Jesus, let's *go.*'

That was me. I stood up.

So did Fielding. 'You're out, Chris,' he said, and drew two fifties from his golden clip.

There is a sense, as you sit in your cab and tunnel through the grooves and traps, there is a sharper sense (there must be) of the smallness of human concerns – in New York, where you always feel the height and weight of the tall agencies. Control, purpose, meaning, they're all up there. They're not down here. God has taken columned New York between the knuckles of his right hand – and tugged. That must make the ground feel lower. I am in the cab, going somewhere, directing things with money. I have more say than the people I look out on, nomads, tide-people. They have no say. Twenty-Third Street, and its running dogs.

I now know for certain that Selina Street *isn't* fucking Alec Llewellyn, or not for the time being anyway. The more I think about it, the more I persuade myself that I've misjudged little Selina. She's faithful to me, that Selina. True, she behaves like someone who is unfaithful to me all the time. She behaves like someone who is hyperunfaithful. But she behaves like that because she knows I like it. (Why do I like it? I do, clearly, don't I. Then why don't I *like* it?) Selina, she just does it to please me. If she were really being unfaithful, she wouldn't behave like that, now would she. She would behave like someone who wasn't being unfaithful, and nobody could accuse her of behaving like *that*. How very cheering.

Hell, it's all good news.

'Yeah?' I'd said warily, expecting Lorne or Meadowbrook or Frank the Phone.

'John? Ella Llewellyn here. I've rung you because there's something I think you ought to know. Bad news, I'm afraid.'

Oh, come on Ella, no need to take that tone with me. I fucked you once – on the stairs, remember? – when Alec blacked out in the kitchen that time. 'Hi, Ella. Okay, tell me,' I said, and I stiffened myself for the worst.

'Alec's in prison. Brixton, on remand. He had it coming. He just wanted me to tell you.'

Bad news? Bad? No, these are excellent tidings in their own right. Well before Selina's sly face had a chance to invade my mind screen, I felt a gulp of innocent, bright-eyed pleasure that my best and oldest pal was in such serious trouble. Mm, it's so *nice* when one of your peers goes down. You know the feeling? A real buzz, isn't it. Don't be ashamed, if you can possibly help it. Now Alec can't get away, he can't escape, translate, burst clear. He can't go up there, with them. He must stay down here, with me. He must stay down here, further down, deeper, much deeper.

The present rendezvous had been riding high on my chart of dreads. How is that? How can a quiet lunch with a beautiful and intelligent girl, in a licensed restaurant, be the cause of dread? Go ask it on the mountain. (I had dreaded the other meetings with her too, hadn't I. Yes I had.) But in the end it soothed me. Only when you are soothed do you realize how much you needed soothing. I was going insane. I was dying. That was what I was doing, dying.

Before we talked about the phantom dinner party we talked

about *aesthetics*. Or rather Martina did. Aesthetics is a topic I have previously discussed only with my cosmetic dentist, Mrs McGilchrist (as in 'the aesthetics are going to cost you on this one'), and with the odd deluded lighting-cameraman who might have his views about the aesthetics of a Bulky Bar dissolve, a Rumpburger close-up, a Zaparama zoom. Martina talked about aesthetics more generally. She talked about perception, representation and truth. She talked about the vulnerability of a figure unknowingly watched – the difference between a portrait and an unposed study. The analogous distinction in fiction would be that between the conscious and the reluctant narrator – the sad, the unwitting narrator. Why do we feel protective when we watch the loved one who is unaware of being watched? Why does the heart hurt when it sees the unattended pair of shoes? Or the loved one asleep? Perhaps the dead body of the loved one expresses all the pathos of this absence, the helplessness of being watched, and not knowing . . . Actors are paid to pretend that they are unaware of being watched, but they of course rely on the collusion of the watcher, and nearly always get it. There are unpaid actors too (I thought): it's them you really have to watch.

I sat cocked on the brink of my seat. I could follow her drift for seconds at a time, until the half-gratified sense of effort – or my awareness of watching myself – intervened, and scattered my thoughts. I felt tense. How tense? Maybe not that tense . . . We were lunching at an emeried chalet off Bank Street in the West Village – licensed, sure, but with a suspicion of health food, of careful eating, of macrobiotics and longevity. Waiters of both sexes eerily serviced the wooden nooks. There went Hansel. There went Gretel. They moved in white like doctors and nurses. The food they brought you was administered as medicine, as elixir. Their grub was of the very healthiest – not like that shit they make you eat uptown. I craved liquor but survived on frequent tureens of white wine. Martina contented herself with a pot of tea, and held her cup with both hands, as girls are bound to do, the fingers spread for all the warmth. When she ate, she dipped her head into each mouthful, her eyes on mine: round, dark, clean.

'Perhaps drunks are like that too,' I said. 'I mean, they don't know they're being watched. They don't know anything. *I* don't know anything.'

'They're also not themselves,' she said, 'which lessens the pathos.'

'Yes, I bet it does. You'd better tell me – about the other night. The suspense is killing me.'

'You really can't remember? Or do you just pretend you can't.'

I thought about this, and said, 'I can't bear to remember. Maybe I could if I tried. It's the trying part that's unbearable. Who was there, for instance?'

'Same as last time. My only friends. Ossie's friends are all . . . The lady from the *Tribeca Times*. Fenton Akimbo – he's the Nigerian writer. And Stanwyck Mills, the Blake and Shakespeare man. Ossie wanted to ask him about the two gentlemen of Verona.'

'Uh?' What a crew, I thought. 'Okay. Tell me.'

Then she told me. It wasn't that bad. I was relieved. Between ourselves, I was even quite impressed. Apparently I had wind-milled in at a quarter to ten, with three bottles of champagne, all of which I dropped in one catastrophic juggle. The kitchen floor, Martina said, was like a jacuzzi. Full of beans, I took my seat at the stalled dinner. Then, for the next twenty-five minutes, I told a joke.

'Oh Jesus. What sort of joke? How dirty?'

'I can't remember it. You couldn't either. Something about a farmer's wife? Yes, and a travelling salesman.'

'Oh Jesus. What then?'

Then I went to sleep. I didn't simply black out at the table, oh no. I stood up, yawned and stretched, and threw myself on to a nearby sofa. There I snored and whinnied and gnashed for nearly three hours, awaking refreshed and raring to go at a little after one. Everyone had gone. I went too. Then I came back again. Then I went away again.

'What did I say to Fenton Akimbo? Did I say anything?'

'How do you mean?'

'I mean, I didn't call him a black bastard or anything?'

'Oh no. You only said your joke, and that was about it.'

'Great.'

'You said something to me though. As you left, the first time.'

'What?'

She smiled, rawly, savagely – not a grown-up smile. A tomboy smile. She had easy access to the girl inside her. The girl was always available.

'What?' I repeated.

'You said you loved me.' And she laughed her laugh, that shocking laugh which turned heads and caused her to blush and put a hand over her naked mouth.

'And what did *you* say?'

'I said . . . let me think. I said – Don't be an idiot.'

'Well, maybe it's true,' I said, emboldened. 'In vino – you know, when you drink you tell the truth, and all that.'

'Don't be an idiot,' said Martina.

Yes, she sounds sane, doesn't she, among all these other people I'm working around? But then she has always had money – she has never not had money. Money is carelessly present in the cut and texture of her clothes, her leathery accoutrements, in rug-brilliance and mouth tone. The long legs have travelled, and not just through time. The clean tongue speaks French, Italian, German. The expectant eyes have seen things, and expect to see more. Even as a girl her lovers were always hand-picked, an elite, far above the usual rabble of irregulars, mercenaries, pressed men. Her smile is knowing, roused and playful, but also innocent, because money makes you innocent when it's been there all along. How else can you hang out on this planet for thirty years while still remaining free? Martina is not a woman of the world. She is a woman of somewhere else.

'Hey,' I said. 'How come you always know when I'm in New York and when I go back?'

She shrugged. 'Ossie tells me.'

'How does he know?'

'He's back and forth from London all the time. He must know people you know.'

'I suppose that figures,' I said.

'How's – your girlfriend?'

'Selina.'

'Yes. How's all that? You're with her. You're together.'

I considered. Then I said, or perhaps one of my voices said it for me, 'I don't know. I mean – you can be with someone and still be alone.'

'. . . She's beautiful.'

'True,' I said. 'How's Ossie?'

She didn't say anything.

'He's beautiful,' I said.

But she still didn't say anything. Instead, she asked me why I thought I drank so much, and I told her why I thought I did.

'I'm an alcoholic,' I said.

'No you're not, you're just a greedy kid with nothing better to do. Aren't you tired of it?'

'Yes, I'm tired. I've been tired of it for years . . . Yes, I'm tired.'

Twenty minutes later we stood outside on the spongy pavement. Before us, across the road, the line of shop windows glistened like a strip of film – Manhattan and its little concerns:

a Thai laundry, a handbag hospital, a delicatessen ('"Lonnie's" – For A Better Sandwich' – 'No Nukes' – 'Sorry. Closed'), a florist's forest, a Zen nicknackery which welcomed all major credit cards, a diesel bookstore. Martina and I performed the uncertain dance of people parting, with its limited steps. She still faced me, but her shoulders had already begun to turn away . . . If you're small and the thing you evade is big (have you ever had this dream?), then the only place to hide is a place where the big thing can't fit. But then you have to stay there, in the small place, or must even shrink to cower deeper. I'm tired of the small place. Me, I've fucking had it with the small place. I'm tired of being watched and not knowing it. I'm tired of all these absences.

'Okay, look,' I said desperately. 'Help! Give me books to read. Point me out a book to read.' I gestured across the road at the blind shopfront. 'Something educational.'

She folded her arms and thought about this. I could tell she was pleased.

'All right?' I said.

Together we crossed the lumpy street. I was told to wait outside. The bookstore window features fanned stacks of the most recent scrotum-tightener from the feminist front: it was called *Not On Our Lives* and it was by Karen Krankwinkl. I scanned the xeroxed blurbs and reviews. A married woman with three children, Karen believed that all lovemaking was rape, even when it didn't seem that way to either of the participants. Her brave and beaming face was duplicated on the reversed covers. Well, Karen, I wouldn't rape you with a ten-foot pole. But then, perhaps all chicks get to look like that, when they've been raped a few thousand times.

Martina returned. She had bought me a hardback. Possibly it was secondhand, but it still looked like five bucks' worth of book, I reckoned.

'What's the damage?' I asked.

'Nothing. It's on me.'

'When can I call you?'

'When you've read it,' she said, and turned away.

Mr Jones, of the Manor Farm, had locked the hen-houses for the night, I read, *but was too drunk to remember to shut the pop-holes.* I stretched, and rubbed my eyes. Was the whole book going to be like this? I mean, did I detect some satirical intent here? Well, that was all right. I can take a joke. I clasped my hands behind my neck, and considered. What the fuck are *popholes*? . . . You see? The bookish, the contemplative life. Martina, she's even cured my tinnitus. Not a squeak for over three hours. The big thing about reading and all that is – you have to be in a fit state for it. Calm. Not picked on. You have to be able to hear your own thoughts, without interference. On the way back from lunch (I walked it) already the streets felt a little lighter. I could make a little more sense of the watchers and the watched. This book from Martina – we split lunch, so it's a present, a proper present, God damn it. How long has it been since I got a present from a girl? I'll call her now and thank her for the book. What could be simpler.

Delicately I reached for the telephone. I paused with my fingers on the plunger. Fatal. And then the whole bomb went off in my face.

'Fat chance, man. No chance. Just you forget it right now. You and her? You? Her? What kind of book she give you, pal? Self-help?'

And he laughed, and went on laughing. His laughter made a terrible sound – nothing to be said about it, really. But my grip tightened and I quietly urged him,

'Get your laugh fixed, boy. Or fixed again. Everyone can tell it's false. Hey. *Hey*. Why don't you leave me alone? How about that?'

'And miss out on all this? Are you kidding? Answer me something. You tell her about Sunday night? You tell her you slept rough?'

'What?'

'Sunday night. Remember? That was the night that just walked right over you.'

'So,' I said, 'you did it.' This had occurred to me, but I'd hoped that the attack had been random. In my state, you're always hoping things are random. You don't want things assuming any shape on you.

'Uh-uh. I just watched.'

'You did it . . . you cruel son of a bitch.'

'No! I didn't do it. With her heels, with her high heels! A *woman* did it.'

The line went dead but oh how my head came alive. A door blew open and the pent sounds burst out fleeing. For a loathsome instant I felt her awkward quivering weight on my back as she found her feet, and her voice saying . . . What? Dah, no – let us abort this memory here and now. I made calls. The airline. Home, with no reply. And Martina, but just to say goodbye. These calls, they gave me no grief. Only Fielding made demands on me. Only Fielding had more penance to exact.

'Spunk,' I said, '– it's an honour.'

I glanced sideways at Fielding Goodney, who shrugged.

'We loved *Prehistoric*,' I went on. 'You were terrific. I mean it. You were absolutely – you were terrific, Spunk.'

I felt Fielding nudge me in the gloom.

'Words fail me. I tell you, Spunk – I, it really got to me, your interpretation there. We want you. We want you for *Good Money*.

Spunk, that's what we're here today to tell you ... Fuck it, Fielding,' I said, 'let's go with Meadowbrook or Nub Forkner or whoever. I don't need this.'

'Good. Very good. Sit down, please,' said Spunk Davis.

We were on the fortieth floor of the UN Plaza. Fielding and I had been buzzed in, cased, X-rayed and heavy-petted by two security guards in plum blazers. 'Davis, Spunk,' the man had repeated ruminatively, among the potted plants and intercom banks and closed-circuit TV screens. 'It's in another name.' He cleared us and we rode the lift's rush of nausea, slurped up, up.

'I'm Mrs Davis,' said the little old lady who answered the door. Well, I suppose she wasn't that old, but her shrunk face was laboriously lined, with deep concentrations round the eyes and mouth. Lined, then lined again, and again. You get this effect when you gaze through a file of London trees in winter, and the naked branches criss and cross until only motes of light remain, in peeping triangles. A worked and working face. But the eyes were bright.

'Oh. Hi,' I said.

'Mrs Davis,' said Fielding gravely. Then he kissed her hand and held it close to his chest. This courtesy, tenderly performed, seemed right out of place to me, but it went down okay with Mrs Davis, who peered up at Fielding for quite a time before she said,

'Are you saved?'

While Fielding dealt with that one ('Oh ma'am, but yes,' he began) I turned to face a kitchen or parlour, plain in its shapes but full of manmade coatings and colours. A dark, low-browed gent sat there in pampered profile, his once-powerful frame encased in a double-breasted needlestripe suit. Spunk Senior, presumably. He glanced at the TV on the chintzy sideboard (bobbing basketballers), he glanced at his watch (the movement limp and stoical), he glanced at me. We briefly exchanged brute stares. We recognized each other for what we were. With tongue and teeth he gave a tight rasp and turned away in boredom or vexation or distaste. Yeah, one look at him and even I had to say to myself – the ladies, the poor ladies. They get it every time. I was in no sort of nick for this encounter, I admit, full of fear and afternoon scotch and the homeward tug. Now I had Mrs Davis's hand on my arm and her pleading face saying,

'And are you saved, sir?'

'Pardon?'

'Yes he's saved also, dear,' intervened Fielding, and I said, 'Yeah. Me too.'

'I'm glad. Spunk's at the end of the hall.'

She led us past a series of dun-walled anterooms through whose windows the burnished leagues of the East River fired off all their flame. I saw a pool-table, a polythene-wrapped three-piece suite, various devotional ornaments and gewgaws with their special pale glow. That glow I didn't need. We entered a dining-room as dark as a cinema with a glistening figure at the head of the long table. Mrs Davis slipped back into the light. It was five o'clock.

'Two years ago,' the actor continued. 'You auditioned me.' He laughed disgustedly. 'For a commercial.'

'Yeah?' I said. 'I really don't remember.' His voice – he had a certain valve or muscle working on it. I recognized that strain. I talked the same way at his age, fighting my rogue aitches and glottal stops. *Glottal* itself I delivered in only one syllable, with a kind of gulp or gag half way through. Spunk here was trying to tame his bronco word-endings and his slippery vowels. I speak all right now, though. But I tell you, it's a tiring ten-year haul.

'I wasn't good enough. I wasn't good enough. For your commercial.'

'No kidding,' I said. 'You remember what commercial it was?'

'No, I don't remember. Put it out!'

He meant my cigarette. 'Where?'

'Put it out!'

'*Jesus,*' I said, and appealed to Fielding. This is just a dramatized hangover, I thought. I dragged mightily and in the mauve gleam I could see Davis more clearly, the bunched muscles in their tanktop. His head had an odd tilt or cock to it, set on the shoulders as if he were looking up from the bars of a drop-handled bike. He was smiling.

'All right,' he said. 'Smoke. Since the word got out on *Prehistoric* I've seen a whole bunch of scripts. Road movies, good-ole-boy stuff, get the girl, happy ending.' He shook his head. 'Now I'm interested. I'm interested in *Good Money*. But let's get some things straight. What's your attitude to this Doug character?'

'Uh, largely sympathetic.'

'He's a degenerate.'

'He's got problems you wouldn't believe.'

'Listen. I won't smoke and I won't drink and I won't have sex.'

'In the film.'

'In the film.'

Well that's that, I thought. But then I thought on a while and raised my finger. 'Will you have hangovers?'

'Certainly,' he said. 'I am an actor.'

'Wait a minute. You had sex in *Prehistoric*.'

'That was a primitive man, Self. Something else worries me. The fight. Tell me something, all right? Why would I want to fight with an old man?'

I noticed that Fielding was also staring expectantly at me. This will be over soon. Like everything else, this is getting nearer to being over.

'It's kind of the climax,' I said. 'You and Lorne, you're fighting over the girl. Also the money. It –'

'Yeah yeah. But you don't fight with old men. Not like that. Not with fists.'

'How about if you *lost* the fight? How about that? Or what if you hit him on the head with a car-tool?'

He looked at me pityingly, a full flat mouth on a chunky chin. 'It wouldn't ever *happen*,' he said. 'I'd take him out some other way. There are other techniques . . . hypnosis, mindpower. Anyhow this we can fix. Herrick tells me you have a first draft two weeks away from completion. You'll come here and we'll talk again. My mother will see you out.'

Half way to the door I swivelled and, as if simply following the script of this particular hangover, strolled back to the table and came to a halt with my hands in my pockets a few feet from Davis's chair. He looked up at me. Yes, even his face was muscular, as though he pumped iron with his ears. I said,

'We'll meet one day.'

'Uh?'

'Room 101.'

'Pardon me?'

'Forget it. You know, I really liked your film. It said something to me. I'll be seeing you, Spunk.'

We stood in the hot sandy bucket of the street, watching First Avenue's wall of death. The road rises sharply here as the tunnel fans out and climbs back into the air. Now the cars thumped and bucked on the ramp, the uptown stampede from the traps of the underpass. Fielding had waved away the Autocrat, and we idled, considering, the producer in his dove-grey suit, the director in boxy charcoal and troubled flesh. You know, the minute we got in there, the studs in my back had started to tickle, to rustle hatefully. Maybe it would be smart to let a medic in on this – there might be dirt in those wounds. Or maybe I could guts it out with penicillin, from my personal supply. In California, how much are backs? A night spent gummed to the plane's polyester would give me the full story either way. Home. Go home.

'So,' I said, 'another nutter. Just what we need. What's all this "saved" stuff? What does *saved* mean?'

'Born again. Fundamentalism, Slick, the most coarse and proletarian of all American creeds. Nicodemus, John 3. Unless a man is born anew, he cannot see the kingdom of God.'

'Uh?'

'The Bible, Slick. You ever read it?'

'Yeah, I read that.'

'Spunk's very religious. The kid's a saint, you know that? He works in the hospitals, he goes down to the projects in the Bronx. All the money his dad doesn't blow on the women and the ponies, Spunk gives to charity.'

'Like I said. Another nutter.'

'We need him. We do need him. With him the mix is just right. He's perfect for us. That kid is going to be very, very big. Spunk's hot, Slick. Hey,' he said, and laughed briefly, 'you think he has a permit for those muscles? Now I know what's worrying you and you can relax. He's controllable. Doris will account for all that in the script and he'll fall into line the second he sees hard print. They all will. Besides, he likes you. They all do. Say, it's too bad you have to get back. Things are moving, John.'

I said, to hell with it, I could do the budgeting and story-boarding just as well in London. If Doris Arthur came through with the script ahead of schedule, he could zip it over in a Poseidon wallet within twenty-four hours. Meanwhile, Fielding promised, he would hire the loft or the studio and line up the auditioning for the bit parts – the waiters, the dancers, the gangsters.

'We'll have some fun with that,' he said. 'The future looks bright, Slick.'

We embraced, a tight clasp with cheeks touching – but dead butch, naturally. Man, did I need that living squeeze. Now the Autocrat was nosing down the kerb. He had me doublesign some contracts on the hood (the usual: once under 'Co-signatory', once under 'Self'). Then he waved, and vanished behind the black glass.

I walked the line of midtown under the sun's red stare. In the Ashbery I was informed by reception that my tab 'was all taken care of' by Mr Goodney, who had moreover reserved Room 101 until further notice. This was a concession of a kind. Fielding deeply disapproved of the Ashbery, I knew, and was always on at me to take a suite, or a floor, of the Bartleby or the Gustave on Central Park South. But the Ashbery was more my speed. And I was settled here now.

So then you pack and do all that. As I slipped Martina's book between the folds of my best suit, Felix knocked and entered bearing a white package the size of a small coffin, flamboyantly fastened with a blood-pink bow. Selina has a bra-and-pants set of just that colour. Selina. I have big plans for Selina. Well, another present, eh?

'Delivery,' he said, straightening. Even in the at-ease position Felix seemed to be jogging on the spot.

'Here, Felix. You've been a real pal.'

He took the note but his face stayed quizzical. 'This is a big bill, man. You drunk?' he asked pleasantly, and smiled.

There are few things better than the reluctant black smile: worth a hundred dollars. Worth more. The slopes of his eyelids were infinitely dark, making the stare louder and the smile more furtive. This would always give Felix a cheeky look, even when he stopped being a black kid and started being a black man. Perhaps I had the same look once, though I've lost it now. At school the masters kept telling me to wipe it off my face. But I never knew I had it, so how could I wipe it off?

'Go on,' I said. 'It's not my money really. Buy a present for your girlfriend. Or your mother.'

'Now you take it easy now,' said Felix.

The black case lay on the bed beside the white box. I tugged the ribbon and lifted the lid and heard myself give a harsh shout of anger and rejection and probably shame. I tore it to pieces with my bare hands. Then I stood in the centre of the room thinking, whoops, hold it, hold on. But there were a good few tears backed up my tracks and now was as bad a time as any. Out it all came. I'll tell you what my present was and I think you'll understand. There was no message inside, only a plastic lady, veal-pale, moist-looking, with open grin.

You know, I've been told that I don't like women. I *do* like women. I think chicks are cool. I've been told that *men* don't like women, period. Oh yeah? Who does then? Because *women* don't like women.

Sometimes life looks very familiar. Life often has that familiar look in its eyes. Life is all vendetta, conspiracy, strong feeling, roused pride, self-belief, belief in the justice of its tides and floods.

Here is a secret that nobody knows: God is a woman. Look around! *Of course She is.*

A BOVE THE entrance to the saloon bar there is a picture of Shakespeare on the swinging sign. It is the same picture of Shakespeare that I remember from schooldays, when I frowned over *Timon of Athens* and *The Merchant of Venice*. Haven't they got a better one? Did he really look like that all the time? You'd have thought that by now his publicity people would have come up with something a little more attractive. The beaked and bumfluffed upper lip, the oafish swelling of the jawline, the granny's rockpool eyes. And that rug? Isn't it a killer? I have always derived great comfort from William Shakespeare. After a depressing visit to the mirror or an unkind word from a girl-friend or an incredulous stare in the street, I say to myself: 'Well. *Shakespeare* looked like shit.' It works wonders.

'Here, Fat Vince,' I said, '– what did you have for your breakfast this morning?'

'Me? I had a soused herring for my breakfast this morning.'

'Lunch?'

'Tripe.'

'And what are you going to have for your dinner?'

'Brains.'

'Fat Vince, you're a sick man.'

Fat Vince is beer-crate operative and freelance bouncer at the Shakespeare. He's been in and out of this place every day for thirty-five years. So have I, in my head anyway. I was born upstairs, after all. He sipped his beer. Fat Vince looks like shit

too, and so does his son Fat Paul . . . I have a feeling for Fat
Vince, partly because he's a fellow heart-sufferer. His heart
keeps attacking him, as mine will attack me one day. Fat Vince
has a feeling for me also, I reckon. Every couple of months
he takes me aside and, his breath sweet with trapped drink,
asks me how I am. No one else does this. No one. He talks
to me about my mother sometimes. Fat Vince is a widower too.
His wife died from being too lower class. She wasn't up to it.
My mother, she just entered a mysterious decline. I used to
get into bed with her after school. I could feel her falling,
dividing. Homesick for America. Too much Barry Self. Fat
Vince doubles as the popular and permissive assistant-manager
of a snooker hall in Victoria. He has a little scullery down
there, where he cooks his mad grub. Fat Paul bounces and
sharks and fills the pie-warmer. On the number-one table, the
cue cleaving his chin, he hunkers down on the cush to draw
his bead on the bone balls . . . Soon after my mother died Fat
Vince took my dad out in a famous fight, by the gents' in the
alley when the Shakespeare was young.

'That's real food, son,' said Fat Vince. 'You wouldn't know –
spent your whole life in a fucking pub. Give you a bag of crisps,
you think you're in heaven.'

'Here, you know Loyonel,' said Fat Paul.

'Yeah,' said Fat Vince.

Now Fat Vince isn't royalty but he speaks with a certain slot-
mouthed restraint. Not Fat Paul – Fat Paul, with his full-breasted
bulk, his impassive sloped slab of a face, his parched pub rug,
and the cruel blond eyebrows which give the eyes themselves
the glint of a veteran ferret who has seen it all in the hare-traps
and rat-pits. Fat Paul, I would say, has few anxieties about his
accent. He doesn't fudge or smudge. Every syllable has the clarity
of threat. You could never do that voice justice, but here goes.

'I seen him in the street Sunday,' said Fat Paul. 'I said – Phwore!

You just had a curry? He said. "Nah. Had a curry Froyday." I said – what you have today then? "Free spoyce pizzas and two Choynese soups." He's only on antiboyotics as it is, for this zit on his armpit and his impetoygo. Next day I seen him down the transport club. You know . . . they got a machine down there, Dad, that sells *chips. Chips.*' Fat Paul still seemed to be reeling at this development. 'Fucking great tank full of gunge, once a mumf some bloke comes along and pours more fat down the funnel. Firty pee a punnet. Loyonel, he's there, leaning on the machine and stuffing himself sick. And these *chips*, I tell you, ah is fucking disgusting. Undescroybable. He's half way frew his forf punnet, he turns to me and says he can't fink why he has all these troubles with his skin!'

'He's fortunate to be alive,' said Fat Vince, 'eating what he eats.'

'Seen the gut on him?'

'His father died at fifty-one. On a diet for five years, he just got fatter. Then they found out he was eating his diet *and* his normal food. What he put away you wouldn't want to think about. When Eva came back she hid his teeth, but he splodged it all up and ate it anyway. He had a bit of money too.'

'Money,' said Fat Paul pensively, 'is not worf two bob, is it, without your fuckin elf.'

The French, they say, live to eat. The English, on the other hand, eat to die. I took my pint to the bar, and scored a bag of crisps – shrimp-and-rollmop flavour – and a sachet of Pork Scrunchies. I turned, eating these, and watched the people. No doubt about it, I'm not a badlooking guy when I hang out at the Shakespeare. I may not rate that high among Fielding and the filmstars, but in here I'm a catch. These working-class women, they're like a sheep trial. It obviously takes it out of you, being working class. There's a lot of wear and tear involved. And pubs can't help. I turned again and leaned on the panelled bar, flanked by the heraldic street-signs of the beer-pull logos, the tureen-sized plastic ashtrays, the furry, nippled mats that imitate wetness even when they're dry. Tacked to the square wooden pillar was the hand-written pub-grub bill of fare, with its obsessive permutations of pie-mash and fry-up, the *ands* and *ors* underlined, the "coffee" and "tea" in their exotic inverted commas. For a while I stared into the clockface of an antique charity-box. Let the Friends of St Martin's Hospital Tell YOUR Fortune. You put in a coin, a wand twirls, and a brief selection of perfunctory destinies is on offer. I surveyed the options: Don't get Gout, Stick to Stout. Luck on the Pools. You'll have Joy, Your next a Boy . . . Nothing forbidding there. And I fear all portents. If the Friends of St Martin's Hospital had been peddling rug-loss, say, or bonk-famine, then they could fend for themselves. I slipped ten pee into the slot and the coin dropped with a contented click. The wand twirled: Money is On the Way. I slipped in another: Beware of False Advice. All right, it's a deal. I looked up, and the wobbly house-of-horrors mirror slipped its planes: the glass door opened, my father stared out and then gestured encouragingly, as if from a touchline. So I ducked in under the trap.

'Hi, Dad,' I said. He was wearing a black leather jacket and a white silk scarf. He's got a good rug, my dad, silvery and plentiful. I wouldn't mind looking like that when I'm his age. Actually, I wouldn't mind looking like that now. I wouldn't have minded looking like that five years ago, come to think of it, or even ten. It's the clock, the ticker. My heart's not right.

'Don't *call* me that,' he said with a flinch. 'We're *friends*. Call me *Barry*. Now,' he said, placing a creaky arm across my shoulders as he led me through to the parlour, 'I want you to meet *Vron*.'

'Vron?' He's doing it with robots now, I thought. He halted me with a tug of my hair.

'Yeah. Vron,' he said. 'Now you behave.'

Vron sounded bad enough when I said it. My father has trouble prouncing his *r*'s, owing to some palate fuck-up or gob-gimmick. Vron sounded a good deal worse when he said it.

The parlour had come on a long way since I was a boy. Now, it was close with money. The ribbed and pimpled gas fire in whose anglepoise heat I used to dress myself for school had been supplanted by a black eggbasket of counterfeit coal. The granny table where I ate my toast was now a cocktail cabinet, with studded plastic, three high stools, a Manhattan skyline of siphons and shakers. Vron reclined on a dramatic sofa of white corduroy. She was a pale brunette of comfortable build, my age. I had seen her before somewhere.

'Pleased to meet you,' I said.

'I've heard so much about you, John,' said Vron.

'Vron's a very happy girl today,' said my father huskily. 'Aren't you, my lovely?'

Vron nodded.

'It's a very special day for my Vron. Show him, Vron.'

Vron sat up, tightening the folds of her kaftan. She reached under the coffee-table and produced a pornographic magazine called *Debonair* . . . Now I know my pornographic magazines: *Debonair* belonged to the cheaper range, targeted at the manual worker's handjob, with many a salacious housewife or spotty-bummed Swede twisting herself in and out of chain-store underwear. 'Sit down, John,' she said, and rubbed the seat beside her with her palm.

Wetting her fingertips, Vron plucked at the pages. With a sigh that was almost a gurgle of gratification, she found the slippery spread. She laid it on my lap in a soft caress. My father sat down too. I felt their arms on my shoulders and their ripe, expectant, human faces very close to mine.

I flattened the mag out in front of me. From the right-hand page Vron's face stared me in the eye. Across her bare throat was the legend "VRON" – again the double quotes with their exotic, their impossible promise. 'Go on, John,' I heard Vron whisper. I turned the page. There was Vron, in the usual silky bonds and tapes, doing all the things that these chicks are paid to do. I turned the page. 'Slowly, John,' I heard Vron whisper. Vron on a steel chair, with a heavy breast in either fist. Vron lying with back arched and legs raised on a tousled white carpet. Vron stretched out on the haunches of a drophead Hyena. Vron crouched over a flat mirror. I turned the page. 'There,' I heard Vron whisper. The final double-spread disclosed Vron on her knees, her gartered rump hoisted towards camera, splaying the busy cleft with magenta-bladed fingers. Now I recognized her: Veronica, the talented stripper, here at the Shakespeare.

Vron started to cry. My father gazed at me manfully. I believe there was a tear or two in his eyes also.

'I'm ... . I'm so *proud*,' said Vron.

My father inhaled richly and rose to his feet. He slapped a hand on the cocktail console. He said explanatorily, 'Pink champagne. Well, it's not every day, is it? Come on Vron! Who's a silly then? Here's looking at you, my love.' He flexed his nose indulgently. 'There you go, John.'

'Vron? Barry?' I said. '– *Cheers*.'

I drove home in my Fiasco, which, apart from the faulty cooling system, the recurring malfunction with the brakes and power-steering, and a tendency to list violently to the left, seems to be running fairly reliably at present. At least it starts more often than not, on the whole. I don't think Selina exercises the Fiasco much when I'm in the States, and of course Alec Llewellyn has no use for it, now that he's locked up twenty-four hours a day ... The ride from Pimlico to Portobello took well over ninety minutes and it was gone midnight when I beached the car on a double yellow line outside my sock. *Why* did it take well over ninety minutes? A rush-hour style traffic jam at 12 p.m. Something to do with the fucking Royal Wedding. For the best part of an hour I sat swearing in a blocked tunnel under Westway. The Fiasco was overheating. I was overheating. Each car was crammed with foreigners and grinning drunks. The tunnel's throat swelled like emphysema with fags and fumes and foul mouths. Then we edged into the blue nightmap of stars. Join the dots . . . London has jetlag. London has culture-shock. It's doing everything the wrong way round at the wrong time.

Selina was sitting up in bed when I went through with my drink.

'What's happening?' I asked.

'Reading my book.'

'Your what?' She had a copy of *Sugar* on her banked thighs. There was also a TV-guide in there with her.

'How was Barry?'

'Oh. Okay.'

'Did you meet his new slag? He says he's going to marry her. He made another pass at me the other day.'

'He didn't. What happened?'

'He stuck his head up my skirt.'

'What?'

'I thought he was kidding until he tried to get my pants off with his teeth.'

'Jesus.'

'Doctor?'

'Uh?'

'Doctor? I think I've bruised my inner thigh. Can you take a look at it please? An oilman offered me fifty petrodollars to blow him in the lift.'

'What did you do?'

'I asked for seventy-five. But then he wanted everything, and

I think he was a little rough with my inner thigh. Would you look at it for me, doctor?'

I told her to forget this doctor nonsense and talk more reasonably – about the oilman and his petrodollars and what he had her do . . . In the dying moments she made a noise I'd never heard her make before, a rhythmical whimpering of abandonment or entreaty, a lost sound. I'd heard that noise before, but never from Selina.

'Hey,' I said accusingly (I was joking, I think), 'you're not faking it!'

She looked startled, indignant. 'Yes I am,' she said quickly.

Intriguingly enough, the only way I can make Selina actually *want* to go to bed with me is by not wanting to go to bed with her. It never fails. It really puts her in the mood. The trouble is, when I don't want to go to bed with her (and it does happen), I don't want to go to bed with her. When does it happen? When don't I want to go to bed with her? When she wants to go to bed with me. I like going to bed with her when going to bed with me is the last thing she wants. She nearly always does go to bed with me, if I shout at her a lot or threaten her or give her enough money.

It works well. It is an excellent system. Selina and I get on like a house on fire. The thing about Selina is, she understands. She knows the twentieth century. She has hung out in cities . . . When we go to bed together, sometimes the conversation turns to . . . While making love, we often talk about money. I like it. I like that dirty talk.

No sleep. No, no chance. I couldn't sleep but Selina could. She's good at that too, an accomplished sleeper, with childish face.

I went next door in my shorty dressing-gown. I poured

myself a drink. I glanced round about myself, on the lookout for clues. When I got in from the airport – yesterday, give or take a week – the flat felt lightly dishevelled, hurriedly lived-in, as if the cleaning-lady's efforts had been briskly cancelled or mussed. There were flowers on the table but no pants in the laundry basket. There was fresh milk in the fridge but old tea in the jar – and Selina likes her tea. She is particular about her tea, and often carries a pack round with her in her handbag . . . She was expecting me. I could tell by the quality of her alarm, which was actressy and overdone. *Where have you been?* I asked her. 'Here!' she insisted, with a chirpy wag of the head. *How did you know I was coming back?* 'I didn't!' she maintained. And I had told nobody, not Ella Llewellyn, nobody. Oh who cares, I thought, and tried to bundle her into the bag right away. I had a strong desire to repossess. She lets me furl her around for a while, and makes those shammy gasps she knows I like, and gives detailed promise of all that cocked and candid talent – before she calls a halt, slithers off the bed, corrects her clothing, brushes her hair, changes her shoes, powders her nose, slides my Johnson out of her mouth and insists on lunch.

We go to Kreutzer's. I eat and drink like there's no tomorrow. We don't have much to say. Nobody asks sticky questions as they are led on all fours up the stairs. I'm not about to spook her, not me. I'm too worried about earthquakes or nuclear warfare or extraterrestrial invasion or Judgement Day coming between me and my reward. All you'll get from John Self is smalltalk, flattery and squealed demands for more drink. After toothache liqueurs I thunder home and abandon the Fiasco in the middle of the street. By now I am a crackling sorcerer of grub and booze, of philtres and sex-spells. Selina walks into the bedroom with her head held low. I give a great hot grunt as I untether my belt.

. . . I picked up the stack of mail from the coffee-table and dealt myself one off the bottom: the envelope that contains my monthly bank statement, with its familiar brown matt and the wax seal like a blob of blood. It's not my bank account any more, of course. It's a joint bank account. Selina has half of it now – to shore up her dignity and self-respect, remember? I broke the seal with my blunt thumb. And the statement, I swear, was *three pages long*. Among the usual laconic entries on the debit side – US Approach, Liquor Locker, Dr Martha McGilchrist, Gas Board, Kreutzer's, the Mahatma, Trans-American, Liquor Locker – there now thronged a host of Selina's new playmates from the days of yore. Christ, what is this crew? It seems that the chick hangs out in Troy or Carthage when she's got a bit of cash to burn: Chez Zeus, Goliath's, Amaryllis, Aphrodite, Romeo & Juliet, Romulus & Remus, Eloise & Abelard . . . I always suspected that Selina spent all her money on massages, rug-rethinks and underwear – but that was when she hardly had any. The telltale entry was the lone item on the credit side: £2,000, from deposit account. I can't complain, I suppose. Such is our deal. Such is our gentle-man's agreement. But that's the whole trouble with dignity and self-respect: they cost you so much fucking *money*.

And now I am one of the unemployed. What do we do all day? We sit on stoops and pause in loose knots on the stained pave-ments. The pavements are like threadless carpets after some atrocious rout of flash-frazzled food and emetic drink: last night the weather gods all drowned their sorrows, and then threw up from thirty thousand feet. We sit flummoxed in the parks, among low-caste flowers. Whew (we think), this life is slow. I came of age in the Sixties, when there were chances, when it was all there waiting. Now they seep out of school – to what? To nothing, to fuck-all. The young (you can see it in their faces),

the stegosaurus-rugged no-hopers, the parrot-crested blankies
– they've come up with an appropriate response to this, which
is: nothing. Which is nothing, which is fuck-all. The dole-queue
starts at the exit to the playground. Riots are their rumpus-room,
sombre London their jungle-gym. Life is hoarded elsewhere by
others. Money is so near you can almost touch it, but it is all
on the other side – you can only press your face up against the
glass. In my day, if you wanted, you could just drop out. You
can't drop out any more. Money has seen to that. There's
nowhere to go. You cannot hide out from money. You just cannot
hide out from money any more. And so sometimes, when the
nights are hot, they smash and grab.

Meanwhile, there are some pretty primitive creatures driving
around with money in their Torpedoes and Boomerangs, or
sitting down with money at the Mahatma or the Assisi, or just
standing there with money, in the shops, in the pubs, in the
streets. They are all shapes and colours, innocent beneficiaries
of the global joke which money keeps cracking. They don't do
anything: it's their currencies that do things. Last year the pubs
were full of incredulously spendthrift Irishmen: they didn't have
money in their pockets any longer – they had Euromoney, which
is much more powerful stuff. There's some bundle in the Middle
East, and a new squad of fiscal space invaders starts plundering
the West. Every time the quid gets gang-banged on the international exchange, all the Arab chicks get a new fur coat. There
are white moneymen, too, English, native. They *must* be criminals, with their wads, the crap they talk, their cruel, roasted
faces. I am one. I am one of them, white or at least sky-grey,
with pub rug, and ashen arm on the Fiasco doorjamb, unsmiling
at the traffic light, fat-brained with abuse – but holding money.
I have money but I can't control it: Fielding keeps supplying me
with more. Money, I think, is uncontrollable. Even those of us
who have it, we can't control it. Life gets poor-mouthed all the

time, yet you seldom hear an unkind word about money. Money, now this has to be some *good* shit.

Ever since I gave up my job and started waiting for the film to happen, I too have felt like a gap in between things. So how can you expect someone like me to deal with the day? I have no ideas on this one. Tell me, please. Money doesn't tell me. I lie clueless in the cot until – until when? How is it that the experience will ever end? Up, get out, do it now – now, *now*. Now! I drift, dither, grope, fumble . . . and there I am at last, half-dressed in the kitchen with cigarettes and coffee-filters. Addictions do come in handy sometimes: at least you have to get out of bed for them. I look through the window – the streets, the sky the colour of wet sugar – and I am simply stumped by this, dumb-founded, nonplussed. The windows themselves, they make a little more sense. They are doubleglazed with dirt. The glass looks like the Fiasco windscreen after a thousand-mile drive, stained with the blackened blood of insects nine hundred miles ago, the dottings of soot, the fingerprints of filthy phantoms. Even dirt has its patterns and seeks its forms . . . When I quit my job it felt like the end of term, it felt like Saturday morning, it felt great, it felt illegal. But the end of something ought to be the start of something else, and I can't yet feel what's meant to be beginning. In my head it feels like nothing, like fuck-all. Selina is an early riser. Her High Street instincts (detectable in the sharpness of her face, even in the sharpness of her teeth) propel her into the world of money and exchange. She has an interest in a boutique run by that useful friend of hers, Helle, down Chelsea way, the World's End. Selina wants me to put money into it. I don't want to put money into it, but I probably will. If I do, I know I'll never get it out again.

So I play patience, and solitaire. Martina's book lies closed on my bedside table: I haven't got into it yet, and I still don't know what *pop-holes* are. I look to the TV, the video recorder. Once I had a pretty decent collection of films on tape, but I can't handle anything continuous any more. I've seen all the video nasties, and I don't need pornography, now that Selina's here. I fill the reels with nightly squirts of random TV traffic. Nature shorts, comedy shows. Football, snooker, bowls, darts. Darts! Dah! Oh man . . . soon I'll look like those fat brutes with the beer mugs and the arrows. And then with shoulders bunched and my eyes on the messed pavement I shuffle off down the drinker, and sit with tankard and tabloid in the corner by the fire.

Russia *is* going to beat Poland up. If I were Russia, that's what I'd do, just to keep up appearances – I mean, you can't let the word start to get about. Seems that Prince Charles had a thing with one of Diana's sisters, way back, before he fingered Lady Di as the true goer of the family. Another pussy-whipped judge has given some broad a ten-bob fine for murdering the milkman – premenstrual tension, PMT. The Western Alliance is in poor shape, I'm told. Well what do you expect? They've got an actor, and we've got a chick. More riots in Liverpool, Birmingham, Manchester, the inner cities left to rot or burn. Sorry, boys, but the PM has PMT. Here is a woman who gave her five-year-old child away to a stranger in a pub for two barley stouts. She's separated from her common-law husband, who is unemployed.

I do the quick crossword. I play the space games and the fruit machines. I feel like a robot, playing a rival robot, for a price. We are both one-armed bandits. Hold, nudge, spin, kick, shuffle, double, win, lose. It's all done for you nowadays – Prizefinder, Holdamatic, Autonudge. The machines nauseate me whether I win or lose. But if they had a hole in the wall here I think I'd put money into it. I go somewhere else and eat junk food and drink junk wine. I hit the betting shop and lose dough perched on a stool. I wander through the newsagents and check out the chicks in the magazines. I go home and lie down and then it all starts again. What is there to help me make sense of things? Time has me dangling on its tenterhooks. I used to run on *energy*. These days, *saying* energy makes me black out with exhaustion. I can't do any storyboarding until Doris Arthur shows with the script. As for budgeting, my first assistant Micky Obbs is on a half-pay retainer until the first day of Principal Photography, along with Des Blackadder and Kevin Skuse. *He* can fucking do it.

Take yesterday.

Eleven forty-five, and I strolled into the Jack the Ripper, the roughest and least local of my many locals. The dump wasn't that crowded: the girl behind the bar just kept disappearing and failing to meet my eye. Two or three new arrivals were greeted, listened to, obeyed, given drinks and change – without any acknowledgement of my cocked fiver and strident *excuse mes*. Well, I'm not one to soldier on with this kind of treatment.

'How about it?' I said loudly. 'I mean, what are my chances, if I stick around for a couple more months?'

People turned, but the barmaid did not turn. She went to the till, which jounced and jingled at her bidding. She swivelled primly – she wasn't one of nature's barmaids – and held up the change just past my face, which was boiling now, as she saw.

'We're not serving you,' she announced. Her face wavered. Then she looked into my eyes. Her face, its small universe, was all present and correct. Along the bar people perked up their interest.

As it was, even when I stepped in here, I wanted a drink quite badly. And that was five minutes ago.

'You're WHAT?' I said. 'Why? Who says? Why?'

'Not after last night.'

'What do you mean, last night? I wasn't even *in* here last night.'

'You don't even remember, you were that drunk. Jerome!' she called. 'Jerome!'

Jerome, the blue-jeaned bumboy with earring and dyed blonde hair, cruised over from his toytown window-display of pie-warmers and bean-blasters.

'Yeah?'

This was Jerome's contribution. The girl had begun to busy herself elsewhere. Over her shoulder she now said, 'Tell him. He was the one last night.'

'What's all this last-night shit?' I said. 'I just told you, I wasn't even *in* here last night.'

'Hang about,' said Jerome. 'Here Flora, it was the night *before* last.'

'Sunday night.'

'What are we today then?'

'Monday,' said Flora. 'It was *last night*.'

'Well which was it?' I said. 'You work in a fucking pub all day, you can't remember either.'

'He smashed the machine,' Flora told Jerome, who crossed his arms unhappily. 'Then he had a go at Mr Beveridge. Then he made obscene suggestions to me.'

'Yeah, well,' said Jerome.

'Hey. Jerome. You. Fuck off,' I said. 'Flora. Come here. Come here.'

Flora also crossed her arms. 'I'm not going *near* that one,' she said.

I dropped my head. I drew in breath. Tears formed. Boy, did I need a drink. I wanted to tell them that I had great trouble with my eyes and rug and heart, and that I was friendly with Lorne Guyland and Butch Beausoleil. More attractively, though, a lumpy clutch of beer glasses stood on the bar before me. With two spread hands I shoved them over the side. They took

quite a time to fall, and by then I was half way to the door.
'You stay *out!*' I heard Flora yell as I shouldered my way into
the air.

There were two more pubs near by, the Butcher's Arms and
the Jesus Christ. The annoying thing was that I was banned from
these joints too. So I checked in to the Pizza Pit. I sat in this
crepuscular caravan with a tub of red wine, and with a Big Sharp
One sizzling unregarded on its platter. Sunday night . . . terrible
to the touch. Or was it Saturday night? I killed another carafe,
then crossed the road in search of some proper grub. With the
aid of a long line of lagers, I consumed three Waistwatchers,
two Seckburgers, an American Way and a double order of
Tuckleberry Pie. But hang on a minute . . . Do you think I might
have left anything out?

After lunch I recrossed the road to the newsagents, and took
my place at the wailing wall of the pornography section. As in
any library, the material is arranged to suit the specialist: there
are magazines featuring chicks with big tits, there are magazines
featuring chicks in silk and lace and garter belts, there are magazines featuring chicks getting roughed up. Boy, are there a lot
of magazines featuring chicks getting roughed up. You'd think
the punters could get by with a mere half-dozen of these monthly
publications, but no, they need more. Pornography has a smell,
a special odour. I think it comes from the treated paper the
barons use. The smell of pornography is arid, acrid, the smell
of headaches and wax . . . I had just taken another look at
Debonair – at Vron, my future stepmother. My future stepmother
has a pair on her, no doubt about it. She could even cut the
mustard in one of the magazines specifically featuring chicks
with big tits. I replaced *Debonair* and picked up *Lovedolls*. Take
it from me, they don't come much dirtier than *Lovedolls*, not in
England, not legally. So there I was, muttering in a low grumble
and torpidly flipping through the pages, shoulders up, head

down – when to the sound of a loud handclap the splayed centre-spread was violently dashed from my grip.

I looked up, in alarm, bewilderment, in terror. A plump, pretty girl, with a sensible scarf, two badges on the lapel of her corduroy overcoat, her face and stance vibrant, unflinching, exalted . . . Browsers paused in their shuffle. Someone near me stepped sideways, beyond the range of my sight.

'What are you doing?' she barked – she snapped. A middle-class mouth, the voice and teeth hard and clean.

I backed off, or veered away. I even raised an arm protectively.

'Why aren't you ashamed of yourself?'

'But I am,' I said.

'Look at that. Look.'

We stared at the fallen magazine. It rested half-open on a low shelf where the normal, the legal stuff was trimly stacked. One of the centrepages was curled over, as if tactfully averting the gaze of the girl spreadeagled there. A trunkless, limp and warty male member dangled inches from her greedy smile.

'It's disgusting, *isn't* it.'

'Yes.'

'How can you *look* at these things?'

'I've no idea.'

At this she gave off a pulse of hesitation. I don't think she had really been hearing me till now. It must have cost her quite a bit too, taking on a man who looks like I look, his fat shoulders and heavy head tensed over the spectacle of her lost or twisted sisters. Yes, even with her strong round face and unimpeachable teeth and her rectitude, it must have cost her something. She had done this before a few times perhaps, but not that many times. Now the full stare of her eyes individualized my human shape, and her questions became questions. She raised a gloved finger.

'Why then? Why? Without you they wouldn't exist. Look at it.' We looked down again. The lovedoll was turned almost inside out. 'What does that say to you?'

'I don't know. Money.'

She turned and walked the long clicking walk down the floor (the shop strangely quenched of sound and movement), tugged back hard on the glass door and with a shake of shiny hair had passed into the random straggle of the street.

There was laughter, a low surge of talk. Amused relief showed briefly on the faces of the two zonked chinks who worked the counter. I restored *Lovedolls* to its rack, then flapped defiantly through *Plaything International* and *Jangler*. I crossed the street and climbed on a stool and lost £20 on the 3.45. I felt awful, ill, all beaten up. Oh, sugar, Jesus, why couldn't you pick on someone else? Why couldn't you pick on someone with a little more to lose?

I walked back to my sock in the thin rain. And the skies. Christ! In shades of kitchen mists, with eyes of light showing only murk and seams of film and grease, the air hung above and behind me like an old sink full of old washing-up. Blasted, totalled, broken-winded, shot-faced London, doing time under sodden skies. In the ornate portal of a mansion-block department store an old man with buttoned overcoat and brown burnished shoes stood talking at the rain. Other old people flanked him expressionlessly and two younger women wearing indeterminate blue uniforms and faces of bleached sincerity underscored or punctuated his address with marching music from pipe and drum. 'It is never too late', said the old man diffidently, unassumingly, as one of God's grim janitors, 'to change your ways.' With narrow lips and eyes he faced the strolling irony of the afternoon crowds, the young, the robed incurious foreigners. 'There is no need', he said, 'for you to feel so ashamed.' You could hardly hear him anyway, what with the drum and all this rain and milk in the air.

Oh, but pal – you're wrong. The skies are so ashamed. The trees in the squares hang their heads, and the awnings of the street are careful to conceal the wet red faces of the shopfronts. The evening paper in its cage is ashamed. The clock above the door where the old man speaks is ashamed. Even the drum is so ashamed.

'How in Christ's name did you get yourself into this state?'

'Right, you bitch, this is it!'

'This is what?'

'You're never fucking here when I call from the States!'

'Can't a girl go to her own flat when she likes?'

'You're never there either!'

'Can't a girl disconnect the phone sometimes?'

'You little actress, you were off somewhere else!'

'Are you going to pretend you don't know why things are in this state?'

'You're cheating on me, you bitch!'

'Why are you so upset? I'm trying to tell you something, don't you understand?'

Selina unbuttoned her coat. She crossed her arms and stood there bristling with all the counter-strength of the street.

'Jesus,' she said, 'aren't you the one. For God's sake go to bed and try and sleep it off before dinner. Where are we going anyway?'

No, I'll be okay, I said or whimpered – just get me some tea or something . . . Selina, she's turned the tables on me somehow, that Selina. I wish I knew how she managed it. Sighing, I lay on the couch with my mug. Selina established herself at the circular steel table: evening paper, teacup, a single, deserved cigarette. She turned the pages briskly, paused, frowned, cleared her throat, flexed her eyelids, and leaned forward in cold concentration. I knew what she was reading about. She was reading about the palimony trial in California. Selina's been following the story. So have I. Palimony sounds like bad news for the boys. As I understand it, the ruling states that if a chick makes tea once a week for the same guy – she gets half his dough. Every evening now, Selina turns straight to the palimony page, and goes all quiet. I hope she won't be wanting any palimony from me.

'Let's be realistic for once, shall we?' she said, later. 'You're too thick to realize it but I'm your last chance. No, not those. They cut into me. Who else is going to put up with you?'

'No, not those. We had them the other night.'

'Look at yourself. No, they need washing. I mean you're hardly a catch, are you. You're thirty-five. Act it.'

'Yeah, that'll do. With these. Put them on too.'

'If you're waiting around for someone better – hang *on*. I've got it – then you're whistling Dixie, mate. Who would take you on anyway? Martina Twain?'

'Wait. Take those off and put these on.'

'She gave you that book, didn't she.'

'What book?' I asked, impressed anew by Selina's witch radar.

'The library book on your bedside table. The one you read the first page of every night.'

'That's good. That's good. It was sort of a present.'

'A present, my arse. Honestly, the ideas some people have about themselves.'

'Face the facts,' she said, later still. 'Grow up, for God's sake. I'd settle for you. Settle for me. I'd look after you. Look after me. Give me children. Marry me. Make a commitment. Make me feel I have some kind of base to my life. At least let me move in here properly.'

'All right. Yeah, okay,' I said. 'You can move in here properly.'

★

So the next morning when the crows in the square were still
making their sounds of hunger I hired a van at the mews garage
and off we chugged down the hill, Earls Court way, to collect
Selina's stuff. Her flatmates Mandy and Debby flitted fanciably
about the place, half-dressed, serving me coffee with the reverence due to a moneyman and debt-settler. I lounged on the
couch in the attic sitting-room, pyramidal in shape with deep-set
windows. Through these chutes of slates you could inspect the
weather, which was making a comeback of the stalled-career
variety, the sun all rusty and out of condition, glowing then
failing suddenly like a damp torch. Selina donned an apron and
put her hair up under a baseball cap and prickled with female
make-do and knowhow, while Mandy and Debby took it in
turns to amuse me downstairs. Mandy and Debby, they look
like nude-magazines too. They look like Selina. Modern sack
artists aren't languid Creoles who loll around the boudoir eating
chocolates all day, licking their lips and purring, their whiskers
flecked with come and cream. No, they're business heads on
business shoulders, keen-sensed and foxy, not young-looking
either but tough, tanned and weathered. Selina falls in and out
of love with these two, as she does with Helle. She once told
me, in a voice full of hatred and contempt, that Mandy and
Debby have been known to do escort work, the deal being as
follows: the punter pays the agency £15 per date, of which the
chick gets two. That's right: two quid. A scandal, isn't it? So
naturally the girls do a bit of business on their own account.
Nothing went on here, though, in this shacky walk-up: what
went on went on in interchangeable intercontinental hotel
rooms, in the private suites of corrupt clubs and thriving speak-
easies, in glazed Arab flats. Mandy and Debby looked the part
all right, they looked tough enough for this, particularly Debby,
who gave me so much eye-contact and hand-on-knee and
dressing-gown disclosure that I almost asked for her telephone

number. But of course I realized that this would be a pretty gratuitous move, under the circumstances. I already had her telephone number.

I wrote out a cheque for £320 to cover various outgoings – kiss-off money' Mandy called it – and marshalled Selina's worldly possessions in the back of the van. She owned pitifully little, really. It would have all gone in the Fiasco, easy, if the Fiasco had been running. But the Fiasco has not been running. Three binliners full of clothes, a teapot, two photograph frames, a soap-rack, a chair, an iron, a mirror and a lamp.

'There you go, girl,' I said at the other end, when I brought in the final batch.

'Thank you, darling,' said Selina. She stood in the middle of my hired front room. 'Now this is my home. Right then.'

Selina had three paperbacks to add to the shelves, *A to Z*, *Common Legal Problems* and *The Guide to Married Loving*. What with Martina's present, my book collection is definitely expanding.

'Don't tell anyone,' whispered Alec Llewellyn, 'but it's really quite cool in here. Don't laugh! They'll see us and think I'm not taking it seriously.'

'Have you got your own cell?'

He sat back. 'No. It's a cell meant for one but there are two other guys in it. We're very overcrowded. They're all burglars and swindlers and things in here. We've got our own little kettle. It's so laid back I can't believe it. On the first morning I woke up feeling great, like a kid, stretched my arms and thought, Now I'll have a cup of tea and stroll out for a –! Then it hit me.'

'Wow.'

'Yeah. But I'm incredibly relieved. With my accent I thought I'd be smashed to pieces or fucked in half after five minutes in here. But it's not like that. It must be the only place in England where the class system still works.'

I lit a cigarette, and waited.

'I think it's to do with the clarity of the voice. Everyone else, including the screws and the pigs, they all talk as if they've just learned how. They can't understand why I'm in here. They're all paranoid of me. The screws are paranoid of me. The assistant governor is paranoid of me. Even the governor comes down to hobnob with me in the cells.'

'What's the food like?'

'Awful. It's all that soya stuff. It fills you up okay but runs you down at the same time. You know, I always thought they put anti-bonk pills in the coffee. But they don't need to. They don't put anything in the coffee. They don't put coffee in the coffee. Butch Beausoleil could live here in the nude and no one would give her a second glance. I suppose they might try and sellotape her to the walls of their cells. All day you feel as if you've just had about ten handjobs. It's the food and the air, and the confinement.'

We sat in a gothic cafeteria. If you lifted your head, it felt like school. Up there among the coach-house windows it was all swimming light, free-style, and tolerance of the noise and warmth of the human commerce below. Below, the prisoners sat at the far side of a rank of yellow-decked tables, with their little visitors – women, kids, the old – ranged opposite on kitchen chairs. No booths or metal grilles. You could hold hands if you wanted to. You could kiss. The older jailbirds were a snouty, ferrety contingent. Some of them looked only half-made. They sat back easily on their benches, their gestures resigned, explanatory. Their women were tensed forward on their seats, almost in a crouch of inquiry or solicitude. The children simply stared and fidgeted, in a high state of nerves – they were on their best behaviour, no question.

'I got you a sleeve of fags,' I said, 'plus twelve half-bottles of wine.'

'Thanks. Did –'

'I was amazed when they told me what I could bring. Half a bottle of wine a day – it's not enough but it's something. I left it all with the guy.'

'Did you bring any books?'

'Uh?'

'Ah you fucking lout! Bring me some tomorrow, okay? Promise. What do you think I do all day, for Christ's sake? All they've got in here is a little heap of Westerns and thrillers with half the pages torn out or covered in tea and snot. I've been reading the fucking Bible for the last few days. Even that would be okay but everyone's beginning to think I'm bananas. Bring me some books.'

'I don't even know what kind of books you like.'

'Jesus, anything. I'll make a list. Novels, history, travel books, I don't mind. Poetry, anything.'

'Poetry? In here?'

'I'll take my chances.'

Alec wore a navy-blue romper suit – the outfit of a French workman, or indeed that of some little new-wave narcissist at a C. L. & S. screening . . . It was the sight of him in his issued clothing that made me sense just how far he had fallen. Not too far, don't take him too far down, I thought. He'll disappear the other way. Everyone in here, they had all transgressed, they had all sinned against money. And now money was making them pay.

'That reminds me,' I said. 'You haven't got six thousand quid on you, have you?'

Alec scratched his scalp. His sharp nose twitched. 'Yes well I'm sorry about that.'

'What happened?'

'I gave some of it to Eileen and tried to double the rest at roulette. Brill, I agree. It wasn't enough anyway. You should have seen me in the dock, man. I was just melting. When that old moron in the wig, when he read out the sentence – oh, I thought, he *must* be talking about someone else. Who, me? And this is just remand. If things go against me on the ninth, then I go somewhere serious.'

'Can I do anything?' I said in a quick voice.

'No. I'd need – with the guarantee I'd need, I couldn't even ask you. What did Ella say?'

'Nothing much. Do you hate her?'

'Oh, you know. When you're fighting and hating each other anyway, it must be nice for the chick when she turns out to have the law batting for her. A judge, five hundred filth and *Brixton* on her side. Instead of throwing an ashtray at you, she throws prison.'

'Christ, I'd –'

'It wasn't her fault. It's all legal stuff to do with the kids. The irony *is*,' said Alec Llewellyn, describing a figure-eight with his neck, 'the irony *is* that Andrew – he's not even mine.'

'How do you know?'

'Look at him. Look at his hair. Look at Mandolina. A completely different order of human being.'

'Are you sure?'

'The month she conceived we were getting on so badly – I didn't sleep with her, not that month. She said I fucked her when I was drunk. But if I was too drunk to remember I'd have been too drunk to perform. Anyway. Ella came here the day after I got in and cried her eyes out. She tried to stop it, you know.'

'Oh yeah?'

'How's Selina?'

'Fine. And as true to me as the day is long.'

'You dupe. You gull.'

I named his prep school. I named his public school. I named his Cambridge college. 'And now Brixton,' I said. 'Wherever next?'

'Pentonville.' He took another cigarette from my fanned pack. 'Well, it's the university of life. You learn new things every day. For instance, there's a contract out on you, pal.'

'Oh that,' I said coolly. 'Yeah, so I've heard.'

'One of the minor villains here told me about it. It's a pretty minor contract, too. Fifty quid or something.'

'Who's taken it out?'

'That he didn't know or couldn't remember. But he remembers the damage.'

'Fifty quids' worth,' I said, feeling oddly hurt or slighted. 'What is it – a clip round the ear? A Chinese burn?'

'One blow in the face with a blunt instrument. Now. I'll make the list. And you fucking get me those books.'

The piece of paper changed hands softly. So did a ten-pound note. It wasn't prudent for him to have more. There wouldn't be a great deal to buy, but money has its powers, even here . . . Soon he was taken away: a uniformed guard simply beckoned to him through the half-open door. Alec Llewellyn nodded seriously at me as he walked off in his blue overalls, Alec, that snappy dresser. I left the way I'd come in. The criminals now embraced and encouraged their women, many of whom were patiently weeping their daily tearfall. The children had been stilled and quietened by fresh apprehensions. I walked through the clearing-house, the bench-lined locker-room, past full trashcans and the rods of old radiators. The next wave of families were gathered in huddles: the next wave of berks, burglars and bunglers was being dredged up from the cells. Shirtsleeved guards moved about with forms – cheerful, overworked. One of the guys at the gate helped me give the Fiasco a push. At many revolutions per second I came down the green slide into Brixton and beyond. But only when I reached the washed sky of the Thames did I dare to pull over and negotiate my fear.

I climbed out. I walked half the slope of Battersea Bridge.

Behind my back the four smokestacks of the power station pointed upwards, the threshold of an unfinished building of inconceivably vast and dreadful size. Beneath me the Thames lassooed and pulsed like a human brain, sending signals, slipping veil after veil as if a heavier liquid had been sent to slide across its face of water, leaving no doubt that rivers are living things. They die, too. I held the bars until the nausea left me, pouring out through the restraining iron and into the open air.

You see, I come from the criminal classes. Yes I do. It's in me, all that, in my blood. Oh, it gets you! Someone like me, I cannot put real distance between myself and prison. I can only put money there. It's in the blood, the blood. When I fly to California for my final rethink, maybe I'll go the whole hog and get my blood fixed too.

California, land of my dreams and my longing.

You've seen me in New York and you know what I'm like there but in LA, man, I tell you, I'm even more of a high-achiever – all fizz and push, a fixer, a bustler, a real new-dealer. Last December for a whole week my thirty-minute short *Dean Street* was being shown daily at the Pantheon of Celestial Arts. In squeaky-clean restaurants, round smoggy poolsides, in jungly jacuzzis I made my deals. Business went well and it all looked possible. It was in the pleasure area, as usual, that I found I had a problem.

In LA, you can't do anything unless you drive. Now *I* can't do anything unless I drink. And the drink-drive combination, it really isn't possible out there. If you so much as loosen your seatbelt or drop your ash or pick your nose, then it's an Alcatraz autopsy with the questions asked later. Any indiscipline, you feel, any variation, and there's a bullhorn, a set of scope sights, and a coptered pig drawing a bead on your rug.

So what can a poor boy do? You come out of the hotel, the

Vraimont. Over boiling Watts the downtown skyline carries a smear of God's green snot. You walk left, you walk right, you are a bank rat on a busy river. This restaurant serves no drink, this one serves no meat, this one serves no heterosexuals. You can get your chimp shampooed, you can get your dick tattooed, twenty-four hour, but can you get lunch? And should you see a sign on the far side of the street flashing BEEF–BOOZE–NO STRINGS, then you can forget it. The only way to get across the road is to be born there. All the ped-xing signs say DON'T WALK, all of them, all the time. That is the message, the content of Los Angeles: don't walk. Stay inside. Don't walk. Drive. Don't walk. Run! I tried the cabs. No use. The cabbies are all Saturnians who aren't even sure whether this is a right planet or a left planet. The first thing you have to do, every trip, is teach them how to drive.

I got drunk and dialled Hire-A-Heap and rented a scarred Boomerang on a budget four-day buy. I bombed around with a pint between my thighs. Bel-Air, Malibu, Venice. Then on the last night I made my big mistake, and hit that bad business I told you about. I don't like to sound judgemental, but it really was a big mistake. I was surging down Sunset Boulevard: purely on impulse I hung a left near Scheldt's, where I've seen these sweet little black chicks parading in tiny pastel running-shorts . . . Anyhow the upshot is, one way or another I'm lying in the front seat of the Boomerang with my trousers round my knees and copping a twenty-dollar blowjob from a speed-fuelled Zulu called Agnes. I mean it's incredibly reasonable, don't you think? What a fine country. What value. With sterling in the shape it's in, that's barely nine quid! But Agnes and I have a problem. 'This is why they're called hard-ons,' I remember explaining to her. 'They're not at all easy. They're very difficult.' Agnes is losing patience and revenue, I've practically got my legs sticking out of the Boomerang window, when there's this heavy handslap on the roof of the car.

I thought: law. The sex police! I straightened my neck. A

glamorous, dressing-gowned housewife was staring in through the open side window, her face framed by my shoes. 'Hurry it up, pal,' she said. 'You're in my drive!' Instantly, as if it were a bad oyster, Agnes spat my dick out of her mouth and started shrieking back at this loathed adversary of hers – Agnes's language, it was unimaginable: even I was grossed out by it. She swore detailed vengeance on the woman, her dogs, her kids, with intimate reference to various feminine rudiments and effluvia that I for one had never come across. 'Okay it's the cops,' said the lady finally, and strode back towards the house . . . I was thrashing and clawing but with Agnes still slumped on my middle and the whisky bottle and everything I couldn't seem to writhe my way upright. Then the door behind my head jerked open, the car light came on like a flashbulb, and there was a seven-foot black pimp snarling down at me with a mahogany baseball bat in his fist.

Well, you don't ever feel more naked than that. No – you never do. Something about the bat itself, the resined or saddlesoaped grain of its surface, offered unwelcome clarity, reminding me why I had stayed away from Scheldt's and the sweet black chicks and their bargain blowjobs. *This is all very serious and violent and criminal and mean. You cannot go slumming, not here, because slums bite back.* As Agnes wriggled out of the far door the big pimp raised his hammer. I clenched my eyes. No quarter. I heard a grunt, a hum of air, a blood-stunning crack, then with oddly exact and flowing movements I sat up saying *'Money'*, took my wallet from its holster, fanned five twenties at the sweating black face, wedged shut the door, made the triple-ring sign, and drove sedately out of Rosalind Court. Next, the machine squeal of sirens on my tail. Leaving a continuous, scalding double-tyretrack in my wake, I rocketed on to Sunset Boulevard, jumped three lights and made a spectacular crash-landing in the lot beneath the Vraimont. I slid out the door and made a dash for the lift. I got to my feet, pulled up the trousers which shackled my ankles, and tried again. Lucky lucky lucky, oh lucky, I kept saying, as I washed the blood off my nose in Room 666. They didn't even notice the smashed front lights and the vicious new welt on the Boomerang doorframe when I slinked back to Hire-A-Heap the following day. I leaned over in my boxy suit and re-signed the credit slip, my bitten fingers shimmering over the scorched trunk. Behind my back, under showboat lights, Sunset Boulevard sailed on down its slope.

An hour later I was fastening my safety-belt at LAX. First class: the Pantheon of Celestial Arts – their treat. Toasting John Self with premixed martinis, I too was a cocktail shaker of hilarity and awe. I had just been reading in the *Daily Minute* about the string of beatings and manslaughters in Rosalind Court: the night before last a Jap computer expert and a German dentist had been found in a parking lot with their faces stomped off. I think I was in shock, or undergoing reaction. 'You're so lucky, you're so *lucky*,' I murmured, staring down at the rocky Rockies or the Smokies or the Ropies through cloud-cover made of snow and contour tracing . . . In the next throne along lounged an elegant young man – summer business suit, Cal tan, thick, unlayered rug: I took him for an actor. He glanced up from his hardback and sipped his champagne. He raised the glass. 'Here's to luck,' he said. 'And to money.' Well, I didn't need much prompting, and soon babbled out all my dreams and dreads. It transpired that he had been scouting at the Festival. He'd seen *Dean Street*, and liked what he saw. And to follow? I told him about *Bad Money* – another short, no big deal. We talked, we made plans, we exchanged numbers, as you do on aeroplanes: it's the booze, it's the canned air and the rich-quick stories, it's the pornography of travel.

'I'll call you,' he said, when our tunnels parted at Kennedy. Oh sure, I thought, as I queued for my ticket to London. Three days later he rang me at my sock. He said,

'We have Lorne Guyland. We have Butch Beausoleil. We have eight million dollars, and climbing. Get your butt on a bird, Slick, and let's make *Bad Money*.'

I can see me now. I'm in the design department over at Silicone Valley. The sun shines but no dust stirs. I move confidently among the technicians, the ideas-men and creative consultants, the engin-eers and fine-tuners. Someone shows me the rough of my new ears and nostrils. I lean over a drawing-board to approve a sample merkin. The heart boys doublecheck on my detailed specifications. I have a preparatory meeting with the rug people. We move on to the gene pool, the DNA programmers, the plasma bank. Occasionally I say things like 'Looks good, Phil,' or 'What's the guarantee on this, Steve?', or 'Yes, Dan, but will it take the strain?' Eventually I produce my wallet, and silence falls.

'Okay, boys, now I want to make this absolutely clear. I'm paying top dollar and I expect the best. I don't care what it costs. I want it blue, I want it royal, I want the best blood money can buy. Go on, God damn it, and give me the *right* stuff this time around.'

Now with Selina Street here the texture of my life has already changed or shaded. With a moan of effort the unloved flat slowly responds to the female presence. Heavily, and with unpractised movements, it straightens up and tries to look courtly, attentive and willing. Only rarely does the leer of insincerity glow through the mask. It smartens its act. It stows its towels. It keeps the batch at bay. Yes, the smell of the place, even to my clotted nostrils, has definitely improved. For this I thank Selina's duty-free perfumes and bath essences, the laundry-fresh tang of her clothes, the costly oiliness of her flesh and its smooth secretions.

She's back in the tub again even now, the amphibious Selina. Soon I'll hear her primping herself in the bedroom, cosseting her curves in silk and lace. We're going out to an expensive restaurant, a very expensive restaurant, the sort of place Selina can dress up for . . . The flat feels better, better-run. It's not that she's much of a hausfrau or hoover-wielder. The cleaning-lady comes once a day now, instead of once a week. But Selina is efficient, is practical. She is cost-effective.

And with a chick on the premises you just cannot live the old life. You just cannot live it. I know: I checked. The hungover handjob athwart the unmade bed – you can't do it. Blowing your nose into a coffee-filter – there isn't the opportunity. Peeing in the basin – they just won't stand for it. No woman worth the name would let it happen. Women have pretty ways. Without women, life is a pub, a reptile bar at a quarter to three . . . Have you noticed, you guys, the way black or blue or red underpants stay clean for days on end, whereas white underpants – what *is* it with white underpants? They barely last an hour. What is it with these exploding, these joke-shop, these trick underpants? Anyway, with Selina here, my life is being lived in white under-pants. They're better, really, I suppose, even though you have to change them all the time.

I went next door with Selina's toy drink. 'Mm,' she said. She stood before the mirror in full brothel gear. What talent. What artistry. She turned. Her sexual features aren't particularly full or plump. They're just incredibly prominent. Bum, box, belly, breasts – just incredibly prominent. She looked so pornographic in her gimmicks that I wanted her to take them off again, or better, much better, push bits of them aside.

'Come here,' I said.

'No.'

'Why not?'

'You know why not.'

'. . . I saw Terry Linex today. He sent his love. Good news about my golden handshake. He says it should be half way to six figures.'

'What's that? Fifty grand?'

'Easy.'

'All the more reason then. Terry Linex made a pass at me.'

'What? When?'

'I thought he was just messing about. Then my eyelashes got caught in his zip. Then he –'

'Christ, enough! Come here.'

She hummed.

'Why not?'

She jounced her black dress. 'You know why not.'

Actually I was by no means sure. We've been fighting about money of late, but then again it might be my face. Never my best feature, my face is still swollen, up there on the left-hand side. That tooth caught fire again. I took my poor mouth to Martha McGilchrist, who exasperatedly drained it for me. Any chick who fancies herself as a feminist ought to go and see Martha McGilchrist. Boy is she butch. She makes me feel like a starlet. Martha McGilchrist – she's a *bloke*. She also said that when my tooth catches fire again, which it will, I won't be able to save it for love or money. That tooth will just have to wait for California, along with everything else.

I shouted at Selina for a while and returned to the sofa and my drink. The television was on. The television is always on. This afternoon, as I passed the square, I saw two dogs skewered together, back to back. Their owners stood around, waiting. The dogs were waiting too: they looked embarrassed, foolish, but stoical. They had been through all this before, or at least their genes had. It is dangerous if you try to separate them . . . On television I watched a nature short about two-headed snakes. Two-headed snakes are rare and don't last very long. They're forever quarrelling about food and which way to go. They keep trying to kill and eat each other all the time. Soon, one head becomes dominant. The smaller head is obliged to tag along but has no say in things any more. This arrangement keeps them going for a little while. But they both die quite quickly.

If there's one thing I think I'm sure of, it's the fact that I must marry Selina. I'm pretty sure about this, I think. Yes, it is time I settled down, grew up. There's no choice really: not settling down and not growing up are killing me. I've got to quit it, being young, before it's too late.

I must marry Selina and settle down and raise a family. I must be safe. Christ, safe sounds frightening. Settling down – that seems a bit adventurous, a bit precipitate, to me. Having kids! That's what takes real balls. To become a husband and a father: no you can't get much butcher than that. Yet nearly everyone shapes up to it in the end. I bet *you* have or will soon. I want it too, I think, in a way.

Of course, something is missing. Ah, you noticed. You are not blind. But it is missing in me, in her, it is missing, it will never be there. Selina and I are very well suited. We get along like nobody's business. I must marry Selina. If I don't, I'll just die. If I don't, no one else will, and I'll have ruined another life. If I don't, I think she might sue me for every penny I have.

Today I made a break with habit and tradition, and took my lunch at the New Born Restaurant. The New Born is a hot little grotto of plastic panels and formica tabletops, half cheap-bistro, half yobs'-beanery, run by an elite squad of Italians together with some straggly irregulars – local charwomen, reformed bagladies, London sweepers. You get all sorts in here, from dustmen to middle-management. The menu is chip-orientated, but the place is licensed. How else could it seriously expect my custom? Today I called for the gravy dinner plus two vedge and a carafe of red – which for me, rotting veteran of Pizza Pit and Burger Shack, of Doner Den and Furter Hut, is the equivalent of a handful of brown rice and a glass of effervescent Vitamin C. (There *are* health-food joints around here, run by aged hippies or unsmiling Danes. But I won't eat that shit. I just won't eat it.) I was sitting there waiting for the grub to show when Martin Amis came through the open door – you know, the writer I was chatting to in the pub the other night. The place was pretty full, and he hesitated until he saw the empty bench at my table. I don't think he saw me.

Martin sat down opposite and quickly flattened a book out in front of him. This kid is going to ruin his eyes . . . Me, I had plenty on my mind, including a desperate hangover, and was in no mood for complications. Last night had been a new one. Cocktails: £17. Dinner: £68. Selina: £2,500. You heard me, two-and-a-half big ones. That handjob I scored at the Happy Isles – I tell you, She-She was giving it away. I'm losing my grip, I'm falling to pieces. A year ago, Selina's two-hour session of candlelit fund-raising would have gained her nothing more than a clout round the ear (I'd have done it nice, mind you, not in the restaurant or anything like that but in the Fiasco or back at the sock). I really am cracking up, I really am deteriorating. I gave her the cheque in the bedroom. She folded it into the cleft of her black bra. Then, boy, did I get mine. An hour later the telephone rang. It was one o'clock. 'Don't answer it,' whispered Selina. But I welcomed the interruption, to the precise degree that Selina deplored it. She and I separated (it was like trying to unpick a mangled shoelace) and I staggered through to take the call. Fielding Goodney, with all kinds of developments: a 'dream script' had come through from Doris Arthur, Caduta Massi and Butch Beausoleil had put their signatures on the line, Spunk wanted in, Lorne wanted out – Lorne

Guyland was going crazy, or was staying that way. Money was falling from the sky quicker than Fielding could catch it. Refreshed, exhilarated, I went next door again, the brandy bottle swinging from my hand, and made Selina curse her mother for ever giving her birth. Two thousand five hundred pounds – now that's a lot of money. But Fielding was talking millions. If everything went through okay, I'd be able to sleep with Selina every night for the rest of my life.

The wine arrived. I had the meal to get through anyway, so I leaned forward and said,

'Fate.'

He looked up with a flash of panic – but then he calmed and smiled. He recognized me. People usually do. I haven't got that problem, the problem of not being recognized. It's one of the kick-backs you get for looking like I look.

'Oh, hi,' he said. 'We can't go on meeting this way.'

'What are *you* doing in this dump? Why aren't you having lunch with your, with your publisher or something?'

'Come on. I have lunch with my publisher every other year. What do you do?'

'I'm in films,' I said. 'Right up to here.'

'Then why aren't you having lunch with Lorne Guyland? See what I mean? It just doesn't happen that often.'

'What made you say Lorne Guyland?' Perhaps he'd recognized *me* – or *recognized* me. After all, I'm tolerably well known in some circles.

'No reason,' he said.

'John Self.' I held out my hand and he took it.

'Martin Amis.'

'Check.'

'Hey,' he said, 'was it – are you the guy who made those commercials, the ones they took off the air?'

'That's me.'

'Ah.' He nodded. 'I thought those commercials were bloody funny. We all did.'

'Thanks, Martin,' I said.

The waitress showed with my heaped and steaming plate. She took Martin's order. He surprised me again by opting for a standard yob's breakfast – egg, bacon and chips. No, I don't think they can pay writers very much at all.

'Toss?' asked the girl, one of the Italian contingent, though her colouring had been exhaustively naturalized by the kitchen spores.

'No, no toast, thanks.'

'Drin?'

'Tea, please,' said Martin.

I gestured at my litre of fizzy red wine. 'Want a drop of this?' I asked him.

'No thanks. I try not to drink at lunchtime.'

'So do I. But I never quite make it.'

'I feel like shit all day if I drink at lunchtime.'

'Me too. But I feel like shit all lunchtime if I don't.'

'Yes, well it all comes down to choices, doesn't it?' he said. 'It's the same in the evenings. Do you want to feel good at night or do you want to feel good in the morning? It's the same with life. Do you want to feel good young or do you want to feel good old? One or the other, not both.'

'Isn't it a tragedy?'

He looked at me with some care. Sadly I followed his eyes, and I too saw what he saw. My snowy cheeks and ruddy lids, the coin-slot of my mouth and its tannic teeth – and the rug, a dry rug, a drinker's rug.

'You still put your money on the evenings, though.'

'Yup.'

'And you feel like shit in the morning.' He glanced with amusement at my wine. 'And you feel like shit in the afternoon.'

'Yeah, well I'm a nightowl,' I said uneasily.

His food came – they don't mess about here – and he reached for the salt. Then, as he started to eat, he said quietly,

'I was in the newsagents' the other day – when you had that set-to with the girl.'

'Yeah?' I said, and felt my blood give a sick lurch.

'I thought you handled yourself pretty well, considering. Nasty business.'

'Yeah, it was fucking embarrassing.'

'Of course,' he said, continuing to cut his food crisply, 'you could have argued that the man was being exploited too.'

'What man?'

'There was a man in the photograph, wasn't there.'

'No. The girl just had this dick in her face.'

'Well who do you think the dick belonged to, brilliant?'

'Yeah but girls don't think that's exploitation. They think that, they think all men want to do that stuff anyway.'

'Well, they're wrong, aren't they,' he said mildly. 'I wouldn't want to do it. You wouldn't want to do it. The men do it for money, same as the girls.'

'There must be some guys who like doing it. When I was younger, I always thought it looked like money for jam. Some girls like doing it too, don't forget.'

'You think?'

'Oh sure,' I said. 'I know one who posed in *Debonair*. She bursts into tears of pride at the very mention.'

'Pride? . . . Yes, I suppose it figures.'

'How?'

'Yob art,' he said, and wiped his mouth. 'Hey look, I've got to run.'

'Come on,' I said, 'you've got to let your meal digest. It's not healthy. Have a drink.'

He shook his head. Before he left, he held out his free hand and I took it.

'Nice talking to you, Martin.'

'Be seeing you, John.'

John. What a name, eh? It means a can, it means a trick. I pushed my plate away and settled back with the wine. I lit a cigarette. I pondered. Yob art . . . *Yeah*. When Vron had sobbed it all out after showing her prospective stepson photographs of herself having a handjob with no clothes on for money, she explained to me – at throaty length and with hot tears still foiling the points of her lashes – that she had *always* been creative. 'I was *always* creative John!' she said again and again, as if I kept impiously insisting that she was creative only sometimes or not until recently. Vron confirmed that she had been good at art as a schoolgirl, often praised by her art master. She instanced her darning skills and her flair for interior design. 'I always knew I'd be in a book one day,' she said, reaching once more for *Debonair*, 'and now, John, that dream has been realized.' She flattened the spread comfortably on her lap: there was Vron, "Vron", on all fours, at three-quarters rear angle, in stockings, stilettoes and a pair of burgundy pants peeled half way down her pocked haunches. 'Beautiful,' I heard my father gulp over my shoulder. 'You see, John,' said Vron, 'if you have the creative . . .' 'Gift,' said my father. 'The creative *gift*, John, then I think you've got to – to give *of* your gift, John. John. Look at this.' She turned the page. Here Vron reclined on a kittenish white carpet, one leg hooked over an elbow, one hand busy in the central divide, a look of appalled transport on the averted face. 'You see how much I'm giving there, John? That's what Rod kept saying to me, the photographer, John. He kept saying: "Give, Vron, give!"' . . . I left half an hour later. Vron and Barry were crying again by that time, crying gratefully, consolably, in each other's arms.

And get this. I'm only going to say it once.

Three years ago, when I started to make some real money as opposed to all that other stuff I'd been making, my father hit bad trouble on the tables and the track and he . . . Do you know what he *did*, that funker? He submitted a bill for all the money he had spent on my upbringing. That's right – he fucking invoiced me. It wasn't that expensive, either, my childhood, because I spent seven years of it with my mum's sister in the States. I still have the document somewhere. It was six sheets of foolscap, thumbtyped. *To* 30 pairs of shoes (approx.) . . . *To* 4 caravan holidays in Nailsea . . . *To* share of petrol to same . . . He tabbed me for everything, pocket-money, ice-creams, rug-rethinks, everything. He enclosed a cover note, explaining in his clerkly style that it was of course only a rough estimate, and that I wasn't beholden to reimburse him penny for penny. Inflation had been taken into account. I'd cost him nineteen thousand pounds.

Anyway, we both behaved in character – the same character. On receipt of my father's letter, I got drunk and sent him a cheque for twenty grand. On receipt of my cheque, my father got drunk and put the money on a horse running in the Cheltenham Golden Shield called, I don't know, Handjob or Bumboy or whatever. The horse was young for a chaser and didn't have much in the way of form – but Barry had a hot tip. 100–8 looked good to him. He placed the bet by messenger. One of his villain mates, Morrie Dubedat, set up the deal and vouched for dad's punt . . . Ten minutes later Barry panicked and tried to cancel. But the bookie was already out hiring frighteners and the bet had to stand. Jackknifed over the whisky bottle, Barry listened to the radio commentary in closing-time light. Sure enough, Bumboy came lolloping out of its stall, each leg going somewhere different, neighing and dumping in its blinkers and Dobbin hat. Eventually flogged into submission by the jockey, Bumboy set off after its vanishing playmates. The horse received the odd joke mention from the commentator, until my father smashed the radio, finished the whisky, and suffered a near-fatal nosebleed.

Barry has since acquired a video recording of the race and still gloats over it even now. Bumboy not only won: it was more or less the sole survivor. There was one of those churning, drowning pile-ups at the penultimate jump. Bumboy tripped snorting through the chaos – and was clear with one fence to beat. The lone horse pranced flimsily on. It didn't leap that last hedge: it just munched its way through. Then, with only flat green ahead, ten yards from the post, Bumboy fell over. The jockey, who was all whipped out by now, tried to remount. Some of his grounded colleagues got the same idea. After about ten minutes – several riderless horses had skipped over the line by now, and another contender had cleared the last jump, and was gaining – Bumboy was finally scourged out of a series of circles and flopped over the line, home by half a length.

Now this bookie was a middleman, not legal, and my dad took Morrie Dubedat, Fat Paul and two shooters when he went to collect his winnings. Also, I had sobered up by then and caused some complications by trying to stop the cheque – until my father came squealing on to the line. He got his money, after a month of gang warfare – not the full whack by any means, but enough to pay his debts, buy out the brewery, gut the Shakespeare, install the pool table, the stripper and the strobes . . . He says he's going to repay me, one of these days. Who cares? It doesn't matter. I'll never get over the grief of that wound. And I don't think he ever meant me to.

I settled the bill – a pretty useful one, what with the line of brandies I had moodily consumed. I returned to my flat and packed a case and started going back to America.

T HE AUTOCRAT moved fast and softly through chintzy prefabs and the continuing scenes of black family life, with its leagues of brothers and stand-offs in the basketball courts, and mothers' shapes behind the insect mesh, calling. Spooked planes buzzed the limo roof at the black spread of water near La Guardia. Pedxing, No Shoulder, Unlawful To Cross White Line, Traffic Laws Strictly Enforced, Stay In Lane, Upgrade – Maintain Speed. Does My Chauffeur Need To Be Told All This? Wouldn't DRIVE do the trick? We came out of the beach-hut belt and slid down on to the barrelling freeway. Now – here it comes again – the gnashed, gap-toothed skyline, the graphics, the artwork of New York.

At the Ashbery I offered the driver a twenty.

'No sir!' he said. 'That's all taken care of. Would you call Mr Goodney, sir, when you're settled in?'

I tried the twenty on him again. He wouldn't take it, so I pressed it on Felix instead.

'I hate to do this to you, Slick, but you got to go see Lorne Guyland – tonight.'

'Oh man.'

He told me why. I was about to ring off when Fielding asked suspiciously,

'Hey, how did you fly? Coach?'

'Yeah.'

'Slick, I'm going to have to talk to you very seriously about your expenses. Shape up, John. It's an embarrassment. It looks bad to the moneymen. Take a floor at the Gustave. Hire a jet and have a weekend with Butch and Caduta in the Caribbean. Go buy a case of champagne and pour it all over your dick. Spend. Spend. You're no *use* to me when you fly coach. Fly supersonic. Fly sharp end. God damn it, Slick, fly *right*.'

I shaved, showered, changed, drank a mug of duty-free and took a hot cab-ride into the East Eighties with Si Wypijewski at the wheel. Or maybe it was Wypijewski Si. New Yorkers will tell you that the surname comes first on the cabbie's ID. But who says? Even with Smith John and Brown David, how can you really be sure over here? I once had a cabbie called Supersad Morgan. Or maybe it was Morgan Supersad. His eyes, at any rate, were brown and terribly melancholy. His eyes were super-sad . . .

My mission? To *go reassure* Lorne Guyland. According to Fielding, Lorne was seriously overdue for reassurance. He had been wanting reassurance for a long time and he hadn't been getting any. 'Do it now, John,' Fielding had counselled. 'You'll save us a lot of sweat in mid-career.' Lorne wanted reassurance about screen supremacy, line ratios and close-up time. Lorne wanted reassurance about his youthfulness, athleticism and general popularity. Lorne wanted reassurance about the nature of his role. Me too, pal. Lorne, I sympathize.

Lorne's role was that of Gary, the nogoodnik father. In my treatment I had, I thought, made it pretty clear what Gary was like. Gary was like Barry, like Barry Self: a lantern-jawed know-nothing, an unreflecting hedonist, a mastermould of brute conceit who none the less exploits a small but tenacious legacy of charm and luck . . . Why do I bother with my father? Who cares? What is this big deal about dads and sons? I don't know – it's not that he's my dad. It's more that I'm his son. I am aswirl with him, with his pre-empting, his blackballing genes . . . Gary, too, had a lot of my dad in him, just as I resembled Doug, the son. When the heroin shows up in the flour, Gary wants to return it to the mob. Doug wants to sell it at its street value, which is two million dollars. They're both bad and greedy, but old Gary is a funker – yes, a lucky funker.

Fielding had told me to expect trouble from Lorne on several counts. Lorne wanted Gary upgraded. Rather than pub landlord or beanery boss, Lorne saw Gary as a celebrity restaurateur. The age question also vexed him. Fielding said that Lorne had even floated the idea that Gary and Doug should be brothers, as opposed to father and son. In this fashion did Lorne hope to make light of the forty-year age difference between himself and his co-star. Then, too, there was the sex.

'I'm Thursday,' said the girl at the door of Lorne's penthouse. 'I'll just buzz up.'

I watched Thursday mince across the hall to her desk. She wore a kind of schoolkid outfit – blouse and tie, cheerleader's pleated skirt, bobbysox. She was six feet tall and looked like a gorgeous transvestite, possibly the beneficiary of some dirty-minded sex-change operation, over in California there. As she bent over the intercom the little skirt went peek-a-boo and you could see white pants cupping her buttocks like a bra. I wondered . . . Fielding maintained that Lorne was 'all fucked out', having gorged himself to the point of decrepitude during his first decade at the top, a common enough syndrome in the movie business. According to Fielding, Lorne hadn't had a hard-on for thirty-five years. Of course one had to remember that Lorne, in his time, had been very big, enormous, colossal. While making *Gargantuan* in Spain during the Fifties (Fielding again), Bullion had chartered sex planes from New York, London and Paris just to keep Lorne in chicks for the five-month shoot. His boast had been that he could tackle a whole consignment with a bottle of brandy and a soft-on. Lorne had been big then all right. All my life I had seen him up there on the screen.

'Mr Guyland. Sir, your director's here!' said Thursday in her singing-telegram voice. She laughed raunchily. 'Sure, lover. You got it.' Then she turned. 'I'm sorry if I seem a trifle flushed. Lorne's been balling me all day. He's right up there.'

I climbed a padded spiral staircase. I climbed from the stalls to the gods. Lorne surged across a cloud of carpet, seventh heaven, dressed in a white robe and extending a broad-sleeved arm through the conditioned air. With silent urgency he swivelled, and gestured towards the bank of window – this was his balcony, his private box, over sweating Manhattan. He poured me a drink. I was surprised to taste whisky, rather than ambrosia, in the frosted glass. Then Lorne gazed at me for a very long time, in ripe candour. I delivered what was to be my longest speech of the evening, saying that I gathered he was keen to talk about his role, to talk about Gary. Lorne gazed at me for a very long time again. Then he started.

'I see this Garfield as a man of some considerable culture,' said Lorne Guyland. 'Lover, father, husband, athlete, millionaire – but also a man of wide reading, of wide . . . culture, John. A poet. A seeker. He has the world in his hands, women, money, success – but this man probes deeper. As an Englishman, John, you'll understand what I'm saying. His Park Avenue home is a treasure-chest of art treasures. Sculpture. The old masters. Tapestries. Glassware. Rugs. Treasures from all over the world. He's a professor of art someplace. He writes scholarly articles in the, in, in the scholarly magazines, John. He's a brilliant part-time archaeologist. People call him up for art advice from all over the world. In the opening shot I see Garfield at a lectern reading aloud from a Shakespeare first edition, bound in unborn calf. Behind him on the wall there's this whole bunch of oils.

The old masters, John. He lifts his head, and as he looks towards camera the light catches his monocle and he . . .'

I stared grimly across the room as Lorne babbled on. Who, for a start, was Garfield? The guy's name is Gary. Barry isn't short for Barfield, is it. It's just Barry, and that's that. Still, this would no doubt be among the least of our differences. Lorne now began mapping out Garfield's reading list. He talked for some time about a poet called Rimbo. I assumed that Rimbo was one of our friends from the developing world, like Fenton Akimbo. Then Lorne said something that made me half-identify Rimbo as French. You dumb shit, I thought, it's not Rimbo, it's Rambot, or Rambeau. Rambeau had a pal or contemporary, I seem to remember, with a name like a wine . . . Bordeaux. Bardolino. No, that's Italian . . . isn't it? Oh Christ, the exhaustion of not knowing anything. It's so tiring and hard on the nerves. It really takes it out of you, not knowing anything. You're given comedy and miss all the jokes. Every hour, you get weaker. Sometimes, as I sit alone in my flat in London and stare at the window, I think how dismal it is, how hard, how heavy, to watch the rain and not know why it falls.

Yes, all in all, a dreadful little show was being staged for me, up here on the twenty-first floor. I knew *that* at least. In his gilt sandals Lorne walked with poised uncertainty from one window to the other, his rapt face upturned, the hands both summoning and offering the revelations which the gods now fraternally distributed. Like all filmstars Lorne was about two foot nine (something to do with the condensed, the concentrated presence), but the old prong was in good nick, you had to admit, with that tan-and-silver sheen of the all-American robot-kings. Yeah, that was it: this isn't a man, I kept thinking, it's a mad old robot, all zinc and chrome and circuitry coolant. He's like my car, he's like the fucking Fiasco – way past his best, giving everyone grief, and burning up money and rubber and oil.

Lorne had gone on to explore Garfield's sumptuous lifestyle, the art galleries he superintended in Paris and Rome, his opera-nut vacations in Palma and Beirut, his houses in Tuscany, the Dordogne and Berkeley Square, his Barbadian hideaway, his stud ranches, his Manhattan helicopter pad . . . And as this fizzy old dog bayed and barked into the night, I spared a tender thought for my project, my poor little project, which I had nursed in my head for so long now. *Good Money* would have made a good short, with a budget of, say, £75,000. Now that it was going to cost fifteen million dollars, though, I wasn't so sure. But I must keep a grip on my priorities here. A good film didn't matter. *Good Money* didn't matter. Money mattered. *Money* mattered.

'Lorne,' I said. 'Lorne! Lorne? Oh *Lorne*?'

'Rubies, diamonds, emeralds, pearls, and an amethyst worth one-and-a-half million dollars.'

'Lorne.'

'Speak your mind, John.'

'Lorne. If Gary's so rich, who cares if he's got a couple of million dollars' worth of heroin in the kitchen?'

'Pardon me?'

'It cuts down on the drama, no? Think a minute. Think a second. If Gary is rich, then so is Doug. Of course they give the heroin back. No problem. No film.'

'Bullshit! Garfield wants to give the heroin back. But the other guy, Doug you call him, he wants to keep it. Why?'

'Yeah, why.'

'Jealousy, John, jealousy. He's jealous of Garfield.'

For twenty minutes Lorne talked about jealousy, how powerful and widespread it was, and how a man like Garfield (I think he even said *Sir* Garfield at some point) was especially likely to promote such a feeling in one as low, as weak, as vile as Doug – Garfield, with his connoisseurship, helicopter pad, erudition,

Barbadian hideaway, and all the rest. This took another twenty minutes.

'*Plus*,' said Lorne, 'he's jealous of what I do for Butch.'

'Why? He can't be that jealous if he's fucking her too.'

'I'm glad you raised that. You know, John, I don't think – and I never have thought – that it's dramatically convincing that he should, that he should fuck her too, John.'

I stared heavily at him.

'It makes no sense. It just doesn't add up.' Lorne laughed. 'If Butch is fucking Garfield, how could she risk that happiness, that fulfilment, John, on a young punk like . . .' He shook his head. 'Okay. Over that we can argue. But my scenario still holds. The way I see it, Butch has never had an orgasm before she meets this wonderful guy, who shows her a world she's only dreamed of, a world of Othello jets and Caribbean mansions, a world of . . .'

I stared on. Time passed. Abruptly Lorne halted in mid-sentence, in mid-spangle, and said, 'I think it's time we talked about the death scene, John.'

'. . . What death scene?'

'Why, Lord Garfield's,' said Lorne Guyland. 'This is how it happens. The mob guys, they're torturing me, naked as I am. I fought like crazy but there were fifteen of the bastards. They want the heroin – they also want my cultural treasures from all over the world. But I tell them *nothing*. Now. As these cocksuckers torture me, Butch and Caduta are forced to watch. Maybe they're nude too. I'm not sure. John, you might think about, about that. And these two women, as they see me, suffering, silent, naked, this guy who's given them everything and who's the greatest fuck they ever had in their goddam lives – these women, these simple, nude women, they forget their rivalry and weep in each other's arms. Credits.'

'Lorne,' I said, 'I've got to run.'

In fact it was another hour before Thursday let me out. The script conference ended with Lorne shrugging his robe to the floor and asking me, with tears in his eyes, 'Is this the body of an old man?' I said nothing. The answer to Lorne's question, incidentally, was *yes*. I just flourished an arm and clattered down the stairs.

Thursday gave a tight smile as she opened the door. 'Is he nude?' she asked coldly.

'Yeah he's nude.'

'*Oh* boy,' said Thursday.

Why do they happen to me, these numb, flushed, unanswerable, these pornographic things? Well, I guess if you're a pornographic person, then pornographic things happen to you.

I slanted west through the pretty East Side, with its decorative dustbins, the paunchy awnings of the low-slung stores, the smell of dark hot trash, and dined blind with Fielding Goodney and Doris Arthur in a loud and airless media restaurant just five blocks from bubbling Harlem. Doris's script was being gimmicked by the typists. I kissed her hand. I called for champagne. I demanded to see the rough. Teasingly they said I'd have to wait-see. There was a lot of teasing going on, I suspected. I was too smudged with booze and travel to be sure. Lorne had given me lots of nonagenarian whisky. I'll say that for Lorne. With additional champagne we drank to Dot's dream script. The place was full of filmstars, more filmstars. Why do I hang out with filmstars? I don't even like filmstars. Jesus, the transparency of actors. The professionals, though, are seldom dangerous. It's the actors of real life you want to watch – yeah, and the actresses. I developed a bad case of hiccups, more like a series of jabbing uppercuts to the chin. One of these blows actually ricked my neck and I had to lie on the floor beneath the table until it was okay to come up again. The angle of the lamp cord on the bar made me think I saw a hearing-aid cable extending from Fielding's ear. My knee brushed Doris's, once, twice, and I thought how wonderful it was when two young people started falling in love. I kept banging my way to and from the can, where they had incredible pictures of nude chicks from magazines all over the wall. I found a woman talking unhappily into a telephone and tried to cheer her up and went on trying even after her boyfriend or husband appeared from somewhere. I disliked his tone. He hurt my feelings. We had an altercation that soon resolved itself with me lying face-down in a damp bed of cardboard boxes at the foot of a hidden staircase. This was bad luck on the lady, who was obviously dead keen. Refreshed, I said hi to a few filmstars, briefly joining them at their tables with a selection of apposite one-liners. Invited into a back room, I shot the breeze with a married couple who said they ran the place. She was obviously a madame of some kind, not that this bothered me too much. She denied it. As Fielding led me back to our table I made a powerfully worded verbal pass at a salacious waitress, who appeared to be all for it but then came down with some deep sorrow in the kitchen, and when I burst through the double-doors to console her two men in sweat-grey T-shirts assured me there was nothing I could do for the poor child. I signed an autograph. Doris looked cute in her sleeping-bag outfit. Under the mussed hair and mace clothes she was just a big-eyed honey, a sack-addict and dick-follower, same as all the rest. She denied it too. You know, I really don't *like* her. I hollered for fortified wines and drank quarts of tongue-frazzling black coffee. Doris cuddled me on the way to the door but she must have let go for an instant (perhaps I goosed her too eagerly) because I went off on a run that would have taken me all the way downtown – further, to the Village, to Martina Twain – if the dessert trolley hadn't been there to check my sprint. The whole restaurant cheered me on as I fought my way out into the night.

I leaned panting against a lamppost, while Doris tenderly removed the segments of toffee orange and chocolate cake that still clung to my suit. Fielding lingered to congratulate – or compensate – the proprietress. What a *long* bit of New York, I thought.

'Jesus, are you okay?' she asked.

'I know you're a faggot and everything but I'll tell you what the problem is: you just never met the right guy. It's that simple. Let's go back to my hotel and fool around. Come on, darling, you know you love it.'

'You asshole.' Doris smiled. Then her face changed and she told me something so terrible, so strange, so annihilating that I can't remember a word she said. Fielding and the Autocrat made their different entrances. People's faces swung sideways as I tunnelled backwards into my cab.

And all this without much in the way of stress. *Stress!* How can people *stand* that stuff?

Waking bright and early the next morning I reached for a copy of *Delicacy* as the most economical means of establishing whether I was still alive. Other questions, no less pressing – such as who, how, why and when – would just have to wait their turn. Having come across no obvious Selina lookalike among the ladies, I found myself completing an editorial stress quiz, delete where inapplicable, in which your nicotine and alcohol consumption was set against various stress-donating hardships you might or might not be falling foul of. So far as *Delicacy* was concerned, I didn't have a care in the world, and yet I smoked and drank like a quadraplegic bankrupt. Then it hit me: stress – perhaps I need stress! Perhaps a good dose of stress is just

what I'm crying out for. I need bereavement, blackmail, earth-
quake, leprosy, injury, penury . . . I think I'll try stress. Where
can you buy some?

You *can* buy stress, and that's what I've started doing. It's New
York, I reckon, the thrust, the horsepower, the electrodynamics
of the Manhattan grid. It just charges you up. Give me a problem,
out here, and I'll crack it.

With a pleasant sense of maintaining the rhythm of the night
before and its various successes and achievements, I went down
to Mercutio's and bought four suits, eight shirts, six ties and a
stylish lightweight mackintosh. These garments now await the
guile of high-priced tailors before transfer to my hotel. Even the
ties seem to need taking out. Cost: $3,476.93. I paid through US
Approach.

At LimoRent on Third Avenue I hired a six-door Jefferson with
cocktail bar, TV and telephone. I drove it straight round the
corner and installed it in a costly carpark on Lexington and
Forty-Third. This would come out better than $150 a day.

I had a hundred-dollar lunch at La Cage d'Or on Fifty-Fourth
Street and a two-hundred-dollar massage plus assisted shower at
Elysium on Fifty-Fifth. Running low on ideas, and tired of shopping, all shopped out, I bought four drunks and three strippers
nine bottles of champagne in a topless bar on Broadway. I considered cabbing out to Atlantic City and dropping some dough at
roulette. I have the perfect system. It always fails. But in the end
I simply cashed my travellers' cheques and dodged the fuming
puddles of Times Square handing out twenty-dollar bills to
selected bums, whores, bagladies and time-cripples. Two
policemen were obliged to quell the minor riot that ensued. 'You,
you're fucking crazy,' one of them said to me, with maximum
conviction. But I didn't bother to tell him just how wrong he
was.

Back in my room, I sat at the desk and considered. Money worries aren't like other worries. If you're $10,000 in debt, it's twice as worrying as being $5,000 in debt but only half as worrying as being $20,000 in debt. Being $10,000 in debt is three-sevenths as worrying as being $23,333 in debt. And if you're $10,000 in debt, and $10,000 comes along – why, then all your worries disappear. Whereas the same can hardly be said of other worries, worries (for instance) about deception and decay.

I sank back on the bed and started worrying about money. I started to get very worried about money indeed. I yanked out my wallet and went through the credit slips and travellers'-cheque dockets. As of now, I don't have any money. And this is really *worrying*.

There was a knock on the door and I wriggled to my feet. An impossibly elegant young black scythed into the room with several polythene bodybags in his arms.

'On the bed, sir?' he asked.

'Yeah. No,' I said. 'I don't want them. I've changed my mind. Take them back.'

He looked at me quizzically, and raised his lordly chin. 'The terms of purchase are on your receipt, sir.'

'Okay. Sling them over here. I was only kidding.'

I gave him a ten and he left. A *ten* . . . For the next hour I took delivery of many additional purchases, the vast majority of which I couldn't remember purchasing. I just lay on the bed there, drinking. After a while I felt like Lady Diana would no doubt feel on her wedding day, as the presents from the Commonwealth contingent started arriving in their wagon trains. A squat kit of chunky glassware, an orange rug of Iranian prov-enance and recent manufacture, a Spanish guitar and a pair of maracas, two oil paintings (the first showing puppies and kittens asnooze, the second a nude, ideally rendered), an elephant's foot, something that looked like a microphone stand but turned out to be a Canadian sculpture, a Bengali chess set, a first edition of *Little Women*, and various other cultural treasures from all over the world. When it seemed to be over, I went to the bathroom and was explosively sick. Stress, it's expensive. There is great personal cost. But out it came, the lunch, the champagne, the money, all the green and folding stuff. When it seemed to be over, I went next door and called Fielding and asked him to give me an incredible amount of money. He sounded as though he'd been expecting my call. He sounded pleased. That evening a large envelope was brought to my room. It contained a platinum US Approach card, a brick of travellers' cheques, and a cash-facility authorization at a Fifth Avenue bank for a thousand dollars a day, if needed. I was so relieved I went to bed for two days. Actually, there wasn't much choice. Steady, I thought, steady. Money holds firm but you have no power. It seems that, whatever I do here in this world I'm in, I just get more and more *money* . . .

And more stress.

'Thanks again for the present,' I said. 'Just what I always wanted.'

'I'm trying to teach you something. Don't you understand?'

'Like what?'

'Many things. Compassion. Self-control. Generosity of spirit. Respect for womankind.'

'Go take a flying – Jesus,' I said, 'I'm beginning to see just how sick you really are.'

He laughed. 'Don't you love this?' he said. 'Say, that was so dumb that stunt you pulled. You can't give money away like that, man. You do it, you do it right.'

'Oh I get it, I've twigged at last. Okay, sickbag, how much do you want? What does it cost to keep you off my case?'

'Wrong. Wrong. I don't want your money.'

'Then what *do* you want?'

'I want your life.'

'Thanks again for the present,' I said. 'Much appreciated.'

'Have you read it yet?'

'Uh? Well, not exactly.' I had read nine pages on the transatlantic flight, but there was still some way to go. 'I've been ill. Look, when can we meet?'

'What do you do all day when you're ill?'

'Mostly I just lie there. Being ill.'

'I'm pretty free,' she said. 'Ossie went off to London again.'

'Great. How about this evening?'

'Will that give you enough time? To read the book, I mean . . . Hello?'

'I'm still here.'

'Come on, don't be feeble. I want a book report. I'm going to test you on it . . . Hello?'

'I'm still here.'

'Well then. You just call me when you've read that book.'

Wait. Watch . . . Yes, here she comes again. I have to tell you that a woman is following me around New York. Yes she is. This woman is fortyish, forty-five, square in the ankles, more than six feet tall on her heels, on her high heels. She watches me through a black veil that hangs from a black hat. Her hair is short, gingery and electrical. Her chin is low and stubborn and insane.

She works at night. I wheel out of a bar and there she is, arms folded in a doorway across the street. I walk along and she keeps pace and distance. I duck from beneath the spastic neon of a porno parlour, spotlit and anonymous, and there she is, eating popcorn or chestnuts from a paper cone. Sometimes, at the intersections, she comes so close that I can feel her breath on the back of my neck. But I don't turn. She reminds me of someone. I can't think who. Now where have I seen that mad bitch before? Wait. Watch . . . Yes, here she comes again.

They make straight for me, these people. They always have. Like animals, they sniff me out, like dogs. When the baglady enters the hushed cafeteria and threads steadily past the skewered tables, when the derelict stands and faces the oncoming crowds and arrives at his soft selection, we all know who they have in mind. I meet their eyes – I can't help it. Something in me says something to something in them. Something in them says something to something in me. What? There is spare material, there are loose components in our heads. We recognize this and move towards it. I think one or two people or things are moving towards me quite fast now.

'Hey my man,' said Felix in the lobby, running a thumb down my thin lapel. 'You know, I like his style. With this guy, it's a week on and a month off. What's happening?'

Auditioning was what was happening. I came down the steps of the Ashbery that morning and burst out laughing at the heat. New York can't be serious about this. I have read, or television has told me, about parts of space where the manmade boomerangs fly. It's hot out there, several million degrees Fahrenheit. Psychopathic heat. In New York, in July, the heat is psychopathic. On bucking Broadway the cabs all bitched and beefed, ferrying robots, bad dogs, uptown, downtown. I grabbed my trap and joined the shunt.

New York is a jungle, they tell you. You could go further, and say that New York is a jungle. New York *is a jungle*. Beneath the columns of the old rain forest, made of melting macadam, the mean Limpopo of swamped Ninth Avenue bears an angry argosy of crocs and dragons, tiger fish, noise machines, sweating rain-makers. On the corners stand witchdoctors and headhunters, babbling voodoo-men – the natives, the jungle-smart natives. And at night, under the equatorial overgrowth and heat-holding cloud cover, you hear the ragged parrot-hoot and monkeysqueak of the sirens, and then fires flower to ward off monsters. Careful: the streets are sprung with pits and nets and traps. Hire a guide. Pack your snakebite gook and your blowdart serum. Take it seriously. You have to get a bit jungle-wise.

Now I was heading, in my hot cage, down towards meat-market country on the tip of the West Village. Here the redbrick warehouses double as carcass galleries and rat hives, the Manhattan fauna seeking its necessary level, living or dead. Here too you find the heavy faggot hangouts, the Spike, the Water Closet, the Mother Load. Nobody knows what goes on in these places. Only the heavy faggots know. Even Fielding seems some-what vague on the question. You get zapped and flogged and dumped on – by almost anybody's standards, you have a really terrible time. The average patron arrives at the Spike in one taxi but needs to go back to his sock in two. And then the next night he shows up for more. They shackle themselves to racks, they bask in urinals. Their folks have a lot of explaining to do, if you want my opinion, particularly the mums. Sorry to single you ladies out like this but the story must start somewhere. A craving for hourly murder – it can't be willed. In the meantime, Fielding tells me, Mother Nature looks on and taps her foot and clicks her tongue. Always a champion of monogamy, she is cooking up some fancy new diseases. She just isn't going to stand for it.

I ungummed myself from the seat, climbed out and paid the driver through his side window – a London habit, and a bad one for New York. The old cabbie sat there unresponsively in his cage.

'Can't change the ten,' he said.

'What?'

'You read?' He pointed to the yellow sign – the one about the driver's helplessness in the face of any bill larger than five. 'Can't do it.'

'That sign must be ten years old. You never heard of inflation?'

'Can't do it.'

'Ah, keep the change. You guys have got to face up to things. You're just not being realistic.'

The cab moved wearily away. I looked up, across the street, and saw a series of sloped garage gangways, minded by the hulks of trucks. On the fendered pot-belly of one of these dead or fossilized machines sprawled the tanned torsos of three young men. Two were stripped to the waist, slabby, downy, while the third was just a leaning patchwork of studded leather and jean rag. The entrance to Fielding's loft, I now noticed, lay directly beyond them, through them, a numbered door between the big black slats . . . With a flourish I fastened the middle button of my new suit (off-white with charcoal seaming: I'm not sure about it – I wish you were here, I wish you were here to tell me it looked okay), eased my hands into my trouser pockets, and ambled loosely across the street.

Now I've never been given any bother by the gays. To an almost hurtful degree, I don't seem to be their type. It just doesn't come up. It just isn't a problem. But as I walked across the jarred and cratered road and sensed the usual quickenings of irony and aggression I also sensed something further – I sensed that my weight, my mass, my meat was being appraised, registered, scaled, not with lust, no, but with a carnal speculation I had never felt before. Christ, is this how you chicks feel? I stared dead ahead at the doorway, with the stirring men present but unpinpointed in my sight.

I walked past them.

'Reader,' someone seemed to say.

I paused. I hung my head. You can walk away but I cannot walk away. I turned, and asked with real interest, 'What did I hear you call me?'

'Breeder,' said the man. He held a kind of grappling hook between his legs. 'Big breeder.'

My head was full of good things to say – but I just snorted, and erased him with the flat of my hand, and walked on. Even this wasn't smart. Even this was jungle-dumb . . . I came through the door. Half-blinded by shadow I made out a steep wall of steps and moved towards it. Then behind me I heard the sounds of footsteps and stiff hinges and the death-rattle of shivering chains. I tell you, I went up those steps faster than a scalded faggot, propelled by a barbarous diuretic terror on behalf of my exposed rear end . . . The heavy door at the top didn't give until the fifth push, but by then I had turned, and seen the shrugging figures as they retreated into the light, and now I could hear only laughter.

I chested my way through and stood panting and blinking in a glass-walled theatre of spacious light, the air so dustless and oceanic that it showed you only the dirt in your human eyes. I steadied. Among the pine supports in the far corner stood Fielding Goodney, looking ridiculously suave and decisive – and somehow air-conditioned – in his jeans and fresh white shirt, in his suit of youth, and his money colour. He was issuing instructions to three workmen or caterers in tublike blue overalls. He acknowledged me with a flat palm upraised.

Waiting for my breath to find its heavy keel I took a turn around the hired loft. I lit a cigarette, whose first jab doubled me up with an unmufflable bark of outrage from my lungs. A tearful itch tickled my lids as spoked hangovers flashed past. Whew, this drinking deal, this drinking life-choice, it's very hard on those who choose it. I wandered on, striving to enjoy the light, passing hospitalic drapes and hoods, loose sections of electromagnetic silverboard, a workbench, a winded pinball table. Hung on the back wall were half-a-dozen milky seascapes. Whoever painted them saw life as clean as toothpaste, or pretended to. I turned, taking the sun full in the face. Up here with the high windows, Manhattan was hidden and you saw only the twin shafts of the World Trade Center, two gold lighters against the strong and pressing blue of the outer air. I shook my head. The mote in my eye, that dead spot where no light lives, wiggled its black finger at me.

'Hey, John. That's some suit. Where you headed? Alabamy?'

'Uh?'

'Anything the matter, Slick?'

'No. I just got razzed by some faggots. On the way in here.'

Fielding laughed, then thickened his brow attentively. 'And?'

'They called me a breeder, Fielding. What the hell is that supposed to mean?'

'Isn't it beautiful?'

'Come on, this is no place to audition. There are going to be little actresses walking through that breakers' yard down there.'

'No, John, they'll come up through the front,' said Fielding, his arm on my shoulder now as he steered me across the floor. 'There's just a gentle little cookie store down there, and a nice elevator. I had you come up the back way.'

'What for?'

'It's educational. Now relax with a drink, Slick, and get yourself ready for the girls.'

This was Fielding's best possible response. We moved on to the shallow stage, where Fielding had installed a raft of video equipment (with two pistol-grip cameras), a stereo, a coffee-table space game, a fishtank, two sofas facing two low steel desks, and a fat little fridge. I like new furniture. I like brand-new furniture. I had my fill of fucking antiques when I was growing up in

Pimlico, and in Trenton, New Jersey. But it has to be plain, you know? Fielding knelt and ticked a fingernail against the sedimented glass of the fishtank. I look into that fishtank, me, and all I see is new furniture of a different kind, studs and beads and zebra flashes, bouncy frills and fruity bobbles, Barry's lounge, Vron's boudoir.

'All the fish respond to the manoeuvres of the alpha fish,' said Fielding, his valved face reflected in the glass. 'That's the alpha fish – there, with the black tail.' He looked at his watch, and straightened. 'Now today we cast the girl, the stripper.'

'The dancer?' I said. 'What about Butch?'

'You know Butch is in. I know Butch is in. You know she's a dancer. I know she's a dancer. These girls, they don't know nothing. You read me, Slick? We're going to have some fun.'

And we did too. What with the jug of Red Snappers that Fielding had prepared, I was feeling no pain when the first candidate came flouncing across the floor. She was a big dark honey with the best . . . no, hang on. Maybe we kicked off with that hot blonde who took her . . . No. It was the black chick whose . . . Anyway, after a while, during that sun-bleached, snowblind vigil of booze and lies and pornography, the girls tended to mangle and dismember in my mind. The routine was the same, and Fielding had them in and out of that door like a chainline vaccinator. It's a time-honoured custom in our industry, the easygoing atmosphere you try to create while auditioning young women for roles of an erotic nature. Terry Linex of C. L. & S., for example, has a particularly telling line. He just says, 'Right. This is a sex scene. I'll be the man' . . . Boy, were they ever eager, these mad, happy, Manhattan girls.

Across the floor they came, edgy as hell but mortally excited, the nerves spiralling to the ends of their hair, each with her special details of shape and shadow, of torque and thrust. We sat them down and gave them a drink and asked them the usual stuff. They didn't need prompting: you see, they really did think it was possible, likely, certain that money and fame had fingered them, that exceptionality had singled them out. They talked about their careers, their crack-ups, their prongs, their shrinks, their dreams. Fielding would let them drawl or quack away for five minutes, before asking, with a strategic glint: '– And Shakespeare?' Well, even I got a few laughs from their replies to that one. 'Yeh, I really wanna do Mrs Macbeth. Or *Anthony and Cleopatra*. Or *The Comedy of Errs*.' One girl, I swear, thought for some reason that *Pericles* was about a car-manufacturer. Another evidently believed that *The Merchant of Venice* was set in greater Los Angeles.

'That's very interesting, Veronica, or Enid, or Serendipity,' Fielding would say. 'Now. We'd like to have you take your clothes off please.'

'To music?'

'Sure,' he'd say, and reach for the tape.

'I'm not really dressed for it.'

'Come on, Maureen, or Euphoria, or Accidia. You're an actress, right?'

And, revealing their teeth first, the girls would go through their hoops. I watched through a sheen of shame and fear, of lust and laughter. I watched through my pornographic sheen. And the girls submitted to it, to the pornography. Professional city-dwellers, they were experienced in the twentieth century. They didn't dance, they didn't tease – they didn't strip, not really. They took most of their clothes off and gave you a lesson in their personal anatomy. One of them simply lifted her skirt, lay on the floor, and had a handjob. She was the best. We received two apologetic refusals in a busy three days. Fielding said it was the Shakespeare that got them going, something to do with the exaltation caused by the tendered handclasp of art.

Every now and then I wondered whether Fielding was

promoting these girls in the other sense. But all he ever said was 'Here's her number, Slick' or 'John, she goes for you' or 'I think you might look good on her.'

'How do you look on Doris?' I asked him, during a lull.

'On Doris? Doris is gay, John. You know that.'

'Where's her script, God damn it?'

'Patience, Slick. Stay icy calm. Oh and – you got to meet with Spunk Davis tonight. You got to ask him something. I warn you, it'll be a bitch.'

'What?'

He told me.

'No way,' I said. '*Oh* no. No. You ask him.'

'You're the one he respects, Slick. He has a hard-on for you a yard long.'

'Oh man,' I said. But by then there was another sexbox cruising down the floor towards us, and I was too fuddled and clogged to argue.

So you see, over these last few days I've had no time for *reading*. I've been too busy *auditioning*.

Mr Jones, of the Manor Farm, had locked the hen-houses for the night, I read, *but was too drunk to remember to shut the pop-holes . . .* I still don't know what pop-holes are. I've asked around. Fielding doesn't know. Felix doesn't know. The dictionary doesn't know. Do you?

'Hi,' said a voice behind me.

I turned. 'Ah fuck off,' I said, and turned again.

I quit reading and looked round about me. This was no kind of place to be caught reading in: a macho gay bar in a five-fathom basement somewhere beneath the charred East Twenties. We were down so deep here, it felt like an inverted skyscraper. Maybe Manhattan would get like that one day – crustscrapers, corescrapers, a hundred storeys underground. Already certain less-than-fashionable New Yorkers have taken up residence in the sewers and subway shafts. They have. They've got little socks down there, with beds and chests-of-drawers. Money has driven them deeper into the planet, money has brought them down in the world . . . Round about me there was womanlessness, jawlines, crewcuts, hunks leathered up like frogmen, Adam in full stubble and muscle and sweat. All you needed in here among the shadows and sawdust was your maleness, your sour testosterone.

'Hi,' said a voice behind me.

I turned. 'Ah fuck off,' I said, and turned again.

Now this wasn't one of the heavy hangouts. I suppose your standard Manhattan faggot might look in here for a final white wine en route to a dungeon appointment or death-pact rendez-vous at the Water Closet or the Mother Load. But this was a dark place of gropes and whispers, of black silhouettes. Their shapes gave off no tremor or threat, more a priestly absorption in the radar of the appetites that had brought them there.

'Hi,' said a voice behind me.

'Ah fuck off,' I said, and turned. 'Oh hi! Sorry about that. How are you doing?'

'Good. You like this place? Look at you, you're terrified. Okay. What do you want to talk to me about?'

I took a deep breath – and heard the tiny tide of protest from the enemies in my lungs. He sat on the stool beside me. T-shirt, veined, tendoned biceps. He ordered a glass of water. Tap water, not designer water. He wasn't going to tangle with those bubbles, not Spunk.

Now I had to remember that this was a complicated young guy. He didn't drink. He didn't smoke. He didn't sniff. He didn't eat. He didn't gamble. He didn't swear. He didn't screw. He didn't even do handjobs. He did handstands. He did push-ups.

He did meditation and mind control. Born again, a true believer, he did charity work: he cared about the poor and the disadvantaged . . . Yes, all my man-management skills would be needed here. I looked into his clenched face and said,

'Spunk? It's about your name.'

'Yeah? What about it?'

'You're probably going to hate me for this.'

'I hate you already.'

'The thing is, Spunk,' I said, 'in England –'

'I know what you're going to say. I know what you're going to say.'

I waited.

'You want me to put an *e* in Davis. Well forget it, Self. Go get a whole new idea. I ain't doing it. No chance.'

'No,' I said, 'the Davis bit is fine. Spunk, you can keep Davis exactly as it is. Davis is fine. It's the other bit we have the problem with.'

'The other bit?'

'Is the problem, yeah.'

'You mean Spunk?'

'That's the bit I mean.'

He looked surprised, wrong-footed. I ordered another scotch and lit another cigarette.

'The thing is,' I said, 'in *England*, it means something else.'

'Sure. It means grit, pluck, courage.'

'True. But it also means something else.'

'Sure. It means fight. Guts. Balls.'

'True. But it also means something else.'

'What?'

I told him. He was devastated.

'I'm sorry, Spunk, but that's the way it is.'

His young face dipped and trembled, with toothache creasing in the corners of the eyes. Why hadn't anybody told him this before? They probably never dared, I thought, and shrugged, and drank my drink.

'I mean,' I went on, 'if you were working with an English actor called, I don't know, Jizz Jenkins or something, you'd have to –'

'To hell with England. What do I care about England?'

'It's a problem, you admit . . . You could just change it a little. How about Spank?'

'Spank? Give me a break. What kind of a name is *Spank*?'

'There are quite a few American names like that. Skip. Flip. Rip. Trip. Hank. Hunk Davis,' I said experimentally. 'Or Bunk, or Dunk, or Funk, or . . . Junk, or Lunk, or –'

'You say one more word and I'll rip my ears off.'

'Or Punk,' I said. 'Or Unk.' I considered. When you come to think about it, it doesn't seem to be a very popular noise, that *unk* sound.

Suddenly Spunk slid to his feet. Holding my tie as if for balance, he let me have his actor's stare, right between the eyes. This went on for a long time. I think he was trying out his thought-control on me, though I couldn't be sure. Then with the chunky knuckles of his right hand he sent his full tumbler of water surfing Western-style up the skiddy steel bar. The glass wobbled to a halt, inches from the edge of the cliff.

'Spunk –?' I said.

But Spunk just walked away.

Coolly I ordered another drink, and swivelled on my stool. If Spunk had been hoping to rattle me by picking this place for a venue, then Spunk was out of luck. I'm used to all that by now. What with the diesels, bull faggots, strippers, cross-dressers and money-lovers I have to work around, I can't get worked up about abnormality any more. The world wavers. Who's straight? Are you? Is Martina Twain? . . . I looked this way and that – the faces, the shoulders, the hands. Me, I have no faggot history whatever.

I have no faggot past. But who knows these days? Maybe I have a big faggot future. As a faggot, I might be a roaring success.

Hey, you guys, you gays who made the break. I mean you out there, not you in here. So you decided to go it alone. You decided to butch it out. What's it like, without them? Just think: no weather. No lunar wind or rain, no biology. A temperate zone. Full of blokes. Humanity having been halved like that, is it reassuring, the sameness of it all? Isn't it strange? Yeah and tell me something I've always wanted to know. Are there times when you *both* can't raise it? Do you get those me-neither nights? Well, it's been your century, you guys, I'll give you that. I heard recently that *Australia* has come whooping out of the closet. Australia! All those pumpkin-faced hicks and tripledecker beach hugies – they're all bumboys now. What's happening, God damn it? Some people blame the women. I blame the men. The first sign of bother, after a carefree fifty million years, and we throw up our hands and go gay? Now is this any way to behave? I mean, how faggy can you get? Come on, you guys, don't run out on me like this. Where's the old cave spirit? Don't surrender. Don't desert. What's the problem. They're only *women*, after all.

I ordered another drink. Glancing sideways I saw something strange, something anomalous: a girl, a plump little bobbysoxer. edging tremulously down the bar towards me. She couldn't have been more than sixteen, this poor lost child, in her brief pink skirt and jean bolero. Gay heads turned. She clambered on to the stool beside me and requested an orange juice from the unsmiling barkeep. I soon realized what I had to do. Why, I could see it all now. Back to her brownstone, an explanatory chat with her mum, a silent, grateful handclasp from her dad, a game of checkers with her little brother, and, as I took my leave, a royal knee-trembler in the rumpus-room.

'Hi,' I said.

She turned. 'Ah fuck off,' she said, and turned again.

Actually, I took her advice. I had a few tyre-sized pizzas in a Mongolian snack-bar, and cabbed back to the hotel. I then had dinner at the Barbarigo, my local Italian joint. Big day tomorrow. I'm seeing Martina, so I've got a lot of *reading* to get done.

Martina's present was called *Animal Farm* and was by George Orwell. Have you read it? Is it my kind of thing? I positioned the lamp and laid the cigarettes out in a row. I then drank so much coffee that by the time I cracked the book open on my lap I felt like a murderer getting his first squeeze of juice from the electric chair. George Orwell changed his name from Eric Blair. I don't blame him. His book kicked off with the animals holding a meeting and voicing grievances about their lives. Their lives did sound tough – just work, no hanging out, no money – but then what did they expect? I don't nurse realistic ambitions about Martina Twain. I nurse unrealistic ones. It's amazing, you know, what big-earning berks can get these days. If you're heterosexual, and you happen to have a couple of bob, you can score with the top chicks. The top prongs are all going gay, or opting for pornographic berk women. At the animals' meeting, they sing a song. Beasts of England . . . I went and lay down on the sack. My head was full of interference. I need glasses. I need a handjob. But I must get on with my reading. The big thing about reading is, you have to be in condition for it. Physical condition, too. This body of mine is a constant distraction. Here I am, trying to read, busy reading, yet persistently obliged to put my book aside in order to hit the can, clip my nails, shave, throw up, clean my teeth, brush my rug, have a handjob, take an aspirin, light a cigarette, order more coffee, scratch my ear and look out of the window. I started reading again. At the animals' meeting, they sing a song. Beasts of England. It was oppressive, it was very oppressive, the heat up here in my room. I went and inspected my back in the mirror. All healed now, except for that wound that got inflamed, enraged. The wound is much angrier than I am. I'm prepared to laugh the whole thing off, but this wound in my back still looks really furious, really pissed. I started reading again. I went on reading for so long that I became obsessed by how long I had gone on reading. I called Selina. Six a.m. over there – isn't it? – and no answer. She'll just say she disconnected. Bitch. I started reading again. At twelve forty-five I'm due across town to lunch with Caduta Massi at the Cicero. But it's still only eleven fifteen. I started reading again – I always was reading, or at least quite a few pages seem to have gone by. I must admit, I admire the way in which Orwell starts his book fairly late in, on page seven. This has to work in your favour. Reading takes a long time, though, don't you find? It takes such a long time to get from, say, page twenty-one to page thirty. I mean, first you've got page twenty-three, then page twenty-five, then page twenty-*seven*, then page twenty-*nine*, not to mention the even numbers. Then page thirty. Then you've got page thirty-*one* and page thirty-*three* – there's no end to it. Luckily *Animal Farm* isn't that long a novel. But novels . . . they're all long, aren't they. I mean, they're all so *long*. After a while I thought of ringing down and having Felix bring me up some beers. I resisted the temptation, but that took a long time too. Then I rang down and had Felix bring me up some beers. I went on reading.

I returned from my lunch break at a quarter to five, in excellent form, having looked in at a bar or two on my way back across town. Three hours and a hundred and twenty pages to go. Ninety seconds per page: no sweat. Caduta Massi didn't give me any trouble either, up in her vast suite. I just sat there nodding along with her old Prince Kasimir (still on the mend from World War II) while Caduta talked like a folksong about kids, mums, birth, the seasons, and her own Tuscan hills, where the grass grows, the wind blows, and the sky is blue. Over there on the slopes of Caduta's homeland, apparently, spring is a time of renewal, the soil gives forth fresh life, the buds quicken and the sap rises in the young trees. 'Now I shall leave the men together to enjoy their coffee and port, free of a woman's chatter,' said Caduta, and disappeared. Kasimir and I sat drinking heavily in total silence for forty-five minutes, until Caduta returned bearing three fat albums devoted entirely to her godchildren. Godchildren are the only kind of children Caduta's got, but, boy, has she got a lot of godchildren. I sat close to her on the sofa and sneaked in many a filial caress . . . By now the book and I were bowling along. This reading lark, it's a doddle. My theory is that whisky helps. Whisky is the secret of trouble-free reading. Either that, or *Animal Farm* must be unusually easy to follow . . . The only thing that puzzled me was this whole gimmick with the pigs. Pull the other one, mate, I kept saying to myself. I mean, how come the *pigs* were meant to be so smart, so civilized and urbane? Have you ever *seen* pigs doing their stuff? I have, and believe me it's a fucking disgusting experience. I checked out these pigs when I was on a farm making a commercial for a new kind of pork-character rissole. I almost walked off the set when I realized what I'd have to be working with. You should see these hairy-jawed throwbacks, these turd lookalikes, honking and chomping at the trough. To eat your girlfriend's tail when she isn't looking – that counts as good behaviour, that counts as old-world courtesy, by the standards of the sty. And when I think of what they get up to in the hay even I have to shudder. I tell you, it's no accident that they're called *pigs*. And yet Orwell here figures them for the brains behind the farm. He just can't have seen any pigs in action. Either that, or I'm missing something.

★

The creatures outside looked from pig to man, I read, *and from man to pig, and from pig to man again; but already it was impossible to say which was which.* Brill. I rang Martina and mellifluously arranged to meet her at the Tanglewood on Fifth Avenue. She made some footling objection – I can't remember what. I showered and changed and arrived in good time. I ordered a bottle of champagne. I drank it. She didn't show. I ordered a bottle of champagne. I drank it. She didn't show. So I thought what the fuck and decided I might as well get loaded . . . And, once that was accomplished, I'm afraid I have to tell you that I threw caution to the wind.

I grew up – or got bigger – out here, out here in the US of A. Between the ages of seven and fifteen I was a resident of Trenton, New Jersey. I did all the stuff American kids did. I stowed my sandals and shorts and scored my sneakers and longs. I had buck teeth, big ears, cropped hair, and a squat bike with whitewalls and an electric horn. I pitched my voice somewhere in the mid-Atlantic. Alec Llewellyn tells me that on occasion I still sound like an English disc jockey. I don't remember everything seeming big out here but I remember everything seeming small when I returned. Cars, refrigerators, houses – pinched, derisory. Out here I collected many subliminal tips on wealth and gratification. I did the groundwork for my addictions to junk food, sweet drinks, strong cigarettes, advertising, all-day television – and, perhaps, to pornography and fighting. But I don't hold that against America. I don't blame America. I blame my father, who shipped me out here soon after my mother died. I blame my mother.

I hardly remember her. I remember her fingers: on cold mornings I would stand waiting at her bedside, and she would extend her warm hand from beneath the blankets to fasten the cuff buttons of my shirt. Her face was . . . I don't remember. Her face stayed beneath the covers. Vera was always poorly. I only remember her fingers, her fingerprints, her blemished nails and the mark of the white button on the contours of the tip. Presumably I couldn't fasten my own cuffs. I seemed to need the human touch. I'm going to burst into tears in a moment but I'm not going to. Actually I was never going to, and never will. I seemed to need something to remember her by, and what have I got? Only her fingers and the difference in the house, the judgement, the shame, when she'd gone.

I liked my aunt and uncle, Lily and Norman, out in Trenton there. Vera, Lily, the sisters: their faces in the lost photograph look questing and American – wide smiles with inward-sloping top front teeth, funny bones, sweet teeth. The sisters look happily conscious of being sisters. There is gene enjoyment. *Here's to you, girls,* I always thought when I saw that photograph (where did I lose it?). *Have a good time.* Also the faces are frightened. They were twenty and twenty-one. I know the feeling. When you're young like that, the deal is – you keep looking confident while understanding nothing. The sisters came to England in 1943. I don't know if English husbands were what they were after, but English husbands were what they got. Lily went home again with Norman. Vera stayed, with Barry Self.

I liked my two cousins, Nick and Julie, who were younger than me. Nick and Julie liked each other too – they were younger, and turned into Americans in a way I never quite managed. Except when they were threatened and I fought or bullied to protect them, they usually preferred it if I wasn't around. Younger, not their fault. Yet I still feel the old exclusion. Where would *I* be in Animal Farm? One of the rats, I thought at first. But – oh, go easy on yourself, try and go a little bit easy. Now, after mature consideration, I think I might have what it takes to be a dog. I *am* a dog. I am a dog at the seaside tethered to a fence while my master and mistress romp on the sands. I am bouncing, twisting, weeping, consuming myself. A dog can take the odd slap or kick. A slap you can live with, as a dog. What's a kick? Look at the dogs in the street, how everything implicates them, how everything is their concern, how they race towards great discoveries. And imagine the grief, tethered to a fence when there is activity – and play, and thought and fascination – just beyond the holding rope.

I have always understood that America is the land of opportunity. Vigorously mongrel, America is a land with success in its ozone, a new world for the go-getters and new-broomers, a land where fortune grins and makes the triple-ring sign . . . Yeah. Or not. Uncle Norman – he started out in the dry-goods business, in a small way, of course. Norman worked hard. The days were long and sweet. Years passed. And nothing happened. He was still in a small way in the dry-goods business. So he sold the concern and poured all his energy into household appliances. He failed again. Household appliances didn't seem to care whether he poured all his energy into them or not. He tried his luck in the timber yards. Failed at that, didn't have any luck. At this point Norman threw a curve: he took a mortgage out on the bungalow and put every cent he had into ventilation engineering. Ventilation engineering swallowed the money up with no trouble at all and didn't give any back. Then he did the really hard thing. He came home.

I was returned to my father, at the Shakespeare, fifteen now and as big as Barry. I went out to work, which suited me right down to the ground. My small family scattered. Lily has married again: she helps her husband run a delly in Fort Lauderdale. Julie is married, too, with kids, up in Canada somewhere. Nick does God knows what in the Gulf – Qatar, I think, or the Emirates. Norman is in a home. I reckon he would have gone there whether he failed or not. A kind, baffled man, always scheduled for great confusions. It was written. Norman is the man that I owe money to. I once sent him some. They sent it back. In a home – that's the only place where money isn't worth anything one way or the other.

I felt big and eager, at fifteen, and willing to use any talent I had. In the early mornings I would hump crates with Fat Vince. All day I ran messages at Wallace & Eliot. In the evenings I would help Fat Paul dribble the drunks out of the public bar, there, at the Shakespeare. I . . . I don't quite see why I tell you this. It's all so far back in my time travel. Points of a journey do not matter when the journey has no destination, only an end. On the streets the women click – they are ticking through their time . . . It happened, but now this is happening. Like the vanished Vera the past is dead and gone. The future could go this way, that way. The future's futures have never looked so rocky. Don't put money on it. Take my advice and stick to the present. It's the real stuff, the only stuff, it's all there is, the present, the panting present.

'What happened to you?' I asked the telephone. I was all prepared to be big about it.

'. . . I didn't show up.'

'Yes, so I seem to recall.' I waited. 'Why didn't you?'

'No point. I tried to cancel on the telephone but you weren't listening.'

I waited. 'I waited,' I said.

Martina sighed. 'You were drunk. You know, it's quite a lot to ask, to spend a whole evening with someone who's drunk.'

. . . I had always known the truth of this, of course. Drunks know the truth of this. But usually people are considerate enough not to bring it up. The truth is very tactless. That's the trouble with these non-alcoholics – you never know what they're going to say next. Yes, a rum type, the sober: unpredictable, blinkered and selective. But we cope with them as best we can.

'Meet me tonight. I won't be drunk, I promise. Look, I'm really sorry about last night.'

'Last night?'

'Yeah. Things got a little out of hand.'

'Last night?'

'Yeah. I don't know what came over me.'

'It wasn't last night. It was the night before. Call me at eight. I'll be able to tell. If you're drunk then I'll just hang up.'

Then she just hung up.

Now I'd felt some queasy queries posed my way as I climbed out of bed, and undressed slowly before the window's span, sensing huge chemical betrayals and wicked overlappings up there in the spilled sky. I had even said to myself, Christ, it's another of those inner eclipse deals – but then Felix appeared with my breakfast, and wished me good morning, and all seemed well. Apart, that is, from the food. My omelette looked docile enough on the plate, yet it soon took on strange powers of life.

I buzzed down for Felix and summoned him to Room 101.

'Now look, kid,' I said, pretty stern. 'Why did you let me oversleep like that yesterday? You're supposed to look out for me. Time is money. God damn it, Felix, I'm a busy man.'

'Huh?' said Felix, tipping his head. 'Man, you weren't even *here* yesterday. I thought you gone away for the weekend or something. You got in last night. Late.'

'Drunk?'

'Drunk?' And here he began his smile. 'Downstairs they don't agree but me I think it was the best yet. You had a party hat on your head. You whole face was covered in lipstick. *Drunk*? They ain't got a word for where you were at. You gone and beat yourself up with that bottle. You were – you were just dead.'

This was a real bitch, no error. I could remember nothing to speak of about last night, yesterday, or the night before. Worse, I could remember nothing at all about *Animal Farm*.

Whatever I got up to yesterday has given me a boil on my ass – and a big 'un, too. I've had some boils on my ass before, but this mother has to be the daddy of them all. Boy, is this a big boil. I thought that these characters had gone out of my life along with circle-jerks and slipped octaves. Apparently not, apparently not. It must be the booze, it must be the junk, it must be all the pornography . . . I feel as though I'm sitting on a molten walnut or a goofball of critical plutonium. Amazing, even flattering, to think that the body still harbours this stinging volatility, these spiteful surface poisons. It fucking hurts, too. If I turn my back on the uncensored mirror, touch my shins and peer through my parted legs, like a scowling pornographic come-uppance, then I get a pretty good view, thanks, of this purple lulu scoring its bullseye on my left buttock. It really means business. It isn't messing about. No wonder they call them *boils*. Oh, brother, sometimes, bathrooms, familiar as the body itself or just rented like this one, with sheets of doublehired reflection, spotty steel, the shower curtain as wrinkled as an elderly raincoat, they take you back twenty years and make you question whether you have travelled at all . . . Lying down is okay. Walking hurts, standing hurts, sitting hurts. Abiding hurts. It must be the booze, it must be the junk, it must be all the pornography.

So my day became a strange one of tracing paper and invisible ink. I sat there reading, re-reading, and sieving my mind and room for clues and taunts. Beasts of England. Boxer, the big drudge. The face-flannel in the bathroom looked like a roller-towel in a busy cat-house: where did that lipstick come from? Whose lips imparted it? She could only have been a professional. No one kisses me willingly any more. Squealer, the liar. It must be the booze, it must be the . . . As I bathed my boil (whew – my ass was never one of the world's great sights but it's a real clock-stopper now) I couldn't help thinking of the Happy Isles: She-She – she did it. I have a confession to make. I might as well come clean. I can't fool *you*. The truth is, I – I haven't been behaving as well as I've led you to believe. No doubt you suspected that it was all too good to be true. I've gone back to Third Avenue, not to the Happy Isles but to places like it, to Elysium, to Eden, to Arcadia – no more than once a day, I swear to God, and only for handjobs (and on the days when I'm ill or unusually hungover I don't go there at all). I go to adult movies on Forty-Second Street instead. I go to porno-loop parlours. There is no kissing in hard core. Come to think of it, there is no kissing in Third Avenue either. There is French and English, Greek and Turkish, but no kissing. I must have paid extra for this perversity. I must have paid through the nose. Ah, I'm sorry. I didn't dare tell you earlier in case you stopped liking me, in case I lost your sympathy altogether – and I do need it, your sympathy. I can't afford to lose that too. Napoleon, the bully: this pig likes his apples. I found a bookmatch in my jacket pocket: Zelda's – Dinner and Hostess Dancing. Where else have I been? Maybe I should ask the woman who trails me around New York. She'd know. I found a three-pack of condoms in my wallet, two joint-ends in my turn up, and a cocktail stick in my rug. Is it any wonder I've got a boil on my ass? It must be the booze, it must be the junk, it must be all the pornography.

You know (and the afternoon is now tilting past me in strictest blue, and the book is also turning on itself and getting nearer to being over), I lie here and cower to a sense of cautionary justice in matters of the body – and maybe there simply isn't any, any justice. Think of the nun who wears her grey skin and its no-sex cosmetic as she twists with curse-pains and life-change in her standardized cell. Certain children are perfectly capable of dying young from old age. Deprived of their zinc or iron, their manganese or bauxite, impeccable stoics start to crackle and fizz. The foes of my body are legion, and far more vicious than my sins. They have the organization. They have the finance (who tabs them?). They have infantry, spies and snipers, street-fighters, minefields, chemical-weapon systems, thermonuclear devices. And they have more than this, for now my body monitor in intensive care is playing space invaders too, with swarmers, mutants, baiters, bristling zipships and twanging smartbombs. Hell, we're all up for grabs. And spare a thought also for the peeping tom with his twenty-twenty vision, the sprinting veering mugger and his good, his excellent heart, the X-rated moviestar with his thick rug and flat belly, the charming child-murderer and his sterling smile.

How can you grow up, with a boil on your ass? Who would take you seriously? A joke is being played, at my expense.

It must be the booze, it must be the junk, it must be all the pornography.

'Actually I quite enjoyed it. What next? *Rupert the Bear*? Come on, give me a break. How about a real book next time? Porker and Squeaky and the rest of the guys. I'm too old for animal stories. I mean, we don't have to start that far back, do we?'

For all its offhand delivery, this speech had been pretty shrewdly rehearsed. I expected Martina to shrug and apologize and put me on to something harder. She would be impressed, a little stung and chastened perhaps, by the restless brainpower she had started to awaken. I met her gaze. Her bruised, active eyes were flooding with consternation, with delight. *Fuck*, I thought. *Animal Farm* was a joke all along.

'You know it's an allegory,' she said.

'What?'

'It's an allegory. It's about the Russian Revolution.'

'What is?'

She explained.

Now this was a shaker, no two ways about it. The Russian Revolution wasn't exactly news to me – well, I gathered that they'd had a major rumble and rethink over there, early on in the century sometime. But this allegory deal had certainly caught me napping. I listened as Martina talked on. That big horse Boxer – he was the peasantry, if you please. Little Squealer – he wasn't just a pig, he was the propagandist Molotov. Did I know that Molotov was a pre-Revolutionary editor of *Pravda*? I did not. To hide my panic (and it *is* panic, panic in the face of the unknown), I threw in my criticism, the one about the pigs.

For some reason Martina had a good laugh about this too. Like most people she has two laughs, the polite reflexive laugh, and the real laugh. Martina's real laugh is the least ladylike I have ever heard – savage, childish, but symphonic, with competing levels and strains. Yes, she likes a good laugh, this Martina.

'I'm sorry,' she said. 'Actually pigs are cleverer than dogs. They have bigger brains relative to body size. That's what counts. Pigs are nearly as clever as monkeys.'

'You don't say,' I said. 'Well I don't know about you but it seems a hell of a way to live. I mean, if they're meant to be so smart . . . I mean, you have *seen* pigs, haven't you.'

'I like pigs,' she said.

She brought me a glass of white wine and parked me on the terrace as she went upstairs to change. It was my first drink of the day. I wasn't hungover. I was in withdrawal – but there were shards of despairing hilarity among all the sourness and static. Martina's terrace had a lot of flowers on it, in pots and tubs and wall-brackets, big ones, small ones, red ones, blue ones, supervised by corpulent bees, their shields as rich and shiny as dark pebbles in running water. Metallic, superdynamated, these creatures of the lower air moved about me like complicit demons, so heavy that when they hovered they seemed to be idling from invisible threads. I welcomed their company. They wouldn't waste their suicide stings on me. Below lay the checkered decks of half-paved back gardens – fishponds and weak fountains, curlicued furniture, an overalled woman with ticking scissors. The birds of New York shivered and croaked among the bent branches. The birds of New York have more or less given up the ghost, and who can blame them? They have been processed by Manhattan and the twentieth century. A standard-issue British pigeon would look like a cockatoo among them – a robin redbreast would look like a bird of paradise. The birds of New York are old spivs in dirty macs. They live off charity and welfare handouts. They cough and grumble and flap their arms for warmth. Declassed, they have slipped several links in the chain of being: it's been rough all right. No more songs or plump worms or flights to summer seas. The twentieth has been a bad century for the birds of New York, and they know it.

'Are you all right down there?'

I tipped my chair back. Martina's face, veiled by the hanging brushwork of her hair, inspected me from an upstairs window.

'No,' I said, 'it's heaven down here.'

The face withdrew silently. And so I sat out on the terrace in the hot dusk, drinking wine among the puppet bees.

We ate in. This spooked me somewhat. I had booked a fashionable table at the Last Metro on West Broadway, and was generally keen to push out some dough. 'Cancel,' said Martina. And I cancelled. She made dinner. Omelette, salad, fruit, cheese. White wine. The two-floor apartment presented itself as the ordered setting for healthy and purposeful lives. Books, paintings, desk surfaces, a typewriter, a chess set, a tennis racket standing easy against the closet door. Upstairs Ossie's fresh

clothes would be set out in lines and stacks . . . The tall Martina
wore a V-necked jersey and a blue denim skirt. She has a useful
hind-end on her, and she's blessed up top too, though perhaps
not as fulsomely as I imagined. No, it's her own body, not built
on any model. 'Let's stay in,' she had said. 'It's just nicer.' May
I be frank? Are you sure you want to hear this? Well I'll own
up now and say that I have always secretly suspected that what
Martina fancied was a bit of rough. That's right – me, in the
sack. It sounds unlikely at first, I agree. But people *are* unlikely
these days. It's happened. Twenty years ago she would have
settled for her home, her interests, her burnished husband. She
would have given me no headroom. But now? You just don't
know any more – you don't know, they don't know. Why has
she persisted in my chaos? I mean, what am I here for tonight.
My conversation?

Mind you, she always appeared to like me. I used to see them
around, in the Sixties, Ossie and Martina, the optimum couple.
He would help her down from the running-board of the Land
Rover they went about in, and the tall pair would advance hand
in hand into the marquee or theatre foyer or converted tramshed
or through the doors of the favoured restaurant or speakeasy or
eel-and-pie shop. They turned heads, those two. Part of their
glamour lay in the firm fact they were so eminently and maturely
a *couple*, rich but clean, while the groundlings were alleycatting
around or blitzed on drugs: LSD, dope – yeah, and penicillin.
Ossie was an actor then. He did Shakespeare. I wonder what she
thinks, now that he's just a moneyman, like everyone else. I knew
Martina from way back at film school, and I used to amble up
with whatever stylist or make-up girl I was squiring and say hi
to the talented team. It did my rep a lot of good. Martina always
seemed pleased to see me. Perhaps she fancied a bit of rough,
even then.

So, towards the end of dinner, as Martina stood at my side

pouring out the last of the wine, I rammed my hand up her skirt and said, 'Come on, darling, you know you love it' . . . Relax. I didn't really. In fact I behaved doggedly well all evening. You see, I'd figured it out by then. Oh, I knew what her angle was – I knew what this Martina Twain character was after. Friendship. Friendship: no sex or duplicity or complication, no money, just frictionless human contact. Well that's no fucking use to me, is it, I thought at first. I was out of my mind with sobriety, teetotalled – I felt lightheaded, I felt downright drunk, eating dinner up here with this sicko who saw nothing in me but myself. Jesus, what kind of pervert am I dealing with now? And yet I steadied, and the talk came freely enough. It takes all sorts, I concluded with a shrug, and resigned myself to the whole deal. Besides, I had this boil on my ass.

I did try a gimmick on her, though, as I took my leave at eleven thirty. The best women, sometimes, are the most neglected, and you never know your luck.

'Oh yeah,' I'd just said. 'Give me another book to read.'

'All right, hang on then.'

It was 1984 – by George Orwell again.

I raised a finger at her. 'No animals?'

'No. Just a few rats.'

'Any allegory?'

'Not really.'

'Say,' I said (and here was my gimmick): 'I had a swell dream about you the other night.'

Normally, with this line, in my experience you get either coy withdrawal or outright panic, depending on the dame. But Martina merely gazed at me with level curiosity and asked,

'Oh yes? What happened in it?'

'Uh – well I was sort of rescuing you from Red Indians. Except they weren't red but white, with fair hair. I was rescuing you in my car. It's a Fiasco. And then the car wouldn't start.'

'What was so swell about it all?'

'Oh, then another car showed up and I drove you away in that. To safety.'

Actually this was my first deviation from truth. I *did* have a dream. What happened was, the Red Indians disappeared or went off somewhere else, the Fiasco was transfigured into a kind of playboy pad, Martina shed her cotton shirt and buckskins – and I loved her up pretty good on that oval sack.

'Yes, it was a real bitch,' I said, 'my car not starting like that.'

'It was probably drunk,' said Martina, smiling as she opened her door to let me out.

The adult movie was a period piece and more thoughtfully plotted than usual, all about a black plenipotentiary (Ottoman? Carthaginian?) and the appetites of his talented wife (Juanita del Pablo), who, with the help of her chambermaid (Diana Proletaria), puts out not only for her husband but for most of his army too, as well as the odd handful of servants, slaves, eunuchs, acrobats and, finally, executioners. He catches Juanita at it in the end, and throws her into some stock footage, where the lions get her. As I shuffled down the aisle with my Orwell and my pint, and as an hysterical voice-over blurbed the coming attractions ('. . . *starring Diana Proletaria, the Princess of Pawwun. Iss whyuld. Iss hat!'*), two black dudes climbed tiredly to their feet, rubbing their eyes.

'Man, I sure could use some of that BC. I wouldn't want to go back *too* long.'

'Yeah. A couple of weeks, maybe.'

'Two, maybe three. I wouldn't want to go back *too* long. But oh man I sure could use some of that BC.'

Five minutes later I was in a gogo bar on Broadway, discussing inflation with an off-duty stripper called Cindi. If you'd asked me how I felt, I would have told you that it was a big relief – to be back in civilization again.

'I want to thank you, John,' said the telephone, 'for our date the other night.'

'Which night was that?'

'Saturday night. Or Sunday morning. Don't tell me you don't remember. We met. Kind of. You were very nice to me, John. You didn't try and kill me or anything. No, you were very dear.'

'Don't talk crap,' I said.

Frank the Phone again, giving me a hard time. Actually I was still deeply curious about Saturday night. The harder I tried to remember – or, let's be accurate, the harder I fought to keep memory away – the more convinced I became that something really bad had happened, something definitive, something life-wrecking. I think that was why I had drunk myself to pieces all through Sunday. To keep that memory away, away. But Frank the Phone I could handle. This wimp couldn't worry me.

'You find a bookmatch in your pocket? . . . Go find it again, John. I wrote a message for you inside.'

'Oh yeah? What?'

'Go find it, John. I want you to see the proof.'

I went to the wardrobe and frisked my suit. I had thrown nothing away. I never throw anything away. Here, the telltale bookmatch, valentine-pink, the colour of sweet lipstick: Zelda's – Dinner and Hostess Dancing. I snapped it open, and I got the message.

'Oh you sick bat,' I said. 'You poor idiot. Will you tell me something? Why are you doing this? Tell me again. I keep forgetting.'

'Oh it's *motivation* you want. You want motivation. Okay. Here. Have some motivation.'

Then he made his longest speech to date. He said to me,

'Remember, in Trenton, the school on Budd Street, the pale boy with glasses in the yard? You made him cry. It was me. Last December, Los Angeles, the hired car you were driving when you jumped that light in Coldwater Canyon? A cab crashed and you didn't stop. The cab had a passenger. It was me. 1978, New York, you were auditioning at the Walden Center, remember? The redhead, you had her strip and then passed her over, and you laughed. It was me. Yesterday you stepped over a bum in Fifth Avenue and you looked down and swore and made to kick. It was me. It was me.'

The Ashbery, Room 101, I sit with my big croc face flickering to the last veils of the late, late movie. I don't –

I don't remember the pale boy with glasses crying in the playground – but no doubt there were one or two, and I was a mean kid. There always are those pale boys . . . I *was* in LA last December, and I hired a car all right. There were near things, there were skids, emergency stops, emergency sprints. There always are those near things . . . I *did* hold auditions in the Walden Center in '78, checking out some models for the big-bim role in a Bulky Bar commercial. There must have been the odd redhead among them, and I was my usual working self (I'm an altogether different proposition when I'm working – I'm not very nice at all). There always are those redheads . . . I was a mean kid in 1978. I was a mean kid last year. And this.

Yesterday I was walking up golden Fifth Avenue towards the tawny gulf of the Park. The powerful stores were in full exchange, drawing people in, easing people out, superintended by the lean Manhattan totems, these idols or rock-statues that stare straight ahead in grim but careless approval of the transactions compounded in the street beneath. It was pouring money. On the pavement the monkeynut operatives and three-card trick artists, the thimble-riggers, hot-handbag dealers, contraband bandits – they all plied their small concerns. A lot of dinky women taking the goods and the air today . . . there's no shortage of big tits in Manhattan. It's not a problem. Nearly everyone seems to have them over here . . . Then I saw something you see pretty often over here too: a have-not, a real flat-earther, a New York nomad lying face down on the flag-stones like a damp log, sideways-on to the streaming spenders in their waves and sheets and racks. As I stepped over him I looked down (the rug as stiff as bark, an ear the texture of pomegranate peel) and said, rather affably I thought, 'Get up, you lazy bastard.' I walked on – and hailed Fielding as he strolled out of a bookstore. Arm in arm we gained the Carraway and met with two more of our moneymen, Buck Specie and Sterling Dun. They were both very excited by the venture and were alike convinced that I had a big future in our industry. Then we ate Jap and they all went off nightclub-bing in the Autocrat, but I was already massive and speechless with rice wine, and so I . . .

Zelda's – Dinner and Hostess Dancing. Inside was the message, the hand forward-sloping, tremulous, not unlike my own. Here in the States, in my day, writing lessons began with you tipping your pad forty-five degrees to the left, in order to promote this wavy, tumbling style. 'Frankie and Johnny were lovers', sealed with a kiss, a full lip-print in sweetest pink.

All in all, I'm none too clear what this guy means by *motivation*.

The new televisual intercom on the steel desk gave off its throt-tled bleep. Fielding pressed the button and waited for the picture to form. He looked mildly startled.

'Who's this?' I asked him.

'That's fine, Dorothea. Thank you. No, you just wait for our call.' Fielding sat down and said, 'Nub Forkner.'

'Good,' I said. With Spunk Davis going AWOL, with Spunk sulking and failing to return our calls, Fielding and I had decided to check out Nub Forkner as a possible reserve. I made a note of the name on my pad, for something to do.

'That's o-r-k, Slick,' said Fielding.

I glanced down at the page. 'That's what I've got.'

'. . . You read much, John?'

'Read what?'

'Fiction.'

'Do you?'

'Oh sure. It gives me all kinds of ideas. I like the sound and the fury,' he added enigmatically.

That's what reading does to you: you start saying things like that. 'Yeah,' I said, 'well I've been reading a novel by George Orwell. *Animal Farm*. Re-reading it, actually. Yeah and *1984* too.' Me and *1984* were getting along just fine.

'*Animal Farm*?' said Fielding. 'No kidding.'

Dorothea or whoever waved goodbye and clicked off to the far doorway buttoning up her shirt. We saw her shrink back momentarily before hurrying out into the hall. Nub Forkner ducked slowly through the entrance and paused with a sigh to re-amass his weight . . . Now I was far from familiar with Nub's work. True, I had dozed and belched my way through two films in which he featured – but at thirty thousand feet, in the refugee darkness of transatlantic aeroplanes. The press handout on my lap confirmed that Nub had played a Pawnee vagrant in *Whisky Sour* and a deaf mute in last year's cackle-factory spectacular *Down on the Funny Farm*. Both the vagrant and the mute, I seemed to remember, were outsize psychotics given to sudden and indiscriminate violence – big mothers, primal-scream specialists. Well, as Nub creaked across the joists towards us, with oil-strike hair shawling his shoulders, throwback knuckles grazing the floor, Fielding and I were clearly meant to think there was something unshirkably elemental about him, his cave shave, primal jeans, noble-savage beerbelly. You didn't need much of an eye for nutcases to tell that Nub was a real fizzer, all set to pop. He was about six five, 300 pounds. Yes, Nub looked pretty useful.

'Hi, Nub,' said Fielding drily. 'Why not take a chair.'

Why not indeed? Nub took a chair and sent it twirling sideways end over end with a negligent whipcrack of his wrist. Next, he picked up Fielding's snazzy egg-timer (used to pace the strippers) and stomped it to the floor. He bent down and extended an arm across the desk, ready to swipe it sideways over the high-tec tabletop. He looked up quickly and I saw that his face was full of expectant ingratiation.

Fielding climbed sharply to his feet. 'Easy, Nub,' he said.

Nub frowned and straightened. 'This is a fury scene, right?' he said in a deep calm voice. 'Male rage. I'm a method actor. I got to get furious first.'

The whole thing was a farce from the start. Nub was a one-role guy, a bearded lady. He was hopeless for us. Who'd believe that Caduta Massi could have produced this room-filler? How would he contrive to lose a fight to Lorne Guyland? Could you see him in the arms of Butch Beausoleil? Forget it. Nub would just have to hang around until the next fat-whacko part came along . . . But we had to test him, and he had to test us. He had to come here to see if his particular brand of rogue chemicals, his particular slant or version, was good for another few bucks. I suppose we sell whatever we have. Actors are strippers: they do it all day long. Fielding gave him the usual bullshit and at last he shuddered off across the floor.

'Great,' I said. 'Back to square one.'

'Don't be so easily discouraged, Slick. You know, Nub and

Spunk are both with Herrick Shnexnayder. I'm going to give Herrick a call. You fix the drinks. It's your turn.'

Fielding called Herrick Shnexnayder. He said he loved Nub's work and wanted to know what his availability looked like. Sums of money, low down in the six figures, were cautiously mentioned.

'Nub's availability looks good,' said Fielding, as he replaced the telephone and turned to the intercom.

'Yeah, I bet.'

'Ah come on, he might do for a heavy – the arm-breaker. Now will you take a look at *that*. Celly Unamuno. Mexican. Nineteen. Word is she's really hot.'

'Christ,' I said, 'I hope Butch Beausoleil doesn't find out about all this.'

'Relax. Hey, what do you make of Butch? Personally.'

'Don't tell me. You've checked her out.'

'I'm too young for her, Slick. She likes mature men. It's you she goes for.'

'The big thing about Butch – well, as she says herself, you know, just because you're young and talented and beautiful doesn't mean you can't be intelligent too. The big thing about Butch is that she's not just . . .' I paused.

'You guessed, huh?'

'What?'

'She's a moron,' said Fielding. 'The big thing about Butch is her ass. Hi there, Celly. Now you just sit down and make yourself at home. John? Where are those drinks.'

Twenty minutes later, as Celly was getting dressed again (she looked like a pornographic cartoon, a comic strip, except for the eyes, which weren't even twenty yet and could hardly be expected to hide their fear or helplessness), I stood up and moved like a ghost to the white window. I held the cold steel of the cocktail-shaker, and, watching the way my shoulders worked, you might have thought that I was shaking it. But I wasn't. I was just wondering, *I'm in hell somehow, and yet why is it hell?* Covered by heaven, with its girls and deceptions and mad-acts, what is the meaning of this white tent? I keep looking at the sky and saying, Yeah, I'm like that, so blue, so deeply blue. How come? I've done it before and I'll do it again. There are no police to stop you doing it. I know that people are watching me, and you aren't exempt or innocent, I think, but now someone else is watching me too. Another woman. It's the damnedest thing. Martina Twain. She's in my head. How did she get in there? She's in my head, along with all the crackle and traffic. She is watching me. There is her face, right there, watching. The watcher watched, the watched watcher – and this second pathos, where I am watched by her and yet she watches me unknowingly. Does she like what she is seeing? Dah! Oh, I must fight that, I must resist it, whatever it is. I'm in no kind of shape for the love police. Money, I must put money round me, more money, soon. I must be safe.

'Fielding,' I said, 'what are you doing to me? What? It's been twelve days. God damn it, where is that script?'

'Tomorrow morning, John. I guarantee it.'

The telephone rang, and I swore brutally – but it was the call that Fielding had been waiting for. Spunk Davis. I returned to the window as Fielding soothed and coaxed.

'Just like I figured. Shnexnayder was straight on to him. You see, Spunk hates Nub with a passion. A long story.' Fielding shrugged limply. 'Yeah, he's in. And Herrick's out.'

'That's good,' I said, and meant it.

'On one condition. Get this. He wants it to be a vegetarian restaurant.'

'In the film.'

'In the film. These guys . . .'

I laughed, and Fielding laughed too, his lovable, his loving laugh. As he showed me his clean back teeth (plump, kiddish, uninjured), I thought numbly, Christ, what a goodlooking guy. When I wing out to Cal for my refit, when I stroll nude into the lab with my cheque, I think I know what I'll say. I'll say, 'Lose the blueprints. Scrap those mock-ups. I'll take a Fielding. Yeah, give me a Goodney. Do me one just like him.'

As I've already mentioned, 1984 and I were getting on famously. A no-frills setup, run without sentiment, snobbery or cultural favouritism, Airstrip One seemed like my kind of town. (I saw myself as an idealistic young corporal in the Thought Police.) In addition, there was the welcome sex-interest and all those rat tortures to look forward to. Stumbling into the Ashbery late at night I saw with a jolt that the room I had hired was Room 101. Perhaps there are other bits of my life that would take on content, take on shadow, if only I read more and thought less about money. But I had no time for reading the next day. I was too busy *reading*.

At eleven o'clock Felix woke me with four smartly-bound volumes of *Good Money*, a screenplay by Doris Arthur based on an original idea by John Self. I ordered six pots of coffee and did my bathroom routines simultaneously, like a one-man band. I D-noticed all calls. I settled down, with the new anglepoise lamp staring interestedly over my shoulder. Reading – it's all I ever do these days. All I ever do is sit about the place *reading*. But this was different. This was work. This was money. '1. INT. NIGHT,' I read, and pressed on, feeling dangerously excited.

An in-form reader, an old hand at reading, I flapped through *Good Money* in just under two hours. Then I burst into tears, smashed a straightbacked chair, threw a full coffeepot at the door and kicked the base of the bed with such savage power that I had to run round the room with a pillow in my mouth until at last I staunched my screams. I couldn't fucking believe it . . .

Fielding was right in a way. *Good Money* was a dream script, wonderfully coherent, with oodles of rhythm and twang. The dialogue was fast, funny and seductively indirect. The pacing was beautiful. You could have gone out and shot the whole thing in a month. I sat at the desk with complimentary pen and pad. I started reading again.

I couldn't fucking believe it. Who's doing this to me? Who? First: Gary, the dad, 'Garfield' – the Lorne Guyland role. In the pre-credit sequence Lorne is glimpsed wearing dank pyjamas, carrying his clothes in a bundle as he is jeered from the marital bedroom. This is pretty well Lorne's best moment. After that it's all downhill. Although Lorne boasts constantly about his erudition, wealth and youthfulness, in reality (we find) he is illiterate, bankrupt and more or less senile. Yes, on his very last legs, is old Lorne. When he eventually blackmails the young dancer into the cot (a richly comic episode), old Lorne can't raise it. Raise it? He can't even *find* it. In his weepy frustration he takes a swipe at the sneering young beauty. She replies with a kick in the balls, and Lorne cracks like a broken stick. In the fight scene proper, an anoraked Lorne Guyland is given the hiding of his life, despite the fact that he surprises his sleeping co-star with a car-tool. His last, abject few lines are delivered from under a mummy-suit of plaster in an intensive-care unit. As for the son, Doug – as for Spunk Davis – well, to start with, his motive for hanging on to the mob heroin is as follows: he needs to fan the wildfire, the sparkling gorse, of his own narc habit, priced at a thousand dollars a day. A chain-smoker, a compulsive gambler, a hopeless lush and (what was Doris up to here?) a haggard handjob artist, Spunk also turns out to be a veritable guru or sorcerer of junk food, presiding over the vats in the restaurant kitchens with various lethal additives and glutinous flavourings. We are left to guess at the full extent of his sexual delinquencies, though in one haunting digression Spunk pays a 'charitable' visit to an orphanage with his mother: in a series of tight close-ups we see him doling out candy bars as he gooses and fondles the staring waifs.

Now for the ladies. If you were searching for a word to encapsulate the Caduta Massi character, then *sterility* would spring to your lips. The key to Caduta lay in how fantastically sterile she was. Boy, was she ever sterile! No extra kids for Caduta. No kids at all: Spunk himself (it crucially transpires) is her adopted son. Despite her husband's well-established impotence, and despite the on-screen celebration of her fifty-third birthday, Caduta kept talking about how many children she would one day bear. There were many symbolic moments in which Caduta gazed desolately at playgrounds full of laughing children or composed herself near jugs of wilted flowers. There was the visit to the orphanage. There was even a dream sequence where the fallow Caduta wandered alone in a boundless grey desert. How sterile can a woman get? Yes, you really felt for Caduta, what with this unbelievable sterility of hers. And Butch Beausoleil – the mistress, the dancer? I had expected Doris, as a fellow feminist, to honour Butch's single proviso. I had expected Butch to be spared the stock domestic chores, the dish-washing, the floor-sweeping, the bed-making. But no. So far as the Arthur screenplay was concerned, Butch could have been a representative figure called Drudgery in a commercial for labour-saving appliances. She peeled potatoes, lined dustbins, swabbed toilets. Even in the nightclub scenes Butch was forever rinsing glasses and ironing G-strings. Her chief dance routine featured a mime with mop and pail. And the other big thing about Butch? You guessed. You were there before me. A confident talker, full of ideas, Butch was none the less a person of sensationally low intelligence. A bushy-tailed, big-breasted meatball. A classic, a textbook dumb blonde: *that* was the big thing about Butch.

'Someone's fucking me *around*,' I said out loud, and felt my
boil burst.

Then I was off and running again.

I moved at speed through the first-floor vestibule where a dozing
flunkey stirred too late, through the antiques and gadgetry of
the tall inner chamber, and right up to the double doors of the
bedroom. I seized both knobs – and tugged . . . Fielding sat at
the foot of the bed in a black dressing-gown, unstartled. Behind
him, naked on the sheets, face averted, lay the hard dark body
of a young boy.

Now I'm as shocked as the next guy when I get a glimpse of
another's true appetites, but I was all fired up by then and I just
thought, So he's a faggot too, is he? *Right*.

'Come here.'

'Something the matter, Slick?'

He didn't look fazed, I'll give him that. He even yawned and
scratched his hair as he closed the door behind him. 'The *script*,'
I said.

'Yeah, don't you love it?'

'It's a disaster and you know it.'

'. . . How so?'

'The stars, the stars! They'll never touch that shit. It's all over.'

'Forgive me, Slick,' he said, pouring coffee from the tray, 'but
you're betraying your inexperience here. You want some? Take
a drink. The stars are all signed up. They'll do it. Or our attorneys
move in on this. You just have to assert yourself, John. You wanted
the realism. God damn it, that's why I went with you.'

'That's not realism. That's – it's vandalism.'

'Don't you see what we're sitting on here, Slick? *Good Money*
will be the only movie of the year, the decade, the era that will
show the real delirium of film, the nakedness of actors, what it
does to –'

'You've got the wrong guy. I can't work like this. Now I'm not fooling around. Doris goes. That bitch is in turnaround. She's sick in the head. I'll get the script I need – I'll get my man in, don't worry. Give Doris her dough and kick her down the stairs.'

Fielding paused and looked away. Here was a man who sees his deepest and most mysterious plans undermined, messed up, blundered with. He said lightly, 'Don't you think Doris should hear this?'

'Sure. Call her.'

'I'll do that.' And he called her. 'Oh, Doris?' he said.

And Doris Arthur came out of the bedroom wearing nothing but a pair of cool pants . . . Now, lit up as I was, this had to be registered and absorbed – and a compelling sight it was too. She walked over to the breakfast trolley, loosely swinging her arms with the ease of a seaside nine-year-old. For she had nothing to hide, nothing, nothing. The pants, on the other hand – and these were useful pants I'm talking about, useful by fetishist standards, let alone feminist ones – the pants contained a good deal: the high trembling rump, the frontal tussock with its own curious pendency, like a plum in a handkerchief waiting to be shined and shared. I suppose (I thought), I suppose she'll get proper tits when she has children, and then the, and then the whole –

'Okay now – right. Yeah,' I said, 'stick to fiction, Doris. You fucked it. You're out. Listen,' I told Fielding, 'it's this simple. She goes or I go. It's me or your chick. Jesus, if Caduta read one word of that crap. Or Lorne!'

'They're reading it now,' he said. 'I had copies limoed over this morning. You, Caduta, Lorne, Spunk, Butch.'

'Okay,' I said. This was my move, my shot. You can do it only once and you have to mean it. 'Now there's going to be a shit-storm from all four directions. And you're going to handle it, pal, because I'm flying out *tonight*. And I'll tell you something else. I'm not coming back. I don't care. I'll go back to C. L. & S. and make commercials and wait for the right deal. She goes or I go. She goes. Do it, or I'm walking out of here for ever.'

Fielding sat tight in his chair. Doris drank coffee unconcernedly, holding the cup with both hands. I turned.

And I walked. Down the long room, past the sofas, the glazed tables. On either side of the far door grey circuitry simmered, key banks and function consoles, a jukeboxful of floppy disks, the many screens showing printouts and readings in squat robot type . . . This walk to the door, I thought – it's good. Keep going. You're on the right track. I *do* mean it. I'll walk through the door and I'll keep walking, all the way to England, and I'll never come back.

'Slick,' said Fielding.

Now a paved park in midtown, with dampness and seepage showing between the flags, despite all the heat could do. The heat had done all it could, and failed. The building at the far end of this block-long concrete bower had a look of some austerity to it, with its strictly channelled cornerstones, but the square was anybody's, street-cultured, with blacks and buskers and birdshit, sax-players, pushers, jungle artists. By my side on the wooden bench, Martina Twain.

She had just been to some museum. Her skin shone with a museum pallor. For all the fruit and nut of her colouring, she has her moments of bloodlessness. Normally, of course, I would attribute this to the fact of my presence and proximity. But there was something else. Consulting my butch radar, I detected Ossie trouble. And I too was thinking of Selina. I had just called London, and the little bag-bantam was home for once. 'Yes,' she even said, 'no, that's good. Come back quickly' . . . This meeting with

Martina – I had called her in full travel flurry, in full escape posture, to say goodbye, and then I thought: wait, slow down. She sounded poorly, more poorly still when I said goodbye. So this silent meeting, with no progress, only presence, and maybe some comfort too. What are friends for, after all? What are they for? I've often wondered.

And I had other spurs to silence. Moviestars, they're evidently speedy readers. When I loped into the Ashbery after lunch, a tribe of adults converged on me and about a dozen things at once seemed to happen to my face. Someone spat in it, someone slapped it, someone swore at it, someone bunched a fist at it, someone waved a writ at it. There was the tearful Thursday, escorted by a Nub-sized black man in minder livery, who introduced himself as Bruno Biggins, Lorne's bodyguard. There was old Prince Kasimir, all set to fix a dawn meeting in Central Park. There was Herrick Shnexnayder, wearing his rug sundae, representing Spunk's interests. There was a hollering ghoul of a human being called Horris Tolchok – Butch Beausoleil's attorney . . . In the end I just made a run for it and holed up in a bar with a telephone on my lap. But it was close to dusk now: Fielding had made the rounds of reassurance all afternoon, and things were slowly calming.

Myself, though, I wasn't calm. Early for my date with Martina, I strolled the bowels of Times Square, the low Forties, the high Thirties. In a murky cross-street I saw a black awning that my legs remembered before I did, because I gave a stagger, and limped forward with my shoulders bent, like a damaged soldier under fire. Zelda's. I came nearer. Dinner and Hostess Dancing. I peered in through the limousine glass. Tables, a hooded piano. It looked dead in there, it looked extinct, with the grey, dry light imparted by dust and full ashtrays. All the staff and clientèle were in their mummies' tombs and vampire coffins, waiting on the night . . . I slipped into a bar across the way and turned my stool to face the forgotten awning.

'Give me a – what are they called?' I said. 'White wine and soda.'

'You sure?' said the barman. He was big, slabby, Irish, in a clean white apron, like a butcher at the start of the week, yet to begin his week of blood. In his arms, in his butcher's arms he cradled a beaked pint of scotch.

'Sure I'm sure.'

Doubtfully he put the B & F aside. 'Where's your ladyfriend?' he asked me, not amiably either – no, far from it. He's going to chuck me out, I thought, and I only just got here.

'What lady?'

'Big gingerhead. The one who had her tongue in your ear.'

'When?'

'How the fuck do I know? I don't know. Saturday night.'

'That wasn't me,' I said, having had cause to use this line before: 'that was my twin brother. Tell me all about it.'

Bleakly he shook his head. I offered him a twenty but he wouldn't tell me more.

'I'm John – he's Eric,' I explained.

'You? A twin brother?' he said, and moved away from me down the bar. 'There's only one of you, pal. One of you will about do it.'

. . . Martina stirred by my side. Our silent meeting was at an end. She stood up, then leaned forward to free a splinter from her dress. She looked at me with her long eyes. And nothing happened. Why should something always be happening? Why should it? We touched hands and exchanged words of parting. I watched her walk down the steps to the sidewalk of Forty-Second Street, between Fifth and Sixth, and head west, soon losing herself in the errand streams.

And so I sit in my manmade mooncave out here in Kennedy, with a triple B & F in my fist and the sky screening a noisy film about the near future – a *good* film, framed by my porthole and really well lit by the director of photography. Around me the people shuffle wearing their airport faces, their departure faces. Coming from all sides, they slowly join their flight details. Earthlings are first-class travellers: they do it day in, day out. *Good Money* . . . Things are happening now all right. I feel fine, I feel formidable, I feel almost adult. I am not just a passenger – I am one of life's pilots. The powers, the force fields that determine things, I've given them a wobble. I may fail, but I know exactly what I'm going to do.

Time to travel. I started moving down the pier toward my bay. On impulse, I called my pal Martina, to say goodbye again. All of a sudden, and without really thinking, it seems quite natural to be travelling first class.

THERE HAS recently been a wavelet of fag murders in my neighbourhood. Well, this is real fag-murdering weather we are having at the moment, and this has always been a fag-murdering district. During the early months of the year, the air was like cold washing-up. Now, with summer well and truly here at last, the air is like warm washing-up. At night, everything is blood-heat, holding sweat but no warmth. There are street celebrations, street rumbles. London is covered in barricades and bunting. The talk is all of royalty and riots.

It is whore-murdering time too. Whores have recently been introduced to my neighbourhood. I don't know who or what introduced them, but here they are: hello girls, and welcome. They stand in ones, twos, threes. They are made of nerves. Guys come in cars. You see these girls bent haggling over the door jambs. The girls are home-grown but the johns are foreign – there is often a language problem. Actually there is always a language problem. 'That's right, No! Twenty *pounds*.' One is a redhead, not yet a woman but dressed like a burgher's wife, with black rat stole and patent handbag, with sharp, arched, chinny face. I have watched her pushy rump as she closes deals through open windows, then slips inside for her lucrative fear. One is a fat blonde in pauper's shapeless winter coat. You're kidding, I said to myself when I first clocked her pacing out her pitch. And yet the chick does useful business, I've got to admit. More than once I have seen her singled out from the group by a waggling dark finger under the yellow lights. One is Persian (I think) and swanks the strip in baby-blue split skirt and filmy top. Now she looks as though she is worth twenty pounds of anybody's money. She has jouncy breasts and brown legs shining from the razor and she seems less bored and frightened by being a whore than her colleagues, who are nervous, nerveless, made of nerves.

Whores having been introduced to my neighbourhood, whore-murdering has too. Three weeks ago a girl was found strangled in a stolen car. The day before yesterday a girl was found knifed in a hotel basement. Yet still they do business in the dusty squares. That *is* the business, isn't it, paid risk, paid fear? The johns, the tricks, they must like and value the nerves, the fear. They give good money. Ah the poor girls – you feel for them. Last night I came home late and paused as I clambered from the Fiasco to stamp out a cigarette and admire the night warmth. Two whores, the redhead and a sturdy stranger with a small muscular head, like a bulb or an onion, were leaning against the railings that trim the fireprone hotel, and I said, 'Hey, I hear one of you lot copped it the other day' – not the best choice of words, perhaps, but kindly, worriedly meant, with urgent fellow-feeling. They turned away, in the manner of non-whores at parties or night-clubs, with civic distaste. 'I'm sorry,' I said. 'Do you want some money. Here – have some money.' I've seen their lousy pimp, Asiatic, standing restlessly on the corner by the Spanish café, with smile and teeth and strides as flared as shark fins, the roll of dough like a dick in the tight hip pocket.

I have a proposition to make: Selina is up to something. This is *my* theory. Yes, she's up to something, that Selina. I just know it – though with chicks, I find, it's very hard to tell what really gives. Yesterday, at noon, I cabbed in from Heathrow. It doesn't half take it out of you, boozewise, flying first class. Selina was attentive, all present and correct, in the spotless sock, as if she'd just materialized, just beamed down. On the sitting-room sideboard flowers stood sleeping. I kissed her. Her mouth evaded mine. Her breath was eggy and metallic. So she's ovulating, the bitch, I thought. Now the deal here is – this normally makes her hot, which normally makes me cold. When she's cold – that's what makes me hot. And I was hot. And she was cold. Yes, she's turned the tables on me yet again, little Selina. Hoping for the best, I whisked her off to Kreutzer's. I sat there with my dick drooling into my bellybutton as Selina talked proudly about nothing at all. Champagne, thick meat, thick wine. A talented total. Skilfully and at high speed I drunk-drove her back to the sock. She wouldn't come to bed with me. That really got me going. It was high time, I mused, that she had her own US Approach or Vantage card – possibly both. She still wouldn't come to bed with me. Expansively, dreaming big, I rehearsed plans to make a sizeable new investment in her boutique. She still wouldn't come to bed with me. Nodding to myself I wrote out a cheque for three thousand quid. Then she offered me a handjob! – well, not in so many words, but that's what it amounted to. We were in the kitchen. I was drinking brandy, while Selina self-righteously sipped her tea. She placed a hand on her throat and hummed as I looked her steadily in the eye. Now I'd had just about enough of this, so when she offered me that handjob (I mean, Jesus, what kind of relationship are we having here?), I accepted, and told her which kit to wear, which routines to deploy, etcetera. 'You are unbelievable,' she said – and withdrew her offer. In the end I decided to play it cool. I ripped up the cheque, finished the brandy, went to bed and had a handjob.

I slept. I slept for many hours, or I think I did. And when I woke I was – I was sprung free from time. My readings and coordinates are still out there among the jetslime and earphones and weather gods of Atlantic space. Time is travelling. Night and day are moving past me in the wrong direction. I am falling behind. I must catch up, get a hold, make sure my grip is tight.

Beyond the bedroom Selina circles, keeping her holding pattern, her distance, her vigil. I called her name. She appeared in the doorway, framed by light but distant, not fully there any more, off in some other film or story . . . Today, at the airport taxi-rank, who should I see but Ossie Twain. I did not greet this tall traveller, as he paid the cabbie and buttoned his jacket with a toss of the head. I backed into the queue and smiled at my secrets. Martina's face, is it still watching me? Yes, it's there, but paler now . . . And now too Selina brings me my coffee, silently, like a nurse, resting the mug on the bedside table, just beyond the reach or range of my breath.

'Hello?' I said. It sounded like a bad line. But it was probably my head that was doing all the fizzing. This tinnitus number – soon I'll have to sack out with a blaring tranny on my pillow. Even when they're deaf, apparently, the ear-sufferers still have this head-noise to listen to. Bad luck. Double bad.

'John Self? Martin Amis.'

'Hallelujah,' I said. 'About bloody time too. I've had a hell of a job tracking you down. I rang your publishers, your agent, the National – you know, the book thing. What's with you? Are you working undercover or something?'

He made no answer. I proceeded carefully. Writers – you have to be gentle with them. They're an odd bunch, sitting at home all day as they do.

'Anyway, thanks for calling. And say thanks to your agent for passing on my message. Okay, now look. You've worked in films, right?'

'. . . Some,' he said.

'Right: kid, this is your lucky day. Now let me try an idea out on you. I've got a –'

'No wait. If you're serious, get on to my agent again.'

'No, listen,' I said. 'This is the beauty of it. We're cutting the agents out. And the studios.'

'Yes, and so is everyone else who packages films in pubs and aeroplanes. And on street corners.'

'No, listen. I had my doubts at first too. But the thing is, my producer, he gets a lawyer to do the contracts, and the lawyer gets a fee but no percentage. This has to be good news. It's all kosher, don't worry.'

He brooded. 'What exactly are we looking at here?'

'Uh?'

'*Money*. I'm in the book. Call me when you know.'

He hung up. I lit two cigarettes and tapped out the fourteen digits . . . It was seven a.m., over in Manhattan there. Fielding had just got back from his morning jog. He was brisk, clipped, oxygenated. He was businesslike, as if this project were one of many. There was also the sense that *Good Money* had lost ground with him artistically, and was now nothing more than a highly remunerative venture – again, one of many, no longer his pet, his baby. It's his new style with me, ever since the Doris Arthur debacle. I miss the human touch but I can survive its withdrawal, I can butch it out, and maybe soon the warmth will return . . . Fielding, of course, had heard of Martin Amis – he hadn't read his stuff, but there'd recently been some cases of plagiarism, of text-theft, which had filtered down to the newspapers and magazines. So, I thought. Little Martin got caught with his fingers in the till, then, did he. A word criminal. I would bear that in mind.

Between the two of us we hammered out a deal – so much per draft, so much per re-write.

'Wait a minute,' I said, 'we can get this guy cheap. That sounds a hell of a lot to me.'

'Not really, John,' said Fielding austerely, and went on to explain. I listened, with the odd admiring chortle. So that's how they do it. The fee sounds outlandish, comical – but really you're paying the guy practically by the page. A draft, a set of revisions, you tell him it stinks and kick him down the stairs. That way we got our script at a 60-per-cent knockdown. Doris Arthur knew the score.

I risked it, and said, 'How *is* Doris?'

'Good,' said Fielding. 'I'm having her novelize that screenplay. You were wrong, John.'

'I was right, Fielding.'

Doris had said something to me outside the media restaurant on Ninety-Fifth Street. I couldn't remember what it was, but I knew I never wanted to hear it again. That was one of the reasons why Doris was in turnaround. One of the reasons. Yes, it was one of the reasons.

'Give the guy a cheque today. Get him writing *now*. How's your flow?'

I said my flow was only so-so. Fielding told me to use the retainer account, which he would shortly replenish.

'Take it easy, Slick,' said Fielding. 'Take it any way you can.'

I fixed a drink and yanked out the directory: Martin Amis was in the book all right – in fact he was there twice, once as Martin, once as M. L. Some people will do anything to get their names in print.

With a premonitory rustle of shopping Selina hurried in through the front door. Her hair was oiled with colour and heat. Sometimes, I swear, Selina's rug ripples like fast-flowing water – it ripples with unguents, with secrets. She said she was tired: she said she was ill. She took a painkiller and went to bed. There was no question of me lumbering in after her. You know, that girl is exceptionally smooth in her inner thigh. The skin is excitingly snakelike there: it shines. If you look, you find silky complicit creases in the tendons near her cleft. You don't often get girls with inner thighs like that.

Selina, she's like a girl in a men's magazine. She probably

is a girl in a men's magazine: there are so many these days, it's hard to keep tabs on them all. Normal girls, they aren't like the girls in the pornographic magazines. Here's a little-known fact: the girls in the pornographic magazines aren't like the girls in the pornographic magazines either. That's the thing about pornography, that's the thing about men – they're always giving you the wrong ideas about women. *No* girls are like the girls in the men's magazines, not even Selina, not even the girls in the men's magazines. I've checked out one or two of them and I know. It transpires that everyone has their human shape, their human form. But try telling pornography that. Try telling men.

How did *I* get to discover this little-known fact? How did *I* get to check out one or two of the chicks in the pornographic magazines? Well how do you think?

Money – that's right.

'Answer me something. Do you sort of set yourself a time to write every day? Or do you just write when you feel like it. Or what.'

He sighed and said, 'You really want to know? . . . I get up at seven and write straight through till twelve. Twelve to one I read Russian poetry – in translation, alas. A quick lunch, then art history until three. After that it's philosophy for an hour – nothing technical, nothing *hard*. Four to five: European history, 1848 and all that. Five to six: I improve my German. And from then until dinner, well, I just relax and read whatever the hell I like. Usually Shakespeare.'

'Yeah, I was re-reading a book the other day. *Animal Farm*. What you reckon?'

'I've never read it, funnily enough.'

'What about – what about *1984*?'

'Oh I'll get round to it when the time comes. I'm not all that interested in the novel of ideas. I don't like coming up for air either.'

'Uh? Hey – how much money do you earn?'

'It varies.'

'But how much?'

He told me.

'Then what the hell do you spend it on?'

I tell you, this Martin Amis, he lives like a student. I had inspected his flat with an adman's eye, mindful of outlay and lifestyle, of vocational expenditure. And there was nothing, no tape recorders or filing cabinets or electric typewriters or word processors. Just his pastel portable, like an ancient till. Just biros, pads, pencils. Just two dust-furred rooms off a sooty square, with no hall or passage. And he earns enough. Why isn't he living right up to the hilt of his dough? He must have a bad book-habit, this character. How much are books? It seems he has the reading thing real bad.

'This feels like a good bit of work to me. It's certainly unusual,' he said. Doris Arthur's screenplay lay cracked out on his lap. He had been flicking through it confidently. 'Are these your jottings? What's your problem?'

'We have a hero problem. We have a motivation problem. We have a fight problem. We have a realism problem.'

'What's your realism problem?'

I told him. It took a long time.

'. . . and so, and so, yeah, that's where you come in,' I said, winding it all up.

'That wouldn't be writing,' he said. 'That would be psychotherapy.'

'Here's the deal.'

'Talk to me.'

I named the sum. That took quite a long time too. Jesus, it sounded an awful lot, for a writer.

Martin laughed. I think he gulped. '. . . Pounds or dollars?' he asked.

Selina says I'm not capable of true love. It isn't true. I truly love money. Truly I do. Oh, money, I love you. You're so democratic: you've got no favourites. You even things out for me and my kind.

'Pounds,' I said, offhand, 'though of course the money's American. How busy are you?' I let him shrug and pout for a while. 'It may eat into your philosophy for a couple of weeks,' I said, 'but that's life. Shakespeare can hang fire. History can wait.' I coolly mentioned the cheque I had right here in my pocket, and tossed in a detail or two about the payment schedule. By now I was thinking – we're just pissing money away on this kid. He'd do it for half the dough, easy. Think of all the books he can buy.

'I'm going to say no.'

Dah! Son of a *bitch*! 'What? Why?' I said with a rush of bitter heat – inordinate, stunning pain, as if a child of mine had been crudely slighted, or me, myself, running home from school in tears. Ooh, the world can still hurt. It's as sharp as ever it was.

'Nothing personal,' he said. 'I just don't know enough about you. I just don't know enough about *Good Money*.'

'I just told you all about it for Christ's sake.'

'That's the trouble.' He paused, and his head dipped. 'This film. Who's directing it? Are *you* . . .? You give me the plot. You sound like a ten-year-old trying to remember a dirty joke. Now that doesn't really worry me. The film industry is full of thriving duffers and speechless millionaires. What worries me is . . . To make a film you need energy, all this energy. That's what film directors are – people with all this energy. Now you, you look as though you're about to check into a sense-deprivation unit. I keep thinking, if he blinks, he'll have a heart attack. I've seen you around and you're really a prodigy. You are something else.'

Happening to have turned out as the human being I am, the first thing I wonder about a woman is: will I fuck it? Similarly, the first thing I wonder about a man is: will I fight it? Three years ago, three months ago, three weeks ago, I would have answered Martin's objections by hoisting him to his feet and nutting him between the eyes. For some ambiguous reason (and I think it's to do with his name, so close to that of my pale minder), I feel strangely protective of little Martin here: in a way, I would hate to damage him, or to see him damaged. But on another level, on another night, I can hear myself – I can smell myself – giving Martin the pasting of his life, a real bad one, roused, blind, with nothing mattering. I sense he senses this sometimes, this stickiness between us. I scare him, for all his talk. Yes, he's clever, and I wish I had his articulation, but I sussed him for a wimp, right from the start.

Sitting back, I let my heartbeat go ahead and take its time. I glanced down at the ashtray before me, a mass grave, with its stools and the crushed corpses of a dozen butts. I said,

'I'm going to double it.' I named the revised figure, and felt a nauseous twinge in my balls. 'And that's just for starting.' I produced my chequebook. 'Now come on. Where do you get off, turning down that kind of money? Do it. Buy a present for your girlfriend. Or your mother. Do it. Come on, save my life.'

'. . . I'll do it.'

'Thank you, Martin.'

'On one condition.'

'What?'

'The cheque doesn't bounce.'

'The cheque's good,' I said, handing it over. 'I'll need the first draft in two weeks. Christ, all you're doing is a re-write.'

He looked up at the tumbling zeros. He said, 'This is – this isn't realistic.'

I stood up sharply: energetically. Martin flinched. His eyes watched me. He knows what's going on between us. Or maybe he thinks he's just being paranoid.

He isn't. He isn't just being paranoid. I can assure him of that.

Now I've started being paranoid too – when I'm out in the Fiasco. I think people are following me. These days I look at the rear mirror more often than I look at the windscreen, and more fixedly. If a car follows me round a corner, then that's okay, I don't mind, happens all the time. If a car follows me round two corners, I narrow my gaze and tighten my hold on the wheel, covertly, like an actor. Round three corners, and it's red alert. That's what paranoia is, after all. Red alert. I lock the doors and shut the windows. I employ diversionary measures. I go round corners to see if they will follow me round corners. I step on it . . . Sometimes I get a contact paranoia from the cars in front: the cars in front might be paranoid of me, in case I'm following them. Sometimes I think the car behind thinks I'm following the car in front. In an attempt to reassure everyone, myself included, I often overtake – or I try. The Fiasco doesn't seem to have the heft it once had. Overtaking takes for ever: it is extremely dangerous and I've had several near things. The Fiasco has lost its torque and twang. I got cut up by a cripple-car the other day. As I grandly cruised along the Bayswater Road towards Marble Arch this toytown three-wheeler lurched out of track and bombed across my bows, heading for the clear inner lane. I changed down and put my foot on the floor – but that gimp just left me for dead. No contest. Yesterday I got paranoid when a cyclist followed me round a corner. I stopped the car. I stopped the car, out of straightforward incredulity. The bike ticked past. It had an old lady on it . . . Today I was driving along and suddenly felt very paranoid. I didn't like it: something was up – it was quiet, too quiet. Then I realized why I felt paranoid. No one was following me.

The Royal Wedding is getting nearer and nearer to being over. London feels like Blackpool or Bognor or Benidorm in bad weather. This is history: the subjects of England converge on the capital, to honour the nuptials of the heir to the throne. This is history, and they want a piece of it. The Turks and Persians and robed boogies, the new London sahibs, they look baffled, affronted – they're not used to being outnumbered by the natives. The pallid celebrants are gaily dressed in the murky warmth of summer. You see them in their pop-art Jubilee wear, squeezed from the heat of the coaches and queueing at the jaws of the sudden hotels. They are loud and happy. Their time has come . . . Three years ago to the month I was in some Mediterranean airport or other, coming home, squiring one of Selina's predecessors, some Dolly or Polly or Molly. We checked in, we drank our mid-afternoon cocktails, we did our thing in Duty-Free. And I moved among them unreflectingly, my people. The airport was a UK shuttle-base, cheap returns to Belfast, Manchester, Glasgow, Birmingham and the remoter London tarmacs. We were all heading back from the sun, heading back to the moon, in great shape really, despite the beerguts and cellulite quilting, the rug glue and snapper sealant. Fleet Street tabloids were on sale at the layered kiosk. The barmen's pub English was laconic but serviceable: they all knew how to say *no ice*. And here we all were, going home. Girls in topheavy T-shirts and sawn-off jeans or else in superfemale parody of indigenous flounce and frill, the matrons also burgeoning in tight angular cords and a flush of freckly renewal, the bronzed brutes twanging their torsos in the bar and enacting their ideal of modern male grace – a mousta-chioed muscle. There is lots of drink and brimming holiday money. Reacquainted with their bodies, warmed, oiled, attended to, they all have the sex tan: it is called *rude health*. And so this shower, this innocent evolutionary catastrophe – them, me, and Holly or Golly or Lolly, the bouncy bim in her wind-whipped dress – we clicked through the mad heat to the noise machine, tensed on its hunkers in a squealing nightmare of toilet strain. With transistors, duty-frees, big tits, white trousers, we climbed up into its trapdoored rump.

Watch. Wait. Here they come again, the people . . . To me in those days traffic was only traffic, anonymous, indifferent – traffic, mere traffic. Now I know a little more about the movements behind my back. The cars are specific, with force fields, meek, hostile or aloof. I see a car's face and a car's eyes and a car's clamped sneer, a car cowering or bristling or not caring either way. And when I look into the crowd, into the human congestion of the street, I don't see traffic but human force fields – rattletraps, dropheads, hardtops, hotrods, the human saloons singling me out with the stare of their lights.

'Charles and Lady Di are getting married on the twenty-ninth,' I remarked to Selina over my coffee and toast. She was wearing her stateliest nightdress. The silk was as rich as icing. It was also bluntly transparent. 'Why don't we make it a double wedding? Wouldn't that be a riot? We could jump in a cab now and pop up to Bond Street and buy you your ring. What do you fancy? An emerald, a ruby, a nice diamond? We could have lunch at Knox's. I'll call the travel agent. After the ceremony we could zip off to Paris for a few days, first class. We'll stay at that new hotel, the one that's meant to be the most expensive in the world. You need a new wardrobe anyway. I also think it's about time you had your own car. The Fiasco's far too big for you. I've heard you say so yourself. Where would you like to go this summer? You might give that some thought. Barbados? The Seychelles? Sri Lanka? Bali?'

'I can't hear you, John. John. What are you doing?'

'Nothing,' I said, but in fact I was doing quite a lot. I was by now straddling Selina's kitchen chair, tuning one of her nipples in my hand and rolling the other round my mouth like a peppermint. 'What do you say?' I said.

'What? *Ow*. Look, get off. Anyway I want to watch the Royal Wedding on television.'

'Fuck *you*,' I said.

'Fuck you too.'

'Fuck off!'

'*You* fuck off!'

'Ah *fuck* it,' I said, and went down the Butcher's Arms.

. . . There was an old lady who lived in a sock. One day, three black boys and two skinheads came calling. They beat her up and raped her and stole all her dough. When the old lady's son showed up with the pigs, one of the black boys was still in bed, sleeping. The boy was sixteen. The son was seventy-two. The old lady was eighty-*nine*, living alone in her sock there . . . An Arab chieftain has been blown away. Suddenly, according to a filler in the *Morning Line*, the Middle East is more volatile than ever, and world peace gravely threatened. Now this raises some serious questions. Will there be a petrol hike? Will the Quid be slapped about and gangbanged on the international money market? Or will it appreciate on account of the oil, thereby devaluing the American dollars I'm going to earn? I demand to know. Or will there be a World War, and all the expense and inconvenience *that* entails . . . TV's Val has been rushed to hospital with a mystery illness. On page five blonde Ulla sports big tits and cool pants. Sissy Skolimowsky turns out to be a diesel, and an ex-chick of hers is suing Siss for galimony. Browsing yesterday through Selina's knicker chest, I came across a pair of briefs I'd never seen before. They were lawyers' briefs: general stuff about common law and chicks' rights . . . Russian tank manoeuvres on the Polish border. I have travelled far enough in Oceania, in 1984, to have my doubts about the joint. I worry about Poland. I worry about Lech and Room 101, about Danuta (you know she's pregnant again) and all those kids of theirs. Me, I think that Solidarity might soon die of overexcitement. Everything Lech does looks reasonable to free men and women, but I bet it doesn't look that way in Poland, where they've got some very tough berks in the saddle. Have you heard the Polish joke that money is telling? It's a good one. Q: What's the only thing worth buying with money in Poland? A: Money. Other brands of money – our money, which is terribly expensive. Isn't it a scream? It's a *good* one, isn't it.

'Barry reckons she has. Fat Vince reckons she has. Cecil reckons she has. Vron reckons she has. *I* reckon she has.'

'Has what?' I asked.

'Done it already.'

'With Prince Charles.'

'Yeah. Well it stands to reason. He's the heir to the frone. I mean, he's got to know what he's getting, hasn't he?'

Another day, another pub. Fat Paul, and the Shakespeare.

Me and Fat Paul – we're like brothers. We were always skylarking and roughhousing, always scrapping and fighting. We stopped scrapping and fighting in our mid-twenties. It hurt too much. He never lost any more. Now I fear Fat Paul and am careful not to be drunk near him. He gets good money for being better at violence than I am. No doubt I would improve, too, if my livelihood depended on it, as does Fat Paul's. Well, he's a professional, I say to myself, and for me it's never been more than a hobby.

'I've just gone off sex,' said Selina this morning, as she finished the tea I'd fondly brought her.

'So?' I asked her.

'God, *be nice*. Use your imagination. It'll pass. I've just gone off sex.'

Then what do you think is the point *of you?* I wanted to say. But I didn't, I resisted the temptation. I looked into the proud drama of her face, the valves and orbits of her throat, the wetlook runnels of her hair, the breasts, heavier than ever, solidly mounted on the ribcage, the naked slopes of the belly, the sudden flaring of the hips, a smell of sleep.

'Then what do you think is the *point* of you?'

'You', she said, 'are unreal.'

It's lucky for little Selina that I've stopped hitting women. If I ever stop stopping hitting women, she'll be the first to know . . . So then I sloped off and spent a dull but necessary morning with my art-director and set-dresser. I had my first assistant come along, Micky Obbs. These layabouts are on retainer now. Fielding has a special numbered account to deal with it all. I went on to lunch with Kevin Skuse and Des Blackadder. They're on retainer too. You should see the way I handle these guys. Martin Amis should see the way I handle these guys. They think I'm God. I can tell by their set smiles and exhausted laughter, the tranquillity of their hate. Next, the Shakespeare, to see my dad, to look for clues to this whole deal with fathers and sons.

'Where's Barry?' I asked.

'Here,' said Fat Paul. 'Take the keys.'

My father was moodily auditioning strippers in the purple-draped crypt of the old saloon. And a sorry lot of chicks they were too – thirtyish, double-nipper housewives, forced on to the stage by money. They even had their kids hanging about back there, yawning nervously. The children reminded me of other children – yes, the prison kids, in Brixton, the little visitors. I didn't want to see all this and sat down heavily with my back to the lights.

'Fetch a glass, John,' said my father, with his brief debtor's stare. 'Who are you then? Emma? All right, my love, off you go.'

I said, 'What's happened to Vron?'

'Don't talk to me about Vron. I can't do a thing with her since *Debonair*. She wants to do a video now. Obsessed by video she is. Stripping's not good enough for Vron any more. Calls herself a *body artist*. She doesn't strip, she does *physical culture*. She did physical culture on stage here last Wednesday and a right bloody disaster it was too. Thank you Emma! Yes, thank you, love, that'll do.'

I turned. Holding her clothes in a bundle, Emma stood nodding under the lights. A pale boy in shorts slipped off the piano stool and moved towards her.

'Next!'

'What happened? Last Wednesday.'

He gave a thick nasal sigh, his eyes level on the stage. He said, 'She had the whole thing *choreographed* by that poof Rod. The photographer. I tell you, he'd better be a poof, or they're both in hospital. He did the lighting, so-called. It was that dark in here, they were spilling drinks, walking into walls. It wasn't the usual – you know, where the girl goes around with a sock afterwards and you give her fifty pee if you feel like it. No, proper seating and two quid entrance fee. Vron comes on covered in veils and scarves and shimmies about a bit in the dark. Then she went off again! They were going barmy in here. I went through and said – get out and take your fucking gear off. She wouldn't do it though, not her. Said that was *it*. I had to give out refunds. Heartbreaking. Thank you, darling! Beautiful. I'll see what I can do for you.'

'Hey, I want to ask you something. Have you got any plans to –'

'*You'll get your money*,' he said and faced me for the first time – the eyes sashed, the lips outcurled.

'It's not about the money,' I said. 'It's about your wedding plans.'

'Oh *them*.' He shrugged and waved a hand loosely at me. 'Do us a favour, John. Look in on Her Royal Highness on your way out. She wants a word with you. Hey. That Selina.' His scrolled sneer deepened, seeming to connect with a sudden light behind the eyes. 'I bet she's a dirty one. Am I wrong?'

'Selina?' I said, with instinctive loyalty, soppy old fool that I am – 'she's filthy.'

He grunted and turned away. 'Off you go, my son. Run along.'

Vron I found watching TV in the marzipan parlour. She lay on the sofa, her body significantly composed, her head held high, like a tray. I saw spiked heels, black stockings, a turquoise kimono with many a mystifying vent and flap. Her black lashes were as thick as epaulettes, the eyes spidery against the mortuarist caking of her cheeks and brow. Vron and the room she lay in, they shared a texture – sweetshops, sherbet, liquorice. As she talked (about Barry, about Rod, about the demerits of the Lady Di hairstyle) she massaged her breasts with her forearms, snugly – 'to keep the shape, John,' she said. From here the conversation turned to her body and how unashamed of it she was. Other people, they might be ashamed of their bodies, but not her, not Vron. 'Why should I be ashamed of my body John! Tell me why. Why?' I had no answer. Vron then inquired whether I had any connections in adult movies or soft video or porno loop.

'No connections to speak of. Not as such.'

'Barry doubts my career possibilities, John. However, Rod has faith in my talent. You're artistic. I respect that, John. Do you doubt me, John?'

'In my experience, Vron, these things can go either way.'

She looked at me consideringly, her hands crossed on the blue lapels. 'I'd be a good mother to you. I would,' she said. 'I would, truly.'

★

'The distance between author and narrator corresponds to the degree to which the author finds the narrator wicked, deluded, pitiful or ridiculous. I'm sorry, am I boring you?'

'– Uh?'

'This distance is partly determined by convention. In the epic or heroic frame, the author gives the protagonist everything he has, and more. The hero is a god or has godlike powers or virtues. In the tragic . . . Are you all right?'

'Uh?' I repeated. I had just stabbed a pretzel into my dodgy upper tooth. Rescreening this little mishap in my head, I suppose I must have winced pretty graphically and then given a sluggish, tramplike twitch. Now I checked the tooth with my tongue. Martin talked contentedly on. Mouth-doctors are just like cowboy decorators or jobbing plumbers. When you're young you think the world of adult services is reliable, proficient and cost-effective. Then you grow up to a life of fatboys and four-eyes, bullies and bookworms, fudgers and smudgers. I sipped my drink and sluiced the scotch round my upper west side.

'The further down the scale he is, the more liberties you can take with him. You can do what the hell you like to him, really. This creates an appetite for punishment. The author is not free of sadistic impulses. I suppose it's the –'

'Hey look you got to give me a deadline. You don't have to stick to it that closely but I got to have something to tell Fielding and Lorne. And Caduta. Davis, too. What about the fight?'

'Which fight?'

'The one between Lorne and Spunk. You know, the big fight.'

'Nobody's going to believe that name.'

'Yeah yeah. We're talking to him about it. You see, lots of Americans are called things like that. They've all got names like Orifice and Handjob. They don't notice. They think it's cool.'

'Well I think it's a problem. Anyway, try this. He *lets* Lorne beat him up.'

'Spunk?'

'Spunk.'

'Why?'

'To show he's beyond all that. Also he's in such exquisite control of his body that he can ride with the punches and –'

'Come on,' I said. 'Lorne won't fall for that. *Lorne* wants Spunk to sneak up on him in an aircraft carrier. Then he wants, you know, he really wants to cream him.'

'Spunk?'

'*Yeah*. See, heroes don't . . . I got to explain something to you. Lorne plays heroes. Heroes don't lose fights. They never lost fights in Lorne's day. Then they started losing them for a while but now they've gone back to not losing them. Heroes, heroes don't lose fights unless it's against ten guys, and they've all got knives and whips, and he'd been sick, and his mother's dying, and his wife's pregnant, and –'

'Yes I read you,' said Martin.

'And even then, they win the next fight.'

'Try this. Lorne lets *Spunk* beat him up.'

'Why?'

'Out of love for Butch. Self-sacrifice.'

'Yeah . . . No but *Spunk* won't fall for that. He doesn't even want to fight Lorne unless it's absolutely necessary. He's got to be goaded and attacked a lot and everything.'

'Then it's unresolvable. Neither party is prepared to lose.'

'You're the *writer*,' I said. 'Use your imagination, for Christ's sake. Put your talent to work on it. What are you guys meant to do all day anyway?'

'If we have two fights then I suppose they'll both want to win the second one. What about no fight?'

'No, the fight stays. We have to have that fight. No, I want that fight.'

'I'll see what I can do for you.'

We then discussed our realism problem, in Martin's sock there, sitting round his book-heaped oval table, with whisky bottle, glasses, ashtrays, writing tools. Martin drinks and smokes a fair bit, or he does now. Generally speaking, he has gone up in my estimation. But the student routine is a downer, I find. You know something: he even rolls his own. How lowlife does he want to get? Outside were skies of salt and the usual sounds of people travelling.

'So the thing is, what you've got to do is,' I concluded, 'you've got to make them behave realistically without them knowing it or minding too much. Just so they'll *do* it. Okay?'

'Well, it's a real bitch,' he said.

I considered. 'Do you have this problem with novels, Martin?' I asked him. 'I mean, is there a big deal about bad behaviour and everything?'

'No. It's not a problem. You get complaints, of course, but we're pretty much agreed that the twentieth century is an ironic age – downward-looking. Even realism, rockbottom realism, is considered a bit grand for the twentieth century.'

'Really,' I said, and felt that tooth with my tongue.

As I walked home through streets the colour of oyster and carbon the air suddenly shivered and shook its coat, like a wet dog, like the surface of worried water. I paused – we all did – and lifted my face to the sky, as a slave or animal might lift its face, fearing punishment but risking it anyway. With banisters of sunbeams a lit staircase now led straight to the blue heaven, far beyond the daily sky of empty eggtrays, full sinks, kitchen mists. 'Okay. Show me something,' I said, and wiped my face with my hand. Up in the clear distance basked a hollow pink cloud, a rosy cusp fastened by tendrils at either end, like a vertical eye, a vertical mouth. In its core lay a creaturely essence, meticulous, feminine . . . *Dah* – do I push that thought away? Issuing from my head, can pornography now shape the clouds and hold all sway in the middle air? Wait . . . the rose, the mouth, the glint. Come on, if that is what it looked like then that is what it looked like. I am probably not alone in supposing that I am shaped by how I see things. And that cloud up there certainly looked like a pussy to me.

Mark you, nearly everything looks that way to me these days. A week I've been back, and still Selina keeps her distance. She keeps her holding pattern, that Selina. Each night, over dinner at progressively pricier restaurants, I get the anti-sex manifesto all the way from soup to nuts. She's in a sensitive state, she says. She's in a delicate condition. At first I thought she was holding out for a really big jackpot or nest-egg or superannuation scheme. I was wrong. I've offered her thousands. I've offered her marriage, kids, houses, the whole deal. Perhaps I lack subtlety, I don't know. She looks at me as if to say, *How could you?* I wish someone would tell me which particular hormone is to blame for all this. It's pinging around in there, that hormone of hers, and playing havoc with my health. If I ever get my hands on that hormone . . . She's not doing any dressing up, little Selina. She's not doing any dressing down. No brothel or men's-mag gear, but no oatmeal tights or hospital pyjamas either. She sleeps in the raw. So do I, so do I.

Tonight, before retiring, I took the precaution of drinking a bottle of brandy, and went into the bedroom just as Selina was emerging from the tub. Brushing her hair with both arms raised, she stood naked by the side of the bed. Patches of moisture still gleamed on her like oceans on a globe. I came across the room in an imploring hobble. I kissed her throat. I knelt.

'Please,' I said.

I listened to the brushstrokes, the Japanese music of her insides, the light whir of silence.

'Ten grand,' I said, '– for the boutique.'

No answer.

'Marry me. Have my children. We could move to a – oh, fuck it, this is – Just shut your eyes! I won't take a minute! God damn it, just come across!'

'If you loved me,' said Selina, 'you'd understand.'

So then I tried to rape her. In all honesty I have to confess that it wasn't a very distinguished effort. I'm new at this and generally out of shape. For instance, I wasted a lot of time attempting to control her hands. Obviously the proper way to rape girls is to get the leg question sorted out and take the odd slap in the face as part of the deal. Here's another tip: undress before the action starts. It was while I had Selina's forearms in my right hand and the belt-clasp in my left that she caught me a good one with the bony fist of her knee. I took it right in the join of my splayed and aching tackle. Whew, that *was* a good one, I thought, as my back hit the deck. Arched and winded, I lay there with the lampshade in my face. I felt I was slowly turning green from the toes up. Then at last I crawled next door like a knackered alligator and roared for many moons into the wind tunnel of the can.

That really was a *good* one, I thought, as I ate an apple in the kitchen, as I limped about the lino wringing my hands. Jesus, now how's this going to look? . . . On my diffident return to the bedroom Selina gave me no more than a cold flick of her eyelashes. She sat there propped against the headboard, the sheets tight beneath her armpits, a buxom magazine on her sloped lap. 'I'm sorry. Oh I'm so sorry,' I said. 'I've never felt this ashamed before.' She turned over and smoothed out a pillow. Gradually – veering, listing, hopping – I shed my clothes and slipped in beside her. I placed a careful hand on her shoulder. 'Selina. Please say it's all right.' She pushed the cold white defencelessness of her backside into my loins, forgivingly. 'It's all right,' she said. She straightened her left leg and put her right hand palm-upwards beneath the smoothed pillow. For a long time I lay there with the breathing bundle in my arms, and sadly listened to the subsidence of her sighs.

Then I tried to rape her again.

In terms of pure technique, of rape knowhow, my second bid was a definite improvement on my first. Different class, really. This time I came at her from behind in a writhing, wriggling rush. The element of surprise took a more central role here, because Selina was fast asleep at the time. You don't get much more surprisable than that. Having learnt the night's lessons, I did the rape-smart thing: I flattened her body and prised her legs apart with my own in a reverse-tweezer action. It worked, too. Fabulous, I said to myself. She's utterly at my mercy. Brilliant. All I need now is a hard-on . . . With her free hand Selina clawed at my side and gave my rug the odd crackling wrench. This I can live with, I thought. It's anti-erotic, true, but it doesn't hurt much either. What now, though? Selina herself brought an end to the impasse. She suddenly found her range and gave me a colossal sock on the cheek with the tensed chisel of her elbow – deep in my upper west side, where that rickety tooth is still living, is still hanging out. I hit the deck even harder this time, but soon stumbled swearing into the kitchen. This rape lark, I concluded, over painkillers and scotch, it's seriously overrated. How do rapists cope with it all? . . . By the time I peered out, Selina had made up a bed for herself on the couch. In she climbed, as into a spectral automobile, the white door closing behind her. 'I'll sleep there,' I said. 'Go to bed.' She ignored me. I shouted at her. For the first time that night I felt I might at any moment turn distinctly *nasty*. As Selina walked across the room (in her woolliest nightdress now), I contemplated one final heroic crack at her. But my good angel urged me to call it a day – to quit honourably, while I was still alive. I had a lunging, flapping night on the hot sore leather (the sheets seeming to bind and tape and measure me) and played host to a hang of frisky new pains as they explored their sudden pleasureground.

When I 'woke up', around ten, Selina had left home for the day. In the morning mail was my bank statement. I opened it with unusual interest and stared at the columns for a long time. Here was evidence at last, here was clear proof that Selina was doing me wrong. In the last four weeks she had spent no money at all.

'*The Usurers. Budget. Consortium.* Words fail me. Thanks, John.'

'What's the matter with them?' I asked. 'They're *books*, aren't they?'

'They've got all this crap in here already. Six weeks I wait for this.'

'How was I to know? You want books, ask your friends from Cambridge.'

'I haven't got any friends from Cambridge. Or from anywhere else, not any more. Why d'you think I hang out with someone like you?'

'How about this one?' I said. '*Animal Farm* . . .'

'What? Oh I read that when I was twelve.'

'Then you probably didn't realize it was an allegory. How could you be expected to? You were only twelve. Now, the pigs, they're sort of the leaders – of the Revolution. And all those other guys, like the horses, and the dogs, they're all . . . Oh Alec. I hate to say this but you look fucking terrible.'

'And I hate to hear it.'

Alec Llewellyn wore the low colour of fear on his face. It's yellow, just like they say – yellow, sallow, sowlike, big-pored. Worst affected were the concavities beneath the eyes, where the murk had gathered in two dark stains, like scabs. The eyes them-selves (once moist, gland-bright, almost fizzy) were the eyes of a trapped interior being, living inside my friend and staring into the distance, to see if it would ever be safe to come out. His hair was long, let-go, flimsy and inward-sloping beneath the jaw . . . Now this was Pentonville, Her Majesty's Prison, and Pentonville wasn't like the other place – it wasn't like Brixton, with its shrugs and apologies, its atmosphere of coping. No, Pentonville was low-morale, dark, damp, the air foul and sullen. Even the screws looked subnormal in their sweat-soaked serge. I waited two lousy hours in a dead classroom with the dangling wives – different wives, not old and dour but young and bored, pissed off, hurting, smarting. These girls, they'd ended up with the wrong guys: criminals. Or maybe there was never much choice in the matter and they just ended up with the wrong criminals.

'The class system,' said Alec Llewellyn, 'it's not so solid here. I'm sharing a cell with a couple of trogs who make you look like the swan of Avon. One's in for looting, one's in for raping. That's the only witty thing about them. John,' he said in a new voice, shakier, rockier, 'you know it's not *meant* to be me in here. It's meant to be you.'

I didn't need this talk. 'What's your problem?' I asked. We sat in the dank sty of a first-floor rec room. It was like a Sixties coffee-bar left to rot, windowless, with bare-filament strip lighting and its heart-attack flicker. Every few minutes I went to the counter and bought Alec another coffee and another chocolate bar. He ate and drank quickly, while the going was good, and without pleasure.

'Listen. It says "Light's Out At Nine". L-i-g-h-t-apostrophe-s. *Apostrophe*-s! It says "One Cup of Tea or 'Coffee'" – *coffee* in inverted commas. Why? Why? In the library, the library, it says

"You can NOT Spit" – cannot two words and the *not* in capitals. It's a mistake, a mistake.'

'Okay,' I said uneasily, 'so the place isn't run by a lot of book worms. Or grammarians. Christ, get a grip.'

'Get me out of here,' he said, his voice steepening now. 'It's a mistake. It's not me, it's you! It's a literal, it's a fucking typo!'

'Hey. Hey. Quiet. Jesus.'

Alec was right in a sense. It's in me, all this. My father's father was an oft-busted counterfeiter. One of his sweated fivers still stands framed above the bar in the Shakespeare. It looks hopeless. It looks like a face flannel. My dad himself has lots of form, a really useful show of prior – it's a funny old London slammer that Barry hasn't seen the inside of. Fat Paul's done time for bodily harm, both actual and grievous. Me, I've spent the odd night in local slammers (drunk and disorderly, breaching the peace, resisting arrest and, on one occasion, assaulting a pig: three months, suspended). Only Fat Vince is clean – Gentleman Vince. And all these guys in here, these dumb berks in regulation boiler-suits, these purplenosed losers, scowling bunglers, hamfisted swindlers, violent throwbacks, they're my kind of people. As best they can they ride their luck in the undertow, where you swim the other way. There's a good deal of money in that business. The hitch is that you go to prison if anyone finds out you're doing it. I looked round the room again. This time, seeing Alec, I expected prison to feel further away. But it didn't. It felt nearer.

I gave him my handkerchief. I patted his shoulder. I wasn't very good at all this. 'Two weeks,' I said. 'Two weeks and you'll be on the out. Two weeks, you and me, we'll be drunk in some casino with a couple of chicks.'

'No I won't. I'll be with Ella and the kids. It's all I can live for now.' He gave me a grin of contempt. 'Drunk in a casino, with you and a couple of slags. Very heaven. You think I haven't had all that?'

I went to fetch him more coffee, more chocolate. Alec had been slumming for ten years. It took him ten years to discover that slums are real, that slums bite back – they bite back, with their mean little teeth. I paid the aproned trusty at the counter. Yes, this was another manworld. You could smell it, the female-lessness, the sour, unalloyed testosterone. *My* time in here was almost up, thank God. Soon I would be outside, with the women and the money.

As I walked back to Alec's table a harsh bell sounded. I remained standing. He saw the relief in my face, and he rallied. He stared at me with the old opposition. He said,

'That contract on you.'

'Oh yeah,' I said coolly. 'The fifty-quidder. One day, when I least expect it, someone's going to pull my hair or step on my toe.'

'I know who took it out on you.'

'Oh really? Who?'

'One blow in the face with a blunt instrument. You ready?'

'I'm ready.'

'Hold tight.'

'I'm holding.'

'– It's your *dad*,' said Alec Llewellyn.

An hour later I sat in another waiting room – Harley Street. As I waited I thought of Selina, on a low bench, piously swearing out a date-rape warrant at Paddington Police Station. But she'd never do that to me, not Selina. There's no money in rape warrants. I felt bad about her. Why? Last night's little show of high spirits would surely soon be forgotten. No – I just felt she was moving away from me. Stop, I wanted to say. Not so fast. Hold on. Wait . . . Mrs McGilchrist impatiently redrained that tooth of mine. She said it was pretty much a goner and would flare up again very soon.

An hour later I sat in another waiting room – Soho, Carburton & Linex. I smoked fags and bit my nails. I suppose all prisons are waiting rooms. All prisons – all rooms. All rooms are waiting rooms. Your room is a waiting room. You are waiting, I am waiting. Everything is getting nearer to being over. At last lean Trudi showed me the door.

Terry Linex sat sprawled in his den, resembling a debauched parky among the fronds and goblets, the darts-trophies and Italian diplomas. It was four o'clock in the afternoon, so he buzzed through for whisky and ice.

'Well old son,' he said, 'how's life in the fast lane? What can I do for you.'

'It's about my golden handjob. Jesus. My golden handshake.' I sipped my drink. I had Selina on my mind. I didn't blush or feel embarrassed. You don't blush or feel embarrassed when you're with Terry Linex.

'It's in the pipeline,' he said.

'How much?'

'Oh, it's got to be half way to six figures. Easy.'

'What, say sixty thousand.'

'Got to be.'

'When?'

'Ask Keith. Things've been slow since you left,' he said sleepily. 'We miss your energy, John.'

'Uh?'

'And your flair. Then there's all this tax nonsense. Here. Are you still with that Street number?'

'Selina. Selina Street.'

'Yeah.' He frowned, and moistened his mouth. 'You and her, you're not still an item, I hope.'

I felt that gravity had just gone heavy, like the weather had been doing for so long now. I felt that gravity had just signed up with the weather gods. It tugged my face down, and my heart, and those neglected bits and pieces, those strangers of the lower air. I obeyed instinct. I said,

'No. That's all over. I aimed her. Why?'

'Good,' said Terry, and yawned. 'Do you want to hear this? . . . I did a swimsuit session last week. The Gallet account. I only pulled the model, didn't I – Mercedes Sinclair. Ever worked with her, John? A woman whose bathwater you'd be proud to drink. No messing about, straight off to Smith's for a – a *cinq á sept*. You know the form.'

I knew the form. Smith's was a bijou little sex-chalet off Park Lane, well known and much patronized in ad-game circles. You gave Didier thirty-five notes and you got a room for an hour plus a bottle of champagne. I used to go there a lot in the old days with my Debbys and Mandys, my Mitzis and Sukis. We all did. They changed the sheets five times a day but the rooms were always shipshape and decently aired. I sipped my drink, waiting.

'It was a busy afternoon. Comical really. All these white-slavers panting at the desk. I got a laugh by shouting, 'Hurry up, Didier, or we'll be here all night!' At the head of the queue is this Selina and a fella.'

'What fella?'

'Tall bloke with fair hair. Sounded American to me but they were both camping it up a bit. Anyway the fella knows the form and asks for evening accommodation – a bed rental. Then Selina does her nut. "I've never been so insulted in all my life." All this. So the bloke pays the full whack. Seventy. And will you be requiring champagne, sir? It cost him a ton in the end and they were only there forty minutes. Me and Didier had a good laugh about it after.'

'The name. The guy's *name*.'

Terry shrugged and stretched. 'Tell you what. After all that, he paid by credit card. It must be in the book somewhere. I'm popping in there this evening. I'll ask Didier. I'm staying the night for once. Mercedes, *cinq à sept* doesn't quite cover it. A real armpit-chewer. I'll give you a bell in the morning. Now Selina, she's a goodlooking girl and a right little mover too I shouldn't wonder. But you're well out of that. She never had any class.'

London is full of short stories walking round hand in hand. In the shuffle of the street you see countless odd pairings, all colours, all ages, all sexes, queens and knaves, jacks and tens, in clubs and diamonds, swords and coins, walking round hand in hand. You see a dull-faced young woman, stodged out on booze or glands, taking the leaning weight of her elderly companion, a man with misangled legs like broken dividers. No relation. You see a punk girl of seventeen, who would resemble a mad parrot with or without her two black eyes, on the arm of a milkman not quite old enough to be her father. Where's the connection? You see a big-shouldered forty-year-old blonde, rowdily flanked by two Lithuanian bumboys in tanktop T-shirts. Now where do they fit in? London is full of short stories, long stories, epics, farces, sitcoms, sagas, soaps and squibs, walking round hand in hand.

And what am I starring in? It feels like slapstick to me. Pornographic slapstick, custard pie, the comic relief with the landlady or bellhop before the real fucking resumes elsewhere. I came barrelling out of Carburton & Linex and marched straight into a telephone box. I had my opening speech all worked out. But Selina wasn't there. She wasn't anywhere. So I vandalized the telephone box. I had been wanting to smash a telephone for a long time. The bakelite splintered obligingly, then retaliated with an electric shock. I got to my feet and left the hot receiver swinging from its mauled base. The Fiasco wouldn't start so I beat that up too. I stomped off a fender and took a brick to the headlights. These deeds turned out to be useful therapy and calmed me somewhat until a six-quid queue-job in a predatory black taxi restored and even topped up my rage. I hurdled the stairs with murder smarting in my bitten fingertips.

The flat was empty, of course – bland, blameless, surprised (quite frankly) to see me in such a state. At first, in the silence, when I saw the envelope marked with a florid *J*, I thought the lying bitch had left me already. Yet her clothes, her elixirs and unguents, her special tea, her smell, her femininity were all still here, had not yet passed on, not yet. 'Dinner with Helle, Back around 12,' said the note. 'Love Selina.' Waiting sounds like a passive thing but this vigil, this waiting, was as active and strenuous as anything I had ever performed. You can kill time in a number of ways but it always depends on the kind of time you're fighting: some time is unkillable, immortal. Whenever I did anything I always wanted to be doing something else but when I started doing something else I found I didn't want to do that either. Smoking and drinking and swearing and pacing were about all I could manage. Nothing for it, then, but to do the waiting. So I drank and paced and smoked and swore for seven hours in my private, in my personal waiting room.

At midnight she came through the door. Selina looked well, she looked happy, with a funny buzz or colour to her that I had never seen before. Greedily I sucked in breath to arraign and denounce her and discovered I was speechless, not with drink but with terror. She knew I knew, you see, and she didn't mind . . . How I hate the truth. I insist on my right, I *demand* not to be told. She ran a bath. She hummed as she made her tea. After a while we went to bed and lay together in the dark, like patients, waiting for the truth to make its rounds.

'I'm pregnant,' said Selina Street.

You know, it takes you by surprise, how you secretly weary of the ungrown state, the childless, the childish state. A man is womanish without a woman, and vice versa. An adult is childish without a child. Kids, change, it's just the next thing, like leaving home or getting to know women and finding your own place and job and joining the dance, the lively and frightening conspiracy. I can't wait, I'm sorry. Of course I know it's a classic setup and there are things missing and we have this boyfriend of hers to reckon with and punish her for – but I'm doing it. Do it! I'm finished with the other stuff, aren't I, clearly? Enough. It's *over*. So when Selina spoke I felt my chin rasp on the pillow as I turned and reached for her, the hot, thoughtful, transfigured form lying in the bed beside me.

'Okay. I'll – I ask no questions. All forgiven. It doesn't matter. Let's get married tomorrow.'

'It isn't yours,' she said. 'And I can prove it.'

Ah, those nights – it's no accident that they happen in the night-time. You couldn't behave in this fashion during the day. You'd start wanting to do something else. You'd switch on the TV, or go down the Butcher's Arms. The night is the time. It took another seven hours, and many scalpels and pincers and gallons of boiling water, but we delivered the truth in the end. The light came on. There was a lot of ugly, quacking talk. There were punishments. I didn't hit her. When you hit girls you go through a door and suddenly it's all fine in the next room, a marvellous place where it's absolutely okay, even rather suave and fashionable, to hit girls as much as you like. I went nowhere. I stayed in that bag and just kept on asking. You know those nights. In the end, she found the unbearable a little less bearable than I did and so, at dawn, with a box of paper tissues trembling on her pregnant breasts, she told me the full answer, the long secret. It was unbelievable, but I believed it.

Selina waited and watched. She didn't know how unbelievable it was, not then, not really. She said,

'You've been good about it, considering. I'll move out this morning. It doesn't matter. You can fuck me now if you want to.'

I wanted to. I tried, Lord love me. But in the end I just crawled the length of the sheets and, with the help of my tears and her slow memories of arousal, kissed that dry purse into a glossy wallet and then into nothing at all.

The telephone rang at eleven o'clock. I was lying in bed, for something to do.

'Before me is a list of names,' said Terry Linex. 'One of them's his. Stop me if you've heard it before.'

After a while I said, 'That's him.'

'Any big deal?'

'No big deal.'

'Here. What does the *O*. stand for?'

I told him.

'Pardon?' said Terry.

I said, 'O-double-ess-i-e.'

'Is there a moral philosophy of fiction? When I create a character and put him or her through certain ordeals, what am I up to – morally? Am I accountable. I sometimes feel that –'

. . . You know, by the way, what the tab on the Fiasco is likely to be? Nine hundred pounds. Yeah. Apparently I fucked the bonnet with that brick, and now it needs a new corner-frame or whatever. Plus the insides are all shot to hell. That's why it wouldn't start. That's why I cut up rough on it, and fucked the bonnet with the brick there.

'And the characters have a double innocence. They don't know why they're living through what they're living through. They don't even know they're alive. For instance, if –'

. . . At ten o'clock this morning Selina walked out of my life and into a whole new story. You've got to hand it to the girl. It hurts, but I take my rug off to that Selina – I do. She's going to hit Ossie Twain with a paternity suit, and she's going to win, too. No contest. For a month now she's employed a team of lawyers and medics and set up an HQ in her box. That's why she wouldn't . . . ah, but you guessed. You're not blind. You know the score. Me, I feel duped, dead – and yet impressively resilient. *Stay strong*, I tell myself. Disappointment breeds an odd determination. That must be why I'm throwing myself into my work like this.

'Go ahead. No, I won't thanks. Oh. I think there's another bottle somewhere . . . Yes, you see, readers are natural believers. They too have something of the authorial power to create life and –'

'Hey, the fight,' I said. 'How you doing with the fight.'

'The fight's all fixed. No problem.'

'– How?'

'Simple. By beating him up, Lorne deliberately provokes Spunk into killing him in order to save Butch and keep Caduta in ignorance. It's beautiful, because *Spunk* wants to redeem Butch and protect Caduta too.'

It took me a while to puzzle it out, but then I smacked a fist into my palm and said,

'Martin. You're a fucking genius. Kid, that's what I hired you for! You started earning your dough at last.'

'I'll have to monkey with the transitions but that's no problem either. It's cute: Lorne gets his death scene but Spunk can kill him any way he wants – thought control, astral karate. Of course we needn't bother the audience with all this. You just use cutaways and out-takes and beef it all up in the editing room.'

'Yeah.' We talked deadlines. Then he said,

'What's up, John? You seem low.'

So then I poured it all out, about the Fiasco. Sometimes I think that the key to my life is to be found in the serial humili-ations I have suffered at the hands of that Fiasco of mine – as I stand over the swindlepoint workbench, with the wide eyes and wide legs of the pin-ups and calendar nudes beaming down on me, and the lupine stares of the grease-bandits glimpsed through angles of axles and jacks, and the guvnor turns to me with a grin of thieving scorn and says 'Now let's think' before conjuring his fabulous fee. It's the Clip Valve, it's the Big End, it's the Manifold. It won't start, it won't steer, it won't stop. I can hear them already laughing as I climb in and go kangarooing off down the mews. The next day I'm back with the towtruck. That car, it doesn't *like* driving. Hanging out in expensive garages is what it likes. I swear, that fucking Fiasco, it costs me more money than little Selina ever could.

'I mean,' I said, 'it's meant to be so flash and everything. But it keeps on breaking *down* all the time.'

Martin considered and said seriously, 'Your car sounds like a bit of a joke to me.'

'Yes. I sometimes think that too,' I said thoughtfully.

'Have you got a girlfriend, John?'

'Have I got a *girl*friend? I – yeah, I got this chick in New York. She's got these degrees.'

'You don't say.'

'Have you got a girlfriend, Martin?'

'Sorry, I never go into my private life. Damn!'

'What?'

He sat up, then suddenly strode the few paces to his little TV at the far end of the room.

'What's on?'

'What's on? It's the Royal Wedding.'

'Ah, give me a break.' I refilled my glass. Selina would be watching the Royal Wedding somewhere, watching from the confines of her new money, her new protectorate – a hotel room, maybe, or the stopgap flat of a silent intermediary. I refilled my glass. 'Don't tell me you're going to sit through all that stuff.'

'Why fight it?'

'God damn it, we're working. Put it on the video and watch it later.'

'I haven't got a video.'

'You haven't got shit, have you, and how much do you earn? It's immoral. Push out some cash. Buy stuff. Consume, for Christ's sake.'

'I suppose I'll have to start one day,' he said. 'But I really don't want to join it, the whole money conspiracy.'

'Do you own this flat? What sort of car've you got? What's the matter with you?'

'Sshh . . . Look at that weather,' he whispered. 'Three weeks of shit and then they give us this. Magic.'

With a soft palpitation the small screen had fizzed into life – and there it was, the Royal Wedding, the crowd-ribbed Mall, the sun, and the horses getting people to the church on time. Blushing and glancing downwards in the glare of all this history, Lady Diana cruised slowly up the aisle, her tottering dad at her side and pocket bridesmaids smirking in her wake. There was Charles, my age, standing uniformed among the ramrod princes. Is Fat Paul right? Has Charles given her one already? He's going to give her one tonight – that's for sure. As I twisted in my seat and muttered to myself I found I kept looking Martin's way. The lips were parted, suspended, the eyes heavy and unblinking. If I stare into his face I can make out the areas of waste and fatigue, the moonspots and boneshadow you're bound to get if you hang out in the twentieth century. Of course, you do see people who appear to be quite unaffected by all this, by the timing of their time travel, not just their own journey but the planet's parallel travel through time. They have a colour. You never see them in the streets, not in the streets plural. That colour, it looks like the sheen of health or sun or gimmicked youth but it is only the colour of money. Money softens the fall of life, as you know. Money breaks the fall. Anyway, Martin hasn't got that colour. And neither have I. And neither have you. Shake. Princess Diana has it. She is nineteen years old, just starting out. There she goes now, gathering herself into the carriage while the horses stamp. All England dances. I looked at Martin again and – I swear, I promise – I saw a grey tear glint in those heavy eyes. Love and marriage. The horses ticking down the long slide.

After a while he dropped a toilet roll on to my lap.

'Do you want a cup of tea?' I heard him ask. 'Or an aspirin. Or a Serafim? Don't be embarrassed. It was very moving in its way. That's right, have a good big blow. You'll feel better for it. Phew! Better? Keep a grip on it. Don't worry. Everything's going to turn out okay in the end.'

At night I hear homeless voices out over the flat rooftops. There are sounds of cramped murmuring. They come, they go, they move on. I sleepwalk in the dark to the bathroom and bend to soothe my parched and aching mouth. Through the window I can see a ragged family or pack, grouped round the fin of a yellow skylight. One of them waves or beckons. I raise a pale hand. They burn candles in the smoky night and mutter with cigarettes moving in their mouths. Beyond, higher up, a big woman sleeps under a creased groundsheet on the flat surface, like a protractor. In Manhattan the underclass live underground, along the half-built subway lines. Here they spill out on to the eaves and sills. How strange to let money just seep us around like this . . . And out there tonight also, in the batteries of the council blocks (looming like God's transistor radios left switched on all over town), an experiment, a breakthrough in vandalism is finding its form. What the kids suddenly like to do now is take *ponies* up in the lifts to the high floors and ride them through the gangways and galleries of council airspace, front doors and windows on one side, a low wall and a night sky on the other. It's true. Where do they get the ponies from? The allotments, the canals? Up they go, to towers of perversity. It doesn't even sound much fun, God damn it. I've been a vandal in my time and believe me, for free entertainment, vandalism is hard to beat. Vandalism is a million laughs . . . Bad for the residents, hearing animal panic. Bad for the animals, whose genes could never have bargained for this kind of nightlife, this kind of highlife. But the ponies can't complain. They've just got to take their chances along with the rest of us. They must adapt, mutate. They can't hide out. No one can. High time, really, that ponies changed their act and did their bit for the twentieth century.

I am a thing made up of time lag, culture shock, zone shift. Human beings simply weren't meant to fly around like this. Scorched throat, pimpled vision, memory wipes – nothing new to me, but it's all much worse these days, not that I ride the planet shuttle. I have to get up in the middle of the night to check out the can. My daily tiredness peak arrives exactly when it wants to, often after morning coffee. Sitting down to eat, I am either ravenous and fat-cheeked with drool – or helplessly sated, for no reason. On impulse I floss my teeth in the middle of the afternoons. Even these would-be handjobs of mine turn out bassackwards, with climaxing coming first. All day I am my night self, spliced by night thoughts, night sweats. And all night, well, I am something else entirely, something else again, I am something overevolved, a salty slipstream thinning out and trailing down over the black Atlantic.

Friday came, and did its thing, and vanished, as Fridays will. I seemed to be in okay shape, considering. I seemed to be hanging in there, alone. Hell, I thought, I can butch this out. I rose at eleven and, wearing jeans and gyms, jogged down the drinker. I ate a lot of pub grub: bendy sausages, ginger baked beans, a trough of cottage pie. I drank a lot of pub drink too. Traditional ales from the handpump, fine wines and choicest spirits. I left nine pounds fifty in the fruit machine and seventy-five quid in the turf accountant's next door. I bought an evening paper and a few take-out kebabs to relish alongside my coffee and toast. I clipped my fingernails with my teeth. I made a highly complicated, demanding, almost experimentalist visit to the bathroom. At five o'clock I fixed myself a cocktail and blacked out for four hours on the couch. I rose again, shampooed my hair, washed up a mug or two, glanced at the *Morning Line*, and went back down the drinker. On my way home I looked in at the Pizza Pouch and had a Big Thick Juicy Hot One. Hard by at the Furter Factory I put three nearmeat Long Whoppers over my belt, and an American Way. And so at the day's end I made a pot of tea and curled up with a pint of scotch and a few video nasties to see me through until bedtime. I slept the sleep of the good. All fine. No problem. The Selina thing turned out to be nothing I couldn't handle. Where do they come from, these reserves of strength, courage and willpower? I was surprised. I was impressed. It wasn't until the next day that I started going downhill.

★

My clothes are made of monosodium glutamate and hexachlorophene. My food is made of polyester, rayon and lurex. My rug lotions contain vitamins. Do my vitamins feature cleaning agents? I hope so. My brain is gimmicked by a microprocessor the size of a quark, and costing ten pee and running the whole deal. I am made of – junk, I'm just junk.

Saturday morning I thought I'd break the routine and treat myself to a burn-up in the Fiasco. Ossie will settle out of court, probably. He has the dough. It won't hurt him if he can keep it quiet . . . On with the cravat and the blazer, and off down Chelsea way, to the pubs and winebars where the county chicks hang out. It wasn't much of a burn-up – traffic, police, the sloth of the refurbished Fiasco. But I did go to lots of pubs and winebars (they were full of county chicks, yes and county prongs too). Driving home, as I sat in a jam on the Bayswater Road, a frazzled wasp flew sideways through the window and twirled out of view between my legs. It was arguable who was in worse shape, me or the wasp. My fist was on the horn as I hollered at the ugly gut of the tourist bus that had straddled the street ahead. I thrashed tubbily about – and the wasp stung me. I pulled into a sidestreet and dropped my pants. There was a little red dot on my thigh. It looked, and it felt, like the mildest cigarette burn. And I thought: is that the best you can do? You've lost the heft, you poor wound-down thing, raised on crisps and pop, on car belch and gutter gook. As I zipped myself up, a pigeon clockworked past on the pavement, eating a chip. A *chip*. Like horseflies and other creatures who direct and star in their own tiny films, the pigeon lived in fast motion. It naturally preferred fast food. City life is happening everywhere. The wasp was dead. That sting was its last shot. Flies get dizzy spells and bees have booze problems. Robin redbreasts hit the deck with psychosomatic ulcers and cholesterol overload. In the alleys, dogs are coughing their hearts out on snout and dope. The stooped flowers in their sodden beds endure back-pinch and rug-loss, what with all the stress about. Even the microbes, the spores of the middle air are finding all this a little hard on their nerves.

I restarted the car and began nipping home the back way. The Fiasco feels better on these sidestreets, where it can show off its acceleration. Then I noticed that a car was following me. I wasn't just being paranoid. It really was following me. It was flashing its lights and parping its horn and generally making with all the swear words and V-signs in the motoring repertoire. I put my foot on the floor and jumped a junction or two at top speed. I must have been going flat out when the car stopped following me. It overtook me instead.

'Would you like to get out of the car, sir?'

The pigs, the fucking *pigs*. 'Sure,' I said, and climbed out. Annoyingly, I tripped and came a cropper on the kerb. But I got up again as quick as you like and dusted myself down, oozing confidence.

'Been drinking today, sir?'

I was ready for this, of course. Absolutely no problem at all. Over the years I've honed down the perfect answer to that question, and I let the pig have it pat. 'Ah now let me see,' I said, sonorously. 'I had a champagne perry and blackcurrant before my lunch and, yeah, a glass of stout with my mutton vindaloo.' It's a good one, isn't it. None of this two-glasses-of-wine stuff. No, you see, the key to the whole gimmick is to confess quite cheerfully to a couple of unserious, feminine tipples, while at the same time deterring the law from smelling your breath. It's a *good* one, isn't it.

'Beg your pardon, sir? Here, Steve – it's not bad going, is it, for three o'clock in the afternoon?'

Annoyingly, I had fallen over again and was having a real spot of bother finding my feet.

'Would you like to come down to the station, sir, and have

another go at saying that? Here, Steve, come on. Looks like we got a dead one.'

I disclaim responsibility for many of my thoughts. They don't come from me. They come from these squatters and hoboes who hang out in my head, these guys who stroll past me like naturalized, emancipated rodents (passport and papers all in order), like gentrified rats, flapping a paw and saying 'Hi, pal', and I have to wait and not mind while they make coffee or hog the can – there's nothing I can do about them. The place I have to shuffle around is a two-room flat with no hall or passage, a student gaff full of books I can't read. The people in here, with me among them, no better and no worse and with complete equality of powerlessness, are like sick bats or threadbare monkeys wearing hippie loons and jaded T-shirts with three buttons up the throat. There's nothing I can do about them, these unknown Earthlings.

You understand, during the past few days (and I am especially displeased with this thought and wish now that I had never given it headroom), I'm finding myself more and more reluctant to face up to the fact that all women's mouths have at some point played hostess to a man's . . . They all have. Every last one. Even the old dears, the sainted grannies, even the twisted relicts who lurk like pub parrots in the corner of the lounge – they've all done it, God damn it. They've all done it, or they will soon . . . I mean, in ten years, twenty, they'll all have done it by then, every woman alive. Sisters, mothers, grans: ladies, what are you doing? What have you done?

I'm not shocked, just disappointed. My tone is not angry. My tone is concerned, tender, grieving. Imagine, please, my fat beady face, my trustful frown. I wince and shrug. I lay it all before you. Quite a number of you girls have done that thing to me. Thanks.

I thoroughly enjoyed it – I was grateful, touched. Thanks again. No, really. But what are you doing? Oh, what have you *done*?

On the other hand, look what the human mouth has to put up with. I'm trying to see it from your point of view. Unimaginable, Third World food-mountains are churned and swirled through that delicate processor – pampas of cattle, fathoms of living sea, horizons of spud and greens, as well as conveyor belts of Wallys and Blastburgers, vats of flavouring and colouring, plus fags, straws, thermometers, dentist's drills, doctor's shears, drugs, tongues, fingers, feeding tubes. Is this any way to treat the mouth, the poor mouth, the human mouth? And so perhaps, after all this, the constant cartoon of pigments, textures and impacts, a man's dick doesn't look that bad.

Ah what the hell. Pretty soon, most of the guys will have done it too, and we'll all be in the same boat, along with you girls. I suppose I might even get round to it myself one of these days – I wouldn't put it past me, what with these perverse thoughts, these crashers, dossing in my head. With their milk cartons on the windowsill and their damp double-mattresses on the floor, they grow in confidence every day. They were nervous at first, it's true, but no one has tried very hard to evict them and they're used to the uncertainty, they're used to living rough. There is historical necessity involved. There is hysterical necessity. In time, all men's mouths will have given headroom to men's dicks too. We'll do it one day, though we of all people really ought to know better. And what a wonderful joke that will be.

I walk more in the streets now. The Fiasco is still in custody. I keep meaning to go along and spring it from the pound. But I can't be fucked. The trouble is, I can't be fucked. Guess how long Ossie and Selina have been doing their thing. Two years. Funny, isn't it. Laugh? I nearly died. The pigs were pretty lenient with me on the whole. There was some doubt about whether the Fiasco could seriously be classified as a moving vehicle, which worked in my favour. I may get off with a drunk in charge. The Fiasco isn't really as quick as I've made out. Ossie has been fucking Selina for as long as I have – longer, in fact, if you count the last few weeks. They were fond of each other at first but then the relationship became purely sexual, after their visit to Stratford that time. The Fiasco is really much slower than I've let on. Naturally I refused to go to the police station and insisted, as is my right, that the pigs send for a breathalyser. I sat on the pavement smoking cigarettes. I also tried another gimmick. What you do is, you take a small coin, preferably a half-pee, and roll it round your mouth like a lozenge. Screws up the breathalyser. Anyway, I only had a fifty-pence piece – and then one of the pigs caught me in the act. As I drew in breath to proclaim my innocence the coin got wedged in my throat. By the time the other guys arrived with the breathbag I had coughed myself black in the face. And, when full, the crystal pouch almost lifted me off the pavement, like a helium balloon. Ossie's eccentric in the sack, apparently. He makes me look like Norman Normal. She doesn't like him that much any more, she said, but on the other hand he does have an incredible amount of money. Me, I haven't got it wet for five weeks now. I'm so despoiled and contaminated with drink that I can't even pull off a handjob around here. Even my handjobs are jokes. What a life, eh? What a joke life. I must face up to something: however painful the realization may seem at first, I must accept that I'm not an alcoholic. If I were, I'd have one of those cool alcoholic constitutions. And I haven't. When I saw the truth I went out and drowned my sorrows. But I can't go on drinking like an alcoholic. Only alcoholics can. They're the only guys who can hack it. Only alcoholics have got what it takes.

I walk more in the streets now. Unemployment is a problem.

I agree. But let me tell you something. Employment is a problem too. My rating on the breathalyser was 339. I called a lawyer who specializes in drunk driving. He has defended a 240. He has defended a 245. He has even defended a 250. He has never defended a 339. He'll defend me, though, providing I give him all the money he asks for. You know how little Selina tabbed her scam? She didn't use my money, or Ossie's either. A girl of high principle, she financed the venture by working like a dog at Helle's boutique. Only Helle's boutique isn't just a clothes shop: it's a sex shop too. Selina swears to God that she just managed the counter, peddling ticklers and crotchless pants and plastic ladies – a vibrator saleswoman and dildo-wrapper, no more. She denies with maximum indignation that she lent a hand with the assisted showers in back. I doubt her word, lawyers' fees being what they are. And who cares. The streets are full of movement but hardly anybody goes where they go through thought or choice, free of money motive. Only people with money do that. At the wheels of the parked Culprits and Alibis sit flustered men with order-sheets and invoices on their laps. Women pollinate the shops. Now that I no longer go to work every day . . . and why should people do this? Who says? Why wasn't I consulted? You give your mornings then creep back with shoulders splitting to the day-home and its afternoon breath. Stop *taking* it. Organize! Fuck your factory! When you go to work every day, you aren't really living. In some ways it must be a great relief. Really living – now that's hard graft, that's nine-to-five stuff (it's like going to work every day). Really living is what I'm doing, and it's killing me. Being a tramp is a tall order. Only tramps seem to be up to it. Only tramps can cope. I subserve the detailed money action, do this, do that, run money errands. I am pussy-whipped by money, but then so is the United States. So is Russia. We are all stomped and roughed up and peed on and slammed against the wall by money. Should the earth enter turnaround tomorrow, nuke out, commit suicide, then we'll already have our suicide notes, pain notes, dolour bills – money is freedom. That's true. But freedom is money. You still need money. We ought to shake money like a dog shakes a rat. Grrrrrr! 'What would happen if you told Martina?' said Selina. I wonder. 'You might do yourself a bit of good there,' said Selina. 'She likes you. Ossie told me.' How is that face? Ah, dear face! Hi, honey. Her face is pale, and worried and watchful.

I walk more in the streets now. I . . . This morning in the sunshine I saw a pale boy, three or four years old or however old kids are these days, wheeled by his father in a hoodless pram. The boy wore thick glasses with thick black rims. Like the pram the specs were cheap. Unhinged, they slipped from the child's pale ears and he groped at this thing on his face, gazing up, appealing to his father, who was thirty-odd, skinny, with long skinny hair, T-shirt, winded denims. The child's face had the gently suffering look you sometimes get among the pale, the small, the hard of seeing: he showed his milky teeth, the expression rapt, expectant, forming a rightful entreaty. The father made his brisk adjustments – not unkindly, no, not at all. The child's pale hand was raised and with its fingertips lightly steadied the darker, busier hand . . . I took this hard, the eyes so old so soon, and coupled to that pale, forbearing thing.

'*You* cried,' I said.

'Well, a bit. Hardly.'

'Yes you did, you liar. I saw you.'

'I wiped away the odd tiny tear, perhaps. But *you* – you were something unbelievable. You were bawling.'

'She's a bloody marvellous girl, she is,' I said thickly. 'Princess Di, she loves her people. She'd do anything for us, mate, anything. Anything!'

'Oh no. I can't bear it. He's going to start crying again.'

'I'm . . . *not*.'

Carefully Martin refreshed my drink. I had a chick in off the streets last night. I didn't do anything. We just talked. I had another crying jag. I gave her fifty quid. The night before, I went rioting. As I flopped out of the Pizza Pouch at eleven o'clock, I saw that Ladbroke Grove was all shards and sparks. I scored a bottle of rum at an Armenian delly and lumbered off into the action. I don't remember much about it: smashed glass and trampled window displays, the ratlife of looters, the riot joy of the chaos kids. The next day I woke up with a back like a corrugated roof, scorched, shrunk. In the passage I found two TV sets – black-and-white, fifteen-quidders. I had a really bad time getting rid of them. Up and down those stairs, staggering through the streets looking for skips. Eventually I wedged them into a pair of warped dustbins. Fat fucking lot of good that did me. Araping and alooting – I don't know who handles their PR, but they're both overrated. Rioting can be a real rip-off sometimes. It's hard work, rioting, just like everything else.

'Hey,' I said. 'I went all the way up the Charing Cross Road the other day and not one of the bookshops had your stuff.'

'Yeah yeah.'

'Only one of the guys had heard of you and he said you were sick in the head.'

'You know how I account for the blackness of modern writing?' Martin asked. 'Like everyone else these days, writers have to get by without servants. They have to take in washing and do all their own. No wonder they're morbid. No wonder they're bushed.'

'You ought to ring up your fucking publisher, mate. Get them on the ball.'

'Yeah yeah.'

The set of the mouth defines the face, as if glimpsed in a bendy old mirror and catching a fault along the parting line – yes, and with a swirl of dust and flecking on the glass. There's no mistaking the century he's from. He drives a little black Iago, a 666. At night, big fast things look especially dark. The blackest thing I ever saw was a mad bus at three in the morning, coming down Westway with no lights and no human driver. I read about it in the *Morning Line*. Someone flipped. Lots of damage. You know those dreams of pursuit when it hurts to run or shout. I get them nightly. I can run as fast and shout as loud as I like. Velocity and volume have been granted in full measure, but I'm still fleeing, and still screaming. Shame is a chick who blew you in the can that time. Ooh, she is so shameless. Watch her make a lunge for your nuts! Every so often fear fucks shame for something to do. He's not frightened. She couldn't care. Yesterday afternoon I fell over in the bath and broke a full pint of scotch. Later, I had a hooker in off the street. Nothing happened. She couldn't have been nicer. Do you know why? Because she thought I might be going to murder her, that's why. This morning, as I finally aborted a catastrophic, neck-searing handjob, the telephone rang. It was *Cleopatra* magazine, asking me to be Bachelor of the Month. Success has not changed me. I'm what I always was.

'It's all nice and tight, don't worry. It's foolproof. Doris Arthur was just trying to give you a bad time. Not me. Things will go smoothly now with those bankable stars of yours. Hey, come on. Lighten up.'

I went for a rug-rethink in Queensway this afternoon. Fifteen quid, just for a feminine touch. That was all I was after. The smocked chick fingered my hair and said in her stupid voice, 'You're receding.' 'We all are,' I said. We all are. We are all receding – waving or beckoning or just kissing our fingertips, we are all fading, shrinking, paling. Life is all losing, we are all losing, losing mother, father, youth, hair, looks, teeth, friends, lovers, shape, reason, life. We are losing, losing, losing. Take life away. It's too hard, too difficult. We aren't any good at it. Try us out on something else. But shelve life. Take life off the stands. It's too fucking difficult and we aren't any good at it.

'The script. When. When?'

If we could spread money shallow it would act like a layer over everything. The world might be softer. But life, life is so hard. Life is so *hard*. Oh, so, it is so – dah. Mah, mother, muh – you never told me, no one said. It, it is, it is so –

'*Easy*,' said Martin, '– steady now. It's all here. Here. Here it is. Just pick it up and take it away. Dry your eyes, old son. Treats are in store. You'll see. It'll all turn out right in the end.'

A T THIS moment in time I am doing something that millions of people all over the planet are longing, are aching, are dying to do. Eskimos dream about it. Pygmies beat off about it. You've thought about it, pal, take my word for it. You too, angel, if you're at all that way inclined. The whole world wants to do it. And I'm doing it. I must say it's amazing how quickly you can cheer up in New York. This is no town for killjoys or cockteasers or spoilsports of any kind. Not much cockteasing goes on in New York. It's not a problem.

I'm giving Butch Beausoleil one. You don't believe me? But I am! Round from the back, what's more. You get the picture: she's on all fours and clutching the headpiece of her neighing brass bed. If I glance downwards, like so, and retract my gut, I can see her valentine card and the mysterious trail of her cleft, like the inside of a halved apple. *Now* do you believe me. Wait: here comes her hand, idling slantways down her rump, ten bucks of manicure on each fingertip. Why, she seems to be . . . *Wow*. Selina herself doesn't do that too often. And I bet not even Selina does it on the first date. Well, true sack artists, they adore themselves, every inch. I'm on my knees too and really going great guns here. I'm in a position to tell you that the camera doesn't lie. I've seen Butch naked before, partially on screen and fully, fully frontally, in one of the whack magazines that feature celebrity indiscretions, but that hardly prepared me for all this costly flesh texture and high-tab body-tone, not to mention the bunk knowhow on such vivid display. It's all top-quality gear and she has this . . . Hang on, she's turning over. I think she wants to turn over. What? Oh yeah. We're off again. As I was saying, I've been at it for a good twenty minutes but I'm still full of running, I think, and really thrilled and awed by the show of form I seem to be flexing. There's an incredible pain in my back, true, and my right leg is all heavy and dead but I'm definitely going to spin this out for as long as I possibly can. What a turn-up, what a treat, what a spree. We just had lunch in the Village and then in the cab she said . . . Hold it. Hold everything. Now wait just a goddamn minute. She wants, she wants to get her – or at least she seems to be trying to . . . Christ, that's a new one on me. That's a whole new concept. Ah *I* see: in fact her leg stays there while she goes crosswise and –[*Dah*. Wait! No, I get it. I'm with you. And then, and then, oh yeah, no sooner had we stepped through the door of her apartment than she fished a bottle of champagne out of the icebox, gave me a line of cocaine the size of a hangman's rope, and led me playfully by the hand into her bedroom, her hall of mirrors. There must be some mistake, I thought. She must be confusing me with another guy altogether. But suddenly she was naked and plucking at the buckle of my own stunned strides. I wised up at that point and took full command. Forget it, Butch, you can't do that. Nobody can, not even you. She seems to be making some sort of attempt to bend her head around from the . . . Well I'll be a son of a bitch. What originality. What control. What pacing. What *talent*. It must hurt, too – or perhaps she works out a lot. I keep looking for the flaw in this arrangement. I mean, it can't be a free offer, can it? She's not doing this for her health . . . Actually she probably is. That's probably exactly what she's doing it for. Over here, you know, they're always looking for fun ways to stay in shape, and Butch has certainly got an aerobics deal going for herself, with the . . . She's not serious. Who, me? Oof! No, please, that hurts. *Ow*.

Whoah, my leg's all . . . At least let me – that's better. That's
a bit better, really quite tolerable. Whew, this is warm work
all right. What with the torched lungs and tom-tom ticker, I
haven't felt as beat as this since that tennis game with Fielding.
And even then no one was using my balls as a test-your-grip
device. Pain barriers opened, and closed again. It is getting
nearer to being over. Each breath is fire . . . At last: she's started
making those noises, like all the crack chicks do. I'm not
entirely sure what the noises portend, but Butch would seem
to be girding herself for some kind of apocalyptic jackpot and,
yes, I'm along for the ride too, panting and jabbering and
holding on for dear life. Now or never. What shall I think
about, to help me jump off the train? I'll think about Butch
Beausoleil. It's working.

. . . Sex is like death, the poets say. It's what the doctors say
too, in my case. And the point of climax, it turns out, is no more
than a half-way stage in the whole operation, as conceived by
Butch Beausoleil. Oh man, some girls – they make you feel like
a real chick. So this is what fellatio is, I thought. All the other
times – that wasn't fellatio, not really. Jesus, the Fiasco must feel
like this when it goes for a carwash. She's not blowing it: she's
rinsing it. She's hosing it down . . . Sounds good, eh pal? Boy, I
bet you're thinking, could I use a little of that. A little, maybe.
But could you use a lot? Half an hour later or thereabouts Butch
murmured,

'John? May I say something?'

'Yeah,' I said unsteadily, straightening up to get a glimpse of
her over my gut. There she was, talking right into the mike.

'I agree with Lorne Guyland, John. We need the explicit scenes.
I think that visually the contrast could be rather beautiful. It has
to be made clear that the girl gives herself to the old man out
of pity and also because of her artistic sense. It is an act of artistic
generosity, of giving. We could have her say something like "You

are old. I am young. You are worn and coarse. I am clear and fresh as the morning. I give myself to you, old man. A gift of youth."'

'Oh boy.'

'Pardon me?'

'Where's your john?' I said.

Worse was to come. But before I tell you about the fight after, let me tell you about the fight before. Something tells *me* I'm going to have to do a lot more fucking and fighting before this deal is done. I live like an animal – eating and drinking, dumping and sleeping, fucking and fighting – and that's it. It's survival. It's not enough.

I had my lunch with Butch. We did some eating and drinking there. I sat facing her, grim, sick, silent, generally at my least seductive. Rug low? On. Dental panic – active. Ticker terror: burning. There was nothing in the air. I upended a brandy on her lap. I cursed at and got cheeked and cheated by the waiters. Silently but irrefutably I farted in the cab back to her duplex. My tongue felt like a flashfried frazzfurter. Midway through the doorman's staged seconds of obsequious lechery, I noted in a hall mirror that my flyzip was broken and that pink-tinged Y-fronts now gazed sadly through the vent . . . I have a theory. They decide, don't they. Girls just decide. It's all decided, it's all taken care of. Those nights you show up with the orchid, and lay on the show and the top-dollar dinner, and they're giving you the gimmick with the eyes and the mouth. Won't do you any good at all unless they've decided. They decide, early on. They have their deep reasons. It's nothing much to do with you. And then, on some night or other, as you sit there burping and scratching your armpit and thinking about money – you get the lot.

But something happened, something happened out on the

street, and this might have pulled Butch my way. I don't know. Whatever it was that pulled her, it wasn't me . . . I paid the check and the revolving doors churned us out into the waiting air. Oh, this is unserious, this is kidding heat. My hangover, which was a week old by now and coming at me with doubling frequencies and full Doppler effect, was of the bloodboiling variety, squeezing the eyes, the throat, the gut. 'You want a cab?' I asked her. Convulsively I waved at the shifting bank of yellow, lost my balance and veered sideways into the snarling ass of an air-conditioning unit, which tried out its hottest bad breath in my face. Now this was Eighth Street, just west of Fifth Avenue, high colour in the August arroyo, and many cabs and Honolulu-shirted cabbies, and jungle movement in its full shimmer of attraction and warning. At the crossroads no cars moved. And then something happened, as it always might in the fire and fumes of high summer in New York.

Fifty feet away a tall untethered man had whirled out with his chain to flog the gridlocked traffic. He was big and white, this chain artist, half naked, with yellow pony-tail. People watched him – there was performance here, but the blocked and lipless face said end-of-the-line things, last things. We could sense the chain's heavy hum as it swooned through the air, then the foundry clang as the iron broke the snouts and spines of the stalled cars, which bellowed and cringed like beasts flinching from the lash in their stall. We moved closer. Through the ugly rumble now came the chirrup, the fruity birdcall of the sirens, and already two hunched cops were running low across the street. They faced off, guns held tight and stubby. The chain artist stood his ground and made wide swathes with the humming links. Uncertainly the cops lowered their guns. They were stoked up too, for this sweaty contact, liking their chances with fists and nightsticks, half-crouched and counting the beats. Ah, I get it, I thought: they'll wait for a full swing, then as the chain goes into turnaround they'll move in together and nail him, like in the movies. That's what you do to guys with chains, and that's what they tried. But this chain artist, he got in several good lashes and followed them up in person with all four limbs twanging. Ach, the jagged insect blur of arms and legs when trouble bursts out like this. He looked pretty tasty to me, but those karate kicks were strictly television and would count for little on the street. Abruptly we lost our vantage as the audience thickened and by the time we were ringside again a shot had been fired, with a query of cordite cloud still hovering, and one cop held the gun above his head while the other (tight-packed with torch and short-wave) jockeyed about beside him. And now at last the chain artist fell to his knees, raised both fists on stiffening arms, dropped his head and, the whole face turning young, sniggered guiltily. All over. No more, not today.

'Don't hit him!' came the sharp shout from the crowd as the cops moved in and flattened the guy on the gooey macadam. 'Don't hit him!' endorsed the Nordic giant standing next to me, some track-suited miracle of push-ups and alfalfa. Others now joined in with their admonitions and advice, and the incensed drivers climbed yelling from their battered cars. A fat old black man wearing a red apron loped importantly across the street to shout out his version. New York is full of actors, producers, creative consultants. But by the time the chain artist had been hurled into the squad car, and another fluting wagon had pulled up, and the last cop had his bullhorn out like an assistant director – 'Okay, the show's over. Move on down a street please. Let's move now. It's all over' – the crowd had levered itself back into the jungle, and I was left with Butch pressing my hand to her breasts and saying,

'Take me home now.'

★

Where was I? Oh yeah, in Butch's can, in Butch's rethink parlour. Actually it was more like a botanical laboratory or plantation hothouse, incorporating only incidentally or forgetfully the standard rethink facilities. By accident I dried my hands on a fold of furry foliage and then almost took a leak into an outsize humidor. Plants, earth, nature, life – all valued commodities out here in New York. Up on some creeper or climber, I now noticed, a burly parrot was eyeing me spitefully from the corner of the ceiling. The air was sweet, hot, rich, good for everything except breathing. I did what I needed to do, and made it back to the temperate zones.

Butch was sitting up in bed watching an adult movie (silent, hard core) on a six-foot screen set into the opposite wall. I joined her. A fat pale guy was giving a bronzed blonde the treatment on a wobbly iron bed. The print was of high quality but production values were low – fixed camera, no variation or close-ups. Quite quickly I realized that the girl was Butch Beausoleil. A little later I realized that the man – the man was John Self. Me, in other words. As you would expect, as you knew already, Butch looked the part. Her closed eyes and the averted curvings of her face showed a flattered delight in the address of the camera: the camera. I judged the angle and turned to my right. There was the video eye, its thermos nozzle quite openly mounted on a table beneath the window. On screen the couple changed position often and strenuously. These contortions, I saw, were gauged to display the female lead to still greater advantage. But they showed you the male lead too, this fat actor or extra or bit-part player, his pocked back, juddering beerbelly and tumescent throat – no, it wasn't the body (we all have *bodies*), it was the face. Ah! the face! The shame and fear of its bared gums, its elderly winces, its terrible surprise . . . Now we came to the blowjob bit and my mug was really something to see. Even Butch remarked on it.

'Don't you like that?' she asked. 'You're a very ugly guy, John. I like that in you, I really do. It appeals to my – this is boring. I'll go fast-forward and then re-wind. No, you really don't like that do you.'

'During,' I said. 'I like it during. Not after. The same, the same goes for all this stuff.'

'It was playing all through. It's geared for simultaneous and delayed transmission.'

The film slowed. Butch was talking now, silently, on screen, singling out the camera with her eyes. My head peered over my gut for an instant, then flopped back again. What was Butch saying? The visual contrast. Youth and old age. I am clear and fresh as the morning. An act of aesthetic generosity. Yeah, I get it.

'Hey Butch. How old are you?'

'I'll be twenty in January.'

'Jesus Christ. Why aren't you home with your folks?'

'I hate my mother and my father died.'

'Okay. Wipe it.'

'Pardon me?'

'The tape. Wipe it. Do it.'

'No I won't do that, John. You see I only ball the same person once. That's why I like to keep it.'

'Wipe it.'

'Fuck you.'

'Do it.'

'Make me.'

So then I beat her up. Yup, I beat up Butch. Nothing dirty – just a few shakes and shoves. My heart wasn't in this, not really: I've lost the old flair for such activities. But guess what. She liked it. Now I know men who hit women are always saying that women like being hit. For the life of me I've never been able to understand why they try this line. It's always been phenomenally clear to me that the women I've hit don't like being hit one bit. If they did, what would be the point of hitting them? They all dislike it intensely, and you usually have to do an incredible amount of grovelling and flower-buying and promising not to hit them again. Perhaps I've just roughed up the wrong kind of woman. Some like it. Practically every human activity has its fans by now. Butch liked it. I could tell. How? After she'd wiped the tape (I had a good twisty half-nelson on her by then), she told me she loved being dominated and tried to get me back in the sack.

'Yeah yeah,' I said. 'If you behave I might bring my laundry bag round for you. Now listen. I don't want to hear any more of your lousy ideas. You're an actress. From now on you just shut up and do as your Poppa Bear says.'

'Okay. Now come to bed, you ugly bastard.'

But I made her get dressed and then I took her to the movies. Then pizza, and a long talking-to. That was all over between us, I said. I didn't want to imperil our working relationship – our artistic collaboration there.

Fielding Goodney straightened his cuffs and sipped his wine. He laughed suddenly, showing his fat back teeth. The usual linen and tuxed flunkies, tasselled menus and twenty-dollar starters, major hoods and numb shiny women – the usual. I made my selection: it was the only dish I could pronounce. I'm one up on Spunk Davis here: he thinks that halibut rhymes with Malibu. If time is money, then fast food saves both. I like these snazzy places out here in snazzy New York, but my gut rumbled candidly for junk. Soon, I'm going to kick fast food and start doing right by my money.

'What did you do to Butch?' said Fielding.

'I gave her a little lecture,' I said. Dead discreet, you see.

Actually I had a hunch that Fielding had been there himself. 'Fielding!' Butch said at one point. 'Is *he* ever weird!' But for some reason I didn't press her for details. Discretion again, I suppose.

'Well whatever you did, keep doing it. She was giving us some trouble while you were gone. They all were. But now? Good as gold. They all are. I don't know how you did it, Slick, but you did it. Lorne and Caduta are crazy about you. Even Spunk thinks you're cute.'

How *did* I do it? I don't know. Films are all luck and anarchy. Yet here I stood, on the brink of something – holding the guard-rail, in fact, and feeling very sober. I said,

'It's the new script.'

'It's some script. How about that guy. You sure he's a writer? You sure he's not in public relations or voodoo or psychotherapy?'

'Uh?'

Fielding shrugged. 'The manipulation. All he's done is take Doris's screenplay and poured treacle in the works. It's just one big cuddle.'

'Ah, but that's the beauty of it,' I said.

True, Martin had retained the Doris Arthur outline. Apart from some structural adjustments he had retained almost everything. The characters were no less mean and venal, the action no less squalid and compromising. He had simply interwedged a rota-system of long monologues, in which each of the four stars was elaborately praised, exonerated and legitimized by the other three. Thus, after Lorne had been jeered from the marital bedroom, the fecund but child-worn Caduta wryly soliloquizes on her failure to satisfy such an ever-vibrant swordsman as her husband. Or again: after Butch has been slapped about by Spunk, she tells Caduta that she deliberately provoked this wayward poet and dreamer as a means of securing the longed-for emotional response, while Spunk himself confides to Lorne about man's tragic propensity to hurt the thing he loves. And so on. Admittedly it looked odd on the page, and *Bad Money* (new title) was by now a pretty baggy and ballsaching read. But the monologues would go straight down the cutting-room toilet, if indeed they were ever filmed, and I foresaw no difficulties there.

'You have to give him credit,' Fielding conceded. 'It's the perfect snowjob. It's almost pornographic.'

Fielding spoke with the sadness of the powerman who sees his constituency fractionally undermined. 'How's Doris?' I asked him.

'Good. Writers,' he said vaguely, 'they have too much power as it is. Well, Slick. You won't be needing me that much any more. From here on in I'm strictly executive. I got a whole bunch of projects from the overflow on *Good Money*. Correction: *Bad Money*. The way the dough's coming in, it's unstoppable. I want you to start thinking about your second feature.'

'You mean that?'

'Fly out your people, Slick. It's green-light time. All you're looking at is blank cheques. Hey, I want you to sign some more stuff before you run.'

Out on the street the black Autocrat was waiting inexorably. The chauffeur stood ready – a different chauffeur, but a fellow member of the zooty, moustachioed, chauffeuring caste. Fielding waved a hand at him and took my arm for a turn around the block. No bodyguard this time. The second guy was a frill, an extra, and even Fielding economized sometimes, as all moneymen do. Yet the driver was wearing his piece: I saw the thickness in his armpit, like a superfat wallet. 'Who's out to get you, pal?' I asked Fielding as we walked along. 'Poor people,' he said with a shrug. So I asked the second question – why the limo? He just looked at me drily. I know why, I think. The hug and glaze they give you is worth the street hate. Maybe it's even part of the deal, the bluntness, the thrilling brutality of money. We turned, and talked a little more, and then Fielding climbed inside, falling slowly into the seat.

I walked back to the hotel. You have to be tough to want a lot of money. You have to be tough to make money, as everyone knows. But you have to be tough to want it. Money means as much to those who have it as to those who don't. It says that in *Money*. And it's true. There is a common pool. By wanting a lot, you are taking steps to spread it thin elsewhere. I'm not sure how tough I am. I'll find out. I know that money means a lot to me. Martina gave me *Money*, and several other books: *Freud, Marx, Darwin, Einstein* and *Hitler. Money* is full of interesting things. Bad money drives out good money, for example. Gresham's Law. The embossing of monarchs' heads on the surface of coins was an ego-gimmick dreamed up by the rulers. When Caligula finally checked out they melted down the entire currency to wipe his face off the loathed dough. You know, they used to use meat for money, and snout, and booze, and chicks of course, and ammunition for fighting with. Now those sound like my kind of market forces. I'd have been happier then, in the old days. You wouldn't have had to pay me in money. You could have used all that other stuff, that bad money. Sometimes *Money* gives me an odd feeling, a worried feeling. It reminds me of the time that Doris Arthur said something unforgivable to me on East Ninety-Fifth Street. I get the sense that everything is ulterior. And you're in on it too, aren't you. You are, aren't you. I don't know how. I'll find out in the end.

I walked back to the hotel. The shadows people cast at night are different over here. Lights are lower, giving you that much more of the sideways presence on the streets at night. In sallow London we have the yellow lamps looming higher, so that the shadow is smaller than the real human being it leads, stalks, dogs or shadows.

The telephone was already ringing when I came through the door of my room. I had little doubt who was jabbing me in the dark like this, nobody I know, nobody you know, but jabbing me anyway.

'Isn't he wonderful?' asked Martina Twain on my first night in New York. 'He's made such a difference to my life, you wouldn't believe. I don't know how I got along without him. I come home and here he is. And I love having him to cuddle at night. Don't you think he's beautiful?'

'He looks great,' I said.

'You look terrible,' she said. 'I'm sorry. Poor you.'

'Yeah. I've had a bad week.'

Since my last visit Martina had acquired a bloody fool of a dog (or a bloody fool of a big puppy), a black Alsatian with tan singlet and tan brows puckered over his beseeching eyes. She had found him bouncing and tumbling about on Eighth Avenue, ownerless, starving, chewed up from fights with other dogs and the random clouts and kicks of the human canines on Twenty-Third Street. She brought him home by the scruff of his neck and had the vet over to check him out. A course of antibiotics was prescribed, and for a week or so the pup was pretty poorly – basketbound, and right off his grub. It was hard to credit all this now, with the animal a twirling hysteric of gratitude and health. His name was Shadow, short for Shadow That Comes in Sight, an old Indian name, Apache or Cheyenne. I very much approved of this. You don't want dogs called Spot or Pooch. You don't want dogs called Nigel or Keith. The names of dogs should salute the mystical drama of the animal life. *Shadow* – that's a *good* name. He took to me at once, of course, as dogs do. I assume it's because I harbour certain interesting dog scents. And I took to him. Boy, was he pro-life. This Shadow could hardly believe his luck. In his dreams, in his wagging, whinnying dog dreams on Twenty-Third Street, he never guessed that life could be as sweet as this, shacked up in a duplex on Bank Street, with a big basket, a lovable and loving mistress, all the food he could bolt, and a handsome new collar of leather and steel which told the world that he had money behind him now and wasn't to be fucked with any more.

'No, he's a beauty,' I said.

She was pleased. She touched my arm as she went upstairs to change, the dog jumping in her wake.

I went out on to the terrace with my wine. I said hello to the puppet bees. I watched the birds of New York, those old spivs. So, Martina. She knew nothing: Ossie was simply *in London*, as he often was. And now I had this fat red trump up my sleeve – knowledge. How to use it? Should I use it at all? . . . In my first ponderings on the matter I had arrived at the following strategy: I would wait until Martina showed signs of depression or listlessness – and then blackjack her with the news. And after that, you know, she'd melt into my arms, all dreamy and tearful. Seeing her again, though, in person, the mouth, the human eyes, I soon questioned the bankability of my plan. Hey, you, you chicks out there. How should I play it? Help me. Should I level with her, man to woman? Or accompany the information with a pally little pass? Or should I just shut up? Well, I don't see the economics in that, quite frankly. I feel I'm owed some kind of kickback on the deal . . . It seems I have a moral dilemma on my hands, God damn it. Moral dilemmas – what do you *do* about them? I have exhausted myself with strictures and provisos. I thought it was going to be easy, telling Martina Twain. I thought it would be like rolling off a log. But I can see her face as the truth comes out. I can see my face as the truth comes out. I thought it was going to be easy. It was going to be hard. I've decided. It's all too complicated. I'm not telling her. You know why? Because it's all too complicated and I can't be fucked.

Just then, Shadow bobbed out on to the terrace. He made straight for me and started sniffing greedily at my dock. Now this was all very well, but hardly the most welcome comment on my personal hygiene. I raised an arm – in warning, no more – and with a crawling wriggle Shadow had rolled on to his back, his head averted, his legs crooked in supplication and fear. I knew then that the dog had once feared somebody very like myself, somebody big, tense and white. I knelt and patted his hot belly. 'Sniff all you want,' I said. 'I won't have you fearing me. I just won't stand for it.' As I straightened up I saw that Martina was watching from the doorway with curious eyes.

Toward the end of dinner in the kind of Village salad-hutch where the staff look like orthodontists, the food carries a live-forever guarantee, and the toilet features an oak tree craning from the bowl, I did something right out of character. And I wasn't drunk. I was grimly making do with frequent, bidet-sized glasses of white wine – no liquor or anything. I put my hand over hers on the bare tabletop and said,

'Maybe you're a little disappointed. Now don't get me wrong. I can say this because I'm so lost in my own life. But you hoped yours would be clearer and straighter. You expected or even assumed it would be. Or not. Or not at all. I don't really know what I mean.'

I didn't, either. It was one of my voices. I often see no reason not to say things, containing all these other voices as I do. Her hand stirred under mine, so I lit a cigarette as she said,

'You think I'm disappointed. I'm not, I don't think. No more than anyone else.'

Her face showed surprise. What else? In it I thought I saw a puzzled and half-reluctant pleasure, an intentness to do with the fact that someone had clearly entertained thoughts about her that must have been . . . well, consecutive, at the very least. That isn't much, I agree, one of the poorest relations of love. But in the family, definitely in the family.

'I'm not being critical,' I said. 'Who, me? I've been a joke all along. But you never were.'

'Everyone's a joke in the end.'

Yeah, I thought, and cuffed my forehead with the meat of my palm. It was a big mistake, that cuff on the forehead business. I must have twitched and smarted quite a bit, because Martina's tomboy smile now grew savage. Often in my nighttime daydreams I see her face as a magic lantern, human, full of trapped light.

'God,' she said, 'all the suffering you do.'

'I know. It's a scream.' Quickly I wiggled my wallet from the sweat-pouch over my heart. But Martina's fingertips (slightly bitten, unpainted, not like Selina's fingertips) had already snatched that tab.

'It's all taken care of,' she said.

That was as close as we got. She knew nothing. And maybe she need never know. It all came down to money – that's all it came down to. If Ossie was seriously loaded, and he was, he could hive off a few grand a year and feel no pain. Presumably he could still stroll over and give Selina a seeing-to whenever he was in town. What a lucky bugger, eh? I never liked the look of him – one of life's actors. But what a lucky funker. Imagine. Martina in New York, running his duplex, wowing his moneymen and, for all I knew, proving a nightly sackful. And then, after a couple of weeks of that, he hops back over the pond to screw the smocks off Selina! Jesus, it's an outrage. It's a scandal. But then money is too. You just cannot beat the money conspiracy. You can only join it.

I walked Martina home and then we both walked Shadow.

My dizzy spell had passed and I was my old self again now, contemplating a goodnight kiss and a sinister hint or two before heading back uptown. Strafed by sense impressions, his face flickering as he busily directed his superfast film, Shadow tested the limits of his leash and the other limits of smell and sight and hearing. Then the dog paused to do his dog thing, in one quaking kneebend. No trouble for Shadow there – not like me, with my *Morning Line*, cigarette, coffee-cup, bullet to bite.

'Good boy,' said Martina.

'What's that?'

'A shit-shoveller.'

'Oh yeah,' I said. 'A pooper-scooper. Christ, you Americans. Hey come on, you're not seriously going to – hey come on.'

'They're fierce about it here,' she said. 'People shout at you.'

'A bit of dogshit never hurt anyone.'

'No, it's very toxic, and children play on this street. Dogshit gives you diseases.'

'What doesn't? I mean, if you look into it long enough, everything gives you diseases. Pooper-scoopers give you diseases. Probably children do too.'

'Look,' she said.

As we reached the cab-swept corner of Eighth Avenue, Shadow came to a halt. He whimpered. He peered uptown toward the sin and death of Twenty-Third Street, Chelsea, the world's end, where everything was unleashed, unmuzzled. There were no collars, no leads, no names on Twenty-Third Street. Shadow tugged, sneezed, pawed his snout. He looked baffled and hungry, momentarily lupine, answering to a sharper nature.

'Every night it gets weaker. But sometimes he pulls really hard and seems to want to go.'

'And leave you? Relax. He knows what the good life is.'

'But it's his *nature*,' she said, and she too looked troubled and uncertain.

We said goodnight. Watched by Shadow's bright and desolate eyes, I hailed a cab and climbed aboard. Without incident. One bar, one drink, and then the hotel room, where the telephone was waiting patiently and sounding its greeting, patient and painful, like pain.

There's a whole backlog of stuff I ought to tell you about that gimp who keeps ringing me up. I ought to tell you, but the trouble is, I can't be – well, okay, perhaps I should make the effort. You may see the point. I don't. With everything going so well now, with my life multiplying and burgeoning as it is, the thin voice at the end of the line is just the voice of street hum, air babble, the voice of the unknown Earthlings – late arrivals, end-of-queue artists – whose sense you can't be fished to catch. And why should you? As threatening telephone calls go, these threatening telephone calls seem comparatively friendly. In California convicted drunk drivers are obliged to attend the meetings of temperance societies, ex-alkie fraternities, and so on. Punishment by boredom. That's what the calls feel like sometimes, though I'm always trying to liven them up.

'How's your chick?' I asked him the other day.

'What chick?'

God, what a dumb voice. This guy, I can run rings around him now. 'The big redhead who wears too much lipstick. The one who had her tongue in my ear that night, in the bar there, across the street from Zelda's.'

He was puzzled. 'So you remembered.'

'Oh sure.'

'You don't remember what she told you. I know that for a fact.'

'How?'

'Because you wouldn't be in New York now, is how. You

wouldn't dare come back. Ever. You'd stay in London with your *little* redhead.'

I was puzzled. 'You got a London office too? I'm surprised you know where London is. I'm surprised you've even heard of it.'

'Big man,' he said.

'Little man,' I said. I keep getting the feeling that Frank the Phone is crippled, lopped, physically diminished in some way. I certainly hope he is.

'We'll meet one day.'

'Oh I know it.'

'We'll meet one day. And when we do . . .'

And he usually winds up with a couple of low-budget snarls and threats. He's like the cheapo frightener that my dad has supposedly unleashed on me. It's hard to take these guys seriously. They've got no money behind them. But he calls again. He calls so often now, especially at night when I find it hard to distinguish his voice from all the other voices.

There are so many voices that another one won't hurt. At least I hope it won't. I hope it won't hurt too much.

The package looks unpierceably firm now, ever since I made my breakthrough with Spunk Davis. I tell you, the kid is putty in my hands. He's even agreed to change his name.

'S. J. Davis,' he said, toward the end of our long talk. 'What do you think?'

'What's your middle name, Spunk?' I asked warily.

'Jefferson. Ma doesn't like it, the S. J. She says I'm breaking faith.'

'Bullshit,' I told him. 'You'll still be Spunk to your friends. Kid, you're born again. S. J. Davis – it's perfect.'

Circumstances did it all for me. I showed up at UN Plaza for a script conference yesterday afternoon – and Mrs Davis answered the door with a blood-soaked handkerchief pressed to her nose. She tried to shield her eyes but I could see that they had been badly blackened. Yes, a hard blow to the bridge had done that, and done it recently too. I felt sudden heat and illness gathering in my face as I caught the smell of violence, the domestic kind, like paraffin.

'Wow,' I said. 'Are you okay?' I reached out and she waved me away in shame. She just stood there holding her face, a little woman, further condensed now. Looking past her I saw Mr Davis fatly slumped in a winged armchair, wearing a vest and holding a beercan in front of the kitchen TV. He gave me his low glance – hardness, exasperation – and raised a finger to his blemished brow.

Spunk I found in the dark and disused dining-room at the end of the apartment. He sat on the edge of the table, arms folded, a look of unwholesome composure on his muscle-bound face. He merely stared at me dully.

'What's up, Spunk?'

'I'm gonna kill him,' he said, in sober explanation. 'I'm gonna kill him,' he confirmed as he came toward me and the door.

I held his shoulders and felt his cocked strength. He *could* kill him, no question of that. He wouldn't, but he could. I saw my chance here, and experienced that surge of authority or eloquence, that high style you need for actors. Then I heard myself shouting:

'You can't kill him! He's you. You are your dad and your dad is you. You're better, but you'll be him one day – *and* the gut *and* the vest *and* the beercan. There's no hiding out from it. Even when he's dead. I know. I got one too.'

'You understand what this is *doing* to me?'

'Tell me. Tell me now.'

He made a childish sound of pain. His face recoiled with effort but he said it in the end. 'It's like my name. It's – no matter what

I do, what I earn, what I act, I'll always be the asshole. I'll always be the guy in the joke.'

'Kid, we all are. It's the twentieth-century feeling. We're the jokes. You just got to live it, Spunk. You just got to live the joke.'

And then we talked for three hours, in the dark there, me and my kid bloodbrother.

'Do you ever get that feeling, Fielding?'

'Why no, Slick, I guess not. I'm only twenty-five, remember, and I don't have any kind of parent problem. I think of all that shit as out there waiting. Tell me, John – I'm curious.'

We were winding up a day's paperwork down at the loft in Tenderloin. Dreary but undemanding – I just sit there signing stuff. Fielding has now established a company, Bad Money Ltd, and employs three girls and an office boy. They work downstairs. A contract lawyer comes in most days too.

'Take a drink.'

'No thanks,' I said.

'Tell me, John. What do you do for ass out here in New York? I can't believe you're true-blue to that little fox of yours.'

'Selina? Oh,' I said slyly, 'she keeps me happy. I get by.'

'There's a thing we can do together. A place on Fifth Avenue. You go in, right? Ambrosia on the rocks with a twist. The Queen of Sheba takes you to her boudoir and with a combination of head and hand gives you the biggest hard-on you ever had. You ever saw. You look down and you think, *Whose dick* is *this*? You look up, and the panels of the ceiling fold back. And guess what.'

'A ton of shit comes down on you.'

'God damn it, Slick, how can you be so unromantic? What happens is, the ceiling opens and this oiled princess is lowered down on a silken rope. She's doing the splits. You understand what I'm saying to you? You connect, maybe half an inch. Then a 300-pound sumo wrestler comes through the door, takes her leg in his hands, and spins her like a top.'

'Christ.'

'A thousand dollars apiece. It'll look good on the expenses profiles. Recreation, Slick. What do you say? We could stop by there now.'

'Sounds good but I think I'll skip it.'

'If you like black stuff there's a place on Madison. Ethiopia. You go in, right? Then what happens is –'

'Don't tell me. I have a date tonight anyway.'

'Oh yeah? Anyone I know?'

'Yeah. No – no one you know.'

You may have noticed that apart from the odd momentary lapse I've managed to quit swearing. I've started stopping doing other things too. All my addictions stand doomed on death row: swearing, fighting, hitting women, smoking, drinking, fast food, pornography, gambling and handjobs – they all cower in the corner now, waiting on the long walk. You know why. It's the new-deal me . . . Stopping swearing is obviously the easiest. That was no problem. I don't miss fighting or hitting women either. As for smoking, well, each time I light up I ask myself, *Do you really need this cigarette*? So far, the answer has always been *yes*, but these are early days. Similarly, when you are a hard drinker it is very hard to stop drinking. Stopping drinking *is* going to be a problem, I can tell. Fast food: the rule here is that I confine myself to one blowout every twenty-four hours, except on the special days when I'm feeling particularly hungry. Gambling has never been a worry for me out here in New York. I can't find anywhere to gamble in. No doubt there are gambling dens, but I can't find them. I look, I search high and low, but I can't find any dens where you can gamble. Now the handjob factor. All my life I've asked around, and this is my conclusion: everybody does it. Girls do it. Vicars do it. I do it. You do it. (Yes, you do it, and *how* old are you? Pull yourself together, man. Come on, sis, it's time to retire.) I'm quitting. Are you? It's a fairly long-term project in my case, I admit, but I've provisionally outlawed those visual aids of mine. This is half the battle. Without pornography, I can't see much point in a handjob. But I'm confident, in a way. No, I am. I'm pretty sure I can flush the junk out of my life. I kicked swearing with no sweat, after all. Who needs these bad habits: I mean, what are they for? Yeah, I could do it. In fact I'm convinced that it wouldn't even be that difficult. The only trouble is – and here, perhaps, we see the root of my problem – the only trouble is, I can't be fucked.

Feeling enviably high-powered and systematic, I took my producer's advice and began rehearsing the stars in pairs: Lorne and Butch, Spunk and Caduta, Butch and Spunk – you get the picture. In human terms it worked out something like this. At first, anyway, before I cracked it. Caduta and Spunk: not bad. Butch and Lorne: bad. Lorne and Caduta: very bad. Spunk and Butch: very bad indeed. Butch and Caduta: really – really very *bad*. Worst of all, though, most arduous and embarrassing by far were the Lorne-Spunk confrontations. At least the ladies had their own female strategies, their own pretty ways. At least they weren't violent. With Spunk and Lorne I was head-doctoring and kissing ass – and refereeing – all at the same time . . . On Lorne's insistence we convened the opening session at the Guyland penthouse on Eighty-Fifth Street. We were trying to do the scene where Spunk tells Lorne that he knows about Mistress and will inform Mother unless Lorne goes through with the heroin deal. Spunk sat there, facing Lorne, and read out the lines with an expression of boss-eyed loathing on his face. Lorne heard him out, turned to me and said, 'John, I don't have to take this shit. From him?

In my own home, John?' Spunk argued, in mumbling mitigation, that the scene was difficult for him because he had always hated his father. Lorne bounced back by claiming that he had always hated his son (a middle-aged accountant, I later learned). Lorne then accused Spunk of plotting to steal his movie. Spunk counter-accused Lorne of trying to turn *Bad Money* into a Guyland vehicle. Spunk was right out of order here, in my view. Christ, I thought, with that script you couldn't turn the *Fiasco* into a Guyland vehicle. Lorne said that he was bigger than Spunk – yes, and stronger, too. Spunk invited Lorne to prove it. 'There, John,' said Lorne, turning to me in triumph. 'I'm threatened by this punk in my own home?' I saw that the first thing I had to do was get the stars on to neutral territory and shift the whole operation to the loft downtown. Then came the transport problem.

Fielding said at the onset that Autocrats were available for both stars. I put this to Lorne, who said that if Spunk had an Autocrat, then he, Lorne, could hardly settle for less than a Jefferson Succès. I put this to Spunk, who scornfully told me that he would be jogging to work, as always. I came back to Lorne, who said that he would sprint or swim or hop-skip-and-jump to work himself, before casually revealing that an inconspicuous Tigerfish or even a little two-door Mañana would be adequate to his simple needs. We settled for an Autocrat, the catch being that I had to pick him up each day and ride downtown with him, an eighty-block journey at nine in the morning, during which Lorne talked all the time. I soon discovered that you could not do this with a hangover. It wasn't possible. I had several shots at it, and got more and more certain that it just couldn't be done.

On the first day, after an hour of immobility on Lexington, the chauffeur drove across the Park to try his luck on the lawless Avenues of the West Side. When Guyland noticed the greenery, or the absence of concrete (about half way through), he seized up in mid-babble and raised a tense trembling fist. 'Anything the matter, Lorne?' I asked. But Lorne sat tight. '*Pull over,*' he snarled, he spat, as we edged out into Central Park West. Lorne slopped back into his seat, almost boneless with relief. 'Never through the Park, John,' he said huskily. 'Never! You tell him. We made it this time but you never take Lorne Guyland through the Park. *Never.*' I asked him why you never did that. 'Helicopters, John,' he said, all calmly now. 'Oh yeah,' I said, and on we drove.

But things went like a dream, like a conspiracy, down at the loft. The key to the whole deal lay in a beautifully simple realization. What each star wanted to do all day was sit around listening to uncritical praise – to the rhapsody-roster that Martin had woven into the script. Well, I couldn't give them that, but I could give them something. Actually I seemed to remember Martin himself suggesting just such a procedure. So I'd kick off by saying, 'Spunk. Why don't we have another crack at your big speech about Lorne.' And then: 'Lorne. How about a run-through of your major speech about Spunk.' One star gushed while the other basked. After a while I began all the sessions this way, and tried it on the girls with equal success. Softened up and spoonfed by these glutinous blurbs, the actors then fell refreshed into the carping, spite-crammed dialogue, which gave them the chance to express their real feelings about each other. These feelings were by now, of course, hideously addled, but the script reflected that too. I was getting some great stuff, particularly from the boys. *Bad Money* was going to be unusual all right. When was the last time *you* saw a film where all the stars were so faint and baffled, so wanton and weak? This was realism. My respect for Martin Amis knew no bounds.

There were problems, naturally, as you'd expect in Problem City. This morning, for instance, I arrived at Lorne's place to find the great man sulking naked in his tent. 'I've never seen him so bad,' said Thursday, who looked at least a generation older in the limelight of day. 'He won't even drink his juice.' Big Bruno, I saw, was also lurking sorrowfully in the hall. I rang Fielding, and had him go downtown to mollify Spunk. Then I walked through into Lorne's opulent brothel of a bedroom. There he sat, in the draped darkness, naked, staring bleakly at the wall. After an hour or two he told me what was up.

'Level with me Lorne,' I'd said. 'Do it. Just think of me as your friend – and your fan.'

'Well, John, it's like this. Nobody knows this, John. Nobody in the whole world. Nobody would ever guess it in a million years. But it's true! The fact is, John, and I know you won't believe this, but the fact is, John, I'm very insecure. I'm a highly ignorant man, John. I don't know anything. It makes me feel very insecure.'

Oh, you poor old bugger, I thought. Where would Lorne be, if he wasn't fluking thirty thousand a day? I know. He'd be out on Broadway, screaming his head off. I placed a hand on his shoulder. It came to me in an instant what I had to say.

'Good God, Lorne. If *you're* insecure, what hope is there for us poor mortals?'

He looked up at me with flickering uncertainty, and then his face cleared like a child's.

'John?' he said, exhaling through his nose, '– let's go make movies.'

After the shunting torment of Central Park South the Autocrat got gridlocked in a theatreland sidestreet. As Lorne told me about his Broadway hits, his love of the stage and whatnot, we grew aware of a faint but persistent ratatat-tat, the sound of a coin pecking on glass. Lorne flipped himself to the floor, like Shadow. 'It's okay,' I said. In the adjacent cab sat Doris Arthur, smiling. Lorne straightened up and composed himself. He peered out: a beautiful girl, staring his way. Grinning, he blew her a kiss, then turned to me in shy gratification, waving absently to Doris, who fixed my eye with terrible meaning and, as her cab peeled off, let her face go slack and her clean tongue loll out in an expression of inanity or mock-craziness, or knowing submission to a mad ascendancy. I felt my heart curl and my scalp hum. Why? I gave up spirits three days ago. Giving up spirits is okay so long as you drink an incredible amount of beer, sherry, wine and port and can cope with especially bad hangovers. I think I had an especially bad hangover. Minutes later we were bucking down Ninth Avenue, not far from Martina's, and I felt – I felt the benefit of it, the nutrition. God, it was like biting into an apple and munching it up with square rustic teeth. I call her from work now, every day. Oh, we chat along about a whole bunch of things. I'm seeing her tonight. Off to the Opera, me. *Otello*. I'm really looking forward to it. I've never been to the Opera before. Do you think it might turn out to be my kind of thing? Martina makes me strong. Why does Doris make me weak? I get the same feeling sometimes when I read *Money*. I've been reading *Money*, and dipping into the other books Martina gave me. Einstein. Now you've got to give him credit. To stare into the world and see its conspiracies, to see the secrets of the Old One. Darwin too. Freud, Marx – what colossal guessers. I haven't given up on the fiction either: I read *The Catcher in the Rye*, a first-class work in my view, most powerfully and elegantly written. As for Hitler, well, I'm consternated. I can't fucking believe this stuff. Look how far he spread his violence. And I thought *I* was aggressive. Boy, Germany must have had some dizzy spell or drunk on, in the Thirties and Forties there, to have given headroom to a sick little gimp like him. I'm consternated. I can't believe this stuff. And you're telling me it's *true*?

Now apparently, for the Opera here, it was some kind of off-season charity gala night, a big deal anyway, and I had resolved to rent myself a tux. Fielding gave me the name of a place on Lexington Avenue and right after rehearsals with Lorne and Caduta I cabbed across town to size up the suit.

'I can't fit you, sir,' said the old extra in gentle despair, after his fifteenth visit to the storeroom.

'You *what?*'

'Not for tonight. Can't do it.'

I kept my temper and dashed off to another joint down the street . . . yeah, and then another. And then another.

Jesus Christ, I thought, and this is *New York*, God damn it, calorie capital, Bulkville, where the superfat bob like barrels over the trampled sidewalks, unregarded, unmocked. Check out that black chick in the beige pants suit, the embossed outlines of her underwear like string on a bulging parcel. Behold the Big Wallies listing through the heat. They don't mind. Nobody else does either. In London there'd be a riot, a revolution of hilarity, if any one of these butter-mountains set a foot outside the door. But over here, in the great mix, you can't afford to find mere oddity funny. Hence the sense-of-humour problem. If you had one, you'd be weeping with laughter all the hours there are. Anyway I ended up in a depressing little place called High, Wide and Handsome or High and Mighty or (let's be accurate) Rent-a-Tent on the very brink of Harlem, and cobbled together an outfit among the beanpoles and longlegs, the girth-raters, butt-trussers and tomato-faced thirty-stoners. I arrived at Bank Street in a fine sweat, parched, winded and boiling for a leak. Martina seemed disconcerted too, though, and before I knew it I was back in the elevator and back in a cab and rolling upriver all over again. We were late. Wearing a plain charcoal dress and a single loop of pearls on the narrow column of her throat, Martina avoided my eye and talked in a sharp and unconvincing voice about the danger of missing the love duets in the first act. She hadn't remarked on my evening wear – the palatinate reefer jacket, the

plump-winged bowtie, the pink cummerbund that had taken
my fancy, the lacquered spats – so I assumed I looked the part.
We hit a magical procession of suspended green lights, then
ran from the beached cab. Like a guilty school playground the
inner concourses held nothing but ringing bells and buzzing
buzzers and a fussy chick who shooed us straight into the stalls.
Late for Scripture, we stubbed and kicked our way through to
the central wedge just as the red sea of the curtain began its
long division.

Opera certainly takes its time, doesn't it. Opera really lasts, or
at least *Otello* does. I gathered that a second half would follow
this one, and this one was travelling awful slowly through its
span. The other striking thing about *Otello* is – it's not in English.
I kept expecting them to pull themselves together and start
singing properly, but no: Spanish or Italian or Greek was evidently
the deal. Maybe, I thought, maybe it's some kind of guinea fest
or beaner evening, a rally for the Hispanics or the Ricans. But
the audience seemed stolidly non-ethnic. I mean, those guys in
buffalo beards and busby haircuts, those six-foot chicks with
tomahawk profiles and Venusian suntans – I mean, they're just
Americans. Uneasily I craned my neck in search of a fellow
tuxedo. The ladies had turned it on a bit, true, but the prongs
were all in office gear. Yeah, I should have dressed down a bit.
Definitely. No bloody wonder Martina was giving out the bad-eye.
It suddenly occurred to me that I would look less conspicuous
on the stage than I did in the stalls.

Luckily I must have seen the film or the TV spin-off of *Othello*,
for despite its dropped aitch the musical version stuck pretty
faithfully to a plot I knew well. The language problem remained
a problem but the action I could follow without that much effort.
The flash spade general arrives to take up a position on some
island, in the olden days there, bringing with him the Lady Di

figure as his bride. Then she starts diddling one of his lieutenants, a funloving kind of guy whom I took to immediately. Same old story. Now she tries one of these double-subtle numbers on her husband – you know, always rooting for the boyfriend and singing his praises. But Otello's sidekick is on to them, and, hoping to do himself some good, tells all to the guvnor. This big spade, though, he can't or won't believe it. A classic situation. Well, love is blind, I thought, and shifted in my seat.

To be honest, all this was far from centre-stage in my own mind. A jungly night in young New York, and the outer heat was proving far too much for the theatre's thrashed cooling systems. I began to notice that an impressively candid odour was seeping from my hired jacket, not one smell but a deadly anthology of fatso emanations, the trail of the thousand soaks and sweats who had used it before me and would use it again when I was done. The people behind, were they getting wind of me? Martina herself now frowned and sniffed. Each time I squirmed in my seat the jacket selected another noxious parallel from its quiver. Either it was paranoia of the nostril or I was getting the lot here: ashtrays, soup-kitchen explosions, used stalls in porno emporiums, magazine wax, booze bubbles. No question, this bit of shmutter had done time on some very fat, hot and unhealthy guys. I scratched my nose. *Pew*. There came another wicked fart from my right armpit. Martina sniffed and writhed. Gently does it, I thought, and searched for a state of fixity and trance.

Fate had given me another good reason for staying put. My need to take a leak – intense enough an hour ago, when in the cab downtown I was obsessively rehearsing a grateful and copious session in Martina's john – was now evolving into a new era of detailed distress. I felt I was sitting with a white-hot cannonball on my lap. I considered barging off to the can, of course, but it clearly wasn't done around here. You're not in the flicks now, you know. People who go to the Opera, they don't go to the toilet, not even at home. And if I stood up in this gear I'd bring the house down anyway. I winced and twisted and tried to loosen the bladder-throttling cummerbund. Smells shimmered. Otello howled for his lost handkerchief. Martina sniffed and stirred. Maybe she thought *Otello* was having a bad time. She didn't know what *Otello* was putting *me* through, the excruciation, the super-suffering endured by the big boiler at her side.

The curtain flooded back. The stalls rejoiced. On soggy legs I followed Martina down the rank and up the aisle. As we came out on to the mezzanine I saw some kind of toilet logo and burst through the black door of my pain. *Dah!* Gimps only! There was an electric pram wedged in the doorway, and a white-suited attendant or medic gave me a righteous glare. I stumbled and turned – and made out Martina, some distance away, sitting alone on a backless sofa, and crying openly as she searched for some-thing in the depths of her handbag. I wish people wouldn't try and do things while they're crying. It's painful enough as it is. I hurried over to her. It's only *Otello*, I thought, and said,

'It isn't real, you know. It's make-believe. Christ. What's the matter?'

I offered her my hand, and she took it and pressed it to her face, badly needing that human touch.

'Don't go away. Please don't go away,' she said. 'Listen.'

She knew everything. She knew far more than me. But then, who doesn't? *You* do.

And you know how it is too, when these things come out, they come out in a funny order, and you're often in no fit state to listen. I sat there, with both knees bobbing like pump drills, bit my lip, and listened. Distant, glowering Ossie had loped in from London that afternoon. There was a confrontation – Martina knew, she had known, really, for two years. They can tell. They can smell. He confessed. Selina, the kid, the trap. He was angry, angry, balked, thwarted. He almost *hit* her, that son of a bitch. He almost hit *her*. Ooh, if I ever . . . She told me that all her life she had wanted children, ever since she was a child herself. Ossie didn't want them, babies, but he'd done his stuff, or he'd tried. They had been *trying* for five years now. They had sat holding hands in research-unit waiting rooms. They had taken courses of powerful wonderdrugs. He had whacked off into test tubes and gone around the house with a thermometer up his ass. No luck, no kids. Incompatibility . . . And Martina had all the money. All of it, always. Ossie pulled down his talented salary – and it was a lot, certainly: why else would you fritter your days away buying and selling money, if not for money? But he had no *real* dough, the stuff that just wallows there inviolably and never goes away. So, she kicked him out. This afternoon. Nothing liberates women like money does. You want to watch them, when they've got money . . . With her hand still in mine (and with the first few groundlings returning from the bar to the stalls) Martina thanked me for being her friend. She was grateful for what she called my disinterestedness. She praised my manly silence over Selina's part in the story. She felt she could tell me all this, she said (and now the first bells tolled, and buzzers buzzed, and suits and dresses flocked past us swiftly), because she realized, as I sat out there by her side tonight, that I too was moved and had the special pain of the deceived, the sufferer's silence . . . Yes, you see? Only human, in all kinds of ways. I looked down at her fingertips and saw how chewed and torn they were. The human pain had spread to the very tips of her fingers, but I never saw it, not really.

'Martina,' I said. 'Sweethead. I –'

'It's starting.'

'I must use the *can*.'

'There's no time. Go on. Quick.'

'Where?'

'There.'

'I can't. It's for cripples.'

'Go on. In you go.'

I emerged two minutes later and we fled back to our seats.

'Are you all right now?' she asked as we settled. 'You look shattered.'

'No I'm fine,' I said. But I wasn't.

I was shattered. I couldn't get the fucking cummerbund off. Jesus, was that cummerbund ever a bad idea. Under the attendant's mirthful sneer I had skipped and cursed and twisted. In the end I merely tautened the noose around the molten melon in my bowels. Martina called from beyond and pausing only to wipe away my tears I blundered back through the door.

The curtains parted, and the same old story began again.

Pain is very patient but even pain grows bored occasionally and wants to try its hand at something else. Even pain gets pissed, and craves variety. Pain doesn't always just want to hang around hurting all the time. After an hour or so I had moved on to a level of self-hypnotic impartiality, of weightlessness: it reminded me, distantly, of the stalled states of buddhist rage I briefly experience while noting (or while being expensively apprised of) some dramatic new shortcoming of the Fiasco's. I can take a joke, I thought, even when the joke is my life, is myself. Me, I often feel like a good laugh. But it's wearing thin, this joke, just like everything else. When I saw that my life had shape and form, I was the first to scream with laughter. Dead witty, I thought. Life's forms and shapes seem droll, until they feel like snares or curses, invalidations, inhuman handicaps. Maybe we are all crippled – or *challenged*, as they call it here. I am. I was challenged and the challenge won. No contest. I am a cripple in my detail, with my many tramp precincts. I am a rug retard, a gut bum, a gum gimp. I have ticker trouble. I know nothing. I am weak, wanton, baffled, faint. I need a new dimension. I'm tired of being a one-liner . . . And now, as the thing on the stage came nearer to being over, as I kung-fued my pushy pain into the corner of submission (oh, this bellyful of tender torment), I heard the woman pleading for forgiveness, alone, in a voice that confesses to all the dangers and addictions entailed by a bodily nature. '*Otello?*' . . . '*Si* . . .' Ah, forgive her, for Christ's sake. Some chicks, some people, they're just double-lifers. One's not enough! They need two! Rough her up a bit, okay, teach her a lesson, divorce her, but don't, but don't . . . He holds the pillow now. I can't bear to watch. A tragedy, a fucking tragedy! Don't kill her, just for her *nature*, I thought, with such plunging urgency that the leak-need now resumed its riot, and the rest of the show, to my eyes, was just acid rain.

'Will you see me to the lift?' she asked, and I said,

'Why of course.'

Martina clicked her way up the steps and across the hall. I followed, at an easy pace. I felt . . . well, there's no use denying it – I felt painfully happy. During the last half-dozen curtain-calls I had told Martina my problem and, in a moment of hilarious intimacy, she helped gimmick the cummerbund before unleashing me into the first bipedal can we could find. The pee itself was pale and blameless, not the incensed ruby or arterial black that I had feared. Then we sailed across the street and sat drinking in the cavernous bar of an old hotel, and laughed about my outfit, and talked with stirring candour of Selina and Ossie, Ossie and Selina. Later, we shunned the shouldering cabs and walked the length of lower Eighth Avenue, past Twenty-Third Street, past Chelsea, without a twinge.

'See you tomorrow?' I asked.

The lift arrived and slipped its accordion doors.

'Yes, but what am I supposed to *do* about you?'

'Nothing.'

Her smile was amused or indulgent or merely friendly, but also warm, wide-mouthed, rich. I moved forward lazily. She stepped backward into the lift and paused and stood her ground. I moved forward lazily. Never stop now. And when her face showed sudden terror my first thought was – *she's over-reacting, surely. I'm not that bad.* But then I felt a hard chest against my back and heard the doors jerk shut: and now there were three of us in the climbing car. I turned carefully. A big black kid, Felix's age, no, older, taller, trembling, with a wide-bladed knife in his hands, eight or nine inches long.

Ah, so it happens. It really happens. Here we all are and it's happening. Now what? The knife, the twanging knife, that's serious. That's all that's serious.

'Okay, kid,' I said. This is my turn. 'You got a problem?'

'Shut up,' said Martina.

'The floor. The *floor*, the *floor*.'

'Seven,' she said. 'The top.'

He slapped at the button with his spread left hand. The car halted, then rode on.

'Money,' said Martina Twain. 'You want money. I'll give it to you. I have seventy dollars in there. Take it. You can take it.'

She offered him the bag on its strap. She raised her free palm. No strings. Here, she was saying, I lay it all before you. The lift heaved upward on its gentle sway.

Martina said to me, 'Give him all your money. Now.'

'Why?'

'*Give* it to him.'

And her face wore pride or anger, all the habits of will showing hard in her eyes. It was ugly for a while, that face, and I knew I had no choice but to defy it.

'Wait a second,' I said. 'He hasn't even asked for it yet.'

The lift stopped and he tugged back the gate. Obedient to a quelling gesture of the raised knife, Martina led the way to her door.

'There's nothing in there. Take our money. Please. I promise, I swear we won't do anything. Just take our money and go.'

Jesus, I thought, it's guilt welfare. People get on just fine with their money, but when someone genuinely needy shows up, with a big knife, they get all these new ideas about the distribution of wealth.

'Open it,' he said, and pointed.

Martina sifted her keys with an audible sob. Good, I thought. Her door had plenty of locks. To keep them out. I turned. What next? We didn't know. He didn't know either, probably, not yet. The guy stood there tensed in shivery readiness, his nerves cocked as tight as they'd go, with this fucking sword in his hand twanging in the light. Yes, everything was trembling. Martina fumbled. From within there came an anxious bark, a reedy sigh. The kid tensed but he couldn't get any tenser than he was already. And as the eyes went sideways toward the door I thought *fuck it* and smacked a fat fist into the cable of his jaw.

For about ten seconds of dream time, nothing happened. He stood there staring at me, incredulous, desolate. Yawn! I thought: I just haven't got the heft any more. Hitting him was one of the worst ideas I ever had. Now he's going to do what he likes to Martina – yeah, after washing his knife in my face. But then, after this interlude, after this long vexed lull, he snapped sideways into the wall, and I was there too, I was along for the ride, driving another fist into the cave of his heart. The head dipped low, the twangy knife still wavering. I'd backed off with the recoil but now I came in again with all my weight tilting headlong at just the right angle and brought my big porky knee up and forward into the bare tray of his face.

While fighting, you really want to make it exquisitely clear to your opponent that he is doing the losing. As in all sports, good morale and correct attitude are crucial – and precarious. Good morale and correct attitude can vanish in one crunchy half-second as, say, your nose is abruptly reversed into your skull. It would take you weeks or months to get over that and back in the mood for fighting – but you've only got the other half-second to do it in. By that time, two smelly fingers have speared your eyeballs and a pocked forehead is coming like a brick for your teeth.

So after the knee in the face I punched him in the balls and then loafed him on the upper lip. There was a doublethump and he slid tidily down the wall. I was manoeuvring, on automatic now, preparing to put in the leather. Another thing about fights – in fact one of fights' few redeeming features – is that if you get the guy on the deck then at least you can expect to administer some leather in your own sweet time. I'd given him an exploratory kick or two when I felt a jab on my shoulder and a wrench on my rug. Oh, not another fight, I thought, and turned to face her.

'You stop now.'

I looked down, panting, steadying. The kid was out of it all right, curled up, the knife dropped, the training shoes pinched quivering together. 'Okay,' I said. 'Call the cops.'

'You nearly got us killed. Do you realize?'

'What?' I stared at her. She had wanted to control all this. She had expected her strength of personality to handle the whole thing. No need for my barbaric intervention, no need at all. 'Oh yeah?' I said. 'You mean *he* nearly got us killed.'

'You give them the money and they're on their way.'

'Haven't you heard? The money's not enough any more. They

want revenge. You can't just pay them off. They take it all and cut you up anyway.'

At this point the kid stirred and tried to arch himself upward. Reflexively I wheeled around and gave him an absentminded boot in the ass.

'You're a violent bastard, aren't you?'

'Yes and you're a fucking prig.'

'A *prig*?'

'*Later*. Just call the cops. Do it.'

She opened the door with rattling keys. I leaned with both palms flat against the wall . . . His eyes were open. The knife wasn't far off but this kid had made his last shot. He wasn't a contender any more, not tonight.

'You alone?' I asked him. He nodded sadly, and so did I. The adrenalin or fight-fuel in my system was going solid on me and I could feel all my weight tugging at my bones. You may win a fight, you may win quite easily in a way, but at my time of life you never win by much . . . For a while I gazed down at him, at his defeated, tearful face. He was much too young and soft for this line of work. On reflection I was surprised he'd had the bottom to take us on in the first place. He didn't look that pilled-up or desperate. But maybe Martina and I didn't look that formidable either – the girl tall but slender-shouldered, yes, and the boyfriend, Bozo the Clown. I tugged off my bowtie. Now Shadow stepped springily into the passage. He said hello to me and, with his head moving like a marionette, checked out our friend on the floor. Having reviewed various options, Shadow gave him a long lick across the mouth. This appeared to be the last thing the kid needed, another downer on a very low night.

Martina returned. She leaned over the boy in the trim-footed posture women use for inspecting each other's flowers and prams.

'Are you all right? Is he all right?'

'Yeah. Did they say how long they'd be?'

'It's Friday night.'

We stared down and he stared up. I shifted my footing and in the flinch he gave I saw that his teeth were far from negro-perfect, dark-flecked and splinted with gold. As a black in New York you'd have your troubles, but dental overheads wouldn't normally be one of them. Bad luck. Like the fat-but-no-tits deal that some girls get saddled with. Bad luck. Double bad.

'Let me go,' he said.

I had to laugh at this. 'Ho no you don't pal. You, you just had a knife in my face. The squad car's on its way and now you want me to – what do you think I am, a liberal? Look at you anyway. You're going nowhere tonight, my friend. Can you believe this guy?' I asked, and turned to face Martina.

It's true what they say: a risky business, being mugged in New York. There's the health hazard and the inconvenience and the entanglement with the law. It can turn out expensive, too, apart from anything else.

I had the devil's own job just getting the guy on his feet. Then I went and put my back out hauling him into the lift. On the way down, the car came to a halt and an old lady with a poodle eerily joined us for the last three floors. I don't think she noticed anything. Perhaps you don't get to be an old lady in New York if you notice too much. You just stand there, and keep a poodle face. Limping three abreast across the foyer, we heard the whoop and gulp of the sirens, and I said to Martina –

'Let's be straight on this. If they're out there already I kick him in the ass and hand him over. No messing. Okay?'

She stood outside, testing the swish of the cross-street murmur. I joined her with my gangling, gurgling load. Down on Seventh Avenue people still churned around the all-night dellies and the porno-hatches of the snout-outlets. Two highstepping greyhounds, excited by their big night out in hot Manhattan, pranced past, tugging hard on their aged charioteer. I looked right, I looked left, I looked across the street. And what the hell did I see but the woman, the gingerhead, leaning on a lamppost with a cigarette raised, her stance the familiar one of defiance and reproach.

I swung the gimp off my shoulder and said, 'Right – make a run for it.' But he'd been mugged once too often tonight. I tell you, he had no future, no future at all in the law-and-order game.

'Help him.'

'I'm trying.' If we can just get him to Eighth Avenue, I thought, he can lie down in a doorway or a puddle and no one will know the difference. 'Help me.'

Now a battered chequer was moving slowly down the street. It was watching us, like a liverish dragon, the yellow eyes grown cautious in their old age. Martina jumped to it, and I followed in my three-legged race as the cab slowed further, and halted. The fat, speckled black driver gazed knowingly out at us.

'Will you take him?' asked Martina, confidentially.

'He sick?'

'No, he's fine,' I said. 'Here's a twenty. Just –' I reached for my wallet and my stance shifted. The kid went down again.

'I ain't doing it,' said the driver. But he made no move. In fact he seemed on the point of falling asleep. That cab of his was a home from home. He looked as though he had been wedged into the front seat for the last twenty years.

'I'll double it,' I said.

'I said I ain't doing it.'

'He's a brother, isn't he, God damn it. He's one of yours.'

'Not my problem.'

'Okay,' I told Martina, 'the cops can take him. They'll do it for free. I've had it.'

New sirens were moving towards us, two or three

intersections away. I could see swivel lights whipping the air above
Christopher Street. Now the driver said musingly,

'Looks like you people want him gone pretty bad. You call
the cops on him, then you change your mind or something.
Looks like I just stick around, and you get to do some explaining.'

My instinct, at this point, was to make a run for it myself.
But with a smooth reverse-elbow action of his dangling hand
the cabbie unlatched the passenger door, and grinned up at me
sleepily.

'And you, sir,' he said, 'now generally I tell you you can keep
your fuckin money. But you gonna give me fifty. And twenty for
my friend in back. Carfare.'

We went dutch in the end, Martina and I. She tried to pay for
it all – but then I did too, for some reason, probably genetic.
After all, she tabbed *Otello*. She's rich, though, remember? Half
way up the steps I took Martina's arm. The gingerhead still kept
her watch. Framed by leaves and lamplight she held a match to
another cigarette, her veil half lifted, the shoulders closing
inwards. She doesn't seem mad now, standing there tonight, I
thought. She seems in control of her strangeness.

'See that woman over there?' I said. 'She's been following me.
She follows me at night.'

'That's not a woman,' said Martina briskly.

'Uh?'

'Look at her hands. And the ankles, the shoulders.'

I looked . . . The calves were slender but welded slopelessly
to the foot, without any curve in the join. The shoulders were
thick. The back was thick. Christ, yes. Look at the hands – they
weren't woman's hands. They were bloody great wanking-
paddles. Now the gingerhead straightened in our gaze. I didn't
know how much fight I had left in me but I started down the
steps and shouted,

'Hey faggot! Hey – no-man!'

The figure backed off with the kind of hesitant confusion that could only seem womanly to me – but would a *woman* back off like that?

'Come on, brother, let's talk,' I said, in fightspeak now (hard-mouthed, urging, eager). 'Hey – cross-dresser!'

No, she didn't like this at all. And as I moved on to the road, fifteen feet away, she stepped nimbly out of her shoes, crouched to collect them, and lifting her dress with one hand ran fast and purposefully towards Seventh Avenue. I stood there and watched him run.

'What did you do that for?' asked Martina, when I returned. 'You hurt her feelings.'

My theory is – we don't really go that far into other people, even when we think we do. We hardly ever go in and bring them out. We just stand at the jaws of the cave, and strike a match, and quickly ask if anybody's there.

I stayed alone on the street and calmed the meaty cops. I had a long wait. The squad car that had panicked me was on quite another errand, what looked like a faggot tiff or atrocity on Gay Street. One of Manhattan's bad puns, a bad joke cracked by Manhattan. 'You know, John,' said Butch Beausoleil during rehearsals, her face lit with surprised self-approval, 'I can't think why they say *gay*. They all seem so unhappy!' Yes, I thought. Fucking stupid. Fielding was right. Now another squad car and an ambulance in its backwash, a man in a blood-brushed T-shirt going quietly, a swollen stretcher and a curled hand waving limp farewell at the grainy black street. Martina appeared briefly, with Shadow, a glass full of scotch and ice, and a key. The old dame and her poodle, they came back too. 'Good evening,' she said. 'Good evening,' I said, right neighbourly . . . My pigs, when they showed, were no trouble to handle. They were swiftly satisfied. 'I got the drop on him but then he made a run for it.' I think they marked me down as a sicko whose sex-plan had boomeranged, what with the outfit and all. 'I beat him up but then he ran away,' I explained. 'Yeh, well you didn't beat him up *enough*' . . . Martina, I found, had made up a bed for me on the sitting-room sofa. I stripped, and for a long time I lay there travelling. Down through the throat of the chimney the noises came. I heard crying, the spokings and unzippings of grief, when the breath sounds as thick as fluid, the weeper gagging on her pillow suicide. Suffering doesn't concern itself with the scale of other sufferings. It has no community sense. It isn't relative, is it. I can't be the only one to have noticed that. Whoever said it first – did they have more to say? The tears could go on for ever but I couldn't. I wrapped myself in a sheet and climbed the stairs like a ghost. I opened the door to the sick room. Shadow was lying in her arms, stretched, agonized – for a second there he looked human, promoted, trapped in another nature. But he soon slipped down to the floor, and shivered with relief, and crept past me into the hall, pleased, it seemed, that a qualified Earthling had come to take over. Nothing happened, and yet this happened. I held her hand. I held her shoulder. I stroked her neck with my fingertips to help her sleep. I can do things that Shadow can't do. I lay by her side in dog-basket warmth, under a roof of rain that came to my ears like distant applause. Oh God, I thought, with fear, my life could turn really serious. Get them when they're crying. Close in when they're crying. They're weak and raw and they can't keep you out.

At sickening speed I have roared and clattered, I have rocketed through my time, breaking all the limits, time limits, speed limits, city limits, jumping lights and cutting corners, guzzling gas and burning rubber, staring through the foul screen with my fist on the horn. I am that fleeing train that goes screaming past you in the night. Though travelling nowhere I have hurtled with blind purpose to the very end of my time. I have lived headlong at a desperate rhythm. I want to slow down now, and check out the scenery, and put in a stop or two. I want some semi-colons. Maybe Martina will be my big brake . . . *I* can't change, but maybe my life can. Mere proximity might do it all for me. Maybe I can just sit back, with a drink, and let my life do all the work.

I opened my eyes and watched impressions take their shape . . . the curtained window and its bluish border of sunlight, the ribbed bookends on the bedside shelf, a spout of flowers on the mantelpiece above the pimply fire of gas, good for baths and winter, the small dressing-table with propped mirror and the bare essentials of the female caste. Details and sacraments, the routines that take no toll. Adulthood might assume this shape. Get to like sleep, get to like milk, get to like the neutral things. Air and water, not earth and fire . . . I turned on my axis: only a note, in her strong lean hand. She had risen early, as grownups will, and would be out all day. Would I make sure the door was locked behind me? Would she see me tonight? Love, Martina.

Having used the bathroom, and sparingly, I sauntered naked down the stairs. Shadow was dozing in a joist of sandy sunlight. With a flip of his tail he acknowledged me drowsily, as an equal – hi, mac. I began to unmangle my hired suit. My hired suit looked even more festively clownish, in the floodlights of day. It can't have looked this bad, surely, in the hired light of evening . . . I sat on the sofa and massaged my face. I felt strange – uncoupled, uncanny. For a good few minutes I thought I must be seriously ill, unprecedentedly, terminally so. My symptoms included a spectral clarity of vision, numbness of head and springiness of limb, and a weird watery taste in the root of my mouth. Whoops, here it comes, I thought, the lung thing, the heart deal, the brain gimmick. Then I realized what was up. No hangover. So this is what morning is. It's not unprecedented. I remember now.

I'll drink to that, I thought. And yet I found the savage craving pretty easy to resist, on the whole. Wearing only a cigarette, I fetched myself some orange juice, climbed into my clothes, bid farewell to Shadow, and made for the door. Shortly I came back again. I took a few turns around the room and, after no more than five minutes of primitive panic, accepted the situation immediately. Martina had locked me in. The front door stood unshackled, with all its clusters, chains and ratchets hanging loose or dangling. But the door wouldn't open, it wouldn't let me out . . . Well, who cared? I had nowhere I needed to be. There was food here, and drink, and shelter. I would be leashed and muzzled all day. But who cared?

After several foulmouthed scourings and spillages I managed to make some coffee in one of the silver utensils ranked like vizors down the length of the kitchen shelf. What is it with me and the inanimate, the touchable world? Struggling to unscrew the filter, I elbowed the milk carton to the floor. Reaching for the mop, I toppled the trashcan. Swivelling to steady the trashcan, I barked my knee against the open fridge door and copped a pickle-jar on my toe, slid in the milk, and found myself on the deck with the trashcan throwing up in my face . . . Then I go and goof with the grinder. I took the lid off too soon, blinding myself and fine-spraying every kitchen cranny. In the end I fought my way out with a mug of tepid but very black coffee which turned even blacker when I added the milk. I got it down somehow. Now what?

I roughhoused with Shadow on the floor for a while, saying things little 'Attaboy, Shadow' and 'Who's the boss' and 'You and me, pal'. But my playmate soon tired, and plodded back to his sunbeam with a sighing yawn. I switched on the television. I monkeyed with the buttons. I jerked the stopsign of the channel selector every which way. All I got was the same silent, fizzy rendering of *The Money Game* – the same cupcake-faced host, the same huge party-tot contestants. I stared out of the window. I

called Fielding, and Felix, and Spunk, and Caduta. I stared out
of the window. I thought of rifling obsessively and methodically
through Martina's personal effects but something about her
human imprint cowed me and gave me pause . . . There was
nothing of any general interest in the drawers of the desk or the
dressing-table, the bedside chests, the cupboards, the filing cabinets, the suitcase beneath the bed and so on, but I did come
across a fascinating item while on hands and knees I completed
my inspection of the downstairs closet. A cardboard box marked
OSSIE, assembled by Martina yesterday evening, no doubt, and
placed here for his collection. It contained various toiletries, a
pair of espadrilles, some soiled shirts, a dead passport (the young
blond face erect with classic vanity), and a travel pouch full of
loose matter: credit-card counterfoils, bills, used tickets, a slip of
notepaper letterheaded the Cymbeline, Stratford-on-Avon, with
a telephone number and appointment time on one side and a
message from Selina on the other. 'O. Oooo,' it said, 'Very
naughty. Bet you don't get that, back at Bank. Till 5. S.'

Now it seems there is a little man living inside me who acts
as minister or propagandist or concessionaire for handjobs. He
champions handjobs: he sincerely believes that handjobs are good
for me, and he is always suggesting that I go ahead and have one.
There is an opposed, paramilitary unit in me too which feels the
opposite way about handjobs and wants to stamp them out altogether. But they're irregulars, the handjob police, always busy
elsewhere just schlepping about and pulling their wires . . . I don't
know what it was, but I suddenly developed a real hankering for
a *handjob*, yeah, a handjob, with full pictorial assist. Of course, I
could have simply trotted up the stairs, dropped my trunks, and
lowered myself on to the treadmill of reminiscence. Oh this tube
of chicks – those Junes, Jans, Joans, Jens, Jeans and Janes. Where
are they: Where is Selina? Funny how Otello there was excited
by Desdemona's crime: the thought of the loved one splayed to

the white man, the other splayed to the other. When I'm old and rich and famous, someone might write my biography. My pornography, though – it's already on the shelves, ghosted by Selina Street with grateful acknowledgements to the many go-getting stylists, footloose talent-coordinators, work-hungry creative consultants and destitute artistic directors who put the whole thing together. Market forces being what they are, there was never a man-pleasing problem, no sir, not in my line of work.

Do you understand what I'm saying to you.

Who needs pornography with a love-life like mine?

I need pornography.

Braced by the challenge, I started sniffing about again. Shadow stirred and looked up, his neck indignantly straightened, as I went padding lithely around the flat, my eyes cold and expert, my senses tuned and vigilant. You see, even in the most staid households a real pro can always come up with something . . . I drew a blank with the mag stacks in sitting-room and bathroom. Just connoisseur and business stuff, art stuff, money stuff. I hardly expected a complete set of *Mouth Crazy* or *Brabursters*, but you'd be surprised how often you find an old *Lothario* or *Plaything*, or at least a *Flair* or a *Sugar*, or failing that, a store brochure or gift catalogue with some kind of knicker range or corset file or girdle spread. Clicking my tongue, I moved on to the wall-sized bookshelves, my fingers poised for the spines of *New York Women, Victorian Lingerie, The Pin-Up, Stay Fit the Workout Way, Underlife, Bordello, Silk, Images* – whatever. But there was nothing, just history, fiction, philosophy, poetry and art! Scandalized, I flapped through the LP covers in search of some cooperatively pouting punk or steaming soul-sister. And what do I find? A deck of Danish landscapes, stylized renderings of animals and pixies, and a lot of metallic old-timers with walrus eyebrows and intelligently

turbid nostrils. Jesus, what kind of household *is* this? I rootled
around upstairs for a while and came across an old album
featuring a snap of Martina in a slithery onepiece swimsuit with
Ossie's bronzed forearm lolling on her shoulder plus a topless
shot of some titless friend of theirs frolicking and shrieking under
a garden shower. Oh, this would never do. I don't know how to
define pornography – but money is in the picture somewhere.
There has to be money involved, at one end or the other. Money
is always involved. Grimly now, I returned to the great bookcase,
rolled up my sleeves, and settled down to business.

An hour later I had assembled the necessary. Pleased with my
work, I made the mistake of humping the whole consignment
up the stairs in one epic stagger. All went well until the top step.
Then I teetered backwards, or tripped, or collapsed unilaterally
beneath the weight of my load. I came to, almost immediately
(I think), and found Shadow barking in my face. He stood there
trembling and nervously smacking his chops, a city snowdog, as
I clambered out from under the fancy avalanche. Eventually I
ferried the gear into the bedroom and cracked it out on the sack.
Pornography doesn't come much softer than this, I thought
shakily as I unfurled my cummerbund, but there we are . . .

It was all down to a three-horse race between *La Femme au
Jardin*, *La Maja Desneuda* and *Aline la Mulatresse* when I heard
Shadow's orgasmic yelp and the sound of sharp footsteps speedily
mounting the stairs. I just had time to flip myself over and
forward in one horrified convulsion as Martina threw open the
door. She stood there vividly, the smile splitting her face . . .
Later, I tried to see what she saw and how it struck her. John
Self, lying belly-down on the bag, one leg coyly crooked, his
expression flushed but diffident as he shyly browsed through a
fanned stack of the old masters. Anyway, here's what she said.

'I locked you in. Where's the key I gave you? You, you're a
deceptive one, aren't you.' And then it was as if a sudden

decision or an old resolve tapped her lightly on the shoulder. 'Why don't you get into bed? I'll have a shower, and I'll come and join you.'

It was eight o'clock in the evening. That was a big sleep I must have had, on the stairs there. And I thought the day had shown a funny colour . . . At ten, we rang out to a delly for cold grub and white wine. I sat up in bed, the food tasting strange and reluctant in my mouth. Another thing I learned that night, a night when I learned many things. Desdemona never did it. She was faithful. She was true. Desdemona never did it – no, she never did.

So now I'm in turnaround, or I'd better be. Me I'm five foot ten and sixteen stone. I have this zooty look, the boxy jacket and the python strides, the bright socks and the black suede shoes, the indeterminate, driven-back hair, the beady scaly face, the face of a fat snake, capable of sudden obedience, sudden revolt. And what else? You're in this too, brother, sister, among the weather, the ageing and the money, the things that move past us uncontrollably while we just stay the same. Only Martina stands outside. And who else? Christ, her eyes are fire to me. When my lips meet hers, so carefully, so critically, it is the kiss of life, it is the kiss of death – it takes two, to kiss. In her presence and her light I sometimes think . . . perhaps, perhaps there is no need, perhaps there is no need to feel so ashamed. Will I stay there, in her light? I can't believe it somehow. I mean, can you? But I'm trying, God damn it, I'm trying.

And it's all happening, everything is happening and I can't stop it. I am a director now and I must do what directors do. I must keep the whole swirl in my head and stop it flying off into the state it loves, which is chaos. I must keep form, I must keep firm. I must balance motivation and character, and be realistic, who, me? . . . Right after Labour Weekend we emerge from the tunnel of Manhattan August and enter day one of Principal Photography. On day one of Principal Photography we start shooting. On day one of Principal Photography I get a cheque for several hundred thousand dollars. Isn't it unbelievable? I'm hoping this will do wonders for my confidence and thrust, of which more later.

Kevin Skuse and Des Blackadder are in town. They flew in yesterday, first class, and are now sullenly ensconced in the Hogg on East Sixty-Fifth Street. By the sound of them they got used to flying first class a lot quicker than I did. But then this is the etiquette of the moneyed and mobile yob – be unpleasant, take it all as your human right. Boy, I wish I had their style. Cecil Sleep, Micky Obbs and Dean Spares are expected tomorrow. The set-men and wardrobe people, the clapper-boy and tealady, the snout gofer and handtowel changer, they're due next week in one great grasping argosy. I'm hoping this will do wonders for my sense of proportion, of which more later.

Fielding and I are now founder lessees of Blithedale Projects, the new studios on the Upper West Side that you've probably read about. Until recently the Blithedale was a retirement hotel: it still looks like a London terminus, or a medieval dream of the final fighting ship, moored to meandering, back-broken Broadway. Last year some property genius managed to boot out the oldsters on a fire-risk loophole, and now the gutted husk has been split cross-wise into four gaping, booming lots. I feel young and small in this dark hot place. As Fielding promised, the Blithedale facilities are superb, state-of-the-art, from the computerized cutting-room in the penthouse right down to the swimming-pool and commissary on the basement floor. Two topflight productions are already on the go at the Blithedale, and one of my fellow directors is another tubby berk from Soho – Alfie Conn. I take great solace from his beerbelly, his sunscorched rug, his bronzed, criminal features. We had a drink together, old Alf and I, and he patronized and one-upped me throughout. Very flattering. In the hallways, the elevators and the games room I tend to mingle with the likes of Day Farraday and Connaught Broadener, Cy Buzhardt and Cheryl Thoreau. You should see the heft I command from the doormen and messenger boys, the production designers and location researchers, not to mention the stars, producers and financiers. You wouldn't believe it. They approach me in the commissary and ask me in whispers about my hopes and dreams. I'm in. I'm welcome. I can handle it all, now that I drink less. I'm hoping this will do wonders for my fitness and self-control, of which more later.

Of course there are star bursts, there are black holes, white dwarves, dead suns. You're bound to get that when you deal with people who want to write their own lives. Yesterday was pretty typical. Butch called me first thing to discuss her doorknob-wiping scene with Spunk. In the script, she wipes the knob in order to erase Spunk's fingerprints, but for Butch this still counts as kitchen patrol. I reasoned with her and she now says she'll do the scene provided Spunk prepares the snack they later share. 'Spunk is a hick, John,' she told me, 'a real lunkhead. He can do it.' I called Spunk and he said he'd be happy to do the cooking provided the meal consisted only of yoghurt and alfalfa. 'Butch is a bitch, John,' he told me, 'just a rich bitch. She couldn't do it anyway.' What he won't do, though, is let Caduta scrub his back while he lolls in the tub. That, said Spunk, was a sick scene. Before I could call Caduta, Caduta called me. 'I want you here by my side, John, while I tell you what I have to say.' I cabbed out to the Cicero. Caduta sat me down and took my hand. Furnished with five shadowy but Caduta-fixated children in the new screenplay, she seemed happy enough with her role. Then she said, 'You understand my deep obsession, John. You are not blind.' Well, I said (I was practically sitting on her lap by this time), I guess it's the kids, not so, Caduta? 'That's right, John. I hate all children. I always have. I cannot help this and it cripples me. I think it best they don't appear at all. Ah, but this you knew! Point two, John,' she said as I tiptoed to the door. Point two concerned the three-second sequence where Butch is glimpsed fussing over a flower arrangement. Caduta found this unconvincing. It was unconvincing, Caduta argued, that a feckless little slut like Butch should be glimpsed fussing over a flower arrangement when someone like Caduta was on hand to arrange the flowers herself. Now if *Caduta* arranged the flowers, that would be convincing. It would convince Caduta, anyway. Then and there I called Butch, who coldly okayed the swap. You wouldn't catch *Butch* arranging flowers, *oh* no. I had just backed out into the hall when the telephone rang: it was Thursday, who demanded that I hurry uptown for a crucial script conference with Lorne Guyland. I hurried uptown. Lorne greeted me with a ten-minute handshake and an anarchical hour-long oration in which were secreted at least a dozen fairly serious demands. He wanted more nude scenes, several zoom-lensed hard-on reaction shots from Caduta *and* Butch, a revised close-up ratio, the introduction of a new female character (a patrician art-critic who loves Lorne with all her heart but has no clear effect on the action), a radically extended dying speech, and a curious interlude – the pre-credits sequence, perhaps – during which Lorne flies supersonic to Paris and back to collect the Legion of Honour for services to international culture. Failure to comply with each and every one of these proposals would result in Lorne's invocation of the Artistic Differences clause in his contract, whereby Lorne indefinitely repaired to Palm Beach at our expense 'until you cock-suckers sort this shit out. As a man of culture yourself, John, I know you'll understand.' By seven o'clock that night we had hammered out a compromise. Lorne would forgo all his demands so long as I cut a single line from the post-coital sequence between Butch and Spunk. The single line was spoken by Butch and consisted of a single word. The word was 'wow'. Lorne seemed pleased – indeed crudely exultant – about the trade-off. As I trudged downstairs Thursday rose from the intercom console and moved gravely across the hall towards me. She was wearing a corset-like pair of tennis shorts and a frilled blouse knotted over her motive midriff. She said, 'Sir, I want for to thank you for what you did for Lorne Guyland.' Then she dropped to her knees, and I felt her large hands smooth my hips. 'Can I help you out here?' she asked. I said I was in okay shape, thanks, and ducked through the door. I think she's a bloke and anyway, the last thing I need is any sexual complication, of which more later.

So I got to Bank Street a little after eight. Next, I . . . well, the evenings are uniform now, and tonight was as uniform as any.

I enter the apartment with my own keys (yeah, my own set), giving the bell a discreet prod just to say I'm home. I knead the hysterical Shadow and kiss his mistress on her dry and tender throat.

I shower. I change. I walk out on to the terrace with a glass of white wine. I tell Martina about my day. 'You're kidding,' she says, or 'I can't believe this,' or 'It's a joke. It isn't real.' She tends her flowers and only half-listens to me. She takes pride in her terrace, Martina.

She shows me around and tells me the names of things. I knew a few flowers already, from advertising logos, chocolate boxes, fruit machines. But now I'm surer of my ground. Those pouting purples with the mouths of waiting fish – they're tulips. Those triplesprigged numbers in freckled orange: tiger lilies. The red creations with the whirlpool throats are roses, as everybody knows. They also come in pink, and in yellow. The thick-stemmed, tendrilled mobcaps – now they're amaryllis.

Stared at closely, the water from her hose looked like all kinds of weather. Like rain, naturally, but also hail, snow, rainbows. Stormy weather. She could fill the air with sun or thunder at the touch of her tap. I always thought that if I ever met the weather god then there'd be hell to pay. I'd demand satisfaction, certainly. But she's my weather god for now, and *I'm* not complaining. In her face I see . . . I see it in her stance, over the troughs of the beds. Let me shift that for you, I might say. 'You're a prince.' There. And I drink my wine.

While Martina makes our meal I stand in the kitchen with heavy arms folded, watching. Her movements are correct and delicate, long-fingered. Yes, she has pretty ways. Even the blots of sweat on the twin cusps of her blue T-shirt are prettily semi-circular. Even sweat seeks its patterns and its forms. Carefully I listen to her soft grunts of effort and concentration and assent.

We eat: omelettes, salads, white meat, white wine. I am watching my glass, I am watching my weight, I am watching Martina Twain. I hold my knife like I hold a pencil. I don't chew right and I talk with my mouth full. It's too late to change. She is a meticulous eater with a modest appetite. I wonder, about her appetite. Coffee? Coffee, or some macabre infusion from the East. She washes and I dry.

Then there is music. Not the hoarse ballads of self-righteous folksongs that Selina sometimes had on last thing – but jazz, Opera, classical. I read my book – *Freud*, say, or *Hitler*. Not *Money*. *Money* gives me panic attacks, even when the guy is going on about Italian banking or the birth of American corporations. I don't know why. We play chess. I always win. I'm good: chess is my chief accomplishment. As a youth I used to hustle for fivers in the Hampstead cafés and the pubs of Bayswater . . . I finish the wine. She empties the ashtray and locks the terrace door. It is all very civilized. It is all very civilized. Then we go to bed, of which more later.

But first I take Shadow for his moonlight ride. I stand there holding the pooper gear while the dog does his thing. The pooper gear I bring along at Martina's insistence. I never use it. The same guy sticks his head out of the groundfloor window and shouts at the dog and me about all the shit. I don't answer. I just say, 'That's it, Shadow. Take a good big dump.' Then we walk to the corner of Eighth Avenue, as it straightens out to frame its share of the New York night. And here Shadow makes his noise of yearning. It starts with an anxious whistle in the sinuses. It ends in moist yelps for breath. Does he have a mother there, sisters, brothers? I smoke a last cigarette as we gaze toward Twenty-Third and midtown, crackling in electromagnetic heat, the place where all life has slipped its leash and now needs no names. 'Did he tug?' she'll surely ask me when I return. Shadow tugs and I tug back, harder, much harder.

'You're a saint,' said Martina.

I placed the tray on the bed and drew the curtains. I take a little sugar in my tea now. Each day in the life needs punctual treats of heat and sweetness. Leaving the sheets' warmth, my dry soul seeks the ghost of candy in the morning brew. Then, on the street and not before, I seal it with the cigarette's fire.

To ride the length of flat-roofed Eighth Avenue – past the lockups and go-downs – is to watch an alien documentary called *The Earthling*, not a good film either, weakly directed and insensitively cut, with no finesse, no overview, the uninteresting given as much space as the interesting. You have to choose. You have to choose all the time.

I hurried through the doors of the Ashbery, past the smiling uniforms, and straight up the stairs. Fourteen flights, fourteen square storm windows, at the run. I came into my room, dropped the key – no further. With breath like a worked zip and the room full of extremity and warning I just stood there, arms slack, shoulders nodding, and ducked my head to a squall of tears. Maybe I never wanted it enough. Christ – no, I never wanted it. I never wanted it anyway.

Later I went to the bathroom, to see what the mirror had to say. *My eyes* . . . They hadn't cried for a long time. They were all out of practice, all out of shape. I looked as though my eyes had wept blood, life blood, everything I had.

The time has surely come for me to tell you. Dah, could I use a little . . . oh, hi, honey. Whew, yeah – that's right. Just along the neck there, with your hand . . . yeah. That's good, that's better, that really seems to help. Don't stop. Don't go.

The time has surely come for me to tell you, to tell you about me, Martina and the . . . Yes, the time has surely come. Hey, brother, give me a drink here. I need it. Let's feel your hand on my shoulder. Identify. Sympathize. Lend me your time.

Well I knew it was never going to be a case of belly-dancing and Turkish delight. I knew it would be serious. What she likes is to writhe and linger, to find the point and then, tuned to the optimum, locked very tight, to dance the level dance with urgency, with address, with – with feeling. She works on direct lines. She likes it this way, that way, but feelingly, humanly.

Such at any rate is my conclusion. It's a rather tentative one, I admit. We've sacked out together – what is it? – ten nights running. And I've yet to, I haven't, I don't seem to be able to . . . There. You've said it for me.

They're very difficult. They're not at all easy. *That's* why they're called *hard-ons*.

Oh me, my, alas and alack. Oh crappy day. What a scream, eh, what a riot? Life is a wag and a funster. Life is the life of the party. It *scintillates*. I've heard this joke before, of course. It *is* an old one. I've had my share of bonk-famines, no-shows and squidge-gimmicks, shoe-horners and sneeze-jobs, twang-strikes and heft-outs. But I've never heard the joke in its long version, in its serial form. I could raise my rope for Butch Beausoleil. I could raise my rope for Selina Street and a snob of a whore on Third Avenue. This old rope of mine has seen action with all shapes and sizes, with the good and the bad and the ugly. But I can't raise my rope for Martina Twain, no sir. It seems she just isn't good enough for this old rope of mine.

'It doesn't matter,' she said last night, for the twentieth time. I lay there, a sixteen-stone teardrop, blinking, smarting, all made of salt. 'Oh yeah?' I croaked. She embraced me and in her hot whisper she said everything that was humanly sayable. 'Oh yeah?' I croaked again. I can't even make it as an animal any more. Even as an animal I'm washed up. 'Jesus,' I said. 'What do I think is the *point* of me?'

The books are for buying, gentlemen. You don't read the books here. Don't readem here. Takem home. Checkm out.

So now I stand in the porno emporium, on the lookout for clues. I flick through the wax-smelling gloss of a cassette brochure. Grannies, kids, excreta, dungeons, pigs and dogs. Oh world, oh money. I suppose there must be people who want all this. I suppose there must be people who like all this. Supply and demand, market forces. Now we're a pretty motley crew, down here on Earth, with no two sets of teeth or fingerprints ever quite the same. Down here, you get all sorts. Odds and sods and no longer any shame, no shame. Everyone is determined to be what they are: it's the coming thing. Women want out from under us men. Faggots and diesels won't be humped by the hets. Blacks have had it with all this white power. Street criminals prefer to go about their business without being vexed by the *police*, who keep trying to *arrest* them and put them in *jail*. Now even the paedophile – the type of human being so keen on violation that only children will do – dares show his shadowed face: he wants a little respect around here. Turn up the lights. Nothing matters. I look around this store of need, at the mag-racks, the private booths, the dark janitoriat saddlebagged with money. I feel singled-out, high-strung and easily spooked but the others in here, they're brisk lunchtime shoppers, quickly attending to their wants and likes. Me, I don't like what I want. What I want has long moved free of what I like, and I watch it slip away with grief, with helplessness. I'm ashamed and proud of it. I'm ashamed of what I am. And is that anything to be ashamed of?

I've taken up handjobs again. You should see me. I'm back with the rest of you – I'm doing it too. Hello again. Well, here we all are, lying flat on our backs and strumming ourselves like bent Picasso guitars. This is *ridiculous* – but what can I do? You know how it is with the street women in hot cities, in concrete jungles. It's not that the weather brings them out. It's just that the weather takes most of their clothes off. In the snarling insanity of high-summer Manhattan, in the staggered ranks of the streets, women move in their extra being of womanliness, all this extra breast and haunch, and emanations, sweet transparencies, intoxi-cating deposits. Men creep palely through the fever. Even Fielding shows the strain. 'It's a bitch,' he says. 'Slick, we can't beat it. So let's join it.' He keeps suggesting outlandish benders, Venusian brothel-crawls, home-delivery women, dialler women, takeout women. There's this chick, that fox, these birds, those diamond dogs. There are dancers, strippers, loopers, hookers. If I heard him right he even said he could swing a weekend on Long Island with Juanita del Pablo and Diana Proletaria. But me I don't need these formal temptations. It's all happening anyway.

You won't believe this. It's the damnedest thing. Suddenly, it seems, half the girls in New York want to get in my pants – yes, *my* pants, the winded Y-fronts with the slack elastic. Is this success? Is this money? Is this promotion, the light shed by Martina Twain?

Loafing around at the Blithedale, I am accosted by little crackers in the commissary and the games room. They come right up to me, packed tight in heatwave wear, and suggest pressing get-togethers at their place or mine. I sit in a bar drinking lite beer and marshalling my confusions – and a big bim will climb up next to me, steadying herself with a hand on my thigh. 'Buy me a drink,' she'll tell me. 'I'm hot.' The other evening, I swear, as I walked up Forty-Third Street in the dusk, a New York woman stood spread-legged in my path and dropped a handkerchief – like so – as I loomed by. There are salacious notes waiting for me in the lobby of the Ashbery. There are salacious women waiting for me in the lobby of the Ashbery. What do you want? I say. 'Can't we discuss this in your room? I'd really like to discuss this in your room.' I fend them off, full of fear and failure. Drink, deep drink, has never looked so sweet. But I get by on wine and Serafim. I look for clues in all this sex bloat and beriberi. And I sometimes think: I'm it. I'm the clue.

The worst news I save until last. It seems – Lord love me, oh, Jesus, give me a break – it now seems that I am developing some kind of gay thing for Spunk . . . Yeah. Isn't it a scene? A couple of days ago I took him up to the Blithedale and bought him lunch at the commissary. His face rippling over the menu, he got into a pitiful tangle with the longhair waiter as he tried to order his foodless salad. It emerged, in a series of stuttering revisions and erasures, that the poor kid can barely read! I almost blacked out with embarrassment and tenderness – and noticed, too, how adorably the muscles on his neck bulged and bunched and burned. Now, when the secretary or the telephonist says, 'I have Spunk Davis for you', I go all clogged and drowsy, as if there were some major chick on the line. I once had a crush on Alec Llewellyn's nine-year-old daughter, little Mandolina, little Mando. It was erotic all right (I loved her touch), and came with classic symptoms (an unkind glance from her and there was, there was nothing, there was suicide) – but the deal wasn't sexual, no, definitely not, not remotely. Perhaps my thing for Spunk is another one of those. Sometimes, I say to myself – relax, he's just giving you a pang of your younger self. Sometimes, among all the fever, the wayward thoughts, I start facing up to the fact that I've probably been deeply in love with Fielding Goodney from the moment we met. Oh man, what to do? I'll just have to weather it, I guess. I'll just have to hope for the best and pray that nothing else too bad goes wrong. I'll just have to butch it out.

Thanks to my shrewd self-projection as a painting-buff, canvas-fancier and general art-artist I have spent a good deal of this turbulent period being exposed to high culture by Martina Twain. Accordingly, I'm in a state of high-culture shock – a panic of bedraggled blackness – as I am led across swirling parquetry, down ulterior corridors, past hidden visions smocked in light. You have to queue, and pay good money, to mingle with vituperative interpreters and flashlight-faced Japanese, balls-talking bumblers, vultures, students, loners, pick-ups, the determined samplers and consumers spun off by the thrashing city. Many of these types, I note, are working class and upwardly mobile, out-of-towners in high-gloss jerkins and biscuit pants-suits. The men are plump clunkers in pastel romper gear, smiling, plodding, nodding. The women are the kind of talking dolls that say *Mommee* and take a leak if you turn them upside down, their faces cute and beady under rugs of taramasalata and meringue. Heroic consumers, they have a slice of most things, and now they want a slice of this stuff too, this art stuff. They seem to think it's all there for the taking. Maybe it is. But for me? I'm from the wrong side of the tracks. I'm from the wrong side of the Atlantic. I'm from London, England. I'm pretty well convinced by now that this gear isn't for me. It's trying. While others look at art or read books or surrender to serious music, my mind just razzes me about money, Selina, hard-ons, the Fiasco. I'm trying, but that's trying too. It's trying, trying.

Me and Martina, we went to all kinds of shows. We went to a constructivist show uptown East somewhere. Twanging maypoles and girder tepees, spastic flexings of concrete and steel, jagged jungle-jims. We went to a modernist show just off the Park. Ripped playing-cards and chess-piece profiles, backgammon battlefields and shards of dice, spoils of trickery, hazardry. I feel obliged to seem enthusiastic about all this but I ran out of bluff and patter long ago and now feign dumb-founded absorption beneath my poker face. Yesterday we went to a show of the classical nude in marble form. It was nice to see some women looking so cool and neutral in the heat. They weren't quite in the altogether, though, these nudes, having been figleafed by a recent hand. It's ridiculous, said Martina, the tiny wraps and sprigs they've added on. Oh I don't know, I said: don't be too hasty – it's good to leave a little something to the imagination. She didn't agree. In my view, of course, the chicks would have looked even better if they'd added stock-ings and garter belts, G-strings and ankle-strapped shoes: but that's aesthetics for you. Tomorrow we go to the big new show by Monet or Manet or Money or some such guy.

So there I am, after a light supper, sitting in Martina's sitting-room, drinking wine and frowning at *Freud*, when the telephone rings . . . I don't feel filial about Caduta Massi any more. I just fancy her now. 'I think of you as a son, John,' she said over tea today. 'That's why I don't like Spunk or Butch Beausoleil. They remind me of children. But you don't have this.' She placed my hand on the electrical cashmere of her lap – and I felt my dick give a sick and fuddled lurch. It was lucky that Prince Kasimir's lungs chose this moment to throttle him awake. Caduta tells me that Lorne calls her *mother* now. They have brave, beaming, soul-rich crying jags together. Lorne would lay down his life for Caduta, but he still wants those nude scenes. 'But mother,' he has said. 'It could be so beautiful' . . . And the telephone rings. The telephone rings, breaking what we must call the illusion of this grownup world I'm sitting in, with my book, the fallen chess pieces, the last act of *Otello* and its gypsy flutes. I *am* grownup and savvy, sometimes. I read sophisticated magazines and go to adult movies. But the telephone is ringing, and it's for me.

'It's for you,' said Martina and handed me the piece, disapproval or puzzlement showing (I thought) in the darkness of the veins on the tender side of her arm.

It's for me – and guess who.

'How'd you get this number?' I asked, with real curiosity. I was sure nobody knew the real truth about my secret life. I was sure everyone thought I was out whoring and alleycatting and getting drunk every night. 'Your gingerhead friend give it to you?'

'She's off the case. I – I don't see her. She says you're no fun any more.'

'Hey, we've got to meet. I'm really ready.'

As I've explained, it is no use hanging up on Frank the Phone. He just calls back for ever. You have to let him speak, you have to let him rage and jabber and sob, until he has said his bit, and steadied, and is willing to say goodbye, exhausted, mollified, all wept out. Frank the Phone likes to lay down the law about what it's like having no money and so on. Frank the Phone doesn't have any money. He doesn't have anything else either. When all the looks and charm and luck and dough were being handed out, old Frank came in at the end of every queue – as I took the chance of reminding him. He countered by itemizing all the neat tortures he was going to visit on me one day, and I heard him out until he was through. Then a silence came, and with a sudden nod I said,

'You're crippled, aren't you.'

'I have a – I have a . . . Yeah,' he said.

Then how do you think you're going to fight *me, scumbag?* I wanted to ask him. But all I said was (and I meant it), 'I'm sorry. I'm so sorry.'

To Martina I played down the whole deal. 'Some disgruntled actor,' I said. 'He keeps ringing me up.'

'Is he the man who dresses as a woman?'

Something of the kind had occurred to me, of course, but now I was surer than ever. 'No,' I said. 'This is a little guy.'

I told Martina my Nub Forkner story. We've hired Nub, by the way, and Christopher Meadowbrook, as the two main heavies. They're a nightmare to deal with but I really believe they're going to make a terrifying pair. Nub, all fat and mad, Chris, all ripe and wasted. Like me and Alec Llewellyn, evening things out here . . . The scene where they threaten Spunk Davis – it *is* threatening. Shoot them in long takes, I say to myself, and let the feeling build. The envy, the bile, the hate, let it build.

I took Shadow for his walk and went to bed with Martina Twain. I don't really want to talk about it. At the moment the gimmick is that we just spoon and cuddle, cuddle and spoon. Like all girls she's a warmth addict: she likes to keep the air-conditioning on and stoke up a counter-heat in the bag. I hold her. I am full of abstract desire and something else I don't understand and can't identify. As I lie there, inhuman, non-animal, nothinged, I scour my mind for kisses and soft impacts, cool caresses. And then they become pornography . . . The screening-room inside my head (exclusive, members only but cheap to join) grows stale and smoky – this old toss-house up here with the soggy seats and the full ashtrays, the ticking film. Nothing happens. Nightly I die a Desdemona death among the many pillows . . . First thing yesterday I tried to spring a morning glory on her. You can imagine how glorious that felt. It didn't work, anyway. I had to go and take a leak. Sometimes I think my dick was traumatized by that boil-up at the Opera. But there's probably more to it than that. Yes, there's probably more to it than that.

Watch. Wait . . . Here I come again. I can see me now. With a happy yawn I rise from the posturepedic mattress of the latest starlet. I take my dick-sized bonk pill and writhe in a whirlpool of Vitamin C. 'Good morning, sir': it's my shower assistant, or my tennis coach, or my poodle groomer, rug guru, youth yogi. I drink my glass of low-calorie, make-you-drunk designer water. The house-to-car therapist takes me by the hand – and I'm off, sailing down Sunset Boulevard, with a scalp rich in astroturf, a mouthful of cobalt and Strontium 90 – and a million bucks of computerized courting-tackle, this bionic bullybag nestling between my thighs. The operation has been a runaway success. We all think it's wonderful, the way I've been able to change.

Ah but you know, you know sometimes I feel as if I've already been to California – and it didn't work out. I feel . . . prosthetic. I am a robot, I am an android, I am a cyborg, I am a skinjob. I read somewhere – or somebody once told me, or I overheard it in a pub or bar or beanery (anyway, it's part of my private culture now) – that a high proportion of Earthlings, one in five, or one in three, or maybe even two in one, is under the impression that all their thoughts and actions are determined by creatures from another world. And these people aren't just mixed-up berks and babbling bagladies: they are haunted tinnitic taxmen, bug-eyed barristers and smart-bombed bureaucrats. Before (and I wish I knew more about that time – before. I don't suppose I'll ever find out much about it now), before, these tribes of spacefaced conquered would brood about God, Hell, the Father of Lies, the fate of the spirit, with the soul imagined as an inner being, a moistly smiling angel in a pink nightie, or a grimacing goblin, all V-signs, bad rug and handjobs. But now the invader is a graph shadow swathed in spools and printouts, and he wears an alien face.

I sometimes think I am controlled by someone. Some space invader is invading my inner space, some fucking joker. But he's not from out there. He's from in here.

We rose late and grabbed a beansprout in some high-priced rabbit farm and took a cab uptown. I had almost forgotten what rain was like, but today rain reminded me. Rain looked as though it had never been away, back where it belonged, in its element. The sunlit beauty of the Avenues, I realized – it's just air, really, nothing, framed with great strictness and symmetry, but only air. Now the vistas vanished into mist – slack-hinged, smoke-breathing jaws. Labour Day Weekend, the streets deprived of their personnel, the few cars stalled and bobbing on the ramps like logs in rapids. We climbed out, and queued under a pink umbrella. On this rainy afternoon Édouard Manet was our man.

The first thing he did was take me back to Paris. You know that one of the girl serving in the stripclub or trapeze bar, her gentle put-upon look, the unopened half-bottles of champagne, the oranges in the thick glass bowl, and, behind her in the distance, the rank of mad tophats . . . I made my Paris debut last year, shooting a commercial for a new kind of frozen horse-meat steak. We used the equestrian studies in that gallery near the river. The idea was: boy meets girl in front of the Degas racetrack, then he takes her off to a swish brasserie for a slap-up dobbin rissole or nagburger or whatever the hell it was . . . Paris overexcited me. I spent a lot of time on the Left Bank boulevards, drunk, shouldering my way through the shopping crowds and circling money-users, stopping dead in my tracks every fifty yards as I saw, framed in the glass canvas of a café window, some haggardly bronzed blonde or pert-haired waif, sitting alone with her beer or coffee and patiently waiting, so it seemed, for someone like me to pop inside and start making with the international language. *'Bonjour, mon petite. Let me buy you a drink. Pourquoi non come back to my hotel. Come on, cherie, you know you love it.'* I must have got chucked out of, oh, a good six or seven places, or maybe even ten or eleven, before I realized what was up. Oh, the chicks have got Paris licked all right. They've worked things so that they can hang around wherever they like without any random drunk or stray coming in off the street to give them a bad time. Well, it's too late now, I thought. What's done is done. But who let them get away with *that*?

. . . And now in wet Manhattan, in the hot gallery where we all smell of damp dog, I look at Martina, staring erectly and with no waste of attention at the form of the dead matador, and I think – yeah, women, they're very different from us, about as different as the French are, say (women, they lean from side to side when they drive and laugh mainly out of friendliness, they hold hot drinks with both hands and hug themselves to keep the warmth, they disapprove of games and sports and say *my* far more than we do, they have what men call self-belief and blame you for your misprisions in their dreams, they are conspiracy theorists, benevolent dictators), but they *are* Earthling, and very like ourselves. Women are more civilized. Chicks, they're the gentler sex. They may give you a bad time in the home but they don't give you a bad time in the street. Men are often urged, by women, to recognize the feminine side of their nature. I always thought that was faghag talk but now I'm not so sure. Maybe that is what's happening to me – I'm getting chicked. It would explain a great deal. I have tried in the past to feminize myself. I womanized for years. It didn't work, though on the other hand I did fuck lots of girls. Who knows? If it happens, it happens. I'm hardly a front-seat driver in all this. I'm in the back seat, or the caboose. I don't know if I ever was in control. But I know I'm not now.

So I looked at Martina as she looked at Manet: the civilized pleasures and sacraments duly celebrated, with nothing pinched or over-correct. Oysters for breakfast, dead fish, deader than the dead man. Women dressing up, the male pride in uniform. The garden as a place for work and rest, then the peonies in their jug. The writer's girlfriend, the writer's vigil at his desk. The world of enough money, the world of enough. I saw all this but I didn't see its shine. Me, I liked the fool-the-eye stuff, the drinks, the bars, the grub, the bim at the picnic, the well-hung blonde, familiar, erotic. I saw all this. I didn't see its shine. But I saw Martina's shine: it filled her eyes, her mouth, her flesh – everything.

Anyway, I then had to leave the girl, God damn it, and bolt across town to clock up an hour or two at a reception in the Carraway thrown by Fielding Goodney for all our moneymen. There are even a couple of moneywomen by now. We have Lira Cruzeiros from Buenos Aires, we have Anna Mazuma from Zurich, we have Valuta Groschen from Frankfurt. It did my old ticker good, I tell you, to see all this dough-power, this moolah-grip, on such raucous display. I mean, *Bad Money* – what is the operation costing now? It has to be better than thirty-five or forty big ones a day, and we don't even start shooting until the middle of next week . . . Through some inscrutable precaution of Fielding's, Spunk Davis had not been invited (and neither had Butch Beausoleil).

But the senior stars were there – Caduta Massi, cosseting the enfeebled Prince Kasimir, and Lorne Guyland, in a robotic dinner-jacket with vampire Thursday on his robot arm. I saw the English contingent, Skuse, Blackadder, Mick Obbs and my whizzkid editor, Duane Meo. They stood scowling in a corner, and for a while I felt like a mother-hen or an orchid-fancier, what with all these souls to tend and soothe. But Fielding took over and worked a kind of flattery contest between artisans and stars, leaving me free to wander through the moneyed crush.

Mind you, they were a surprisingly unostentatious mob, lacking the glow – poorly shod, some of them, and crying out for a few grands' worth of rug work or complexion fixative. There was a lot of jazz and jabber in the air, what with the good champagne, the prettified canapés, the tuxed tapsters, the money, and swapping the odd smile or wave or shout I moved among them, free as water. They all seemed to be talking about acting, fairly specifically too – working, resting, availability, auditioning, projection, all the usual stuff. Well, I thought, they're all amateur producers, or they are now. And being rich is about acting too, isn't it? A style, a pose, an interpretation that you force upon the world? Whether or not you've made the stuff yourself, you have to set about pretending that you merit it, that money chose right in choosing you, and that you'll do right by money in your turn. Moneymad or just moneysmug, you have to pretend it's the natural thing . . . I never felt I deserved it, money, for what I did (it was a big embarrassment), and that's probably why I pissed it all away. I won't be able to piss this lot away, though. There isn't a can deep enough, and there's simply too much money. Then I'll have to join them, the money artists.

★

I awaited Fielding's grave, complicit nod and then, after a hand-squeeze each from Lorne and Caduta, slipped outside and caught a cab downtown. We hit one of those weird relays of lights over on Ninth Avenue, fifty blocks without a brake, the green eyes fuelling my agitation by saying, yes, go, it's okay, you can do it, when for once this backseat traveller longed for limit and drag, longed to cut right in off the fast lane. So I ditched the car and walked the last mile to ease my itching heart, across the Chelsea teen streets to Eighth, past the slumped bars in their blue or purple light, past the black antimatter recesses of heartbreak hotels (some boxy black chick doing a tough rap at the desk), and then paused in perfect Manhattan twilight, the air now holding its components of grey, silver and yellow, and watched through diamond wire as eight kids bobbed with their ball beneath the flapping hole.

Martina stood silent on the terrace, in T-shirt and useful shorts, one arm akimbo as she trained her hose . . . We ate out there on the wet raft, salad, bread, cheese, that toy white wine again, the musky, flanky odour of drenched mulch and peat. Later, Shadow drowsed in supplication to his mistress, the features, in repose, formed purely for anxiety and the sighs of sleep. I sat with *Hitler* on my lap – night of the generals, scorched earth, collapse and humiliation and death: a happy ending. Now I would have to start reading *Money* all over again. Martina had given me these books. Martina had given me a how-to kit for the twentieth century. And yet that was what I was giving her too – in person. She was observant. She had been watching me these past weeks no less keenly than I had been watching her. She was learning quite a bit about her planet's travel through time. She had osmoted some with this limp fatso, his mind in freefall and turnaround, a rag-and-bone man, hollow, stuffed, made out of junk, junk.

I said, 'Hey. You've got to tell me.'

'What?'

'Why are you letting me hang around like this in your life? It just isn't convincing. I mean, who would believe it? Would you?'

'Oh,' she said. 'You're not so bad, you know. You're here, and no one else is. You're trying. I just like you.'

'Why?' Because I'm so twentieth century? 'Why?'

'You're like a dog.'

I tensed a little here. I'm still not happy about this kind of thing. With girls I normally demand to be taken very seriously at all times. But I do see I'd be asking quite a lot here, especially these days, when I can hardly keep a straight face myself.

'You've already got a dog.'

'Now I've got two. What do you think about when you aren't thinking about anything else?'

'I'll have to think about it,' I said. At that moment I craved whisky so badly – there's no use denying that fear plays a big part in all this, in these transactions down at Bank Street. Fear of the unknown, fear of the serious. There was a glass of white wine left in the bottle. But you don't get much courage from a glass of white wine. I said,

'You tell me yours first.'

'Losing things.'

She fell silent. I reckoned she was thinking about losing things. I stared into the bruised whites of her eyes. Yes, her crying muscles were well developed all right: those eyes had pumped a lot of iron in their time. She talked on. She meant losing people, not losing things. She had been losing people for some while now, at the rate of one a year. Her grandparents had taken care of the mid-Seventies. Then she lost her mother (cancer), her best friend (car crash), her father (suicide), and, last year, her only brother (drowning, drowning). That was a summer ago, up there on the Cape. I knew none of this.

'Christ,' I said. Of course the rich leaven death by leaving you things. It's the other way around where I come from. You're always having to dig into your pockets for debt settlements, funeral fees. 'Still,' I went on gropingly, 'you haven't lost anyone this year. So far anyway.'

'Yes I have. Ossie – for good.'

'Oh yeah.'

'You, what do you think about all the time.'

I felt my face go puffy and stupid, then I shrugged and said, 'Money. It's either that or fear and shame. It's all I've got to use against people who might hate me.'

'Poor you,' she said. 'But maybe you're not so special.'

We went to bed. We went to bed in that grownup way – you know, as if it were just the next thing. No mood-qualifiers or tone-deepenings, no goatish grunts or frisky yelps and giggles, no props, brandy, brothel gear, thongs, thumbscrews, third parties. She stripped swiftly. Her pants are pretty talented, too, but you hardly ever get a decent look at them. On her long brown legs, the form of the inner thighs endearingly curved like the join of a pincer (the hips broad-banked, the back deep but unsturdy, raisined, rich), Martina strode to the bathroom. Then her return, full and frontal, the flesh showing the first interesting looseness, the first prints of time, of death, making you sure that if you were ever lucky enough to – you would certainly have been with a woman. That was a woman, no mistaking her. I said,

'God, while all this has been happening you've still had all your stuff to think about. I never thought. I'm sorry.' And I glimpsed all her other thoughts, too, up there, like her face, way over my head.

I stripped and joined her in the linen. We kissed, we embraced, and I know I'm a slow one and a dull dog but at last I saw what her nakedness was saying, I saw its plain content, which was – Here, I lay it all before you. Yes, gently does it, I thought, with these violent hands . . . And in the morning, as I awoke, Christ (and don't laugh – no, don't laugh), I felt like a *flower*: a little parched, of course, a little gone in the neck, and with no real life to come, perhaps, only sham life, bowl life, easing its petals and lifting its head to start feeding on the day.

'Should I let him go? What do you think?'

'Yeah, let him go,' I said. 'He's cool.'

'He might run.'

'You've got to try it some time.'

Washington Square, Labour Sunday in New York, with the air as heavy as drips on a blue kitchen wall. Another big date in the jungle calendar, full of tribal turnout, the wise kids on skates dodging to a dozen different beats, the frisbying faggots all jump and stretch (their spun dish would hang for ever in the thermals of the haze), boardgames, drug burns, spells and curses, two police cars with all four doors open, the pigs' cocked traps ready for the first incautious paw. And no shame, anywhere. Some menace and some desperation, and great hardness showing itself best in the ginger grip, rake and bristle of the cops' facial hair – but no shame . . . The dog was twisting himself inside out to be off and away among all this risky human colour. We untethered him. At first he ran in widening circles, with his tongue practically thrown over his shoulder like a scarf. Then he paused, and sat in profile, erect and civic-minded, the posture of a chess knight waiting quietly on the third rank, in sober contemplation of the choices to come.

I bought a few cans of lite beer from the superette. We sat on the stone bench and talked, Martina wearing white (white skirt, white shirt), me with a band of wincing, gloating agitation wound tight around my heart. Upward movement along the chain of being, social mobility – it's great stuff but it isn't half tiring. Just keeping a handhold and staying where you are, not slipping, even that takes tons of balls. As Shadow looped about us, returning ever less frequently for that encouraging touch, I picked a topic and asked Martina about philosophy. Not her philosophy – just philosophy. She gave me some examples of the sort of thing philosophers got up to. Like, how can you tell that the *Morning Star* and the *Evening Star* are really the same thing? I bounced back by saying that surely they *weren't* the same thing: even if they shared a parent company they were still two separate titles and would therefore be considered quite distinct for budgeting and tax purposes and so on. Martina smiled and nodded in agreement. She gave a laugh, a new one, which seemed to express simple happiness or resignation. Philosophy's a doddle, I thought, and I said,

'Okay. Do me another one.'

But her face changed now and she stood up suddenly. 'Oh no,' she said. 'Where's Shadow?'

This had been bothering me too. Shadow hadn't shown for a good few minutes and I had been secretly straining to get a glimpse of him in the human whir. Saying nothing, we zigzagged through the square, skirted its border, then retraversed the thriving, mugging heat. No dog, no Shadow. We split up and ran in widening circles, returning ever less frequently for that encouraging touch.

An hour later I was running alone down Seventeenth Street, my hammocked gut bouncing in its pouch, a terminal jogger, all peeled eyes and peeled breath. Martina kept saying, as we linked up and parted again, that the dog had been stolen. But I knew he had cut and run uptown, back to the cross-stream of Twenty-Third Street and beyond. At first I felt, Christ, let's just *find* the little bastard – then at least I get a lie-down and a drink. For a while I even developed the idea that it would do me no harm if Shadow left the picture after all. But now as I staggered at speed through the grid I had a dire certainty that my fate was closely bound up with the dog's, that with Shadow gone I too would be back on Twenty-Third Street among the human canines. No more gentrification for me. Just inner city, cold-water, walk-up. I thought I saw him, dashing knee-high between the gaps of parked cars, meter posts and hydrants, but when I dodged through the traffic to the far pavement I found only a split trashcan flailing in the breeze. I ran on now, up Eighth Avenue towards the world's end.

I found him on Twenty-First Street, one of the turbid inlets off the old Limpopo. My instinct was to holler and sprint forward, but I slowed, and edged watchfully toward him. Shadow stood bemused in a weak cyclone of detritus – you know the way trash has in cities of playing ring-a-roses for helpless hours in a pocket of wind: food cartons, snout packs, beercans, all in their afterlife of headless chickens . . . I came nearer. He looked to be in a queer state, Shadow, shaking and clicking the long trap of his mouth, a limp paw pointing, pointing uptown. There was a physical difference in him, a vital detail, that I couldn't locate. His collar, his collar was gone. One hour in the jungle and Shadow had already been mugged, ripped off – stripped of all he had, no-named. Now he turned to me with incurious eyes, and looked away dully. He was about to tiptoe off into the rush of the Avenue but I barked his name with all the power left in my lungs, and he turned again, with effort, and came towards me low across the kerb, shoulders bunched in extreme surrender, the abject maximum. I didn't hit him. I seized his scruff. I carried him home. Martina was waiting on the stoop. She hadn't wept before but she wept now.

And as she thanked me and held my hand to her face I thought – she really loves him, it, she loves Shadow, this dog. Yes, she's been deceiving me, Martina. She's just human, only human. It turns out she's all too human in the end.

★

And one, and two, and three, and four. I'm lying on the fourteenth floor of the Ashbery, wearing tacklebag only and wiggling my legs in the air like an upended beetle. What am I doing? I'm exercising. Poop strength and gut flex are the immediate targets, but other considerations obtain. I'm staying in shape for Martina. This is the new-deal me. This is my metamorphosis. And five, and six, and seven, and eight. I'd go right through the pain barrier if only I could find it. Besides, I know the real muscles are up in my head somewhere, the muscles of mortification. Whew, I hope they're still there. I hope they haven't atrophied. I hope they're not too drunk. I need to get my brain trained is what I need. I need some sadistic singlet-and-dumbbell artist to sweat my brain into peak condition. I need my brain to feel the burn. Tomorrow sees day one of Principal Photography. I get a big cheque. Everyone will have to start taking me a lot more seriously – including you, mister, yeah, and that goes for you too, lady. Yesterday I need tell you nothing about. It seems that all you've got to do is be nice to them, and candid, and faithful, and then you get all this. What a deal.

I rolled on to my chest and did a push-up or two. The first one went remarkably well. Exactly half way through the second, though, both arms snapped out co-instantaneously, and the carpet shot up and loafed me on the nose. As I lay there swearing and mumbling and spitting the fluff from my mouth, the telephone rang. I had spoken to Martina ten minutes ago, and was half-expecting Fielding or Frank the Phone. Old Phrank, that gimp – how can he hurt me now?

So this was a double surprise.

'Hi! . . . Hey – it's me, remember?'

'You're kidding,' I said. 'Are you in New York?'

'You bet.'

'You can't be.'

'Why not? Let's meet and I'll fill you in. Lunch?'

I couldn't manage this, so we arranged to have drinks at the Bartleby on Central Park South, two thirty. I lay back blinking in my white body. All my lags and jumps and switches, all my reality levels are getting snarled up. You'll never guess who that was – or maybe you will. Why, little Selina.

But now it was into the suit and off to lunch with Butch Beausoleil and Spunk Davis, a final peace-talk, gee-up and reassurance-rally in preparation for the big day. I thought I'd take the kids to the Balkan Coffee Shop on Fifty-Third Street . . . First off, there was a minor rumble at the door, due to the informality of Spunk's outfit (actually he looked smarter than I'd ever seen him: silk skirt, designer rompers, leather shoes), but I laid a fifty on the manager's wide palm and he siphoned us into a booth near the bar. I should have known something was up when Spunk allowed Butch to precede him into our nook, making quite a show of this courtesy, and then fondly torched her cigarette. Next, with an eye on the lady, he goes and accepts a glass of champagne! Well, after this (and after a glance at Butch's stoked body-tone and Spunk's furtive and queasy pallor), I couldn't pretend much surprise when they leaned forward, hand in hand, and asked me to be best man at their wedding. Jesus, can you believe these characters? Two weeks ago they were hawking all over each other. I know my gay thing for Spunk had died quietly enough (ditto my straight thing for Butch: they never really started), because my first thought was – Beautiful: this is a million bucks' worth of free publicity. My second thought, on the other hand, was – Calamitous: this wrecks the whole package. I'll never get anything out of them on the set and as for Lorne Guyland, he'll flop down dead the instant he hears the news . . . But you know how it is, I hope. I was feeling a hell of a wise and sexy old bastard, after my weekend in heaven there, so I played it diplomatic. I told them to wait, and keep it quiet. They seemed a little stung of course, as I talked grandly on throughout a meal of what looked and tasted like a fresh haul of seal jizz and eel helmet. Yes, I was very persuasive, very passionate. And I meant it all too. I'm thirty-five, I realized, sitting there, and I'm a frustrated father. Maybe I should have had kids when I was young, before I had time to think.

As Spunk slid off to the men's room Butch eyed me meaningly, paused for a couple of beats, and said,

'I'm pregnant, John.'

Great, I thought: now Caduta has a nervous breakdown too. Then something else occurred to me. 'Are you sure it's his?'

'Not positive on that, no.'

'But you're on the pill or whatever, surely. You got a gimmick in there or something.'

'Answer me this, John. Why is it always the woman who takes the precautions?'

Uh? 'Because it's always the woman who gets pregnant.'

'I thought I was sterile.'

'Who?'

'I was sterile.'

Oh yeah – rhymes with Beryl over here.

'And I already had two abortions this year. Spunk doesn't know.'

'About the abortions.'

'No. That I'm pregnant.'

'Careful now, Butch,' I said. 'Remember Spunk's religion. They have this right-to-life deal where you –'

'It's okay. He doesn't buy that crap any more. He doesn't know anything, John. And I want to tell the whole wide world.'

You do that, I thought, and *I'll* tell the whole wide world – on the front page of the *Daily Minute*. She stretched and shivered happily. No doubt she was fired up on cocaine, as well as on clueless self-approval. Yes, a mad, dumb, coked bitch is what I had on my hands here. But I got her to swear to silence for the

time being, and when Spunk returned she hit the can h
looking vastly assured. In fact she was gone so long I thought
she might be having an abortion there and then.

Spunk was gazing at me trustingly. 'I know what's on your
mind, John. You're thinking this is going to affect our work on
Bad Money. You're wrong.'

'Reassure me.'

'We've been rehearsing together. That's how it all happened.
In the script, you know that, that beautiful speech where Butch
talks about the journey of my soul.'

'Yeah,' I said uneasily.

'It's poetry – it's music. And you know that beautiful speech
I have, about Butch being one of life's children? As we worked
we came to see that the meaning of our lives was a kind of a
dual flowering that –'

'Look, Spunk,' I said, 'why don't you just fuck her a lot for a
while and forget this whole marriage bit.'

He was about to take a swing at me but I was ready for him
with my adult stare. I couldn't take any more of that stuff, that
soft-voiced leisurespeak, and I was glad to see the old opposition
in him.

'You don't understand,' he said. 'She's teaching me how to
live.'

There was no question of that. He looked terrible. By his
standards he seemed debauched to the point of imbecility. God,
with the dope and the champagne and the high-tec playbacks
and whatever else Butch had in her larder, imagine what these
two youth-users were getting up to in the cot. The very thought
of it made me pant with exhaustion. Still, this suited me in a
way. I didn't want Spunk looking too bland or healthy, up there
on the screen. Give the guy a month more of this, plus some
darkener under the eyes, and he'd look as whacked and wasted
as I could possibly wish.

always had money, right?' he said. 'She knows
.oney, she's taught me that money is just some-
You know I never carried any money, no change,
.ever wanted to forget what it was like to be poor.
Bս․   ⸱r. That's shame. Why *not* forget it? I'm through all
that now ⸱ɪd I feel good about my money.'

So this philosopher had frowned his way to a conclusion. The
pity was that the whole of tabloid and letterhead America had
reached it before him. 'Well,' I said. 'Now you know.'

He was up as straight as a ramrod for Butch's re-entry, and
over coffee and cake they snogged and canoodled like a couple
of sweaty college kids – no, not like that, more like a
couple of actors in the pre-credits sequence of an adult movie.
I watched their breathy squirmings with the neutral curiosity
conferred by my own sexual peace, or wealth. I felt the same
way about my meeting with Selina – that Selina . . . The waiter
gave me a benign and elderly smile as I flicked my Vantage
card on the offered tray. The romance would be all over town
by tonight anyway. And, yes, the script could accommodate
this body heat all right, with a little smudging here and there.
I'd have to settle for the free publicity and find some way to
pacify Lorne. That aristocratic art-critic of his. Another nude
scene. Another torture scene. He could step out of the shower
and slip on the soap for all I cared. Christ, what a psychotic
industry. Not even an industry – a conspiracy, a money
conspiracy. I also reflected, not for the first time, on the sinister
adaptability of the new screenplay. Fielding was right. You
could do what you liked with that script: it had an obscene
plasticity. That script was Juanita del Pablo or Diana Proletaria:
she took it everywhere.

'Your card, sir.'

I looked at the tray – and felt the sweat of shame spread like
ice across my chest. Like hot ice, like cold sweat. I got to my feet.

In the burning gloss of the salver I saw the waiter's waiting face – and my Vantage card, neatly snipped into four.

'Where's the fucking manager! Hey you, come here.'

'Company policy, sir. We checked your card on the computer. There's a recoup out on it.'

'Well the computer fucked up, didn't it. You know who this is? Butch Beausoleil! You know who this is? Spunk Davis! You know who I am? I could buy you out ten times over. I could –' And lots more of the same. Nothing this bad had happened to me for at least a couple of weeks. I roared on for a while, but really – the whole mess was so ludicrous that I couldn't stay angry for long. It would be something to tell Martina, and chortle over with Fielding . . . After that three-day weekend I seemed to be down to my last few tens and fives, but then Spunk produced a toilet roll of hundreds from the back of his jeans and scathingly tossed two bills on to the chocolate cake. We filed out in good order. I only lingered at the tasselled lectern and coolly asked the *maître d'*,

'You get money for that. Am I wrong?'

'On recoup? Fifty dollars a card, sir.'

I fished my fifty out of the crested tit of his blazer, where I had seen him stow it on our arrival, and wiggled the note in his face. Then I dropped the money and walked out into the street.

What a joke, eh? Company policy . . . by the time I got to the Bartleby on the scorched reactor of Central Park South, I wasn't sure that I could even be bothered to call the Vantage people and give them a blast. Yeah. I'd get some chick down at Bad Money to do it all for me.

'Fucking and shopping,' said Selina Street: 'they're the only things that girls should be allowed to do much of. Don't you think?'

She sat surrounded by the ritzy capsules and hampers of Fifth
Avenue loot. Selina was dressed in her own heatwave gear: a
childishly flounced tutu plus a bra-sized half-shirt, dappled here
and there by her spicy sweat. Was she thickening slightly around
the waist? Maybe, just a bit.

'I'm puffed,' she said. 'You look different.'

'How?'

'Have you stopped drinking or something? More in control.'

'So do you. You look the same, only more so.'

But she did look different. She had acquired what she had
wanted all along. You see it climbing in and out of cars or behind
the sheen of jewellers' shops or in the foyers of hotels like this
one. It is the glow, doubleglazed against time and weather. She
had the colour now, the money tone.

Selina sat back and talked. New York was just how she'd
always imagined it. I flailed for waiters in the busy aquarium
of the lobby. It was one of those showcase fairgrounds where
America breathes deep and flexes its corporate wealth, where
the scenic elevators surge and swoon through fountains and
foliage and computerized purity – a stand in the Great
Exhibition of the future that would one day be christened
Money . . . She had been in Long Island for a week, doing God
knows what with God knows who: she looked tangy, rusty,
with a salted sharpness of tooth. Among other things she was
over here to firm up her settlement. Ossie was in town too,
somewhere. Although it was finished between them, he
continued to be very *good* about it all. She flourished: she was
equal to it. She was equal. Selina was also prospecting for what
she still called the boutique, which thrived and prospered,
which prospered and thrived. As she talked, Selina scratched
her thigh with a forgetful fingernail, slowly crossed her legs
and turned her head aside to frown at a blemish on the halter
of her shirt. I accepted the opportunity to review the

perspective of her legs, and the white pants, curved like a sail at the vista's end.

'You know, it's funny how, how sentimental I am about you.' She leaned forward. Her eyes moved softly across my face. 'The other night I was in bed with someone. I won't say who. And he turned me over. You know, to fuck me from behind the way you like to. And I had to stop. I couldn't go on.'

She shook her head, as if such constancy were indeed to be marvelled at.

'But you started again,' I suggested. 'You went on later.'

'Yes of course, I soon got over it. I went on later all right. He's so rich. I've been shopping all morning. I meant to get you a present. I feel I owe you one. You were very good about every-thing really. But I ended up just getting presents for me. Look. Isn't this nice? I know you like plain white or black but these sharp reds can be good too. I wouldn't usually pay as much for something like that. This was expensive too. It clips up between my legs. You know that little thing cost a hundred dollars and it's so tiny. It hardly weighs a thing. Feel. They're presents for me. But they could be presents for you too. I was thinking of trying them all on. Here. In my suite. I'll call down for some champagne. I'd like to give you something to remember me by. My suntan. Do you want to come and watch?'

I looked carefully into her face, into her High Street eyes. They have a glow too, the light of shopping malls at six o'clock, business ending under a tripledecker light of silver, bruised blue and the oystery gloss of the necessary commerce. The set of her face was sentimental, but the eyes were not sentimental, weren't even kind. I felt danger – my very armpits hummed with it. Not the danger of discovery but of reversal, of turnaround, of harsh, suspended laughter. Selina was right: I *had* changed. I saw her offer and the attempt, the attack it made on me. And so with my vows to Martina still warm on my lips I smiled with regret (you'll never know how much), and shook my head, and paused before saying, 'You bet.'

Three twenty-five. The champagne was on its way. Yeah – where's my champagne? The show was over but the other show had already begun. It's a show all right, and high on spectacle, this performance of the sack artist. There is time for thought among all the unfeeling, time for reflection among all the reflection. Reflection is what keeps the dancer on the ramp, it keeps the actress in the gun-lights' sights, the mirror game of withheld applause. This is just the private performance, the most private performance that is theirs to give.

'I want to be on top.'

'Anything you say.'

Her shape and its mouldings loomed above me. She shut her eyes and let her head drop back. I viewed the culverts of her throat, the staring, saucer-sized spectacles of her brassière, one eye open, one eye shut, but both staring, the waist measured by a thin golden chain, the showcase hips packaged in their ribbons and bows. Her skin is like superskin that encloses a single organ. She is like a hard-on, she is like a dick, sitting there on me . . . And so – why the fear, why the shame? I know I won't feel good until I'm back in my strides. I should be in *my* pants, not in hers. But there she squats with a breast in each hand. And you can't teach an old dog new tricks. Selina, she really has the franchise on these old loins of mine. Authentically corrupt, seriously vulgar, intensely twentieth century, she will always be the ghost writer of my poor pornography – little Selina, that Selina . . .

Now she leaned forward with her hands on my shoulders and let a breast slide into my mouth. Time passed. Time passed, until the outside world – the real one – knocked on the door of the neighbour room. '*Yes*,' she said fiercely, '*come on in*,' then more softly, 'The champagne – they'll leave it there,' then more softly still, 'Don't stop.' But I started to struggle even as I felt the double doors waft open and the third presence enter our space.

In one movement Selina sat up and turned, straightened a leg and swivelled like a gymnast to her feet. I raised my neck and stared.

A pretty adult situation, no, wouldn't you think, with Selina now tightening the belt of her sheer negligée (and gazing down disclaimingly – even *she* won't forgive me), and Martina fixed in the frame of the doorway, in a suit of light-grey worsted, black shoes together (and what did she see? Brute hard-on, gut, the frightened face) – and me, the decked joke, flummoxed, scuppered, and waving his arms? I've had some naked travel but never quite as naked as this, not even in the Boomerang off Sunset Boulevard, sprawling under the pimp's bat.

A pretty adult situation, and yet Martina looked like a child. She looked like a child who has suffered more reverses in a single day than ever before in living memory, and is now poised between refusal and acceptance of the fact that life might be significantly worse than she thought, that life was unkinder in its essence, and no one had given her fair warning.

Her eyes dropped and wandered. She shook her head. I think she even stamped her foot. She said,

'And I've lost Shadow.'

'Oh no!'

'Over the rooftops.'

And then she ran too, across the outer room and through the door and down the length of the padded passage behind my head.

*

At last I rolled over and reached for my clothes – the pants, the dead suit. It took for ever to crawl into those dead clothes of mine.

'What was all that about?' Selina was saying in her tightest voice. I couldn't look at her. 'No, don't tell me. You've been fucking her, haven't you. You've been fucking her. You. What a joke.'

At last I walked past her, my hands raised in submission or defence. At the door I managed to turn and say,

'What was she doing here?'

'How should I know!?' said Selina. 'It's Ossie's suite. Ask him. Ask her.'

In the fluttering ballpark downstairs I drank twelve bourbons – yes, that's it, drink your hemlock – and called Martina's number until my ripped fingers bled. No answer. No answer. Engaged. Engaged. That hateful sound. Busy, busy, busy. And as I sat slumped at the bar, fumbling with the last of my money as drunks will, I heard something that in all my life I never expected any pleasure from, the sound of my own name – *John Self* – paged on the public address. I moved to the pink telephone. And I thought: *it's her*.

'Yeah?' I said.

'The end. All over.' The gimp voice. The gimp laugh.

'*You*,' I said. 'Oh please, come on, let's do it. Now. Now. I'm ready.'

'Okay. Listen. There's a carpark back of that porno store where you hang out. Take a right at the booth and walk fifty, sixty yards to the trashbags stacked by the busted door. We'll meet one day. And when we do . . .'

'We'll meet now.'

'Yes. Now.'

I came out on to the silo of Sixth Avenue, Avenue of the Americas, where the stick-legged scrapers waited on their pads.

Time and temperature flashed above. 'Ninety-nine,' said the man at his stall. 'Son of a bitch.' I moved forward, and rocked on my plinth, and felt that my heart would take fire and that I too would squirt off in a dying spiral toward the kindled sky. All the million windows of New York glared down at me, the infidel. Oh Christ, my life was serious for about ten minutes and now it's a joke all over again. Well let's lend a little viciousness here. Let's make the joke turn as nasty as it wants, I thought, and started running south.

Ready, I was ready. I jogged down the defile, past the slatted toilet windows of the sex emporium, where paid girls swirled on their loops of hell taking it this way that way for ever for money. I jogged through the furnace of the carpark, where the Tomahawks and Boomerangs all took it in the face, hating the heat, hating the hate. I waved to the boys in their baseball caps. They waved back, encouragingly. Go on, go on, you're on the right track. I jogged right, fifty, sixty yards. There were the black sacks, as ripe as bodybags, and there was the sawn-off metal door of a flat-roofed go-down. Yeah, this was a good place for fighting. My cigarette seemed to ignite spontaneously as I hated and waited. No fear. What could he take away from me now? I was ready, very ready. And then there was the sense of shadow dropping down on me as a heavy thing fell lightly to its feet and two long arms snapped shut across my heart.

No sweat, I thought, after the first volts of shock had been squeezed from my systems. A straightforward heeljob on the right instep will sort this lot out. Then an elbow in the face and Bob's your uncle . . . But now I sensed with a gasp that my feet were off the ground. There was no kick-purchase in my legs and with both arms trapped all I could try was the reverse head-butt – and where was *his* head, for Christ's sake? I couldn't find it. Things suddenly got much worse as he started to jounce me up and down, his pelvis stirring my rump, and ape-sex noises and spluttered laughter and the torch of his breath on my neck. For the first time I felt the full foundry of his madness and I thought, no contest, this guy has some other power sources, this guy has strength to burn . . . But I'm strong too, God damn it, and I've never felt madder than I feel today. Just then he took me a foot too near the facing alley wall. Beautiful: the very thing I'd always wanted. I lifted both feet and with a balls-splitting shove sent him sprinting backwards into the metal door with all my weight on top of him. He straightened, no loosening, no quarter. With a fierce twist of the jaws he took a bite out of my hair, and spat, and laughed, and jounced me harder . . . Only one outcome now. Here's the last hug. I felt my face purpling – and it was this other fight, this fight for air, that showed me how. That cigarette was still in my mouth, bent but glowing between the clamp of my teeth. I turned my gouged face until it would turn no further. It was inches away and my strength was just hissing off me now like leaked gas. But then he made his mistake, as he had to do. He went too far. He put his tongue in my ear and I knew for sure that this could not be borne. That was the only certainty: this could not be borne. So with an audible wrench of the neck I drove my fuming mouth right into the bare cusp of his throat.

I was free, I was dancing on air. In one staggering swivel I turned and caught him full in the face with the back of my fist. I gave six, eight, ten doublehanded smashes to the head and shoulders, down, down like a tentpeg into the earth, and as I swung my foot for the final blow I saw the face too late – too late, for the boot was travelling so fast now, and when I kicked that face (and I didn't want to, I didn't want to) there came a sound so eloquent of dead-on damage, the knock or thwack a pintable makes when it salutes the silver ball: *Thwock!* And you know what I'd done? I had kicked the face of a woman.

'Hey,' I said, or 'Okay', or 'You okay.'

Wait. Watch. The thing turned on its side. Bits of half-digested meat and broken dental pieces came from its mouth. Our eyes met horribly. I had seen those eyes before, but not in that face. Now the hair fell away, disclosing the ginger matt. There it shivered, in its indeterminate smock.

'Who are you?' I said, dragging deep on the buckled cigarette.

It was no woman. The voice was male, like the rest.

'Oh damn dear go,' he seemed to say. 'Oh and you man dog.'

Now I sit in my room at the Ashbery, under a new net of nausea long suspended, long feared. I was drinking scotch and reading *Money*. I stood up. On my slow legs and with my slow hands I assembled a ballpoint pen, a sheet of paper, the Dictionary. I took out the tranquillizers that Martina had given me. She said they were less addictive than all the Serafim I was putting away. The label tells me: MARTINA TWAIN – TO BE TAKEN AT NIGHT . . . I sat down. On the sheet of paper I wrote out a list of all our moneymen. I sipped my drink. I cross-checked with the index of *Money*. Ricardo, Gresham, Biddle, Baruch. I looked up *cowrie* in the Dictionary. I sipped my drink, and spat it out again. I looked up *valuta* in the Dictionary. I got to my feet and opened the window and stuck my head out of it. I looked up *dibs*, and *dun*. I got to my feet and went to the bathroom and vomited noisily. I came back. I took three tranquillizers with as many swallows of whisky. There was a single tap on the door and Felix eased himself into the room with sudden speed, the way cigarette smoke surges around corners into the draught.

'Felix,' I said thickly. 'Have my shirts come back. How are you. I haven't seen that much of you this time here.'

And then I had to ask him, 'What's the matter?'

'It's over. What have you *done*, man?'

With dry lips and voodoo heat in his eyes Felix told me that all America was interflexed by computer processors whose roots spread ever outward from the trunks of skyscrapers until they looped like a web from city to city, sorting, clearing, holding, okaying, denying, denying. Software America sprawled on a humming grid of linkup and lockout, with display screens and logic boards of credit ratings, debt profiles. And now all the States were keying in my name, and the VDUs were all wincing like spooked electro-encephalograms. America played space invaders with words john self. I was a money enemy. And the tab police were on my tail.

'Don't make me laugh,' I said.

'Pack a bag.'

'It's just some cock-up.'

'Pack a *bag*.' His eyes were incensed, imploring. His eyes were supersad. 'Right after Labour Day they do a check. They ran your name through ten, fifteen times. They called their people in. I tell you, man, you are out for a whole lot of money.'

We heard the juice of the lift. The uncoupled telephone spoke to me in its new voice. I didn't answer it. I didn't even pack a bag. Felix took me down in the staff elevator, and out through the kitchens. The workers in their low-caste T-shirts among the sinks and kilns gazed at me steadily. They saw all my danger. We walked up into the trash of the alley. These deep stains on the paving – they would never come out, not in a million years. We turned to face each other for the last time.

'Okay,' said Felix.

'Thanks.' I put a hand in my pocket. Two bills – six bucks. Reflexively I gave Felix the five.

He glanced at the note in his hand. He gave it back to me, and I took it.

'No, man,' he said with a snort. 'You don't understand. This whole thing it's all over.'

I am something unbelievable going forward, sixteen stone of flash and hurtle. I am the express at the end of the dream. You sit in your train at the siding and look up startled from the page as I bellow by, bringing with me that chute of black air which takes your carriage by the lapels and shakes its windows loose from their putty. And then I'm gone, and your calm returns. I'm gone, but I'm still going, still fleeing, still screaming.

In through the Carraway foyer and up the stairs with my head down. The double doors were open, to air the sick room. On its brink stood two security guards, a hotel maid, a big guy in a cheap business suit bent listening to a deaf-aid intercom, and a tall old lady, wearing an anorak and brown stretch-pants and a badge saying, DAISY'S: RETIREMENT LIVING DOESN'T COME ANY FINER.

'I'm Beryl Goodney,' she confided. 'The mother. Are you the poor man?'

I walked past the sad women, the awed and whispering guards. With a sheet over his shoulders Fielding sat at the window on a straightbacked chair. He turned slowly as he sensed my approach. The rusty hair netted flat to the skull, the swollen mouth, the loss of something vital in the line of jaw. The jaw's gone, I thought. And that was where his life once lurked.

'The money,' I said. 'Where's the money.'

'There's no fucking money.'

I opened my hands at the room and its furniture, at the computers, the drinks trolley, at the chandelier, at New York. 'Who's paying for all this?'

'You are.'

'Oh, what have you *done*?'

He looked at me drolly. Something jagged lisped in his mouth as he said, in explanation, 'I'm forty-five, Slick.'

They couldn't stop me at the door, not with the momentum I had on me then, and I clattered panting into the street and slipped, and steadied, thinking which way to run. At the corner a yellow cab sharked to a halt and Doris Arthur climbed out of it. She turned, measuring herself against me and the big hotel.

'I warned you,' she called. 'I tried to tell you.'

I came up and took her by the collar and swung her into the sidestreet. I don't know why I have this hangup about hitting women. It couldn't ever feel more natural than this. But I just held her jaw in my right hand and said,

'Ah, you bitch. You were in it too.'

'You don't listen, do you, meatball?'

'Why? You went along with the whole thing. What for?'

She pulled my hand from her mouth, and I let it happen. 'Sex,' she said.

'Yeah, you chicks. You writers. Same old story. You're full of talk and then some good-fitting dick comes along.'

'You asshole,' she said, and smiled. 'You won't ever guess right. In bed he's a woman.'

And then I heard a deep and serious shout from behind me. The tall operator with the crackling deaf-aid stood ready at the corner. And Doris was gone and the world was travelling past me at full speed all over again.

And I went on running. You know something? I'm really good at running. I am. If only I could run away from America – I could do it. I've got the legs. But I haven't got the wings. I haven't got the money.

The next place where I did a lot of running was in the flat dark bowl of JFK, down there in the crater ringed by the steel-eyed terminals with crucified planes fleeing and screaming above my head. I had just cheated a cabbie out of twenty-five dollars: and he wasn't the usual zebra-chewing throwback but an earnest young earner from Israel, saving for college and helping to keep his folks in modest retirement, out in Jerusalem there. As we approached Kennedy he asked me about my own spangled life-style – London–New York, New York–London – and I was saying, well, there were interesting contrasts between the two cities, and nice driving, kid, and I'll just slide across the seat here, and what do I owe you, and . . . I was out of the door and over the wall. I took the ten-foot drop on elbow and pelvis, my feet found me and I was running again, into the black spools and printouts of fences, sliproads, cable lines. No pursuit. All I heard was his baffled 'Hey!', the voice so weary now, so sick and tired of these tab-beaters, bad-cheque and bent-plastic artists, the money thugs of New York . . .

The first terminal I tried was Trans-American. Straightening my suit, I walked briskly up to Ticketing. 'No problem,' said the peanut from under his hat. Economy, aisle-seat, smoking: even a so-so movie to look forward to. Suavely I handed over my platinum US Approach card. He keyed in my name and number, said 'Just one moment, sir,' and backed away through the low door. Whistling, hands in pockets, I strolled from the bay and took up position near the glass gates to the forecourt. Yeah, sure enough, my guy emerged, flanked by two plainclothesmen – airport security? Agency boys? No, just money police: dicks, pigs, filth. Money filth – and I was out and off and running again.

I panicked at the PakAir desk but managed one more bid at British Albigensian. This spelt the end of my Air Budget card and also involved me in a protracted chase sequence – twenty minutes, pissing for my life along the running track of the outer circle with a whippetlike oldster on my tail. Manhattan, JFK, you know these are suddenly very different places when you have no money. You change, but they change too. Even the air changes. I felt it the instant I stepped out of the Carraway. With money, double-dazzle New York is a crystal conservatory. Take money away, and you're naked and shielding your Johnson in a cataract of breaking glass. Each sound and smell and stare is that much harder to hold. It's a tough town. I see that's all true now. Tough? It's a fucking shitstorm! Near the knuckle is the only place where things really happen. It is a lot more vivid, a lot more realistic down here. And you need to deal with new kinds of moneymen, talented milers in sensible suits, who jink with change and moneykeys as they run grunting in your wake.

With my legs crossed beneath me I perched on a can in Air Kiwi and went through my pockets looking for money or a means to it. Already I am thinking in terms of selling my watch, wallet and Y-fronts, a spare kidney, the gold in my teeth. I can bus out to Canada and wire my dad for dough or work my passage on some bugger-tub right through the icing of the globe . . . Nah, I'm not going back in there, into New York, into America. I'd sooner try a skyjack. I'd sooner swim it. I'm not going back to America. Ever.

Now I am of that breed of men who tote their paperwork and money-bumf around with them in the saddlebags of their chests. There was a whole life-story – not a good story either, a really depressing one – crumpling and curling here on my lap. A gas bill, Opera dockets, cigarette coupons, passport, telephone messages, tax demands, rosters, shooting schedules, bills and credit slips from Kreutzer's, the Bartleby, the Happy Isles, expenses forms, a drunk-driving summons, a Manet postcard, a note from Martina, no money, an unused airline ticket . . . I fingered this last item for quite a while before I permitted myself to register what it was. An unused airline ticket. Airtrak. New York-London. 20 Kilos. YAP 1Y. OK.

Okay? Christ, I'd been running without luck for so long now – I hardly recognized its upright thumb, its farcically winking face. Remember that time out here, way back, when Fielding gave me the first-class ticket at the Berkeley? The bomb hoax, all that? Well, I never used the Airtrak ticket I bought the same day with my own sweet money, and here it was, a little crinkled to be sure, and smudged with carbon fingerprints, but still valid, still honest, still good.

A remarkably affable porter had me know that the Airtrak kiosk was housed in the next satellite along. I slinked right over, shielded by a prowling coach. Ten thirty-five, and there were seats to burn on the eleven o'clock flight. My big-mouthed bim flapped through the red bunting and said,

'Yes. This ticket's good.'

'Oh sweetheart, I believe it. You know for my money this is the best airline in the skies. No contest. You can take all the others and – you're the *people's* airline, God damn it! You took on the bigshots and you won. Yeah I've heard about your financial problems but you'll make it. You're all right, I reckon. Yeah, you'll do. I'm always going to fly Airtrak from now on. You'd do anything for us, you would. Anything. You're the only one that really –'

I might have jabbered on like this indefinitely, I later realized. I know it took a heavy handclamp on the shoulder to shut me up – it wasn't the cops or anything, just an Airtrak official whose astonished stare and words of grave reassurance at last persuaded me to wipe away my tears, take a few falsetto gasps for breath, and head off through the garden gate. No bags, me, no strings. I was all greased and streamlined – I was as travellable as air. In the departure stall the bar was closed but fate or justice had sent me an airport sweeper, a child of God, with a rack of miniatures and a wheeled fridge – and I blew my $6.75 on three warming B & Fs. I felt so strong and proud that I wanted to call Martina and sort out the whole misunderstanding. But I'd spent all the money. I had to go and spend all the money. That's right. I couldn't spare any, I couldn't even spare a dime.

Soon I was strapping myself into the window seat of an empty three-pack. What value. What service. I gave a harsh shout of joy as the big bus promptly shrugged and shivered, and lumbered off into the ring. I watched the pools of light, the fleeing dumptrucks; and felt the slackening grip and glare of hard New York. No, you can't catch me now. We took our slot in the cartridge belt, then raced with screaming purpose down the black tube and out into the night.

As the plane levelled I lit my last cigarette. Slowly I sipped its fire – no snout was ever sweeter. I had a one-man party all mapped out, the seating, the menu, the entertainment: cocktails, dinner, the late late movie. There was a money problem, true, but I could always burn a cheque on them, or submit my non-platinum US Approach card, or overpower the hostess. I was going to get *drunk* tonight, up here in the land of duty-free. I wrenched myself around in search of the pushcart. And then three things happened at once.

First, as an opener, someone kicked me in the face – but from the inside. My head wagged with this boot of pain, this uppercut, no-nonsense, straight to the maximum. Meanwhile I felt a whole jacuzzi of cud and poison start to slop around my gut. Three bolted B & Fs on a scoured stomach, all that fucking and fighting, all that hiding and cheating and churning. At the same time – I had always known that there were creatures of the middle air, weather gods, cumulus leviathans of ampère and spore who flailed their lives away at thirty thousand feet. Something vast and full of rage now took us in its chaos. The jaws above our heads fell open in amazement. People spoke in strange tongues: even the pilot's voice yodelled and tremoloed in the spasms. There are devils up here, I thought, fallen from heaven. No, it's *New York*, it's still New York, reaching out to tickle our hearts with its thick strong fingers. Defying all warning I got to my feet and pingponged to the rat-cans in the rear.

I don't think I've ever felt emptier, as I rode that bowl with my chin in the sink. Sixteen stone? I'm not even sixteen ounces. I'm a dead tooth on a fart of air. Everything I have is leaving me and falling, down past the plastic glasses, the dog-ends and scraps of air food, past the hurry, fear and thwarted homing, down into the weather and the black Atlantic . . . At last the plane panned out. And so did I. The pilot's voice came back on the line. Weepily I too ran my damage checks and wound reports. The pilot had his problems – but haven't we all? He could drill the crate into the North Pole for all I cared. Once again pain walked my upper west side. Pain is nature's way of telling us that something is wrong. Patiently, pain goes on telling us this, long after we've got the message. That tooth is dead, they informed me – it's out of it for ever. That tooth is dead, but I am still alive. And here was this second message coming through. I had no choice now but to listen.

'You'll notice we're going into a wide turn at this time. It looks like I'm out of a job too, so . . . Ladies and gentlemen, I have to tell you that this is Airtrak's last flight. They've pulled the plug on the whole operation. We'll be re-encountering that turbulence on the way back to JFK. Please fasten seatbelts and, uh, extinguish all smoking materials. Thank you.'

I got back to my seat as we came lancing in over the bay, just in time to see the stretched arcs of silver and slack loops of gold, the forms and patterns that streets don't know they make.

'Towards the end of a novel you get a floppy feeling. It may just be tiredness at turning the pages. People read so fast – to get to the end, to be shot of you. I see their problem. For how long do you immerse yourselves in other lives? Five minutes, but not five hours. It's a real effort.'

'Yeah yeah,' I said. 'Now, Martin. Listen. I tell you, this is fucking embarrassing. Guess what.'

'We're in turnaround.'

'Yeah. How could you tell?'

'Well, Christ, couldn't you see it coming?'

Then I bawled it all out, in no particular order – Fielding, Frank the Phone, the fight at the rear of the porno hall, the dead room in the Carraway . . .

'Why?' I asked. 'Why did he do it? Where's the motivation? On the phone he was always saying I'd fucked him up. How could I have? I'd remember. Even with the blackouts and everything, I'd remember.'

Martin considered. I felt a squeeze of warmth for the guy as he said, 'I think that was all a blind. You never hurt him.'

'Really? But then it's senseless.'

'Is it? These days? I sometimes think that, as a controlling force in human affairs, motivation is pretty well shagged out by now. It hasn't got what it takes to motivate people any more. Go for a walk in the streets. How much motivation do you see?'

'Why me? That's what I want to know. Me, why me?'

'Well, you fitted the bill in all kinds of ways. But I've got a hunch it was to do with your name.'

'What about my name?'

'Names are awfully important. Anyway, you'd better get going, hadn't you? I'll give it some thought and we can meet up later if you like. Don't worry. It'll all come out in the end.'

'Well you're laughing,' I said. 'You got your money. Or half of it at least.'

'I never cashed that cheque. Here. You want it back?'

'Christ, you just haven't got any money sense, have you. Look – hang on to it. Some of those moneymen might have been legit. There might be some dough around at the end of all this.'

'You don't understand. The moneymen didn't have any money either. It's clear what they were.'

I looked at him until he said,

'They were all actors.'

The streets sing. Yes they do. Can you hear them? The streets scream. You're told about street culture. There isn't any. That's the point. This is as far as it goes. Where does the song end, the scream start? And in the monologue malls and choric alleys of London West the screamers sing and the singers scream. They face the breath from the grills of the all-night space-game parlour, the all-night supermarket, the middle-earth hypocaust of the all-night city. Like the places that they haunt, the screamers are twenty-four-hour, round-the-clock, we-never-close. They never close. That brown-legged woman – Christ, her strength! – jack-knifed in doorways, at all hours, in all weathers. Along with the rest of the choir she rehearses for ever the single grievance, the lone conspiracy, the one betrayal. It ends in obscenity and hurried movement, self-hating, as if she could no longer bear to be near herself. Oh mother . . . The song the screamers sing is a song to what they cannot bear, defining and miming the meaning of the word *unbearable*.

Have you noticed, now, the way people talk so loudly in snackbars and in cinemas, how the shelved back gardens shudder with prodigies of talentlessness, drummers, penny-whistlers, vying transistors, the way you see and hear the curses and sign-language of high sexual drama at the bus-stops under ghosts of clouds, how life has come out of doors? And in the soaked pubs the old-timers wince and weather the canned rock. We talk louder to make ourselves heard. We will all be screamers soon.

Television is working on us. Film is. We're not sure how yet. We wait, and count the symptoms. There's a realism problem, we all know that. TV is real! some people think. And where does that leave reality? Everyone must have, everyone demands their vivid personalities, their personal soap opera, street theatre, everyone *must have* some art in their lives . . . Our lives, they harbour form, artistic shape, and we want our form revealed even though we only move in our detail, with keys, spongebag, coffee-cups, shirt drawer, chequebooks, linen, hairstyle, curtain-rod holders, fridge guarantee, biros, buttons, money.

I'm looking for money, I'm looking for money. Give me some. Go on. Do it. *Here, have some money* . . . I tried to cash a cheque this morning. All went like a dream, a good one too, until the very last minute: then I got nixed by the chick in back, a single headshake over the wooden palisade. I ransacked my sock. I expected crinkled quids in old tennis shorts, fivers in the pockets of jeans, tenners under the sofa cushion, twenties in the jar on the shelf. All I found was ninety-five pee. At the wheel of a nervously bounding Fiasco (petrol gauge just under the red), I drove to the Soho offices of Linex & Carburton. I don't know what's in store for me but I know I'm going to need money to help protect me from it. Otherwise some money god will just swoop down any second and take a big bite out of my rug. I went into Terry Linex's den and said, 'I want my golden handshake. Give me my fifty grand.' Terry had promised that my payoff was going to be half way to six figures. And Terry was as good as his word. Mind you, he'd had a spot of worry himself, had old Tel. He poured me a bottle of scotch as he gave the lowdown. Dodgy tax-dodges, fiscal freeze – I was none too clear on the ins and outs. We shook hands. He wrote me out a post-dated cheque. Terry had promised that my payoff was going to be half way to six figures. And it was. It was three figures. A hundred and twenty-five quid.

An hour later I was drinking last year's cherry brandy in Alec Llewellyn's kitchen. We sat hunched like gamblers over the square table. We had faced each other like this so many times now. Neither of us said much because there wasn't much to say. Alec Llewellyn owes me several thousand pounds. But what can you say? There was no money here. I could tell. There was only red money, minus money. I didn't say anything about it. He knew, though. The money radar was still working in the remains of his pinched, sensuous face. He knew why I had come, and he feared me.

This was the last fear I'd ever get from Alec Lewellyn. So I sat back and let it climb.

I expect you're wondering how I escaped from New York. So am I, in a sense. I expect you're wondering who tabbed my flight. Martina? No. Alas, no, not Martina.

Airtrak just pooped us out into the terminal at half-past midnight. It was a twentieth-century scene all right, planet panic, photojournalists, men with clipboards and name-tags, the loud grief of refugees. Did the people's airline provide its people with alternative travel? It did not. All it gave us was a soft-drink coupon and a bun voucher. I was about to pass out anyway when who should I see trampling through the swirl but Big Bruno and Horris Tolchok. Good! Do it, take me, I thought. But I was off and running again, dodging Bruno, Horris, the money filth, dodging all America . . . I spent the night holed up in the PakAir toilet. Every few seconds I burped bleakly, and waited for that tooth to nut me in the face. There was an aspirin dispenser, there in the can. But I had no money. I didn't have any. If I could have killed myself that night, I would have done. But suicide, like aspirin, like everything, costs money and I didn't have any. Unless you're really brave, suicide is always going to set you back a couple of bob. I tried Martina's pills. I couldn't keep them down. And I had no booze to help do the job right. Around five in the morning I reached a point where I felt an outsider's sadness for that poor tooth of mine, which after all was suffering its own death agonies, dying young and violently and by its own hand, long before its time.

At eight I rang the Bartleby collect. That was the hardest bit, persuading the hotel chick to defy company policy and accept my call. Selina Street cabbed straight out here, that heroine. She picked me up at British Albigensian (Arrivals: I thought it would be safer there) and whisked me off to brunch at the Welcome-In near La Guardia. One look at my face and she knew the score. It pleased her. Jouncily she led the way into the considerate darkness of the hotel restaurant. I followed her, this high-assed dick-brimmer in her summer frock. I felt no bitterness. Who, me?

'Yesterday, with Martina,' I said, as I removed the celery, marrow and watermelon from my first bloody mary. 'It was a set-up, wasn't it. You set me up.'

'Yes. I'm sorry,' she said.

'How!'

'Oh it was simple.'

Yes, it was simple. Martina and Ossie had arranged to meet at three thirty in his suite. Strictly business. Selina then told him that Martina had called and asked for a postponement. She packed Ossie off to see his lawyers – and then had her drink with me. Martina was punctual, as always. Martina is very punctual. We all know that about her.

'Why?' Typical Selina, I thought. The set-up was simple but the acting was great art . . . No it wasn't. It was only what was necessary. It was pornography. All she did was show me her soft core, her eighth avenue. And I did the rest.

'You know, it can be good fun deceiving people,' she said, and lit a rare cigarette. 'You don't see that because you're no good at it. You haven't got the talent. When you lie, it's just a joke. Ossie and I had a lot of laughs bringing you two together. It was neat. It meant we could crosscheck on your movements. He was horrified by how things turned out. We were both horrified.'

'In your different ways.' The waitresses in this dark place had been obliged to squeeze themselves into wench outfits – bibs, stockings, all *that* again. Market research had no doubt established that this was the most common male fetish. They also said *enjoy your meal* and *have a nice day* and *you're welcome* the whole time. People think that's a natural American foible, a natural winsomeness. Don't they *understand*? It's just company policy. They're trained to say it. They're programmed. It's all money. God I can't wait to leave this moneyworld.

'And a dessert, sir, to follow your steak?'

'Thank you, but I –'

'You're welcome.'

'But I think I'll just have a brandy.'

'Easy now,' said Selina.

'Did you love me? To do that, you must have loved me a bit some time.'

'Not necessarily,' she said. 'It's all fun and I suppose I'm hooked on it.' Then she gave a shrug that expressed not indifference but a self-girding, a shoring-up. 'I wouldn't want you to be happy with anyone else. And not with her. What did she see in you anyway?'

'I don't know.'

'I'm sorry. It was cruel. Would she have made you happy?'

'I don't know.'

Then she said something that I can't bring myself to pass on, not for now. I was sinking fast, under the lies, the candour and the darkness. Selina booked a room and led me there like a mother with smaller kids to care for. I probably tried to have her join me in some act of comfort or revenge – sex, hitting, weeping, rape: I don't remember which, and there seemed no difference anyway. I fell down on that bag and was out of it by the second bounce.

And so I came home. I woke up to find that a day and a half had moved past me in the night: I found also that Selina had settled the bill and left me the standby fare plus thirty dollars drinking-money, like the good moll she was. The heat was off at JFK. I flew Trans-American just like everybody else. I rode a tube from Kennedy to the United Kingdom, and then another one from Heathrow to Queensway, paced up the curling colon and wandered out into the meat-eating breath of a London morning. With milk carton and newspaper, Martin Amis was waiting on my stoop.

I'm home. I'm home, but I'm still running.

'I've just put two and two together,' said Alec Llewellyn, with pleasure and some alarm. 'Here's this sweating mute sitting here. He's come because he wants his money. He needs his money. Fair enough. I haven't got any, but fair enough. Then I ask myself – *why* does he need his money?'

I coughed for a while and said, 'Forget the money. Pay me whenever. I want to hear about you. Let's hear about you.'

'Oh you want to hear about me, do you. Okay. Well take a look. Here I am, home. I haven't had a drink in three weeks. Just one blinder when I got out of the Ville – and that was it. I'm defying about nine injunctions just by being here. If I so much as uncap a tin of cider or stay too long in the bathroom, if I don't make her come one night she can dial 999 and I'm back in fucking priz . . . don't get me wrong, I'm thrilled to be here. I'm looking for jobs, but who isn't? There *aren't* any. Ella works and I run the flat. I can smoke and swear and that's it. I'm a fucking househusband is what I am. You'll notice I'll be putting on my pinny in a minute to make the kids' lunch.'

He did, too, when he heard Ella on the stairs with the children. And in it came, the family, colour and complication, changing everything: Ella, her legendary rug now sheared to a boyish bob to tell you how tough it all was these days, little Mandolina, my goddaughter, a green-eyed cat with a wicked tongue on her – and Andrew, bringing up the rear. Andrew has had difficulties. Andrew still has them, and always will. His elderly yet fresh-born face said this: I'm new here and I'm not sure I like it. No one made things clear to me. I should have been told, I should have been warned. I want to go back. Perhaps you can fix it.

I levered myself to my feet. Normally I would get to kiss Ella hello and exchange a few nuzzles and murmurs. Comfort would be exchanged. After all, I gave her one out on the stairs a few years ago, when Alec had blacked out that time. Does Alec know? Unlikely, because not even Ella knows, not any more. There's been a re-write and it never happened. Times are hard. No kiss even. No smiles, no ribbons in the hair, no county flounce in the dresses, as before. She's wearing the pants now, the long pants.

'So how's the film mogul?' she said.

'Medium cool.'

'You look terrible.'

'No kidding.'

'Say hello to John,' said Alec, as Mandolina sidled towards us. In her hands she held a broken umbrella.

'Hello, will you fix it? It's new,' she said, and gave me the dead thing. 'I'm ten now.'

Girls always know they are girls, right from the start, but children don't seem to know they are children. Children know nothing about time. Christ, I'm so paranoid of kids, especially the girls. I keep thinking that they will stare into me, that something young in them will feel unknown distress. They will see all my time, weather, money and pornography. I always give money to Mando. She has fearless things to say to grownups. I wouldn't want her saying those things to me. I think that's why I give her money . . . The toy umbrella dangled from my hand. It was cheap and knew it wasn't meant to last long. It knew it was meant to break. They say everything wants to persist in its being. Even sand wants to go on being sand. It doesn't want to break. But I don't know. This umbrella looked relieved that it had broken, had broken out of the world of definition and was just a sprig of plastic tackle again.

'I'll buy you a new one,' I said. 'But now I've got to run.'

Alec escorted me to the stairs. Yes, that's where it happened, on the landing there.

'Hey,' I said, 'you couldn't lend me some money, could you? No – just a fiver or something. I left my wallet at home and I've got the Fiasco down there with an empty tank.'

Alec was gone some time. I heard tethered voices deepen in cadences of recrimination and demand. I heard the patter of the children as it slowed and ceased. This was all bad, surprisingly bad. I've suffered some long moments, some slow travel, in the latest run of time, but none longer or slower than these. The door opened. Andrew stood there with tears in his eyes.

'What's the matter?'

'Do you like me?'

'Andrew! Oh *sure*. I –'

Alec now stood over him and softly masked his face with a wide hand. The boy slipped back into the silent flat. His father shrugged and held out three pound notes

'Thanks,' I said. 'I really appreciate it. I fucked Ella there. Once. I'm sorry.'

'I know. So does Andrew – sort of. I fucked Selina.'

'Did you? When?'

'Whenever. A lot. All the time. Christ, I can tell. You're almost finished, aren't you.'

The Fiasco gave out on Maida Vale. It just coughed and whinnied and clawed its way exhaustedly to the kerb, like a struggling swimmer. I hoped it might be the fuel count but it felt a lot more basic than that. Besides, I'd just put three quids' worth of petrol into the tank. Maybe the clutch was broken. Maybe the manifold was broken. Maybe the big end was broken. Maybe the fucking *car* was broken.

I left it there at the side of the road and went on travelling south.

Ten to three in the Shakespeare. Ten to three in the reptile house, with two races already lost, the parched breath of noon booze and scraps on the floor from feeding time. I was drinking the strong beer that makes you weak. My fat pal Fat Paul had slipped me a tenner. I was now putting the last of it into Moneymaze, the warbling fruit machine by the door to the gents' and its briny, tidal air. These bandits do everything for you. Autohold. Maxinudge. Scramblematic. You just stand there and keep the money coming.

Ten past three in the Shakespeare. Fat Paul was gathering glasses and calling Time. No Fat Vince – and I could have done with his hand on my shoulder. I pushed through the vault of mirrors into the back room. Vron was there. She was lying on the sofa, drinking pink champagne. An ordinary magazine rested on the lap of her pornographic housecoat . . . The room, I saw, had been further padded and primped, in sweetshop colours, raspberry and chocolate and lime. Even the walls hurt my teeth.

I loomed bulkily in the doorway. I said, 'Where's Barry?'

'Down the better.'

My voice was thick but so was hers. Only the lower jaw moved. It moved slowly, as if the hinges were over-oiled, and might slip. She straightened herself and looked at me with a different lens.

'You want your money, John?'

'How long will he be?'

'Ages,' she said. She turned to the spiky clock. Her elbow slipped and she laughed without meaning. 'Time for my rehearsals.'

'For what?'

'For my glamour work, John.'

'You rehearse?'

'You have to, John. You should have put me in that video, John.'

She gathered her gown. She lifted the glass, three swallows, four swallows. She moved at an angle towards the staircase. She leaned heavily on the banister, the guardrail, the restraining divide. She took my hand.

This is the room where my mother slept. This is where she died. On the bed, another bed, coated in silk of piercing green – the silk of men not worms, wet-looking, with glossy deposits like puddle visions on hot macadam – Vron lay deep in the royalty of her robe. She didn't look at me, not Vron. With stern application she addressed herself to the valentine mirror on the facing wall. To me the faulty glass gave only a grey sighting of the gristled clouds. But for Vron it simply framed her raw material.

'It depends on the book, John,' she began. 'Some books are more – adult than others, John. More – explicit.' Her eyes never meeting mine, Vron sat up and full-throatedly untethered her hair. The robe slackened at the shoulders: with a two-handed gesture of explanation or disclosure she strained the frilled divide. 'In some books you give more than others. And it depends how much you've got to give, John.' Now she knelt and stretched her back, and I could see her full pageantry – the long-spiked shoes, the chainmail stockings, the silver holster of the pants, the double-barrelled brassière. Now the robe slipped from her shoulders 'Some books move with the times, John. But you can still be artistic too.' She reached behind her back with both hands, the neck taut and distended. As she uncoupled herself – her wings raised for flight – the soft frame fell readily and even slithered to the floor on its own slick current. With empurpled fingertips she smoothed her breasts as if coating them with an ointment of spectral costliness. 'But in the best books, John, you show the art of loving your own self – your *self*, John!' I stumbled forward a pace or two but it was hard because hard core makes the air so thick. Hard core makes the air as hard as concrete or steel.

She lay back on the bed and after a tranced pause her hand trailed down until the fingers began to impend over the muscular divot between her legs. 'They say you don't do the writing in the books, John. That's not true. You write the words, John. I've done it. I know.' The hand had slipped beneath the silver flex, the last leash, the last restraint. After a while there was a faint ticking sound, moist and regular, the sound of gum being chewed, '"Vron,"' she said, with a different voice, '"Vron, in all her full majesty. The poetry of Vron's body gives a vision of true beauty.

Pleasure is Vron's philosophy. Joy is her religion. Love is her art . . . *Vron*.'" She turned over. Her neck strained to keep erect. There was another mirror: Vron could see what I could see. A woman on all fours, a set of fingers gripping the silver band, and tugging. 'There,' she said. 'Do it there, John. The rest is Barry's.'

'Jesus Christ,' said Martin. 'What the hell happened to *you*?

I waved a hand at him.

'Have you seen a doctor? Listen. I've got the Iago outside. I'll take you to Casualty at St Martin's.'

'It's okay,' I said, and drained my glass. 'Nothing's broken. It looks worse than it is.'

It looked terrible, I had to admit – like a volcanic goitre. And my face felt crushed from jawline to eye-socket. Anything could be happening in there. I hear cartilage grating when I stretch my mouth. I feel tissue fizzing when I turn my head. A yawn would be a bad idea. Oh, very bad. The cheekbone itself is deceptively untender to the touch – for now – but it seems different, structurally different. It'll take me some time to get over the grief of this wound. Yeah, and the other wound, the deep one.

'I see,' he said, 'so you're just going to butch it out. What happened?'

'I was in this pub,' I said.

'What happened?'

'Me and this bloke had a little disagreement.'

'What happened.'

'I don't want to talk about it. Can't you talk about something else?'

'. . . Okay. Actually I'd like to return to the motivation question. It seems to me it's an idea taken from art, not from life, not from twentieth-century life. Nowadays motivation comes from ~~i~~de the head, not from outside. It's neurotic, in other words.

And remember that some people, these golden mythomaniacs, these handsome liars – they're like artists, some of them. Let's look at another recent phenomenon: gratuitous crime. I'm sorry. Are you with me?'

'Yeah yeah.'

What happened was *this*.

I stood swaying by the green bed. My thing with Vron – it was all over in less than a minute – oh, easily: it was, it was forty-second street. There was a headsmell of scorched poly-thene, spitsnuffed candles, a smell of sulphur or cordite. As I grappled with my pants I was almost flattened by a fresh draught of excruciating nausea. The spasms of hard core, they get you deep in the guts. They get you right in your hard core. Vron lay belly-down, eyes and mouth open but so corpselike that I tensed and waited for the sound of her breath. Its slow tide was joined by a faint ticking, moist and regular. I turned. Barry Self stood at the bedroom door. He was chewing gum. 'There goes your money, John,' he said drily, and pointed with a finger.

I pushed past him and ran down the stairs. I waded through the mirror doors. I knew it wasn't finished, not yet, not by any means.

The talented Fat Paul stood waiting in the empty bar. He was ready. He held a black sock in his hand. I knew what this meant. My legs felt like legs seen through water. The back door – would they have locked it? No matter. You can run, but you can't run. You do that, and you get beaten like a dog, yes, a real fascist kicking. I was in no shape to run. I was in no shape to stand, but I had to stand.

'Well,' Fat Paul explained, 'you can't walk away, can you. Not from that. Fair's fair, John. I mean they only got married Tuesday.'

Thinning his pale lips, he nodded. He walked to the pool table.

The balls dropped like bombs and hurried in a mob to their gate. In his hand he showed me the black and the white.

'Come on, man,' I said. 'Leave it out. Jesus, we're like brothers.'

You don't often hear laughter from Fat Paul's mouth – his mouth is not made for laughter – but that's what I heard. He paused. He considered. He let the balls roll on to the bed of piercing green and walked through the trap to the curved till. A bell sounded. Round One. No. Round Fifteen. He took two tubes of bank-packed coins. He dropped them into the sock and tugged on the dark scrotum.

'Weighs about the same,' he said interestedly, 'but with the coins there's a little more give. Know what I mean? Should mend quicker.'

'Fat Paul, listen,' I said. 'Money. What's he giving you? Fifty quid or something. I'll give you a grand. Let me run.'

Fat Paul frowned. 'No, I'll get a drink out of it. No real notes. That was just Barry sounding off down the Fancy Rat. Come on, John. Be realistic.'

He came towards me. There was a faint ticking sound – regular, but dry this time.

'Where?' I asked him.

'The face.'

'How hard?'

'Full arm.'

'How many?'

'Just the one. But it's got to be clear. All right? Sorry, John.'

I stood my ground, to make the next thing happen sooner, to make the next thing nearer to being over. From above I heard the shake of rage and fear – but it might have been laughter, just laughter. I saw the arm start its swing. In the air the long black bag kept its distance. Its swing could come later, when the arm was at full stretch – the second swing.

After a while I heard the bolts being cracked back, and there was Barry Self helping me out into the mist and the flare. I fell again. He looked down at me with scorn and delight. The scorn had always been there but the delight was new. He had waited a long time for that delight. Thirty-five years.

'Well old son? Now we're quits.'

'You,' I said. 'You're my fucking father.'

'I'm not your father,' he said, and he told me who was. 'Oh, fat John. Oh, you great pillock. Don't you know *anything*, you bitch's bastard?'

I feel better now, funnily enough. No, I do. I feel better for the whole experience. I feel a solid and stately calm. Now I know I'm perfectly capable of dealing with my life. Yes, everything is coming up roses. In fact the future looks really bright, now that I've decided to kill myself. I've decided. I have decided. Ah, it's so simple. Deciding is the hard part, and life has decided for me. Tonight. I've got the doings, here in my sock. Tonight, alone. Last thing.

'Thanks again for coming over,' I said.

Martin stirred. 'I suppose I ought to run,' he said, 'and let you get on with it.'

'No, stay! . . . Go on, stick around. Just for a couple of hours.'

He sighed, and tilted his head.

'Go on. Just for a couple of hours. I know I don't owe you any favours. Okay, I fucked you around. But I'll never ask for another. Go on, be a pal.'

Martin stared dully round the room. He looked at his watch.

'I just, I've just been reading this book about Freud. What have you been reading?'

'Reading's overrated,' he said. 'As overrated as Shakespeare's women. I shouldn't bother your pretty little head with it if I were you . . . What's that? A set of skittles or something?'

'That? It's a chess set, for Christ's sake. Onyx,' I said.

He selected a piece at random from the jade box. 'What's this? A king or a queen?'

'It's a pawn. What's wrong with it?'

'You play much?'

'Yeah. I used to. You play, do you? Are you good?'

'Naturally,' he said. 'How about a game? It'll pass the time.'

'Okay, sure,' I said, and felt the heat of sudden excitement. What was it? The prospect of exoneration, revenge? I'll fucking show him, I thought, the little smirkbag, the student, the abstainer, with his facetiousness and his degrees. He's got me down for a know-nothing. But *he* doesn't know I'm a chess artist. I'll show him. 'Right,' I said. 'We're playing for money.'

'*Money*? What do you think this is, a game of darts in the Jack the Ripper? You can't play chess for money.'

'Ten quid. With doubling. We're playing for money.'

'. . . But you haven't *got* any money.'

'Oh yeah? This set alone is worth five hundred quid. I've got a cashmere overcoat in there that's worth a thousand easy. And,' I said, straightening a finger, '*and*, I've got the Fiasco. Okay, what's so bloody funny?'

'Nothing. I'm sorry. Look, are you sure you wouldn't rather a game of snap or noughts-and-crosses? No? All right. But it's serious. Yes?'

'Oh it's serious, mate. And you're in for a nasty surprise. Come on, let's do it.'

I took the numbered dice from my backgammon set. I adjusted the two-faced clock: one hour each. Amis drew white.

'Hah!' I said. I. P–QN3. I ask you. 'Where'd you learn that. Some book?'

You won't catch me playing by the rules but most of the

opening lines have by now been embossed on my repertoire. I
didn't think any player could really disconcert me before the
middle-game: as early as the fifth move, though, little Martin
here drove right out of lane. He went on a meaningless sortie
with his knight, prancing round the centre of the board while I
jabbed him with my evolving front line. There *is* an opening like
that, but it's a defence, not an attack. He's a total rabbit, I thought,
and doubled him. Then he beavered me! I stared down at the
redoubled dice . . . Chess is a meeting of minds, a shock of
private cultures, and there's a rich seam of shame in it somewhere.
I ottered him. He racooned me. I moled him. The doubling dice
read 32. That was it for now.

'I've been thinking about your little adventure in New York,'
he said, as his knight scuttled back to the second rank. 'I think
I've got it all worked out. Do you want to hear my theory?'

'Shut up a minute. I'm concentrating.'

Now I was way ahead on development but my pawn structure
looked distinctly ragged. The game went quiet for a couple of
moves as we tended our own gardens, both briskly castling,
kingside. I was searching for blueprints, for forms and patterns,
when he launched into a tedious series of pokes and prods at
my extended pawns. This was no sweat to counter in itself, but
I had to wheel my guns away from his sparse kingside, back from
the centre too, where Martin was beginning to establish a couple
of minor pieces – that knight again, a useful black-square bishop
. . . Oh Christ, I thought, it's turning into one of those games.
Within the space of three moves I had been nudged into a position of intricate inertia, my pieces cramped and clustered, misled,
cross-purposed. It would take at least two tempos to find any
freedom and I never seemed to have a beat to spare. My every
touch was a bit of fine-tuning, delicate repair-work in shrinking
space.

'Fielding Goodney,' he said,' – everything went his way until

I entered the picture. *I* was the joker in the pack. I don't know how – how realistic his scheme was, but it might have gone something like this. Double,' he said, and moved.

His second bishop lanced out, trapping my knight against a queen already smothered by her paranoid underlings. Oh, this was hell, an awful dream of constriction, of pins and forks and skewers. I gulped scotch and looked for exchanges. There were two on offer, each with its strong disincentive – a doubled pawn, an opened file giving gangway to his centralized rook, which would then . . . Man, I could lose right away! This is really *serious*, I thought, and raised a hand to my damaged face.

'Given the stars he'd signed up, given their neuroses and delusions, the Doris Arthur script was designed to be absolutely unworkable. Watching you trying to coax them into it would have made quite a spectacle. But you held out. You weren't as wasted as he thought you were. You had some strength he couldn't undermine.'

'Go on,' I said. Suddenly I was seeing light and smelling air. If I could inch my queen on to the third rank than I could cover the knight and release the bishop *and* threaten his . . . yeah. All I needed was a tempo. Leave me alone, you son of a bitch. God damn it, stay off my case for a single move. Keep talking. With a glance at the clock and a show of flurry or dither I edged my queen out of her hive. Martin considered, then tamely pushed a pawn.

'Go on.'

'Those girls you said were chasing you last time out. They were on the payroll too. Either that or they were – they were auditioning. But you weren't as dumb and drunk as he hoped you'd be. You held out. That girlfriend of yours, the one with the degrees. Maybe she was a joker, just like me. Maybe she was the second joker in the pack.'

At last I was back on terms with a glimpse of some counterplay. And, well, it's hard to describe, but the other end of the board just turned all limp on me. I seemed to have tempos to burn – it was like playing *Selina*, with white forming pretty patterns on distant squares. There was no, there was no opposition any more. Idly Martin continued to push his queenside pawns, apparently unmoved by the bursting arsenal I was amassing to his left. Now my linked bishops threw out their searchlights towards his king, and my chubby rooks were all set to gun it down the single open file. Time, too, was on my side.

'Fielding's original notion might have gone as follows. Did you study the paperwork? Obviously not. Hogtied by the Arthur screen-play, which is little more than a witty, four-pronged character assassination, the stars renege on you. Fielding comes down on them for breaking contract. No big deal. Nuisance claims. Happens all the time. The stars are all insured for this so there's no real loser, except John Self. Fielding had non-completion insurance too. But then you screwed it all up by bringing *me* in.'

'Double,' I said. I turned the dice from 64 to 16 – the usual highrolling practice. 'Sixteen hundred quid. Okay?'

He just wasn't interested, I thought. His moves are waiting moves – but waiting for what? I had it all my own way now on this squared field of power. Martin could wait as long as he liked: he'll have black in his pants before he knows it. When the knight is poised I'll go straight for the crotch of his defence. Yes, me and my rooks, we'll tear the joint to shreds. I haven't got him good. I've got him beautiful.

'How he managed the money, well, that's another story. What's the phrase? "The mad agility of compound deceit." You said he had a lot of computer equipment in his room. Clearly he was hacking – you know, a spool artist, riding the software and the memory circuits of banks and conglomerates. He couldn't keep the balls in the air for ever. But he had his hands on money at some point. He could make money. But he didn't care about money. Not as *money*. Double.'

And neither does this guy. Am I missing something? Quickly I reviewed the disposition of his pieces and their possible flare-paths. Zero – no bookish sacrifice or swingeing combination, no discovered brilliancy. The advanced queenside pawns might give me a few headaches later on, but . . . Later on? Jesus. They say that pawns are the soul of chess. This might explain why I never pay them much mind, not until the endgame anyway, when you can't help but think about your soul. Those four white skinheads were coming down towards me like space invaders on a churning screen. Black's broken battlements just stood there, gaping, as once again my forces entered turnaround.

'The wonder is,' said Martin musingly, 'the wonder is that Fielding didn't cut and run at an earlier stage. Probably he was too deep into his themes and forms, his own artwork. The illusionist, the lie artist, the storyboarder – they have a helplessness. And then of course there was the underside of his character. All that had to have its play. Why didn't he let you walk out of the door at the Carraway? Because he was hooked. On the fiction, the art. He wanted to get to the end. We all do. A failed actor, he wanted an actor's revenge. He took it out on real life.'

Now there was some warm work out on the flank as the pawns began to strut their stuff. This must have given us a taste for carnage because the central bloodbath, when it came, was all smash and grab. Those vanished pawns breathed new powers into his sleeping pieces: I watched it all come down, nabbed what I could, and huddled whimpering on my own back lines. The wound dispatches were telling me that I was only a pawn to the bad, but I had two pieces under threat and his fat rook lurking on my second rank. If I can just survive, I thought, if I can just survive. I don't expect to beat this guy. I won't let him beat me, though – I won't take another loss.

'Can you remember,' he asked, 'can you remember what

Fielding said, in the alley, after the fight? He said something. Can you remember what it was?'

'I don't know. You – new man dog. Something like that. It didn't make any sense.'

'Could it have been *inhuman dog*? . . . Fascinating. Pure trans-ference. Oh damned Iago. Tell you what. You're better than I thought but this is still money for jam. If you win, I pay up. If we draw, you win – I'll give you the game. If I win – I just take something from you. Anything I want, but just one thing.' He pointed to the dice. 'The money's sort of a joke by now anyway, or a symbol. Sex, status, phallic. Have I left any out?'

The cunning bastard, I thought. Oh, I caught that reference to his own little rattletrap. He's definitely after my Fiasco.

'Okay?'

'Okay.'

And I did survive, more or less. All right, so I lost the exchange – knight for rook – but I regained my lost pawn and tiptoed into the endgame like a street dog heading for home – and food, warmth, shelter. It was this way. White king, pawn, rook: black king, pawn, knight. Pawns opposed on the queen's bishop file. Now theoretically he might have had winning chances – but I had something else: I had the clock on my side. Martin, *he'd* done all the talking, and he'd done it in his own good time. There were nineteen minutes on my clock, and less than seven on his . . . Our pawns met head on, escorted by their kings. His rook made broad sweeps, came in close, backed off again. My knight held its ground. It was gridlock, diversion, no thoroughfare: all his decisive moves seemed to lay him open to a king-rook fork. Time ticked. I even ventured out with my knight, innocuously splitting his rook and his pawn.

'This is exquisite,' he said – and made a waiting move with the king.

Greedily I stared at the board. His rook was there for the

taking. Exchange, then locked pawns: a draw. All over. I think I even incurred a minor hard-on as I leaned across the table and said, 'I hope you mean that, pal, because you're not having it back. Double.'

'Double.'

'Double.'

'Double.'

I sank back in the chair and feasted on my drink. Ah, such luxury, in this clubbed face, in this hired sock, even in this extremity. I wanted Martin to see it all coming. I would take his rook with my knight. He would recapture – or resign. That would leave the opposed foursome, his king to the left of my pawn, my king to the right of his. When I had his cheque in my hands I was going to tear it up and throw it back in his face. 'There's your payment,' I would say, and point towards the door.

'Sixty-four thousand pounds,' he said. 'I don't think you'll quite run to that. But I'm going to take what I'm going to take. You won't miss it. You never even knew you had it.'

'What were you after? It was the Fiasco, wasn't it.'

'You don't understand. Your car's just a joke. I think I've worked out how Fielding did it, moneywise. How much are you out on the whole deal? Personally?'

'I don't know. Not that much. He paid for nearly everything.'

'Wrong. It's finally come to me. And it *is* beautiful. You signed a lot of documents. My guess is that you signed them all twice. Once under *Co-signatory*, once under *Self*. It was your *name*. The company you formed wasn't Goodney & Self. It was Self & Self. It was Self. The hotels, the plane tickets, the limousines, the wage bill, the studio rental. You were paying. It was you. It was you.'

I shrugged, dead cool, and just said, 'Let's play.'

I captured his rook. He captured my knight. The four pieces stood locked in their formal pose. We climbed to our feet, and stretched, facing each other over the square table. I offered him my hand and said,

'A draw.'

'No. I'm afraid you lose.'

'Come on, there's nothing doing.' I gestured airily at the board. And saw that he was right. My only moves were king moves, and they were suicide. He could capture, and keep his own pawn in range.

'Zugzwang,' he said.

'What the fuck does that mean?'

'Literally, *forced to move*. It means that whoever has to move has to lose. If it were my turn now, you'd win. But it's yours. And you lose.'

'Pure fucking jam, in other words. Dumb luck.'

'Hardly,' he said. 'The opposition itself is a kind of zugzwang in which the relationship between the kings assumes a regular pattern. There is such a thing, though, as the heterodox opposition. In composed positions you could call them conjugated square studies. You see, the –'

I clamped my hands over my ears. Martin talked on, shadowy, waxy, flicker-faced. I don't know if this strange new voice of mine carried anywhere when I said, '*I'm the joke. I'm it! It was you. It was you.*'

I didn't see my first swing coming – but he did. He ducked or shied or stood swiftly aloof and my fist slammed into the light bracket above his head. I wheeled sideways with a wide back-hander, fell against the low chair and caught its shoulder-spike deep in the ribs. I came up flailing. I hurled myself round that room like a big ape in a small cage. But I could never connect. Oh Christ, he just isn't here, he just isn't there. My last shot upended me by the rhino-hide sofa, which kicked me full in the face with its square steel boot. The boil in my head now broke or burst. The room tipped and tunnelled and fled screaming into the night.

When I awoke, Martin was still in the room, and still talking.

When I awoke, Martin was gone and there was no sound anywhere.

Just after dawn I walked out into the streets for the last time. Then I returned. What is there to say? The sneezing policeman, the tragic traffic warden, the bald black postman in his running shoes. And the people, one by one, leaving night for day on the usual errand. Then I returned. What is there to say? What is there to say?

I lined up the bottles of scotch, Martina's tranquillizers plus forty more from my kitchen pill-jar. I wrote a suicide note, a short one this time. It just said, 'Dear Antonia, Don't go into the bedroom. Go home and call the police. I'm sorry about your money. I'm sorry about all the mess.' I downed the pills in fist-fuls. You'd be amazed how quick it is. At first the mist looked like love, it did, like love you won't find on this world, and I wept and said, 'Do it. Take me. Oh, quick – take me.' But then I felt the last shame coming. Dah. My life was a joke. My death will be serious. That must be why I am so afraid . . . Don't be like me, pal. Sister, please find another way. Soon you and I will no longer exist. Come on, let's feel a little fear together. Give me your hand. Shake . . .

DECEMBER, JANUARY.
1981, 1982.

G UESS WHAT. *I fucking nearly killed myself the other day. Yeah. It was really close. The culprit? You're right. The Fiasco.*

I was bowling along at 25mph. On reflection, maybe it was more like 20, or 15. The Fiasco doesn't like it when it's cold. The Fiasco doesn't like it when it's hot either, or when it's rainy. To tell you the truth, the Fiasco nearly always screws things up when it comes to getting you anywhere. For all its virtues, it's never been much of an A-to-B device. What it likes – what it's really incredibly good at – is staying put . . . The main roads were seamed in furrowed slush. It was the sort of traffic that cars hate most, the streets slowed by a thousand reaction-times, after you, after you, after you. I hung a sharp right, an experimental shortcut, a new angle sliced from the outer grid. The Fiasco was perhaps the first vehicle to have tried this street all morning. The macadam looked wet but felt dry. I accelerated towards the junction, touched the brake, and found myself on a frictionless chute of black ice. For a microsecond or two I even felt a throb of gratification that the Fiasco was at last showing some form. Pushed on to a purer plane of travel, a sleigh on seized wheels, we took the long slide into the toytown street – Whee, I thought. Now how's this going to turn out?

I sailed into the main road, sailing on a silent scream. And the street so normal! A fat bus snorted in astonishment. Someone cartwheeled off a bicycle. The caged crate of a milk van shuddered and froze. The Fiasco half turned on its skates, surfing sideways through the slush towards the metered cars on the distant kerb. Among the colour-blocks of the jarred traffic I grappled with the meaningless wheel. Broadside on, like a ship finding its dock, the Fiasco drifted into the narrow bay, jolted to a dead stop, and stalled.

I climbed out. The street stood and stared. I put a coin in the meter and walked straight through the opening doors of the Princess Diana, ordered a double scotch and let the bar take my weight as I nursed the grief of my imaginary wounds. Jesus Christ. I fucking nearly killed myself.

It is Christmastime in London. In London, Christmastime is the time when cabbies' change feels as hot as coins coughed from the bowels of fruit machines, when office duds try their hands as wits in the pubs and on the long tables of cheap bistros, when in the dead days before New Year people show their presents to the world in buses and tube trains: collars grip the neck like a cold compress, gloves lie on the lap as stiff as pickled octopi, watches and fountainpens flash their signals in the hired light. Christmastime is the time when all girls talk about things being lovely and warm.

The first annual snowfall caused dismay, breakdown, anarchy, as it does every year. All week I've been walking through the London streets and wondering what they look like. They look like something terribly familiar. People are wiggling on their faulty gyroscopes. Whoops! we all go on the hoof-marked brocades. We stare at the pavements to find our footing but we can't tell what the pavements look like. For fifteen minutes the snow was crispy white and squeaky clean. Then no colour at all – no-colour, not even grey. What does it look like? With its murky scurf and banked channels of glint and scum, it looks like washing-up, it looks like London skies. London summer skies – that's what the winter streets look like. Summer skies: that's what they look like. And so is everything the same?

The second annual snowfall caused dismay, breakdown, anarchy, as it does every year. This second snow stayed white and hard for a lot longer. It was better-quality stuff: it obviously cost more. The snow surprised everyone, as it does every year. It surprised me. But then, snow surprises. Snow is surprising! It is the element of surprise. For a while the world was lunar. It was silent. It was snowjobbed. It was hushed the next morning until at last you heard the apologetic sounds of whispering cars. We all tiptoed out of doors and blinked at the world. Everyone seems to think that everything is all their fault. But we give ourselves credit too sometimes.

Credit? I haven't got any and maybe I never will again. Yes, I'm busted. Do you know of any cheap flats? Can you lend me some money – just until Thursday? I'll pay you back. Honest. Martin was right. I'm the last to know as usual, but my lawyers have finally established who was tabbing the whole psychodrama, from cab fares to lab fees, from soup to nuts. Me. Muggins here. Fuck! Why didn't I look at all the stuff he made me sign? Oh, I was a pup, let's face it. Still, he charmed and gulled lots of other people too: I have proof of this, because until recently I was being indicted by eight or nine of them, including Lorne Guyland, Caduta Massi, Butch Beausoleil and Spunk Davis. In the end I called all four stars and just sobbed out my story. Caduta dropped her suit quickly enough but went on to give me the hardest time person-ally. 'I, who gave you a – why, John. Why? Will you tell me why? Why? Why did you do this to your own – why? Why?' If I had a nickel for every time Caduta has asked me why, I wouldn't be in this fix. And I have no answer. The real turn-up was Lorne. He couldn't have been sweeter – or calmer. 'Well, John,' he said, 'these things happen.' But do they? 'Oh all the time, John.' Do they? Really? Spunk proved no problem, as expected. Prehistoric was a big hit in New York, and Spunk's been signed up for a series of romantic comedies. You've probably heard of him: he's called Jeff Davis now. His estranged girlfriend Butch Beausoleil, in contrast, is still very much on my case. Horris Tolchok torments me daily by post and telephone. 'I have a video of you nude,' he recently announced, 'beating up on my client.

That's rape rap, pal.' But my lawyer thinks we can pin the whole deal on Goodney. Fielding is now undergoing psychiatric tests at a correctional facility in Palm Springs. Do you want to know why Fielding did it? You really want to know? Okay, call Beryl. Ring up his mum. I'll give you her number. She'll tell you why. She'll talk for hours and hours about his motivation. She'll even call you back. If you really want to know why Fielding did it, call Beryl Goodney. Her number is 2210–6110. The code's 215.

Without money, you're one day old and one inch tall. And you're nude, too. But the beauty of it is, there's no point in doing anything to you if you haven't got any money. They could do things to you. But if you haven't got the money, they can't be fucked. On the other hand I now face criminal as well as civil actions. There are proceedings underway to extradite me – get this: it's a good one – on charges of Recklessness, Unjust Enrichment and Gross Indifference. My lawyer says we can fight these actions and have every chance of prevailing so long as I give him lots of money. As things stand at the moment, I ought not to go to America. But I don't want to go to America. I can't afford to go to America . . . And the hold of all this is weakening so fast on me. My life is losing its form. The large agencies, the pentagrams of shape and purpose have no power to harm or delight me now.

Fat Vince has found me a job, working as a minder for a Hyde Park icecream van. It starts in the spring. He thinks I may have a future in the bouncing business. One day, perhaps, I'll go back to the ad-game. The ad-men, they love it when you fail, and they like to show their love. My name is muck for now. This is part of the price they will charge for having me back. They'll have me back in the end. But sometimes I think, no, I'm not going back. When I watch the ads on the television I feel nausea, right in my soft core. TV being here, TV being the religion, the mystical part of ordinary minds, I don't want to be working in this sensitive area, I don't want to be selling it things. If we all downed tools and joined hands for ten minutes and stopped believing in money, then money would no longer exist. We never will, of course. Maybe money is the great conspiracy, the great fiction. The great addiction too: we're all addicted and we can't break the habit now. There's not even anything very twentieth century about it, except the disposition. You just can't kick it, that junk, even if you want to. You can't get the money monkey off your back.

I still cry and babble and holler a lot, but then I always did. I drink, and have fights, and gangway through the streets. I am still a high-risk zone. I am still inner city.

As for my suicide bid, well, the whole thing was a total disaster, as you've gathered. I finished a bottle and a half of scotch and swallowed my ninety tranqs. For a while I felt bloody marvellous. This suicide lark, I thought, it's a doddle. I sat and waited. Then fear came. It was like shrinkage – as if the world were growing bigger and blacker while I grew small and pale. Boy, I said to myself, do I need a drink, or a tranquillizer. Suddenly I cheered up again and started looking on the bright side. I put my boot through the TV and stomped the hi-fi and the video. I was going to run downstairs and take it out on the Fiasco too, but I was falling over a fair bit by that time and, besides, I half-remembered abandoning the car in Maida Vale. It was then that I must have had my first major rethink. Look, I didn't mean it, I kept shouting. You know how it is. So I had a few drinks and things got out of hand. I was hasty. Can't a guy make one mistake? I jogged on the spot and tried a press-up or two. I ran a cold bath and fell into it with most of my clothes on. I drank a pot of French mustard in the kitchen. I practically fingerfucked my own tonsils – with no joy, no joy at all. I thought I could feel grabby death ducking and feinting round my head, looking for its opening, its passage. So I just paced and paced for as long as it took . . . By mid-morning, with the day calmly trundling on its track beneath my window, I felt so pooped that I thought I might as well hit the sack, come what may. After all the excitement, I poured myself a drink. I was so frazzled by then that

I might well have taken a tranquillizer before turning in. I don't think we can rule out the possibility that I even attempted a handjob. Some hours later, at any rate, I was roused by a pig and two ambulancemen. Me, I felt like death. I kept thinking – maybe I did it, maybe it's happened, maybe death is just like life, the same old stuff only iller. They wanted me to go for a pump, but I wasn't having any. I borrowed ten quid off my cleaning-lady. I did the butch thing and just pubbed the day out somehow. You know what saved me? Martina's tranquillizers, I suspect, were placebos. I recall dissolving a couple of them one time in New York and thinking how like aspirin they looked and tasted. I have also been poring over my pill-jar with growing scepticism . . . Here then, tentatively, is the recipe for my suicide bid: a hundred fluid ounces of scotch, fifty aspirin, a week-long course of antibiotics, and twelve yeast pills. No wonder I felt so bad. It was nearly a week before I could say with any confidence – yes, I'm sure I'm alive again.

Now you'll understand that I don't remember much about that night and that dark morning, and yet it was a time when I did a lot of remembering. Rogue memories that I had often tried hard to tether – they just came to me, one by one with their hands in the air. I suppose I was walking the blackout line and had full access to all the hidden things. I wrote them down. I wouldn't have remembered them otherwise. I don't remember remembering them. I don't remember writing them down. The handwriting on the pad was unrecognizable as mine, much more upright and correct, which shows you how far gone I was.

I remembered that time in the Berkeley Club, where I always suspected something terrible happened. Something terrible happened. Fielding took me to the can to cool me down. Then he turned from the stall with his dick in his hand. He said, 'Real drunk, huh Slick?' – and gave me a swipe of pee right across the front of my strides . . . I remembered that time up on Ninety-Fifth Street, when Doris Arthur led me from the media restaurant and, answering my invitation to come back to the hotel and fool around, placed her lips on

my cheek and murmured, 'You asshole. It's all a joke. Fielding's
taking you. It's a game, a ride. Step off the train. Step off!' . . . I
remembered that time in the Irish bar opposite Zelda's (Dinner and
Hostess Dancing. The worst moment? Perhaps), being kissed and
petted by the gingerhead with Fielding's eyes. 'You know who I am?'
it whispered. 'It's me. I'm it. I'm your producer.' And me sitting
there nodding, smiling, stupefied, cretinized, zugzwanged . . . And
I remembered Martin, here in my flat, standing over me and saying
again and again in a clogged and wretched hush, 'I'm so sorry.' He
kept saying it. 'I'm so sorry. I'm so sorry.'

All that morning when death felt so near and life seemed such good
stuff – I never called for help. I have wondered why. I can only put
it this way. Bear with me, please. My life has been a fight between
shame and fear. In suicide, shame wins. Shame is stronger than fear,
though you still fear shame. You still fear fear, in my case, and suddenly
you want to call the whole thing off. In the finished suicide, shame
wins, but you wouldn't want anyone to see it winning. Suicide is so
shameful. I would have hated anyone to see me at it. No, I wouldn't
have been seen dead in the bedroom there, committing suicide like
that.

I've got a new girlfriend, thank Christ. She's called Georgina. She
works as a secretary for a dry-goods firm in White City. She's a big
girl, sort of a fat nurse, basically, which is just what the doctor
ordered. You'd like Georgina. I'm grateful . . . I met her in the Blind
Pig, or was it the Butcher's Arms? I was face-down at the time,
having just been rather thoroughly decked by a very fit, extremely
sensitive and incredibly sober Australian. She took me back to her
sock and with her own hands put the meat to my eye. I courted her for
over a week. She's about my weight and we really hit it off. Georgina
has got big . . . She's got a big heart, that Georgina.

I write to Martina about twice a week. Each morning I mount
the cold lino, on the lookout for that envelope of red, white and blue.

Nothing yet. I still hope. My love letters may not be great works of art, but they're fucking sincere, I tell you that. They have to take you back, don't they, if you love them enough? If you open everything wide and love them enough, they have to take you back. No? They just have to. At first I was too busy to feel bad about her. Now it comes to me daily, a punctual pain, punctual, like the girl herself. She's the best. She's the best and I want it, I want the best . . . Do I? Did I ever? Perhaps I never really had what it took to want the best. Culture and all that – it's not, or not only, that we aren't cut out for it, some of us. We sort of hate it, too. I'm trying. I read quite a bit. It's the only diversion I can still afford. Reading's cheap, I'll give it that. I've read all the financio-sexual thrillers on Georgina's shelves. I hang out in the Library. The Library is a good place when you're unemployed. It's warm and free. There is shelter.

I have written to Selina too. That might be a more realistic ending. She'll have a nipper, an income, and a house. A house is not a home, I know. But at least it's a house. Ossie won't stay with her. If he's got any sense, and if she'll have him, Ossie will go back to his wife, on all fours. I hope she finds her Shadow, that Martina . . . I wrote to Selina care of her gynaecologist. I intend to raise that child of hers as if it were my very own, even though it'll be a lot more upper class than I am. Princess Di is in the family way too now. The world proliferates. Try and stop it. In her chatty, chirpy reply (London postmark, no return address), Selina told me that she will name her child after the royal baby, providing the sex is right. I suppose it'll be something like Mary or Elizabeth, or George or James. I approve. But I won't get a glimpse of Selina until I'm back at the money.

The Fiasco is still running, though not at the moment. The Fiasco is my grand folly. The Fiasco, it's my pride and joy. Between ourselves I don't know whether I could have pulled through all this without the Fiasco. I clean it often now, out there on the street, with the bucket, the rag, the tranny. That motor will be back on the road again, oh, don't you worry. I'll stick by the Fiasco. I choke up about that Fiasco of mine. We've been through a lot together. We'll go through a lot more, the Fiasco and me.

As for the other court case – the one for driving while drunk, or, rather, for drunkenly possessing a non-stationary vehicle – my lawyer is trying to postpone the case indefinitely. This costs me, and earns him. A technique favoured by other lawyers in my employ. What money I have goes straight down the can of legal fees. I'm on the kind of underdole they reserve for alkies, screamers and prongs of the road. My main source of income is my sock. I moved out, into a basement shitbox off Ladbroke Grove, and hired my hired flat to a polygamous sheik and his caravan of kids. It was easy: I just stuck an ad in a fagshop window along with all the other cards saying FRENCH GREEK & TURKISH LESSONS GIVEN and DO YOU DARE PHONE THE BAYSWATER BITCH. I'm especially reluctant to learn what TURKISH is, after seeing the state of that sock of mine. I go round every Thursday to pick up the rent. Impassively the gowned colossus hands me my wad. I peer past him into an unfathomable atmosphere of silenced grannies, scorched wives and scourged daughters. There's only one little boy in there: no kid ever had it so good. The flat is a ruin but the oof is top dollar and keeps the lawyers sweet. Also, my old dad slips me the odd ten or twenty, when he's flush.

A cigarette millionaire, I blew it all away. That's in the past now – I've cut right down to less than two packs a day. It's all I can afford. I even roll my own, God damn it. I hardly drink any more: just a Barley Stout, two Particular Brews, a Whisky Tak and a few Ginger Perries. Either that, or a bottle of Cyprus sherry or Bulgarian port to lower me into the night. It's all I can afford. I'm economizing on pornography too. No more nude mags or assisted showers. They're too expensive. I still score the occasional handjob, every now and again. Who doesn't? Say what you like about handjobs, slag them off all you want, but they couldn't very well be cheaper or more readily available. In the end you've got to hand it to handjobs. They're deeply democratic.

I don't see Terry Linex any more because he owes me money. I don't see Alec Llewellyn any more because he owes me money. I don't see Barry Self any more because he owes me money. I don't see Martin Amis any more because I owe him money, in a sense. Money, it's always the money. I once thought he and I might be friends. But there's nothing between us, now that there's no money between us.

Mind you, I did see him once. I was down the drinker, the London Apprentice or maybe the Jesus Christ, drinking beer and patiently feeding the last of my dole into the fruit machine. Our eyes met as he came through the door: he looked at me in the way he used to before I ever met him – affrontedly, with a sudden pulse in the neck. I achieved two damsons and swapped them for a doublenudge on the flashing Switchmatic. There were three tulips on view for a two-quid jackpot. I gambled the nudges and got the four I needed. Shunning the Winfinder, I chose to do the nudge-work manually, in sentimental tribute to the old crafts, the old skills. Anyway I goofed and made two cherries on the left. Twenty pee. Then I felt his force field behind me. I didn't turn. 'Hey, what are you doing here?' he asked. 'You're meant to be out of the picture by now.' I just glanced over my shoulder and said – I don't know why: some deep yob gene must have prompted me – 'Fuck off out of it.' In the bendy mirror behind the bar I saw him leave, woodenly, stung, scared. I gambled my win to 30, to 50 to 70, to £1.40. I gambled again. The robot paused, went numb, and spat out a ten-pee piece. Drunk, I put the coin into the Token slot by mistake. It got stuck and I was thrown out as usual for beating up on the machine . . . You'd think dole money would feel extra precious, wouldn't you. You'd think it would feel like the last money on earth. It doesn't. It feels like trash, throwaway stuff. It feels like nothing.

Money, money stinks. It really does. Dah, it stinks. Pick up a wad of well-used notes and fan them out in your face. Pick it up. Fan it. Do it. Little boys' socks and a porno headache tang, old yeast, batch, larders, damp towels, the silt from purses' seams, the sweat of the palms and the dirt in the nails of the people who handle this stuff all day, so needfully. Ah, it stinks.

I went to see Mrs McGilchrist about that long-suffering tooth of mine. I sat there under the lead vest while she X-rayed my face. She pronounced the tooth dead but still viable. I know just how it feels. She drilled and drained and did her squeaky work. Later she invoiced me but I bounced back with a new gimmick: I didn't pay her. What can she do? What can she do? It doesn't hurt any more. It just seems hollow, light, without substance. I chomped a toast rind with it the other morning, and discovered, when I came to, that it still has a lot to offer. I lost another tooth last month, a front one, right in the heart of midtown, right on Central Park South. It was loafed out by an Arab in the One Off the Wrist, a new cocktail bar in Queensway. Who was it who told me that Arabs were no good at fighting? Ooh, if I ever catch up with whoever it was . . . Actually, this set me thinking. I only had one more fight after that. I reckon I've only got one more fight left, at the most, and then that's it. I'm going to kick fighting before it kicks me. Despoiled with drink and rage one night, I tried to rough up Georgina. Bad idea. You see, she's a big girl, that Georgina. She's not like these cool small ones who squeal for mercy the minute you flex your fist. No, she hit me back, if you please. I woke up with a swollen ear and another black eye. Georgina brought me tea in bed and asked if I was ever going to try that stuff again. I said – no sir. You can't be doing with fighting at my age. At my age, when everything is needed and nothing is renewed. There's no more Mrs McGilchrist either, so I must now rely on what Fat Paul calls the National Elf. That back tooth is dead, but I am still alive. That front tooth is gone, but I am still around.

I opened my eyes today and thought, whew, I've never felt as old as this before. And yet that's accurate, isn't it. I've never been as old as this before. And so it will go for every morning of our lives. You too, brother. And you, sister. How are things? Are you all okay? . . . Pretty soon now I'm going to look in the mirror and find that my nose has exploded on me. The grog lichen will steal across my face like verdigris. Then the inner works will start their failing. My fat pal Fat Paul once said that money, it isn't worth anything if you haven't got your health. Yeah, but what happens if you haven't got your health or any money either? When you haven't got your health, that's when you really need a couple of bob.

I can't complain, though. Thanks to Georgina I'm a lot fitter than I used to be. I went to see my doctor the other day, not my mouth doctor or my dick doctor but my general practitioner – my time doctor. The old ticker is steady enough. All in all, shares seemed rocky but holding, over at Rug & Gut & Gum. He asked about fags and booze and so on. I lied through my tooth and he was still astounded – by what I needed, by what remained.

Late this afternoon I showed up at Georgina's with a bottle of Desdemona Cream. It was to be the usual kind of evening: spaghetti, day-chat, her little telly, comfort in the cramped bed. I was early, because the Fiasco went ahead and started, against all the odds. Georgina wasn't home yet, and I keep losing the keys she gives me. She has a spacious bedsitter up there, above a betting-shop on this pushy street.

It was cold, but not that cold. The second snow still neatly frilled the pavements. I sat myself down on a bench, near the charred bridge, near the open mouth of the underground station. I was wearing my old donkey-jacket – I'd fished it out of a forgotten cupboard, and I do believe it's actually warmer than the cashmere, for which I got £215, by the way, from an old shafter in the Portobello Road.

The fourth of January, 1982. The world has started working again. From the aromatic trap of the underground (its breath somewhere between the hot burp of a hamburger stall and the damp, carpety spice of an Indian takeout) the people come surging in five-minute intervals, heading intent with midwinter faces for warmth and food and their human shift. Georgina would be among them, heading for the same things, all in the one room.

Life is pretty good over here in England but this is a tough planet and don't you tell me any different. In the best, the freest, the richest latitudes, it's still a tough globe. If you ever go to Earth — watch out. You probably heard that the Poles went under. Yeah. Military rule. Martial law. A guy with a name like a hangover cure is running the deal now. The first thing he did was triple all the prices, that popeyed little son of a bitch. You don't hear a lot about thin-lipped, deep-chested Lech Walesa any more. Danuta had her baby okay, but she's on her tod now, fending for herself and all their other kids.

Where is the girl? They sometimes make Georgina work late, without overtime. A scandal, I agree — but then everyone is huddled up a bit now, with recession coming, and the bosses play on fears and just feel civic-minded. They sweat too, I suppose, and they have more to lose.

I want money again but I feel better now that I haven't got any. There are these little pluses. You, they can't do much to you when you haven't got any money. There's no money in it for them. So they can't be fucked. I've been rich and I've been poor. Poor is worse, but rich can be a clunker too. You know, during that time of pills and booze, during that time of suicide, my entire future flashed through my head. And guess what. It was all a drag! My past at least was — what? It was . . . rich. And now my life has lost its form. Now my life is only present, more present, continuous present.

Well, I'd like to sign off with some words of wisdom. I'm closer to you, I hope, than he'll ever be. But if I'd had any good advice to give you, I would have taken it. I would have kept it all for me. Do you want to know the meaning of life? Life is an aggregate, an aggregate of all the lives that have ever been lived on the planet Earth. That's the meaning of life.

Oh yeah. I think I've cracked my age problem, my time problem — sussed it, not solved it. A product of the Sixties, I was led to believe *that being young was quite an achievement. Everyone seemed to encourage me in this apprehension, especially the old. An iconoclast, I had no time for mortality. I used to stand around denouncing you all – you old fucks – and you just nodded and smiled. You seemed to think I was wonderful . . . Come to think of it, I didn't look too bad in those days. My rug was frizzy but strong and electrical. My gut was flat, my teeth were white. I was better then. But they told me I was everything, and they were lying, those old fucks.*

One other point. This isn't of much general interest or application either, but it's the only thing I know I'm right about. Should you ever find yourself in a paternity or maternity mix-up, should you ever have a child who isn't really his or isn't really hers, tell the kid. Tell the kid soon. Do it. If you're a girl, then you are your mum and your mum is you. If you're a boy, then you are your dad and your dad is you. So how can you live seriously if you don't know who you are?

Few fathers have abused their sons as Barry Self has abused me. But Barry Self is not my father. Fat Vince is my father. In a sense, then, my life has been a joke right from the start, right from the womb, right from the first twinkle in Fat Vince's eye. I used to think I could take a joke. Can I take this one?

I uncapped the Desdemona Cream and enjoyed a festive swig. Well, it's the New Year, isn't it. Lispingly I whistled and sang – and babbled of Fielding, Lorne, Caduta, Butch and Spunk, the turnaround, the whole hysteria, the whole conspiracy . . . I've settled the motivation question. I supplied it all. The confidence trick would have ended in five minutes if it hadn't been for John Self. I was the key. I was the needing, the hurting artist. I was the wanting artist. I wanted to believe. I wanted that money so bad. Me, and my no-confidence trick. 'Confidence' I now regard as a psychopathic state. Confidence, it's a cry for help. I mean, you look at all that out there, and what you feel is confidence?

Fat Vince and I have had our confrontation. We wept it all out in the back room at the snooker hall. 'You should have told me, Vince,'

I said. 'It wasn't for me to tell you, son.' 'But when you saw no one else was going to, you should have told me.' I stared into his face, his flummoxed, his snookered face. 'Don't get me wrong,' I said, and finished the bottle. 'I'm proud to call you father.' And I am. He's a great man in his way, Fat Vince. He loved my mother, which is more than Barry ever did. I'd say he's a definite improvement.

And Georgina loves me. She does. She said so. Tonight I'm going to make it clear just how grateful I am. Without Georgina, I'd be a dead man. She will shine with pleasure, if I do it right. Selina shined to money, Martina to paintings but most of all to flowers . . . Georgina would probably shine to flowers – and money too, come to that. I can't afford to give her any. And when I can, I tell myself, Georgina won't do any more. I'll be off with someone like Martina (no. No. That won't happen again) or Selina or some other Tina or Lina or Nina.

All afternoon the sky has looked like an empty eggtray, with maybe an egg here, an egg there. Then the sunset's streaky bacon. Now in the far west the night clouds are gaunt and equine, like doorkeys at an angle or Spanish locomotives. But the clouds obey their natural functions and do not know or care how beautiful they are. What does know, what does care about its own beauty? Only beautiful women – oh yeah, and artists, I suppose, real artists, not the sack, piss, con and bullshit varieties that I've always had to work my way around. I am an artist – an escape artist.

That time in the Welcome-In near La Guardia, with the darkness, the hired wenches, the fleeing planes, you know what little Selina said to me? She said: 'This may sound cruel, but I knew you'd never make money. Right from the start. You always smelled wrong for money. You never had the right smell' . . . It's colder now. I feel it, and I feel the need of shelter. Give me some. Where does the wind come from? Why does it blow – the stars, the myths? Who can tell? If I stay poor then Georgina may stay in luck. Is luck quite the word I want? I'm good to her. I can't afford not to be. She loves me. She told me so. I think she must have had a pretty rough run of guys, that Georgina.

With a soft salute I removed my cap. My cap, my cloth cap is designed to keep my hair in some kind of order. I can't be doing with these twenty-quid rug-rethinks any more. Georgina cuts it now, humming like a gardener over my quilted, brooding form. Here – I drink, I sing, I babble with my missing tooth. The people hurry from the underground, very mortal, the young half healthy, the old half shrewd – quarter beautiful, quarter wise. Humans, I honour you.

And then I felt a light and sudden plop on the loose covers of my groin. I looked down: among the soiled prisms of the lining, a ten-penny piece nestled in my cap. I looked up: a compact lady moved beyond me with a brief and lively smile. Well, you've got to laugh. You've got to. There isn't any choice. I'm not proud. Don't hold back on my account. Now here's that Georgina at last, moving clear of the crowd; her smile is touching and ridiculous – delighted yet austere, and powerfully confident – as she ticks towards me on her heels.